THE DECISION

THE DECISION

JOE SALERNO

abundance
collective

Published by Abundance Collective
PO Box 43, Powell, OH 43065

LCCN: 2024915078
Paperback ISBN: 978-1-965419-03-8
Hardcover ISBN: 978-1-965419-04-5
e-book ISBN: 978-1-965419-05-2

Available in paperback, hardcover, and e-book.

Any Internet addresses (websites, blogs, etc.) and telephone numbers printed in this book are offered as a resource. They are not intended in any way to be or imply an endorsement by Igniting Souls, nor does Igniting Souls vouch for the content of these sites and numbers for the life of this book.

This is a work of fiction. Any resemblance to actual persons, living or dead, or actual events is purely coincidental. Names, characters, places, and incidents are either the product of the author's imagination or are used fictitiously.

Dedication

There are many people who have played a significant role in bringing *The Decision* to life. The amazing team at Abundance Collective provided tremendous support and guidance throughout the process, and I am very thankful for their efforts.

The inspiration that led me to sit at the keyboard and begin writing came after losing my father to Alzheimer's and while watching my mother battle valiantly with dementia. Their bravery in the face of this devastating disease is the spark that ignited my desire to undertake what has become an unbelievable journey.

From its infancy, this project has been championed by my incredible wife, Missy. Without her, none of this would have been possible. Her unwavering encouragement from day one was critical in propelling this story across the finish line. LYTM

This is for them…

A portion of the proceeds from this book will be donated to the Alzheimer's Association.

Prologue

Jonathan has won a number of cases here, but this courtroom has never been his favorite. It's poorly lit, small, and located in the bowels of the 200-year-old courthouse. His steady hands smooth the front of his Hugo Boss three-piece suit, the one he saves for closing arguments, as he scans the gathering. Jonathan's eyes stop briefly on his parents and Emily, who are eagerly anticipating the tale he will expertly weave.

After taking a deep breath, Jonathan strides confidently across the courtroom to stand in front of the captive audience in the jury box. "Ladies and gentlemen, the right decision in this case, exonerating my client, leaves the plaintiffs without further recourse. That may seem harsh, but it's the right decision. The only decision."

As he continues reviewing the facts of the case with the seven women and five men, he keeps their thoughts on the importance of always doing the right thing, even when doing so might feel wrong. To emphasize his point, he randomly gestures toward the image of the blindfolded woman holding the scales of justice carved into the wall behind the judge.

Suddenly, the judge stands and stares with annoyance at Jonathan. "Decide," she demands.

The courtroom seems unfazed by the interruption. The court reporter continues to capture every word while the jury watches him, awaiting his next point.

Jonathan is fazed, though. He shifts his weight between his feet and looks to the judge, working to mask the confusion caused by the unexpected demand. The frustration of losing the momentum of his closing arguments comes through in his response. "What decision are you looking for me to make, Your Honor?" he asks through gritted teeth. Being an experienced attorney, the agitation quickly diminishes, and he forces a smile, swallowing his pride.

"How dare you!" the judge snaps. "You know what it is, Mr. Silverman. Do not disgrace yourself before this court by pleading ignorance." She opens her robe to remove a handgun. Spectators begin gasping and ducking in desperation to hide themselves from the bewildering danger.

For a moment, Jonathan wonders how she got the gun past the metal detectors, but then his eyes flash toward his family, who are sitting in the corner with their hands folded in their laps, pleading with their eyes for him to do whatever the judge demands.

Jonathan opens his mouth, but nothing comes out. The eloquence he exhibited in his statements to the jury disappears the second he grasps the gravity of his situation. Fear clouds his mind.

The judge smirks in disgust, then points the gun at his family and pulls the trigger. The thunder of the shot ricochets around the courtroom.

1

It's 4:17 a.m. Jimmy Rizzo returns from the bathroom and crawls between the blood-red silk sheets on his king-sized bed next to the blonde, who's probably half his age. He didn't ask her age before he brought her home last night, nor does he remember her name—and doesn't care. He'll be sleeping next to a different woman tonight. There are many standing in line to spend the night with someone as powerful as he. And he's earned it.

Joey Battaglia gave Jimmy his first job, and that's all he needed to find his way into what would become the rest of his life. He didn't care about anything else. He quit going to school and gave up everything he ever cared about. Except his mother. No good son turns their back on their mother.

From his early days to watching the prayer card burn in the palm of his hand as he became a made man, Jimmy eagerly did the grunt work no one else would do. He stole, lied, cheated, ran numbers, loan-sharked, and eventually killed on his way to the top. Wet work never bothered him, even when he had to take care of Joey Battaglia after Joey slept with the wrong guy's girl.

Jimmy views himself as no different than any other CEO of a large business. He meets with colleagues, makes decisions, sets strategy, delegates problem-solving to those below him, and drives financial success. These days, he focuses on the long game, watching the dollars closely, knowing diversification is the key to financial security.

Others thought him a fool when he rolled the dice on a costly plan a few years ago. He'd look like the world's biggest chump or go down in history as the smartest boss of all time, and the finish line is now in sight.

Jimmy turns slightly, putting his feet on the sleeping girl's back, and shoves her violently out of bed. She hits the floor with a muffled thump. "Get the fuck outta here!"

The blonde's grogginess barely registers with Jimmy, but the longer she takes to gather her panties and $500 shoes, the more annoyed he becomes. As he's about to escalate his invitation to her to leave, she huffs and stomps out of the front door.

As the waning moonlight streams in through the window and the city starts to come to life, Jimmy closes his eyes and grins at the ceiling. History awaits.

2

It's the end of the quarter, and Michael Riccio, CEO of the biotech firm Propentus, is sitting at his desk long before anyone else arrives for the day, his tie undone and the sleeves of his heavily starched dress shirt rolled up. He's staring at the graphs in a PowerPoint presentation. Despite knowing every financial and operational detail by heart, the quarterly board updates cause Michael's blood pressure to reach dangerous levels.

He's invested his entire life in Propentus, and he knows the questions about Antsalemab will be the board's focus today. The company's recently FDA-approved treatment works to stop or, at a minimum, slow early-onset dementia and its devastating effects. The board will also be demanding an update on the status of the IPO.

The initial success of Antsalemab has put Propentus on the global stage, and the pending IPO will make them all wealthier beyond their wildest dreams—not that money was Michael's priority. The notoriety for achieving something others have failed to do will make him famous. Everyone will know his name.

The pressure's immense. The process, however, is not moving fast enough for anyone, particularly the investors. The irony isn't lost on Michael that the current status of the IPO flies in the face of the company's namesake and mantra: *propero eventus,* meaning "accelerated results."

As he's finalizing his notes, Joyce Kramer, the Senior Vice President and General Counsel for Propentus, sticks her head into his office and knocks gently on the door. "How goes the prep?"

"I have no idea what I'm going to say about the IPO. It hasn't changed from last quarter. With the FDA approval behind us, the growth of Antsalemab and the IPO launch is all anyone cares about."

Michael recruited Joyce from Wallace, Connors, and Ramirez, the law firm that helped guide his prior employer, Genomics, through its IPO. Joyce is an engaging, highly intelligent woman with an uncanny ability to find and exploit loopholes in the complex world of Securities Law. Michael found a key partner willing to push the boundaries, which is critical for any start-up wanting to differentiate itself from the competition, and successfully entice prospective investors.

Joyce glides fully into Michael's office. "You know you get like this every time, and you dwell on every potential negative comment and ridiculous question the board may ask. It always comes out fine."

"It comes out fine *because* I dwell on every potential negative comment and ridiculous question." Michael snaps. He catches himself and takes a breath before continuing.

"But this one feels different. Everyone knows the time to strike is when the iron's hot, and it doesn't get hotter than it is right now. They're going to take one look at the financials and hammer me about the IPO."

"The response is simple. We are guided by Andrew Billington, our lead investment banker, who coincidentally was recommended by members of the board. And he says there's still too much volatility in the market at the moment. The board's always been supportive. That's not going to change, particularly since they can see the light at the end of the tunnel."

She smiles and attempts to lighten the mood. "And I am sure one or two of them is saying to themselves, 'Show me the money!'"

Michael hates that movie. He's never been a fan of Tom Cruise, and hearing the line pisses him off. "This is about building a legacy, about a potential Nobel Prize, not about making the goddamn investors, nor the board, filthy rich."

Joyce rubs her hands together, carefully choosing her next statement. "We have investors to keep happy," she said almost apologetically. As her eyes darted nervously around the room, like she was concerned someone might overhear them, she whispered, "We can never forget that." Michael's reddened face tells her all she needs to know.

Michael glares at Joyce's exiting back as if trying to burn through six inches of lead with his eyes. He grumbles about the investors to himself before returning to his preparation. He needs to focus on transforming Propentus into a global powerhouse. But, to do that, he must get the investors and the board off his back. The IPO will take care of that.

3

Joyce is walking briskly down the hallway toward her office, shaking off the encounter with Michael when a buzzing in her Louis Vuitton handbag causes her to stop and hunt for the annoying item. The shocking recognition of the number causes the phone to slip from her hand onto the bland office carpeting. "Damn it," she grumbles and reluctantly bends to retrieve the dangerous item. Before answering, she sprints down the hall to take refuge behind the closed door of her office. She doesn't get a chance to say hello.

"Wake up. You have work to do."

Joyce's hand trembles, and she fights to keep her voice steady. "I'm awake."

"When's this gonna fuckin' happen?"

"I'm working on it," she insists as she searches through the mess on her desk for a legal pad.

"You've had three fuckin' years."

It's actually closer to two, but she's not stupid enough to point that out. "I was just speaking to Michael about this."

"That ain't no fuckin' answer."

She has only one out. "We're close. I'm gonna make some calls today."

"I want a fuckin' answer, or I will recoup my investment in a different way, and you and your little friend ain't gonna fuckin' like it. Capeesh?"

She's irritated by her inability to keep the tremors from her voice. "Understood."

The line goes dead. The phone slowly slips between Joyce's fingers, making a thud as it bounces off her desk and onto the tiled floor. Her shaking hands prevent her drooping head from matching the phone's journey.

4

Thirty-eight-year-old Jonathan Silverman sits up suddenly, gasping for air in the darkness, momentarily uncertain of where he is. His heart is racing, and the sheets are soaked. He has no idea what triggers the dream that leaves him sopping wet as if he just ran a marathon.

He sits on the edge of the bed, using the top sheet to wipe the sweat from his face, as Emily Watkins, the love of his life, rubs the sleep from her eyes with the palms of her hands. He watches as she gets up and shuffles toward the kitchen, wearing nothing but his Syracuse Law School t-shirt, the one she commandeered the first night she slept at his apartment. It's never been returned.

As she walks back into the bedroom and hands him a cold bottle of water, she asks the question Jonathan knows is coming. "Is it the same one?"

"Yes," Jonathan replies, dejected and frustrated. He opens the drawer of the bedside table and grabs the notebook, where he captures what he can remember. While his doctor claims it will help him understand the genesis of the dream, it seems like a waste of time. But he's willing to try anything at this point. Today, instead of observations, he adds questions: *Why always in a courtroom? Judge? Work? Parents? Emily? Gun?*

Jonathan stares at Emily padding barefoot across the hardwood floor, where she grabs a clean set of sheets from the closet.

He can't suppress his frustration. "I'm sorry I woke you up again. It's always the same, and I still have no idea what the hell it means."

"You'll figure it out." Emily smiles at him gently as they move to change the linens in silence.

5

W alt walks into the office, grinning from ear to ear. "Good morning, Jonny, my boy!"

Jonathan sighs without looking up from his work. He hates being called Jonny but allows only one person to get away with it. Walter Erickson is Jonathan's best friend from law school and the one with whom he risked everything when they hung out their own shingle. "Mornin' Walt. You ready for today?"

A bombastic, certified genius with a photographic memory, Walt smiles and scoffs as he hands the large file he has under his arm to a passing paralegal. "Me? Ready? Please... I'm always ready." he says before taking a long drink from his oversized Dunkin' iced coffee.

Today, Walt begins what will be a long and grueling trial, which he's handling pro bono. His client's accused of killing another man during a fight over a woman at The Last Inning sports bar, a well-known mob hangout. Walt told Jonathan he believed he had a good shot at a self-defense argument, given the deceased reportedly started the fight. There's just one hurdle: his client's well-known reputation, complete with a lengthy rap sheet highlighted by multiple assault convictions.

Jonathan is envious of Walt's carefree approach to life. At work, Walt's memory allows him to be less structured at trial, freeing him up to focus his efforts on giving the jury the "aha" moment they've come to expect from watching crime dramas every night on TV. That approach doesn't work for Jonathan. He tried it Walt's way once. It cost him and his clients dearly.

Jonathan should buy stock in 3M, given the number of colored Post-It notes scattered across the wall of his office, which increases dramatically as the trial approaches. He takes painstaking effort to create a meticulous outline that any juror, regardless of their level of education, experience, or background, can follow to achieve the result he wants.

Walt takes another sip of coffee. "Looks like you've been here for a while."

Jonathan looks up and laughs at the cream cheese gleaming off of Walt's burgundy tie. Walt always has something on his tie. "Yup, I have to find a few paying clients to support your benevolence."

Walt snickers and heads for his office. Jonathan shakes his head while turning his cellphone's ringer off. He hates distractions during trial prep.

Three hours later, Jonathan listens to the voicemail from his mother—twice. There's something about her tone, and she mentioned they'd love it if he and Emily came to the house that evening four different times. The telltale sign is her enticement of lasagna with meatballs, Jonathan's favorite. He's convinced something's terribly wrong and calls Emily before returning his mother's call. If he's honest with himself, he can't imagine life without the woman he never saw coming.

• • •

They met one night at The Jury Room, his favorite bar near the courthouse. It has the best chicken wings and gravy fries in Boston, which are staples when he's on trial. He prefers simple pleasures. They speak to his upbringing and the way he lives his life.

Walt was returning to their table with another round, but Jonathan's attention was elsewhere, awestruck by the understated beauty sauntering in.

The smell of hot sauce wafted across the room as Walt snapped his fingers in front of Jonathan, whose gaze never left Emily. Realizing what was happening, and before Jonathan knew it, Walt wiped the blue cheese from the corner of his mouth and sprinted back to the bar, glad to be away from the heat of the wings. He sent a round of drinks to Emily and her friends… from Jonathan.

As the group moved to leave, Emily walked straight toward them with an easy flow for a tall woman. Jonathan found himself wondering what her business suit would look like on his bedroom floor as she thanked him for the drinks.

After erasing the pornographic thoughts from his mind, he mumbled his own name and asked Emily for her number. She smiled and quickly threw ten digits over her shoulder as she retreated toward the exit to rejoin her friends. He wrote the number on a napkin covered in wing sauce, anticipation racing through his body. As Jonathan watched the long, toned legs walk out the door, his victory quickly became the agony of defeat; he never got her name.

After some goading from Walt, Jonathan mustered enough courage to call the next day, beginning what he refers to as the best chapter of his life.

• • •

"Hi, babe. How goes the battle?"

Jonathan smiles like a schoolboy with a crush. He loves the sound of her voice and her calling him babe. "It goes. Listen, I only have a couple of minutes before a deposition. Mom left me a strange message asking us to come to the house tonight. She asked four different times and offered to make lasagna and meatballs."

The concern in Emily's voice elevates his own. "Four times? That definitely sounds like something's up. I can make it, but can you change your trial prep schedule for the night or at least part of the night?"

"It doesn't sound like I have a choice. I'll let Mom know we can be there at 6 p.m. Does that work?"

"Yes... and I know these are wasted words but try not to worry."

Jonathan smiles at the comment, knowing that's exactly what he'll be doing. "I will. I'll be home by 5:30 p.m., and we'll head over to their house. Sorry, gotta run. Love you."

"I love you, too."

After he hangs up, Jonathan's anxiety skyrockets. It's something awful, but what? Cancer? A brain tumor? Something worse? He's convinced one of his parents is dying.

He grabs his files and heads for the conference room, knowing tonight will be about much more than lasagna.

6

Joyce is on Michael's heels as he leaves the boardroom and steps into her office. While hers is large and opulent, it's nothing compared to Michael's. But both stand in stark contrast to the bland, white walls of the adjacent research labs where researchers are forced to share a bench and where the real work arguably takes place.

Joyce grabs a bottle of water from her mini fridge and heads for the couch. "That went well."

Michael tosses his file onto the glass coffee table. "Those vultures only care about one thing. I mean, the meeting went fine, I suppose, but as I warned you, all they wanted to know is what we can do to expedite the IPO's launch."

"Yes, you did, and you answered them clearly and concisely."

Michael loosens his tie. "Jenkins is an ass. It doesn't matter how many times he asks the question; it isn't going to get finalized any quicker."

"He wants to show off in front of the rest of the board. He's an asshole and everyone knows it. I'm planning to make some calls regarding the IPO, later today."

Michael moves to leave. Contemplation on his face, he turns back toward Joyce. "I'm sorry, Joyce. I know you're aware of how damn important this is to me, the board, and certainly the investors. We have to get it done."

"And we will."

He's almost out the door when he hears Joyce rifle through the stack of mail on her desk "Oh shit!"

Michael spins like a top and walks to the front of her desk. "What's the matter?"

Michael watches as Joyce lowers her head, struggling with the millions of thoughts racing through her mind. He knows Joyce and this isn't good. He braces himself as he sees her take a deep, calming breath before sharing the news, "It's a class-action lawsuit."

Michael explodes, throwing his arms into the air. "Are you fucking kidding me?"

"I wish I was."

Michael immediately goes back to the question he fielded from that jackass Jenkins during the board meeting. "Did Jenkins know about this? If not, his asking if there's anything that hasn't currently been accounted for… Something that will delay the IPO further… makes him fucking prescient." He paces back and forth as he digests this news, fearful of what it'll mean for the IPO timing.

"Take a breath. The lead plaintiff is Melissa Cosgrove. You remember her, right? The sixty-three-year-old who claims her chronic kidney disease is a direct result of taking Antsalemab," Joyce says, trying to interrupt his rumination.

Michael starts wringing his hands. "I thought you quashed that?"

"I did," Joyce replies, trying to keep her voice calm. The blame will fall on her if things go sideways. "When we received the letter from that dumb-ass ambulance chaser, I called him and told him to pound sand. Said they wouldn't see a dime. The FDA approved the drug, etc. It's been radio silence for months. I figured they got the hint."

"Well, guess again… Goddamn it!"

Michael stands in the middle of the room, looking more like a lost child at Disney World than the CEO of an up-and-coming biotech firm that has the newest treatment for a disease that affects over six million individuals in the U.S. "You know our resources are thin. Adding a law firm that bills out at $850+ an hour to handle this isn't gonna help."

Joyce sits behind her desk and says with an optimism that isn't fully reflected in her tone, "We can win this. Strike that. We *will* win this. They've got nothing."

Michael shakes his head as if to clear the cobwebs. "I want to meet the attorney before you hire them. I want to make sure it's someone who'll work with us. You understand what I'm saying?"

Joyce glowers at Michael, obviously displeased. "Yes… I know *exactly* what you mean. Let me put out a few feelers."

Michael's compassionate mood of a few moments ago is long gone. "It's important that nothing interferes with the IPO. Nothing."

1

"This is absolute bullshit," MJ Fernandez mutters to herself for the thousandth time as she sits cross-legged on her couch with her beagle's head in her lap and jazz playing in the background. She's wearing her favorite comfy sweats, the ones with the hole in the butt, and the Red Sox t-shirt she got from the 2018 World Series. No bra.

At twenty-nine years old, she's pleased she doesn't need one, although she knows the day's coming. Time has a way of doing that. To add to the speed of that eventuality, she has lousy eating habits and drinks too much, which she blames on the job, although she knows better.

MJ blames being single on the job, too, but that doesn't bother her—she has her dog for company. Snoopy was the happiest dog at the pound the day she'd gone to pick out a companion. She knows his name is a cliché, particularly for an investigative reporter. She uses words to tell stories, and that's the best she could come up with?

As she reflects on today's argument with her editor, Eric Spagnola, MJ pours herself another glass of Sauvignon Blanc, one of her favorites from a little winery in New Zealand. She has the liquor store order it for her by the case. It's cheaper that way. At least, that's how she justifies it to herself.

Earlier, MJ grabbed the backpack that held her laptop before leaving Spagnola's office, closing the door hard enough to let everyone know she was pissed but not so hard as to be described as slamming it—a fine line. She's had lots of practice.

MJ walked briskly to the elevator and slapped the down button, grumbling in frustration, "A pity assignment?" She didn't want any assignment from Spagnola. She prefers finding her own projects. It's what she does.

Today sucked. Spagnola told her they wouldn't be running the final story she had worked months to pull together. It would've given her the front-page ink every reporter covets. Adding to her frustrations, he had encouraged her to continue at each update but sang a different tune today. Based upon what he *didn't* say, she's convinced he's afraid of the political ramifications.

"Chicken shit," MJ says under her breath.

As she rubs Snoopy behind the ears the way he likes, her thoughts shift to what she'll tackle next. She can't sit still for long. She has to be on the go, chasing down a story. It's ingrained.

Being an investigative reporter is all MJ wanted since she watched *All the President's Men* for the first time. Her paperback copy of the book is tattered from repeated readings. She loves the way the story unfolds and the doggedness of the reporters. The fact that it's based on a true story makes it even more appealing.

She stares at her mahogany-framed diploma from the S.I. Newhouse School of Journalism, pondering her reality. She hasn't accomplished anything close to what she set out to do seven years ago. An idealist, she had a shiny new diploma in hand coupled with a voracious appetite for the truth. She vowed to make a difference but, the real world is much more complicated.

Reality doesn't always allow MJ to do what she does best—plow forward, a trait that's earned her the nickname "Pit Bull" by her peers. Her total disregard for anything but the truth has landed her on Spagnola's shit list on more than one occasion.

MJ's strategy is simple: follow the money and the smell of bullshit to their points of origin, and you'll find the truth. It's as easy as that. Okay, maybe not that easy, but she isn't built for political games.

MJ takes another sip of wine as she closes her eyes to listen to *Elevator to the Gallows,* one of her favorites by Miles Davis, starting on Spotify. It fits her mood if she'll actually let herself feel it. "I'll start looking for my next project in the morning," she resigns. Tonight's for good wine, great jazz, and the comfort of an unwavering companion.

After half an hour of getting lost in the music while petting Snoopy, MJ pulls up the e-version of a competitor's newspaper, interested in seeing what others are focusing on. An article on the front page catches her eye. *Propentus IPO in Jeopardy?*

She becomes intrigued by the young CEO who's apparently done what no one else has been able to do: find a treatment that slows the progression of dementia. How does a thirty-six-year-old discover a crown jewel, one that's eluded the brightest scientific minds for years, despite billions of dollars in research?

MJ mournfully recalls her grandmother, who suffered from dementia at the end. She was secretly glad her grandmother didn't live long after the diagnosis. It was gut-wrenching to witness the ravages of the disease first-hand.

As MJ's mind races with possibilities, she pours one more glass of wine as the music changes and decides to start looking into this wunderkind CEO and his magic medicine. Tomorrow.

8

Jonathan and Emily stand nervously on the front stoop of his childhood home with a bottle of Ruffino Chianti, one of his mother's favorites. The cozy three-bedroom cape in Canton is where his parents have lived most of Jonathan's life. It's the home his father surprised his mother with on their third wedding anniversary.

Jonathan gives Emily a quick kiss before they knock on the door and walk in.

Jonathan calls out. "Hello?"

Nancy races to meet them, taking off the apron that didn't help keep the sauce off her blouse as she put the lasagna together. "So glad you're here!"

Her response makes Jonathan hesitant, something he's never felt before, at least not with his parents. "Hi, mom. We brought your favorite."

Nancy stands on her toes and gives Jonathan a hug and kiss on the cheek. The hug is normal; the kiss is not. "Thank you, sweetheart."

Emily carries the wine and follows Nancy into the kitchen while Jonathan heads for the living room, where his father is watching the Red Sox pre-game.

"The Sox really suck this year," Jonathan starts the conversation, wondering what the real topic for the evening will be.

Joe keeps his eyes locked on the screen. "Yeah, they should've done more to stabilize the pitching staff during the off-season. They shouldn't have traded away... Um... You know... What the hell's his name again? Anyway, they got two minor league outfielders. Useless. You can't win if you can't pitch."

"True enough." Jonathan hears something strange in his father's voice.

"But you know me. I'll still watch every pitch."

They both chuckle at the obvious.

Jonathan and his father continue their unusually strained conversation. Jonathan wants to cut to the chase, but knows he has to let them deliver whatever their message is in their own way, at their own time. It's not long before he hears his mother's voice in the dining room as she and Emily get everything ready. He pulls his attention from the Sox game and sees Emily bringing the lasagna pan from the kitchen, the aroma of the meal filling the air.

Nancy yells out, "Okay, boys, let's eat."

Jonathan pours wine for his mother, Emily, and himself—his father has never been a big drinker. He looks over at Emily, who's trying to communicate something to him with her eyes. She fails miserably.

After a quick blessing, Nancy starts to fill the plates with steaming lasagna and homemade meatballs.

Jonathan closes his eyes. The smell transports him to his favorite Italian restaurants in the North End or on Federal Hill. This really is his favorite meal. But it's hard to enjoy it tonight. The very uncommon tension in the air is stealing his joy. When his mom passes a full plate to each of them, she refuses to look Jonathan in the eye. This convinces him that the bad news is about her.

After his dad complains about the Red Sox—again—his mom decides to jump in and talk to Emily. "How's it going at the bank, dear?"

Emily looks at Jonathan before answering. "Things are pretty good, although I had to let one of the branch managers go the other day. Her touchy leadership style, which she refused to modify, made the tellers uncomfortable."

Jonathan watches painfully as his mother forces a smile. This isn't going to be good.

When everyone is fully sated by the wonderful meal, Jonathan and Emily carry the sauce-covered plates to the kitchen, hoping to get a moment alone, but his mom follows them, grabbing the peach cobbler she made for dessert from the oven.

She asks, "Anyone want a cup of coffee?"

Emily and Joe decline, but Jonathan accepts. He needs to be on his toes for whatever's coming next.

As they finish the cobbler, Jonathan and Emily try again to steal a private moment. They take the dessert plates into the kitchen, where Emily sneaks him the one piece of information she was able to gather.

"I think it's really bad. Your mother was crying when I walked into the kitchen earlier. I almost got her to tell me what's going on, but she stopped mid-sentence, wiped the tears from her cheek, and walked into the dining room."

Jonathan's fears are already raging like a wildfire, and Emily's information adds jet fuel to the uncontrolled blaze. He stops short of slamming his fist on the counter. "Shit!"

They head back into the dining room, maintaining the brave faces they've been wearing all evening.

Nancy stands, apparently wanting to delay the discussion, as if delaying it will make it easier. "Why don't we take our coffee into the living room where it's a little more comfortable?"

Jonathan sees the weight of what's to come pressing down on his mother as they step toward the next room.

Nancy nervously sits on the edge of the loveseat and clears her throat. "We have something to tell you." She begins to squirm. "Do you want to tell them Joe, or do you want me to do it?"

Joe plops into his recliner, the seat farthest from Nancy, creating more distance from what she's about to say. "Jesus, Nancy. Just tell 'em."

Nancy looks at the floor, and in a voice barely above a whisper, she delivers the devastating news. "Your father has dementia."

The room goes silent as if sound never existed. The air's thick, making it hard to breathe. Jonathan and Emily are dumbstruck. This isn't one of the possibilities Jonathan contemplated. Words escape them. They stare at each other as the tears start to roll down Nancy's cheeks. Each tear seems to release a little more of the weight she's been carrying. Emily brings her the tissues from the end table.

After what seems like an eternity, Jonathan finally finds his voice. He shifts toward his father as the questions pour out like bullets from a submachine gun. The words are shell casings bouncing all over the carpet. "Dad, is that true? Do you really have Alzheimer's? How long have you known? Why didn't you call me before this afternoon? How do you feel? How do you know for sure? You're so young. Old people get Alzheimer's, right? What are the treatments? This can't be right... Are you sure? Did you get a second opinion?"

His father is outwardly steady, the rock Nancy and Jonathan have always known him to be, but Jonathan senses the fear his father feels inside and stares at him like he did when he was a child.

Joe adopts a stoic expression and holds his hand up. "Yes, the doctor said I have dementia. He told us yesterday." The crushing impact of the words is clear to all in the room.

Jonathan notes his father's response. Not an admission but a statement regarding the doctor's diagnosis.

Emily reaches over to hold Jonathan's hand and then turns to Joe. "I'm so sorry."

Joe waves dismissively as if swatting away a pesky fly. "Stop it. I'm fine." Joe uses a tone designed to convince himself and the others that it's true. It doesn't seem to persuade anyone, least of all himself. He reaches for the lever on the side of the recliner, pulls it, and puts his feet back up, returning his world to its normal position.

Jonathan gets up from the couch and takes a couple of steps toward his father. He doesn't know what to say or do. His mind's reeling. He knows his father hates them, but Jonathan thinks about giving his father a hug. Is it because he wants to or because he thinks it is the right thing to do?

The news is a python slowly squeezing the breath from its prey. Lost in his own circular thoughts, Jonathan turns and sits back down on the couch, only to jump back up immediately. He must get out of the room. Grabbing his coffee cup, he blurts, "I'm getting more coffee."

Jonathan stares at his feet as he walks across the carpet, which now feels like quicksand. He didn't ask his mother if she wanted another cup of coffee; he felt ashamed.

The thoughts come faster as he gets to the kitchen. His father's only sixty-five years old. How can this be? He would've seen signs if his father had Alzheimer's, wouldn't he? Did his mother notice anything? The doctor must be wrong. Dad needs a second opinion. Why is this happening? How does he make this better for his parents?

Jonathan refills his cup and mindlessly takes a gulp of scalding coffee. He almost spits it across the kitchen. Instead, he makes a fish face, sucking in air in an unsuccessful attempt to cool it down before swallowing it with a wince. The pain steadies him as he begins organizing his thoughts. He's smart. He'll do whatever it takes to fix this. He can handle this.

Jonathan walks back toward the living room slowly to give his mouth a chance to cool down and to allow his mind to quiet.

As he walks back in, Emily is giving Nancy a hug. She whispers, "How can we help? We're here for both of you."

Nancy pulls away from the embrace, reaching for more tissues. She takes a couple and hands the box to Emily, who also needs one. Between sniffles, Nancy works to pull herself together, looking intently at Jonathan, unsure of what to do.

Jonathan takes control. "Now that we know, let's all sit back down."

9

Joyce has put this off for as long as she dares. She's dreading making the call, particularly given his attitude this morning, but she has to be the one that tells him. She dials the number she memorized from the Post-It she found under her windshield wiper a couple of weeks ago. It's picked up on the first ring.

She didn't give the other person a chance to speak. "We have a problem."

"Why you tellin' me? Go fuckin' solve it."

"The company was served with a class-action lawsuit that claims Antsalemab caused chronic kidney disease in a sixty-three-year-old woman and others."

"I repeat... Why you fuckin' tellin' me?"

The shaky hand of this morning returns with a vengeance. "It may cause some to rethink the timing of the IPO."

"Were you fuckin' listenin' this mornin'?"

"I was." Less is more at this point.

"No more fuckin' delays." The phone line goes dead once again.

Joyce's shoulders relax as she lets out a small sigh. The call went better than expected. She's been answering to him for years, and was bracing for his usual barrage of expletives and accusations. Screaming about how he thought she was smarter than that. Blah, blah, blah. Does he think she can see the future?

Her breath catches with panic as she breaks into a cold sweat. She knows *exactly* what the future holds if she can't quash this lawsuit quickly and get the IPO launched.

10

Jonathan sits forward, putting his forearms on his thighs. He's not sure what to say, or how to say it. He wants to be gentle, the way his parents taught him to be, but quickly falls into cross-examination mode. "What's the actual diagnosis?"

His father refuses to acknowledge the question. Jonathan's mother retrieves her purse and pulls out a folded piece of paper. She gives it to Jonathan silently, handling it as if it's one of the Simon Pearce wine glasses Emily bought for their anniversary last year. The ones she refuses to use because they're too delicate and too expensive.

It's a doctor's personal stationery. It reads, "Early onset dementia." Beneath that: "Dr. April Mancini, Head of Neurology at Massachusetts General Hospital," with a phone number at the bottom. Jonathan looks to his mother, knowing he has to get involved with his father's treatment. His mother will be emotional, and she'll struggle with every aspect, and that's not helpful for anyone. Jonathan looks at Emily, working to gather strength from her caring yet determined eyes.

"Why don't I call Dr. Mancini in the morning and set up an initial appointment?"

Joe's well-known stubbornness reappears. "I told you, I'm fine. Sure, I forget things. I'm old. Everyone forgets things."

Jonathan knows fighting him at this point will not be beneficial. "Maybe you're right. The first thing we're going to do is ask Dr. Mancini to confirm the diagnosis. It's always good to get a second opinion. The sooner we know what we're dealing with, the better."

Jonathan watches his mother wipe away the occasional tear leaking from her now bloodshot eyes, her fear creating an electricity in the room. "I know you're both scared..."

Joe's heard enough. "I am *not* scared. There's nothing wrong with me. End of discussion."

Jonathan flashes back to the thousands of times his father used this phrase when he was a child. He knows pushing further will only serve to strengthen his father's resolve or, worse still, outright anger him. Jonathan isn't going to ignore this, but one step at a time. He must digest this news and carefully craft a game plan. It's what he does.

The conversation's been shut down, and Joe clearly wants to be left alone, so the evening draws to a close. Jonathan and Emily say their goodbyes. Nancy holds them a little longer and a little tighter than usual.

Once in the car, Jonathan slams the palm of his hands on the steering wheel. In a voice just above a whisper, he lets out some of the emotion he's been swallowing. "Goddamn it!"

Emily reaches over and takes Jonathan's hand. "I'm sorry."

Jonathan yanks his hand back and raises his voice, the anger he concealed from his parents breaking free. "Why are you sorry? He's burying his head in the sand. I mean... I understand he doesn't want to admit it... Who would? This isn't like having a cold. A little chicken soup, and he'll be all set. Stupid son of a bitch!"

Emily tries to bring calm. "Maybe he just doesn't want to burden anyone. He doesn't want to worry you or your mother."

Jonathan barks again, albeit at a lower decibel. "That's bullshit. I'll do whatever it takes to get him what he needs. I have only one concern right now." His mother's tear-filled face flashes before his eyes. "Strike that… Two concerns."

Jonathan backs out of the driveway slowly, staring at his childhood home. This house has been a safe haven for more than forty years, where nothing bad has ever happened. That ended tonight.

Emily rests her hand on Jonathan's thigh as he drives. "Do you want to stop for a drink?"

His anger dissolves. "I can't. I don't know how the hell I'm going to do it, but I have to go back to the office and continue trial prep."

He turns his head to the right, catching Emily gazing sadly at her lap and realizes how selfish he's being. Over the past couple of years, Emily's developed a close relationship with his parents. She's hurting, too.

He smiles, returning his eyes to the road. "Fuck it! It's only 9:15 p.m. Let's find a bar."

Emily leans over as much as the center console will allow and puts her head on Jonathan's arm. He leans over and kisses the top of Emily's head. He loves the floral scent of her shampoo. He takes his right arm and drapes it over Emily's shoulder, giving her a small squeeze.

Tomorrow, he begins the fight for his father. Tonight is theirs.

11

Anticipating he'll need to adjust his schedule in the coming months, Jonathan confides in Walt once he arrives for the day.

"I'm sorry, bud. What can I do?"

Say what you will about Walt, but he's always there when the chips are down.

"Nothing at the moment." Jonathan knows he looks like crap; the bags under his eyes scream lack of sleep. "Hell, I don't know what to do. I've spent hours researching dementia and still feel like I don't know a damn thing about it. Our first appointment with the neurologist is next week."

"That's good. You don't want to hear this, but you really do have to take it one step at a time."

"I know, but patience isn't a strength for me."

"Don't I know that?" Walt smiles, trying to lighten the mood, even for a moment. "Now, get back to work. I hear the boss is a real jackass if he catches you goofing off."

Jonathan's wearing a weak smile as he returns to his trial prep. He's lost a lot of time, and playing catch-up is another thing he hates. His office phone rings as he opens a new package of Post-It notes, fluorescent green this time. Each color has a different meaning.

Julie, the office manager, picks up the call. Jonathan can't make out what's being said on the other side of the door, but it sounds like Julie's taking someone to the woodshed. He's trying to focus when there's a knock on his door. Everyone knows not to bother him when he's preparing for trial.

Jonathan's sleep-deprived mind has to work extra hard to keep his annoyance under wraps. "Yes?"

Julie opens the door and sticks her head through the crack. "Sorry to interrupt, Jonathan. There's a call for you. The woman refuses to leave a message. She says she's an attorney and is threatening to keep calling until you speak with her. She says it's 'critically important.'" Julie rolls her eyes, making air quotes as she says it.

Jonathan nods and manages to flash a sympathetic smile. "That's okay, Julie. You don't get paid enough to deal with all the crazies. Give me a second." Jonathan can't imagine who this woman is. She must be something if Julie can't handle her. He takes a few minutes to let this woman cool her heels. He'll take the call on his terms, not hers.

Jonathan walks around to his desk and sits down. He takes a quick swig from a warm energy drink sitting on the corner. He's been living on these and chicken wings from The Jury Room. He takes a deep breath and picks up the call using his best irritated tone. "This is Jonathan Silverman."

"Mr. Silverman, my name is Joyce Kramer. I'm General Counsel for Propentus, a biotech firm in Cambridge."

Jonathan will always defend Julie. "Ms. Kramer, berating the office manager to get me to take your call is unacceptable."

"Yes, that was unfortunate. I'll apologize. I'll do whatever you think is best, but I have an urgent matter."

Jonathan's tired and only half listening. He's scribbling a trial detail on a Post-It. "You can apologize to Julie a couple of seconds after this call ends. I'm preparing for trial. Candidly, I don't have time to take this call."

"Understood. We've been served with a class-action lawsuit. Let me … Strike that … Would it be okay if I sent you a copy of the complaint?"

"Ms. Kramer, I'm not trying to be confrontational, but what part of 'I don't have time' are you not understanding?"

"Mr. Silverman, I've done my research. You're exactly who we need on this one."

"Again, Ms. Kramer…" He stops mid-sentence, his attention pulled away from the bright green Post-It as the front page of the newspaper flashes through his mind. "… Ms. Kramer, is this connected to the article in the *Globe*?"

"Yes."

He hesitates, waiting for her to say something more. Surprised when she doesn't. "Okay, Ms. Kramer. Julie will give you an email address… *After* you apologize. I'll take a look." Trial doesn't start for a few more days, and Jonathan suddenly finds himself very interested in treatments for dementia.

"Thank you, Mr. Silverman. Please transfer me back to Julie."

"Goodbye, Ms. Kramer." He's intrigued. This may be a drug that can help his father, and besides, he can always say no.

12

MJ's sitting on the couch in her usual position, legs crossed, her laptop balancing on her knees, and a Yeti full of black coffee on the side table. Long before she hits the streets to investigate a story, she spends hours trolling the internet for information. She wants to be prepared when she asks her questions. She may only get one shot, and she wants to make the most of it.

She excels in this and actually enjoys what others call tedium. Her friends, the handful she has, are convinced she's crazy. Who the hell takes joy in surfing the internet day and night, looking for all the little details? When they give her grief, she reminds them their phones are for more than texting and posting pictures of their meals to social media.

MJ is shocked by the number of articles generated by her entering "Propentus" into the search field. The company has been the subject of hundreds of articles in the past twelve months. After a few minutes of sifting through the list, she finds the *Globe* article that initially piqued her interest. She reads it again, taking notes. Eventually, she'll transfer the information onto one of the external hard drives she keeps in the industrial safe she has secured to the floor of her bedroom closet. It's the size of a small refrigerator. Just like her sources, MJ doesn't mess around when it comes to protecting her research. She needs it for personal reasons, too. Where else would one keep a birth certificate and a passport?

Next, she finds the lawsuit's case name and docket number, which allows her to begin her search of the public court records. She enters the case number and takes a sip of her coffee.

After bookmarking it she reads the entire complaint four times. The lead plaintiff is Melissa Cosgrove, a sixty-three-year-old mother of two and grandmother of five, who alleges she suffers from chronic kidney disease as a direct result of taking Antsalemab for early-onset dementia. MJ knows there are a few more plaintiffs waiting in the wings; otherwise, it wouldn't have been filed as a class-action.

With a little more typing, MJ begins her medical education, learning Ms. Cosgrove has three options: dialysis multiple times a week, finding a donor for a kidney transplant, or dying slowly as her kidneys fail to clear the toxins from her system. None of those sound appealing.

Since it was sued in Ms. Cosgrove's name and not the name of her estate, MJ rules out option number three. With a dementia diagnosis, she wouldn't likely be a candidate for the national registry, which means her only options for a transplant are to get a new kidney from a family member with a compatible blood type or a directed donation. With no mention of transplantation in the complaint, MJ concludes Ms. Cosgrove is receiving regular dialysis. A shitty way to live.

MJ has read plenty of complaints over the years, and this one's horribly drafted. The attorney representing Ms. Cosgrove, Mr. Schneider, is a stereotypical ambulance chaser. She's seen him, with his lousy-fitting suits and even worse-fitting toupee, advertise on late-night TV. She doesn't sleep much.

Something draws MJ to this story. First, the poor woman's been diagnosed with early-onset dementia, which is bad enough. Fortunately, she can afford the newest available treatment, but after taking the drug for a while, she's diagnosed with chronic kidney disease and now requires regular dialysis. To make the entire situation worse, Ms. Cosgrove has declared war on the biotech firm that discovered the treatment with an attorney better known as "The King of the Fender Bender."

Her mind begins to swirl in its customary way, generating question after question. Why didn't Ms. Cosgrove go with one of the power players in the plaintiff's bar? Did she try, and none of them would take the case? If not, why not? Did the big firms learn of something that suggested it would be a losing battle despite being a story that pulls at the heartstrings? How did Schneider land a case like this?

MJ then thinks about this guy swimming with the sharks. Does he know that's where he's at? Does he care? Or is he looking for a quick settlement, even if it means selling his client short?

Rage swells in MJ. As a self-proclaimed fighter for the underdog who'll do anything to find the truth, she decides that Ms. Cosgrove deserves better, and who better to help her?

13

The Last Inning is a sports bar where Jimmy has spent the majority of his adult life. He remembers the day he bought the place. He never blinked when he cheated the "missing" owner's wife on the price. It's what he does.

He slaps on the cologne he keeps in his desk, locks the door to his office, and heads out to find the brunette he met a couple of weeks ago. The eighties rock song "Pour Some Sugar on Me" by Def Leppard is blasting from the speakers hung on every beam. As he struts toward the front door, his brooding mood sending a clear message, he sees Vinnie Napolitano standing at the bar in his Propentus security uniform, looking like a child waiting for their parent to pick them up from school.

"What the fuck do you want?"

"Jimmy, I wanna…"

Before he could continue, Jimmy's anger erupts as a violent back-hand. "Shut the fuck up you worthless piece a' shit. I put you in a primo fuckin' job. What do I get for my effort? Not a fuckin' thing. I gotta hear shit from others."

Vinnie rubs his face. He reaches for a bar napkin and in one swig finishes the whiskey sitting in front of him, the alcohol stinging his split lip. The liquid courage makes it possible to try to defend himself. "Jimmy, whatta ya mean? I tell you stuff?"

"I shoulda left you in that fuckin' parkin' lot. Woulda saved myself a shitload of trouble."

Vinnie stares at the floor still dabbing his lip, and whining like a toddler in a check-out line begging for candy. "Jimmy. I've helped you…"

"Shut. The. Fuck. Up!"

Jimmy raises his hand again, and Vinnie flinches to avoid having his lower lip match his upper, but he never completes the swing. The glare of anger on his face turns to one of disdain. Without another word, Jimmy resumes his interrupted trip to find tonight's bedfellow.

• • •

After Jimmy wanders away, Vinnie orders a double, wanting to blot the interaction from his mind and dull the pain from his pulsating lip.

The huge bartender in a Last Inning t-shirt that's two sizes too small takes pity on him. "Why don't you go home, man?"

"Just give me my fuckin' drink!"

The bartender scoffs at the demand. He shrugs and walks to the other end of the bar, ignoring Vinnie, who's sitting with his head in his hands, his elbows leaning on the bar. He's disgusted with himself as the night that changed his life plays in his head like a bad movie.

It was a cold, dark, rainy night, the type of steady rain everyone loves because it helps the lawn. It was a little after 2 a.m., and Vinnie was sitting in his patrol car with his lights off in a place he wasn't supposed to be: the parking lot behind

The Last Inning. He'd told dispatch he was Code 7 at a diner across town.

It was closing time, and he hoped to catch Tina leaving at the end of her shift. Vinnie had chatted up the blond waitress the last time he was there. She was somewhat attractive, and she seemed interested, so he figured he'd ask her out. A real date, not just sitting at the bar with him buying her Appletinis, like last time. He didn't even get a goodnight kiss for his efforts.

After arriving at the bar, Vinnie popped a piece of Trident into his mouth and waited. As he began to settle in, someone stumbled out the back door of the bar. He wasn't expecting anyone but Tina. Vinnie peered through the rain-covered windshield and turned the car's spotlight toward the back door. The guy was bombed. Not really walking. Shuffling was a more accurate description.

Vinnie looked at his watch. His limited window of time was quickly closing, and this guy was fucking everything up. Vinnie opened the car door, grabbed his baton, and nearly slipped on the wet pavement while getting out of the prowler. As the rain soaked through his uniform, he hit the baton against the palm of his hand to get the drunk's attention. "Hey, shut up before you wake up the whole neighborhood."

"Fuck you, sasshole… I'lls wake every damn body up if I wanna!" The drunk began to trudge toward Vinnie.

Vinnie got pissed. "Stop!" He slammed the baton into his palm again. "Listen, man, just fuckin' go home." He turned on his heels and walked briskly toward his police cruiser. Two thoughts ran through Vinnie's head as he jumped back into his car: *Tina's not worth the bullshit,* and *I need to get back to work before I get caught.*

With the rain coming down heavier every moment, Vinnie started to back up and maneuver in the small area behind the bar. As he was swinging around to return to the main street using the alley next to the bar, a twinkle of light coming from the door the drunk had emerged from caught his eye. *Tina's kinda cute… So…*

He felt it before he heard it. The car rose up and then returned to the pavement. The sledgehammer of realization hit as he slammed the gearshift into park.

"Motherfucker!" Vinnie leaped from the car to find the drunk under the cruiser, blood, and air bubbles gurgling from his lips. Vinnie remembers him trying to say something, but neither words nor air came out. Nothing, just the drunk's glassy eyes staring upward as the rain mixed with the blood leaking from his mouth.

Vinnie stood in the pouring rain, eyes wide open, not blinking. He'd been distracted, looking toward the glimpse of light. It happened in a split second… Fucking Tina! The drunk must have slipped on the pavement as Vinnie had almost done moments earlier.

His head began violently swinging back and forth in search of potential witnesses. Finding none, he decided to get the body out of sight. It'd be hours before anyone found it, and the rain would wash away the evidence of his transgression. As he dragged the body toward the dumpster, Vinnie learned the true meaning of "dead weight."

The rain continued to pelt his face as the back door swung open fully, light again briefly covering the parking area. It wasn't Tina.

• • •

Vinnie sits up and throws back the rest of his drink as the worst part of the memory comes into focus. He closes his eyes with the realization that his life mirrors the famous line from The Eagles' "Hotel California."

The sliver of light was a young Jimmy Rizzo leaving for the night. Despite the downpour, he never hesitated, walking straight toward Vinnie without a word. Jimmy stopped short, noticing a red trail on the pavement. Without saying a word, he followed it to its endpoint, carefully tip-toeing around the blood.

Just then, Vinnie's radio crackled. "Base to 21-33."

Everything fell into place quickly. Jimmy stepped from behind the dumpster, gave Vinnie a smirk, and played it perfectly. "Listen kid, get the fuck outta here before you lose everythin'. Come back an' see me tomorrow night around closin' time. I'll take care of the rest."

Time stood still. Each raindrop akin to being struck with a ball pein hammer. The weight of the last five minutes crushed Vinnie's future into an uncertain, singular option. Without warning, Vinnie's defeated voice fights its way through the wind and rain. "I'm workin' nights this month."

Jimmy laughs. "Okay, asshole, come an' see me in the mornin'. Answer the call, get yourself outta here, and find somewhere to get the blood off you and the car."

Vinnie reached up to his collar mic, slowed his breathing, and responded to the dispatcher: "This is 21-33... Sorry... Was in the can. 21-33 is 10-14."

And with that, his fate was sealed.

Suddenly, Vinnie slams his empty glass on the bar, frustrated by the stupidity of youth. The passing of twenty-five years has seen him doing whatever Jimmy demands. He's used police databases to give Jimmy information on his rivals, stolen drugs from the evidence locker, helped Jimmy avoid raids, fucked with evidence, and broken the bones of people who owed Jimmy money.

Vinnie's done everything short of murder; he has morals, after all.

14

Jonathan has a lot of jobs today: supporter, listener, note-taker, mediator, and advocate, but none more important than son. He arrives at his parents' house early, fearing that getting his father to go to this appointment will be harder than getting a teenager up and ready for school. He knocks on the door and enters cautiously. "Good morning."

"Good morning, sweetheart." Nancy's wearing an eggshell-colored blouse with a blue pleated skirt. "Do you want a cup of coffee?" She's rushing around cleaning the kitchen.

Jonathan wonders why she feels compelled to dress up today. "That'd be great. Where's Dad?"

"In his chair, watching the news." A conspiratorial voice Jonathan's never heard before follows. "Don't tell him I told you, but he didn't sleep well last night. He tossed and turned like the bingo balls in the spinning wheel at church."

Apparently, Jonathan wasn't alone. Part of it was work, but the real reason was today's appointment. Knowing the answer based on what she's told him, he asks anyway. "How'd you sleep?"

"I slept okay. Although I was up early today." She isn't convincing. Nancy walks over and gives Jonathan a one-armed hug. With the other, she hands him a steaming mug of coffee.

As his mother lets go, he decides it's time to bite the bullet and say good morning to his father. His confidence isn't there, but he can't let that show… not today. He walks toward the living room, smiling and silently wishing he was there for a different reason.

Fox and Friends is on. His father switches back and forth between that and CNN. Jonathan has heard it his entire life. *Between the two, the truth's in there somewhere. The challenge is finding it.*

"Mornin' Dad."

Joe shifts in his chair and grumbles. "Mornin'."

Thankfully, his mom was able to get his dad dressed in a polo and khakis. Jonathan wasn't sure what he'd find. One hurdle cleared. "How'd you sleep?"

"Fine."

Jonathan's internal struggles find him defaulting to the obvious. "Watching *Fox*, huh?"

"Yup." Joe takes a sip of his coffee.

This isn't going to be a fun day. Jonathan has to remember his mother and father are both scared. Yes, he's scared too, but that doesn't matter. It's about the two of them. End of discussion.

"We need to leave in ten minutes."

More grumbling. "Whatever. Let's just get this over with."

Jonathan turns and heads back to the kitchen. "That was like pulling teeth."

Nancy smiles weakly as a tear trickles down her face. "Yeah, barely says two words anymore. I'm really scared."

"Of course you are." He almost said, "We all are," but remembers who this is really about. "It's a scary time. We'll find out what's going on, and then we'll figure out how to tackle it."

She wipes the tears from her eyes with a tissue she'd tucked in her sleeve. "I'm glad you're here," she says with a sniffle.

"Where else would I be?" He gives his mother another hug. This time, she wraps both arms around him. He swears she's going to crack one of his ribs. "Mom, why don't you get your things? I'll get Dad."

She looks up at him and squeezes him tighter still. "Good luck with that."

They share a brief chuckle. It's nice to see her smile, even for a moment. She heads to the other room to grab her handbag as he returns to the living room.

"Come on, Dad. It's time to go." Jonathan's bracing himself for "Hurricane Joe."

"Fine." Joe throws the lever, returning the recliner to its upright position, turns the TV off, drops the remote in his chair, and heads toward the door. "Are we going or what?"

Not wanting to lose momentum, Jonathan places his coffee cup on the counter as they get to the kitchen. He begins to walk toward the door when he feels his mother's gaze. Wearing a sheepish look, he steps back, empties it, and puts it in the dishwasher. Emily's constantly on him about that, too.

As everyone gets in the car, he sadly embraces the fact that this will be the longest, most heartbreaking journey of his life, and it starts with this car ride. Second hurdle cleared.

It's a Friday in July. The traffic is lighter than normal. A lot of people are down the Cape or in New Hampshire enjoying their vacation or working from their summer home. Jonathan's thankful for the small favor. His father doesn't tolerate traffic on a good day, and today's not going to be a good day.

They arrive at Dr. Mancini's office twenty minutes early. Jonathan had planned for any contingency except the ones he got: total compliance from his father and zero traffic.

Jonathan smiles. "We're a few minutes early, but let's go in. There's always forms that need to be filled out."

"Fine." Joe unbuckles the seatbelt, opens the car door, and jumps out as if his display of dexterity proves nothing's wrong.

Jonathan's already gotten out and opened the door for his mother. She smooths out her skirt after getting out of the backseat.

Jonathan's determined to bring something positive to this day. "Mom, you look great! Doesn't Mom look terrific, Dad?"

Joe turns his head and looks Nancy up and down. "Why are you all dressed up? We're going to the doctor's, not a wedding." At least he didn't say funeral. Jonathan's thankful for small favors.

Nancy immediately snaps back, "I want to look nice. Is that okay?"

Everyone's on edge. Maybe it's time for Jonathan to put on his mediator hat?

"Whatever." Joe starts stomping toward the building.

The three of them get in the elevator, and Jonathan pushes the button for the fourth floor. They ride up in silence, lost in their own thoughts. Jonathan checks his father in ten minutes early and is politely handed a clipboard holding a number of documents.

"Here, Dad. You need to sign this. It allows the doctor to bill Medicare directly. I already filled in the other details." He passes the clipboard and pen to his father.

Joe's body language is clear as he scribbles his signature across the line Jonathan identified without looking.

A few minutes later, they're escorted to the exam room. Joe leads the way in another attempt to demonstrate his well-being. Even with this next hurdle cleared, Jonathan knows they're a long way from the finish line.

As they wait, Jonathan considers the information Emily pulled from the Internet. Dr. April Mancini received her medical degree from Harvard University and did her residency at Johns Hopkins in Baltimore. According to her research, she's one of the best.

Emily found an article written when Dr. Mancini was named the Head of Neurology which provided more personal background. April Mancini was valedictorian of her high school graduating class and got into Harvard with her perfect SAT scores. According to the article, April had dreamt of being a doctor from a very young age. The photo accompanying the story captured the old stethoscope her pediatrician gave her when she was five years old, hanging proudly in her office.

There's a gentle knock on the exam room door. Dr. April Mancini walks in, bringing calm and warmth with her. "Good morning, Mr. and Mrs. Silverman."

Jonathan steps forward. He was standing in the corner of the small room. His father sits stoically on the exam table, ramrod straight and maintaining his self-imposed silence. His mother sits in the small chair that had been in Jonathan's corner with her purse in her lap, fiddling with a tissue.

"Good morning, doctor. I'm Jonathan Silverman, Joe's son. This is my mother, Nancy, and of course, my father, Joe."

They shake hands briefly. "Pleasure to meet you," she says and quickly turns her attention to the person she came to see. "How are you feeling today, Mr. Silverman? Can I call you Joe? Do you prefer Joseph?"

That gets Joe to smile. "The only time someone calls me Joseph is when I'm in trouble."

Jonathan smiles and shakes his head. He's heard that line a million times.

The doctor chuckles at the response. "Okay, Joe it is. How are you feeling today, Joe?"

The brief smile quickly returns to a tight-lipped, blank expression. "Fine."

Nancy leans forward, unable to remain quiet. "He always says that."

"Thank you, Mrs. Silverman."

"Please call me Nancy."

Dr. Mancini smiles affably. "Okay. Thank you, Nancy."

So far, Jonathan's impressed. As the Head of Neurology, whose calendar's undoubtedly packed with meetings and appointments, she's amazingly calm and unrushed.

"Your file says you were referred by Dr. Robinson. Is that correct?"

Nancy puts the tissue away and engages fully. "Yes, that's right."

Dr. Mancini takes an understanding breath. She glances at Jonathan, who gets the unspoken message. He puts his hand on his mother's shoulder, leans over, and whispers in her ear. Nancy nods.

"Will you answer a few questions for me, Joe?"

"Sure."

Jonathan knows he's trying not to be ornery, but his tone fails to convey that.

"Do you know what day it is, Joe?"

"Friday, I think. I don't really pay attention anymore. I'm retired. Gave up my watch, too."

Jonathan twitches at his use of the phrase "I think." Nancy doesn't notice because it is, in fact, Friday.

Dr. Mancini offers a reassuring smile. "Thank you. Can you tell me where you are?"

"The doctor's office."

"Do you know the address?"

"No, my son drove, but I think we're in Waltham."

Nancy cringes, leaping to correct him. "No, Joe. We're in Newton. I told you we were going to Newton this morning, remember?"

Dr. Mancini doesn't even blink. "That's correct, Nancy. We're at my offices in Newton. Joe, I'm going to ask you to remember these three words for me… banana, tricycle, and clock. Can you do that?"

"Sure. Banana, tricycle, and… um, clock."

"Right. Very good."

Dr. Mancini asks a number of questions about Joe's medical history, and after capturing the answers, she returns to the prior question: "Joe, can you tell me the three words I asked you to remember?"

Jonathan holds his breath, repeating to himself: *banana, tricycle, clock.*

Tension fills the small exam room as Joe looks at the floor. He looks back up, smiling. "Clock… I know one of 'em's clock."

"That's right, Joe. Do you remember the other two?" Dr. Mancini's encouraging tone wills Joe to answer.

"I think one was bicycle."

"Very close. It's tricycle. That's a kind of bicycle, right? What about the last one?"

Jonathan sees a well-understood redness creep onto his father's face. Joe's frustration's about to boil over. He shifts on the table, the sanitary paper crinkling like wrapping paper at Christmas.

Nancy moves to protect the love of her life. "It's banana, Joe. Remember? It's banana."

Joe whips his head toward Nancy, his rage just below the surface. "Of course, I remember."

Dr. Mancini enters a few notes into her laptop and then places it on the counter. She pulls a small pad of paper and a pen from the pocket of her lab coat and hands them to Joe. "Can you please draw a clock that shows 2:15 for me, Joe?"

Joe scrunches his face at the odd request but takes the pen and starts writing. He draws something reasonably resembling a circle. He starts adding numbers to the clock inside the circle. He writes the numbers one through twelve in the correct order, but they are bunched up in the space where you'd expect to see twelve through eight. The arrows are the same size but close to the requested position.

He hands the pad back to the doctor. "Well done, Joe. That's it; no more questions for today."

The stress in Joe's shoulders visibly fades.

Dr. Mancini grabs her laptop and stands. "Excuse me for a moment." She walks out of the exam room, closing the door gently behind her.

Reality begins to take its inevitable toll as Jonathan digests what he has just witnessed. His father has been the bedrock of the family—never sick, never one to complain, the one whose sole focus has been providing his wife and son with whatever they needed or wanted.

Now, it's their turn to take care of Joe. Jonathan sympathetically places his hand on his mother's shoulder, recognizing the same emotionally devastating thoughts are likely flooding her mind.

Joe smirks. "See… Told you I was fine."

Jonathan's crushed as his mother's querying eyes silently plead with him. The past twenty minutes have been excruciating. He isn't sure if she's looking for him to confirm what she hopes; that Joe's fine, or that Joe isn't fine, but everything will be alright. It doesn't matter. He smiles lovingly, allowing her to choose the answer she seeks.

15

Vinnie's anxiously sitting outside Joyce's office, his tongue darting along his scabbed-over lip. He'll feel better once he's back in Jimmy's good graces, and Joyce is the key.

The door opens, and Joyce sighs. "I'm busy, Vinnie." She steps aside and points toward her office, an invitation to enter.

"Hey, Joyce. How goes it?"

"Do you read the papers, Vinnie? What do you want?"

Vinnie puts his hand on a chair in front of her desk. "Mind if I sit?"

"Yes, as a matter of fact, I do."

Vinnie never lets her rebukes interfere with the mission. "Well... Just wondering if there are any concerns with this new lawsuit?"

The redness creeping up Joyce's neck conveys to Vinnie how pissed she is. "No concerns. The FDA approved the drug, and we're confident we'll defeat the class certification and the litigation in its entirety."

Vinnie has no idea what "class certification" means and doesn't want to look stupid by asking. He's always had a thing for Joyce, but she sprinted in the other direction the first time he suggested spending time together outside the office. Besides, it doesn't matter. Today's about getting information. "Okay. You need anything from a security perspective?"

Her neck's in full bloom at this point, and Joyce makes her eye roll obvious. "No, Vinnie. I'll let you know if I need anything. I have to get back to work." She dismisses him the same way she invited him in.

"Sure. I'm here if you need me."

He has no choice but to smile and leave empty-handed. Jimmy's expecting him to deliver. He looks to the heavens for guidance and is struck by a lightning bolt. He tries not to run.

Harold Johnson, PhD, VP Head of Research, and Renee Spencer, PhD, lead researcher for Antsalemab, are sitting in Harold's office when Vinnie arrives out of breath. Harold is complaining about his horrible personal situation again.

Vinnie's excited. Questioning these two is no different than his years as a detective when he had a suspect "in the box." Harold's office is better lit, but it's about the same size, and equally as inviting.

Vinnie leans his shoulder on the casing of the open door with his hands stuffed into his pockets. "Mornin', team."

Harold takes his eyes off Renee's long legs and looks up, probably hoping Vinnie didn't overhear him. "Whatta you want, Vinnie?"

"Just makin' my rounds. Crazy about the lawsuit, huh?" It's a lousy segue, but these two are lab geeks. Vinnie doesn't need to be tricky.

Renee's neck starts to get blotchy, and her left leg begins bouncing. She looks at Harold, silently begging him to do the talking. Vinnie's excited by her change in appearance, knowing she gets flushed and her leg bounces uncontrollably when she's nervous. She'll definitely give him something worth taking to Jimmy.

There's no love lost between Vinnie and Harold. "It's common for these types of lawsuits to be filed. It was going to happen to Propentus sooner or later." Harold's dismissive tone reflects an air of superiority he doesn't possess.

Vinnie decides to divide and conquer. "Hey Renee, you're the lead researcher on Antsalemab, right? What do you think about the lawsuit?" Vinnie's instincts are confirmed by the speed with which Renee turns to look at Harold.

She swallows hard. "Like Harold said, happens all the time."

Vinnie pushes himself off the door casing with a grunt. "If you say so. See ya around."

He confidently strolls toward his office to devise a plan to get Renee alone... She's the weak link.

16

After the passing of a few quiet moments, there's a light knock on the exam room door. The nurse who walked them in and took Joe's vital signs at the beginning returns.

"Dr. Mancini would like to see you in her office where it's a little more comfortable. Please follow me."

Joe slides off the exam table, bringing most of the sanitary paper with him. He turns as Nancy nervously picks the paper off the floor, trying to put it back in place.

The nurse smiles reassuringly. "That's okay. Please don't worry about that. It happens all the time."

They're led to an office, where Dr. Mancini sits behind a desk that holds a single file. In front of the desk are two matching chairs and a folding chair.

Dr. Mancini motions toward the seats. "If you'll indulge me, I like to share why I do what I do." She pauses as the three take their seats. "In short, it's to honor my grandmother, who was diagnosed with dementia right after I started medical school. My family and I cared for her as her journey progressed, and that served as the defining moment for me, directing me to pursue neurology as a specialty. As someone who believes in fate, at least a little, I knew this to be my destiny. From that moment forward, this has been, and will be, the focus of my efforts."

Jonathan's impressed with her willingness to give them a look behind the curtain and openly share her personal pain. Today's interaction has told him everything he needs to know about the doctor now treating his father.

She lets those comments hang in the air for a moment. "I reviewed Dr. Robinson's findings before your appointment. I understand what they say, and what's been communicated to you."

Nancy stiffens. Joe looks at the doctor blankly, and Jonathan squirms like a little boy who's about to tell his parents what he's done.

"While I use the information, I don't trust any diagnosis I don't make myself."

Jonathan knows what's coming next, and the glimmer of hope he sees in his mother's eyes is about to be violently extinguished.

"Joe, I'm sorry to say you possess the indications of dementia. It's commonly referred to as 'early-onset' or 'young-onset' dementia if the patient is sixty-five or younger, which you are.

A lone tear trickles down Nancy's cheek. Jonathan knew she'd been praying Dr. Robinson was wrong. Dr. Mancini offers Nancy the box of tissues she pulls from her bottom desk drawer. Tools of the trade.

"Thank you."

Jonathan places the "advocate" hat squarely on his head. "Doctor, the questions you asked my father, they were part of a test, right? And his answers lead you to conclude he has early-onset Alzheimer's?"

Dr. Mancini adopts the tone of a professor in front of a class. "First, dementia is a more encompassing term.

Alzheimer's is the most common form of dementia, representing about 70% of all dementia cases. I'd want a couple of additional tests before I'd make an actual Alzheimer's diagnosis." She lets that settle for a moment.

"Secondly, yes, it's the Mini-Mental State Examination, sometimes called by the shortened name 'mini-mental,' or the Folstein test. It measures orientation, memory, attention and concentration, language, and the visual orientation of objects. It's used extensively in the diagnosis of dementia."

Jonathan recalls seeing this mentioned in some of the literature Emily had pulled together. "Sorry. I thought all dementia was Alzheimer's."

Dr. Mancini remains the professor, encouraging her student. "Most people believe that."

Jonathan plunges forward. "Is that the test where a score is generated?"

"Yes. It's a 30-point scale. A score of 23 or lower is indicative of dementia. The lower the number, the more severe the status of the disease."

Joe reaches for Nancy's hand and regretfully looks her in the eye. "I'm sorry, Nance."

Jonathan watches as Dr. Mancini works to calm the anticipated emotions before they burst forth. "Joe, I tell you this as a board-certified neurologist. You've done absolutely nothing wrong and, therefore, have nothing to apologize for. The true cause of this disease has been a mystery, and despite recent therapies and billions in annual research, a cure remains elusive."

Jonathan asks the next logical question, steeling himself for the response. "What was Dad's score?"

Without hesitation or remorse, she gives them the facts. "His score's on the cusp. He scored a 23. However, I'd be remiss if I didn't tell you the MMSE isn't 100% conclusive.

There's a very small number of false positives. I don't want to give you false hope, but my job's to be honest and transparent."

Jonathan continues to be impressed by Dr. Mancini. She's straightforward without being harsh and isn't one to conceal the truth to avoid emotional fallout. He's pretty sure she could tell someone to screw off, and they'd thank her.

Not wanting to fall into his own spiral of depression, he presses on. "What tests would you want to perform before you're sure?"

"I'd like to get a PET scan, possibly an MRI, and a spinal tap. Are you willing to do that, Joe?"

Jonathan appreciates that she focuses on the patient.

Nancy jumps in. "Of course, he is. There's still a chance he doesn't have dementia, right?"

Before the doctor can answer, Jonathan continues his questioning. "What will these tests tell you?"

Dr. Mancini makes the information understandable. "The scans can show the loss of brain mass, which is associated with Alzheimer's disease and other types of dementia. And we're looking for a protein called 'soluble amyloid precursor protein beta' or 'APP-beta' in the spinal fluid. That's also an indicator of Alzheimer's."

Jonathan's still trying to wrap his head around all of this. "So, in addition to the protein, you're looking for some type of brain shrinkage?"

"I wouldn't put it that way, but essentially, yes." She shifts her attention. "Nancy, I haven't forgotten your question. While it's theoretically possible these tests will come back negative, indicating a false positive on the MMSE, I can say with a high degree of medical certainty that Joe has early-onset dementia."

Joe's sorrowful look shakes Jonathan to his core.

Tiny pieces of tissue paper fall onto the floor in front of Nancy. "But there's still a chance?"

Jonathan grabs the "protector" hat. "Dad, it's your decision, but you don't need to make it this second, right Dr. Mancini?"

"Not at all. But I'd like to complete these tests sooner rather than later. Joe, do you have any questions?"

Joe looks down, summoning strength from the floor, and responds with conviction. "Nope. Might as well just get it over with."

"Good. I'll ask the Imaging Center to prioritize the scans. Please check with reception before you leave."

Dr. Mancini pauses, allowing her patient and his family to begin absorbing the life-altering devastation her news has thrust upon them. "I encourage you all to learn about dementia. I'll answer your questions honestly and directly. But there's a lot to this. The National Alzheimer's Association is a tremendous place to start. I also know there's a MA/NH chapter. Both are amazing resources and great places to continue learning about the disease. You should also know there's an 800 number available day or night. It's manned by highly-trained counselors 24/7/365 prepared to provide guidance and answer any and all questions you may have. And there's never any cost to you. You can find more information at www.alz.org."

She hands them a pre-printed card as her tone switches from physician to a caring woman who's been through what they're about to face. "My family and I found these services invaluable. Please don't be afraid to use them. And above all, please know you're not alone in this."

Fascinated by Dr. Mancini's ability to make each one of them feel heard and supported during a gut-wrenching discussion, Jonathan's mind fixates on her last statement. As he prepares to lead this fight for his parents, he's never felt more alone.

17

When Jonathan arrives at the office the next day, Julie hands him a pile of pink message slips and lowers her voice. "I'm sorry to hear about your father."

Jonathan's surprised. He hasn't told anyone, but... *Damn it, Walt!*

"Please don't be mad at Walt. You know we both care about you and Emily and while he won't say it out loud, you're his family."

Jonathan knows she's right. "Thanks, Julie. Please don't share this with anyone."

Julie winks at Jonathan and heads back to her desk. "I'm a vault."

He walks into his office and hangs his suit jacket on the coat rack in the corner. Some people like the warmth and security a blanket brings. His litigation files are his blanket. He knows it drives the paralegals nuts when they have to search his office for a file, but he does it anyway. A benefit of being the boss.

Sitting on top of another file in the middle of his desk is a copy of the Propentus complaint and a non-disclosure agreement. There's also a note from one of the paralegals: *No conflict identified.*

Jonathan remains standing, looking out the window. Why would he need to sign an NDA to review a complaint that's public record? He pushes that to the side and grabs a new legal pad and a pen with blue ink. Seeing comments written in red feels too much like reading a high school term paper after the teacher graded it. Not his style.

He begins reading the poorly written complaint, making notes along the way. The first thing he notices is the plaintiff's attorney is "The King of the Fender Bender." How the hell did he secure this case? The lead plaintiff, Melissa Cosgrove, is a sixty-three-year-old woman diagnosed with early-onset dementia. Jonathan can't help but wonder what her "mini-mental" score is. Timing was on her side. She's one of the first individuals to have been prescribed the newly FDA-approved treatment, Antsalemab. He knows from his own research that the drug has an annual cost in excess of $36,000. He also knows Medicare hasn't yet agreed to cover the treatment. How's she paying for this on a retiree's income? In no time, he has three pages of scribbled questions.

The complaint asserts the drug was providing benefits after four to five months, but there's nothing that speaks to why or how the plaintiff knows that. After seven months of treatment, the plaintiff's bloodwork reflected potential kidney problems. A month later, the plaintiff's diagnosed with chronic kidney disease, allegedly as a result of taking Antsalemab.

He's just finishing up his initial review of the complaint when his phone buzzes. "Ms. Kramer's on hold for you."

Jonathan is torn. Should he take the call now or push her off? Based on their initial interaction, he isn't sure delaying is an option. "Persistent" is the nicest word he can use to describe her.

With a sigh, Jonathan accepts the call. "Hello, Ms. Kramer."

"Good morning, Mr. Silverman. Have you had a chance to review everything?"

"I just finished my initial review of the complaint. You know Leo Schneider is 'The King of the Fender Bender,' right?"

"I noted that. Wonder how the hell he got a case like this?"

Jonathan has seen this situation play out before. "Not sure, but either way, he's likely not going to be around for long. You'll throw money at him to go away, or one of the big boys will see this and reach out offering a fat contingency to take it over. No matter the choice, he won't be the one you have to worry about."

"That's probably true. Before I go much further, did you get a chance to review the NDA?"

"No, it seems premature. It won't be needed if I don't take the case, and I could've gotten my hands on the complaint as a matter of public record."

"Fair point. I like to be efficient. I apologize."

"Ms. Kramer, I'm not sure I'm your guy for this one. I start picking a jury in a couple…"

Before he can continue, she interrupts. "I appreciate that, Mr. Silverman, but you should know up front, we're not going to throw money at this to make it go away. It'll be around for a while. The only aspect you may not feel comfortable with or have time for is preparing the initial responses within the requisite twenty-one days. I've reached out to Mr. Schneider to request an extension."

Jonathan can't help but wonder why she's seemingly insisting his firm take on this case. "Ms. Kramer, forgive me for asking but, why Silverman Erickson?"

"Not Silverman Erickson. You. I've done my homework, and your name continues to be on the mind of many as the right attorney to handle this. I read the *Ackerman v. Dow Chemical* motion you authored, challenging the class certification. It's extremely detailed, which tells me you're thorough. And your argument was strong enough to get a judge to deny cert."

Flattery rarely works with Jonathan. And it certainly isn't going to work coming from a woman who makes her bones handling IPOs. He's done his homework, too. "With the same commitment to read every word on every document, I'm sure anyone could have put that motion together."

"Don't sell yourself short. What'll it take to get you on board, Mr. Silverman?"

Joyce Kramer isn't messing around. Jonathan knows this will be a great case for the firm but doesn't want his newfound personal connection to the disease to dictate his response. He's still digesting the meeting with Dr. Mancini, not to mention grappling with his own emotions. And there's this little matter of a trial on the immediate horizon.

"Ms. Kramer. This matter would tax our firm. We're not a national firm with hundreds of lawyers and paralegals at our disposal. If I was going to consider this, and that's a tremendous 'if,' I'd need to talk it over with my partner."

"Understood. Will you be speaking with him this evening?"

Jonathan's mind swirls with adjectives. Pushy, demanding, overbearing, directive, obnoxious, pain in the ass… Does he really want to deal with this every day? "Ms. Kramer. I've told you; I'm preparing for jury selection. My focus tonight and every night will be that case until the trial concludes."

Without skipping a beat, Joyce says, "Mr. Silverman, I'm authorized to offer a $250,000 retainer that can be wired to your escrow account before the end of the day."

Jonathan's blown away by the amount but quickly collects himself. "Ms. Kramer, you may find this interesting, particularly coming from an attorney, but it isn't about the money."

"I understand, Mr. Silverman. How about this... I'll wire $25,000 to the account of your choice before the end of the day. You commit to speaking with your partner, and only your partner, before you start trial. If you decide you can't take the case, no harm, no foul. You keep the full $25,000 for your time. If you do take the case, the $25,000 will be outside the retainer. It's yours no matter what."

Jonathan is glad this proposition is telephonic. He feels his face react to the offer as he considers it. $25,000 for a brief conversation with Walt, although no conversation with Walt is brief, is pretty good for a day's work.

He feels the urgency to get back to his trial prep and buckles. "Fine, Ms. Kramer. I'll transfer you back to Julie, who'll provide you with the routing information. I'm sorry, but I really have to get back to my prep."

Jonathan barely hears Joyce start to say "thank you" before he transfers the call to Julie. It's the easiest $25,000 he and Walt will ever earn.

Suddenly, a phrase his father is fond of saying comes to mind: *If something seems too good to be true...*

18

While on her morning stroll with Snoopy, MJ decides to go into the office. She can't hide forever, but she isn't going in without something to pitch. She's begun her research, and her "spidey senses" tell her there's something off about Propentus, Antsalemab, and this class-action lawsuit. After she gets yelled at, she'll start her investigation the same way she always does—by following the money.

The elevator arrives on the floor where she and Spagnola, the chicken shit, sit. She's scrolling through information on her phone as the doors open, and without looking up, steps forward, almost colliding with Spagnola. Fortunately, they both stop in time. Being covered in hot coffee would be a shitty way to start their conversation.

"Glad to see you decided to join us today." His tone makes it clear he's in no mood for her antics.

MJ makes a feeble attempt to defuse the bomb. "I know how much you miss me, and I didn't want to deprive you another minute."

She feels like a schoolgirl reporting to the principal's office—a familiar activity from her youth—as they remain facing each other in front of the elevator doors as they close.

Spagnola breaks the silence after taking a sip of coffee. "I need to speak with you about your little tantrum the other day, but I'm late for a meeting. Will I find you at your desk when I get back?"

She leaves her wit in her pocket this time. "Yes."

As he boards the elevator, MJ walks through the glass doors with the paper's logo and heads to her desk without speaking to anyone. She likes getting shit done, and chit-chat gets in the way. It's about finding the story and identifying an angle no one else sees. The one that'll land her the front-page byline all reporters crave.

MJ drops her laptop bag onto the floor next to the decent-looking leather chair she paid for herself. The chairs the paper usually provides are from the fifties. They creak and have absolutely no padding where it counts. Her ass deserves better.

As she rifles through the clutter overflowing her desk, MJ finds three energy drinks, all half-full and the remaining half of an onion bagel, still in its Bruegger's bag. She prefers Bruegger's. Dunk's is so cliché in this town. She drops the fuzzy green science experiment into the trash, then combines the contents of the three different cans and pensively takes a sip. The stuff can probably withstand a nuclear event.

MJ kicks her bag under her desk and puts her laptop into its docking station, allowing her to take advantage of the two 27-inch monitors that take up most of the desk's available space—at least the paper got that piece right—and signs in to find 100+ emails in her inbox.

She's on email number forty-eight when Spagnola shows up at her desk. With a look that says it all, he returns to his office. Thankfully, he can't see her roll her eyes while she's digging through her desk for a pad of paper and a pen.

As MJ enters his office and moves to take a seat in the single chair in front of his desk, Spagnola closes the door. He jumps right in as he walks toward a large desk covered with books and what looks like a thousand pages of paper.

"MJ, your little show the other day was unacceptable." He doesn't raise his voice, deciding to lean against his desk rather than sit behind it. "This isn't the first time we've had this conversation, and I'm at a loss. Since I'm unable to figure it out, I've decided to go straight to the source. What can I do to get through to you?"

MJ quickly adopts her usual approach, although he didn't start by yelling at her. She apologizes, commits to not repeating the offense, a little more yelling, and they move on. "First, I'm sorry. I was upset you killed the story I worked on for months. One you supported. And you didn't discuss your decision with me." She knows it's his prerogative as editor, but starting with an apology always turns the heat down.

His voice remains steady and calm. "Thank you, but you didn't answer my question."

He must be really sick of her shit this time. MJ decides the safest approach is to take control by asking questions; otherwise, the discussion will get away from her. She re-positions herself in the chair. "I'm not sure what you're getting at. I told you I'm sorry. What else are you looking for?"

Some of the ire Spagnola had been suppressing leaks out. "Damn it, MJ. I'm looking for you to tell me what I need to do to get through to you. I've given you free rein. You come to me with proposed stories far more often than I assign you one. You come and go as you please. Your attitude and actions in this office need to change. Period."

MJ knows she has it good. She's also aware her idiosyncrasies drive him mad, but he tolerates her because she always delivers. Always. "You know I can be emotional. And I'm really committed to my work." Will he bite on the commitment angle?

"I do. But expressing that emotion through unacceptable action has to stop. This is the last time we're going to have this conversation, MJ. Do you understand what I'm saying?"

She loves this job, so she swallows hard. "Yes."

After letting the silence make MJ squirm for a bit, Spagnola relaxes his posture. "So… Where've you been?"

Okay, that wasn't so bad, MJ thought. *Although he seems serious this time. Let the nauseating politeness begin.* "Mostly at home. I think I have a story, and I'd like to run it by you."

Spagnola rarely says no. She has the special skill all great investigative reporters have: she's a pure bloodhound when it comes to sniffing out a good story.

"You have five minutes. I have to get back to the meeting. I came down to speak with you before you left... Again."

Ouch. MJ smiles and takes the shot. "Did you see a local biotech has been sued over the side effects of its newest drug?"

"Yes. Happens all the time. Next."

"Well, the CEO of the company is only thirty-six. He somehow solved a problem that's eluded researchers for years despite billions in research. Looks like he used his own money to start the company, somehow raised \$350 million in capital, and then BOOM, he hits the motherlode with a drug which treats early-onset dementia, something that affects millions of people across the globe."

MJ's boss seems unimpressed and is getting antsy. "And…"

"And the company's reportedly on the verge of launching an IPO, and suddenly, this class-action lawsuit falls from the sky. You know I don't believe in coincidence." MJ can't control her excitement and leans forward. "Is someone trying to stop the IPO? How'd he convince investors to give him \$350 million to search for a treatment that's been elusive for decades?

If the allegations in the complaint are true, how the hell did this drug ever make it through the FDA approval process? There's a lot here. I can feel it."

Spagnola narrows his eyes the way he usually does when he's mulling over a pitch, making her squirm for a painfully quiet two minutes. "Okay, you have one week to bring me something more than questions. And remember what I said about your attitude." Without warning, he pushes off the desk and leaves to return to his meeting.

MJ remains for a moment. She doesn't put up with shit from anyone and knows that's both a blessing and a curse. She's also aware not everyone finds her form of wit charming. She trusts that maturity and wisdom will someday help her balance both.

Until then, she returns to her desk with a single thought: *Let the games begin.*

19

Vinnie loiters at the lobby security desk, waiting for Renee to leave for the day. He needs to find out why she was so nervous earlier. He can't tell Jimmy he's trying to get information. Jimmy doesn't like trying. He likes succeeding.

Within a few minutes of arriving, Vinnie spots his target doing a 180 spin on one of the screens. "Hey, Renee!" He yells more loudly than he should have, his voice echoing in the foyer.

As he rushes to get out from behind the desk, he trips, causing an aluminum garbage can to clang against the inside portion of the desk. Quickly, he regains his balance. He's going to speak with her today, come hell or high water.

His breathing is reflective of too many cheeseburgers as he makes the short jog around the corner. He calls out again through labored breath this time. "Hey, Renee, glad I caught you."

Renee cringes. "Oh, hey, Vinnie. I was just heading back to my office. I forgot my yoga mat."

"That's okay, I'll walk with you," Vinnie says and matches pace beside her.

Renee unlocks her door and crosses her office, quickly retrieving her yoga mat. Vinnie recognizes the look on her face and is caught off guard by what he sees: the glare of a cornered animal, openly prepared to fight to escape.

She heads toward the door with determination. "Sorry, gotta run."

Vinnie doesn't move. "You looked upset earlier. Just wondered why you're concerned about this lawsuit?" He knows he's pressing too hard.

"Lawsuits happen all the time." She dodges the question again and steps toward the door with an unexpected confidence.

Vinnie adopts an aggressive tone. "What are you worried about, Renee?"

Renee twists her body to squeeze past him, somehow making it through the tiny sliver of space without touching him. "I can't be late." Renee never looks back. Her pace would qualify her for the Olympics in speed walking.

As he chases her down the hallway, Vinnie's tone becomes one of desperation mixed with fear. "Jesus, Renee. I'm just tryin' to have a conversation here."

He stops as she flies through the turnstile at the entrance of the building, bending over and leaning on the security desk with his left arm as he works to catch his breath.

20

Melissa Cosgrove sits quietly with her eyes closed, contemplating what her life's become as the dialysis machine removes the waste and toxins from her blood. The room has a sterile hospital feel and smell, although they've tried to make it less so by painting the room a soothing yellow and hanging a few photos of sailboats in the Boston Harbor. She has no choice but to spend a few hours, three times a week, sitting in this ominous room, surrounded by others battling for their lives and enduring the same treatment.

Melissa was to move into her daughter Alexa's home once the dementia robbed her of the ability to remain safely independent, but her kidney issues trumped that timeline. Watching Alexa add dialysis and neurology appointments to a calendar filled with soccer and hockey games, dance recitals, and dental appointments brings shame and guilt while crushing her vivacious spirit.

After a successful career in finance, Melissa opted for early retirement. Her dementia diagnosis came nineteen months later. She watches her 401K hemorrhage to pay for

Antsalemab but considers herself lucky for having the means to pay for the newly approved treatment, which insurance denied. In an effort to defray some of the exorbitant expense, Alexa established a GoFundMe page on her mother's account, but beyond a few small contributions from family, friends, and former colleagues, it's been of little help.

The joy Melissa felt as Antsalemab delivered promising results became fury with her chronic kidney disease diagnosis. Ever the optimist, Melissa doubled down on her positive attitude. Her grandchildren were watching, and she refuses to teach them that giving up is an option. Although she's considered discontinuing Antsalemab, stopping won't return her kidneys to their previous functionality, and it's still helping with her cognition. Now, it looks like her body will give out before her mind will.

To add to the crippling stress that shrouds her daughter's small three-bedroom home, the two fight often about Melissa's choice of attorney.

Melissa liked what she saw on TV late one evening when she couldn't sleep. The next morning, she called 1-800-FENDERS, and Leo Schneider showed up an hour later. He spent less than thirty minutes with her and left with an executed retainer. Melissa knows her dementia will eventually rob her of her decision-making ability, but she's not there yet, so she remains firm in her conviction.

Now, Melissa is transfixed on the seed of doubt about her chosen attorney that Alexa planted. They agree that if Melissa wants to go to war, she should have the best army possible. Their debate centers on whether "The King of the Fender Bender" fits the bill. He certainly isn't an army. A simple question echoes in Melissa's head. *Can Attorney Schneider stand toe-to-toe with the type of law firm Propentus can afford to hire?*

She leans her head back, once again praying she gave her daughter the correct answer.

21

Vinnie's excited by the unexpected start to his day.

"Hey Joyce, what can I do you for?"

As he closes the office door, he experiences a sense of relaxation he hasn't felt in a while. Something good's finally coming his way. He undoes the button, straining to keep the jacket closed around his stomach, and sits in one of the chairs in front of Joyce's desk. He doesn't ask this time.

She's all business. "I need you to look into a couple of people."

Vinnie loves digging up dirt. It's one of the things that's kept him out of the trunk of Jimmy Rizzo's Cadillac on more than one occasion. "Sure, who?"

"I need background on the two partners of a law firm I'm considering relative to this new lawsuit."

"Okay." He pulls a small notebook and pen from the breast pocket of his sports coat. Some habits are hard to break. "Names?"

"Jonathan Silverman and Walter Erickson. I need more than I can get from Martindale-Hubbell."

"You lookin' for anything specific?" A focused search is more likely to find a pot of gold at the end of the rainbow, and Jimmy loves gold.

Joyce struggles to maintain eye contact. "Nope. Just a firm I was told might be a good fit in this situation."

"When do you need this?"

"Tomorrow morning, 11 am."

"I'll have to work through the night to get you anything meaningful."

"I appreciate it. Thanks." Joyce's gaze drops to the open file on her desk. She flips a page, signaling she's done with the conversation.

Vinnie leaves with an extra lilt in his step. He'll call a couple of people who owe him and still have access to certain databases. Then, he'll order pizza, roll up his sleeves, and break out the shovel.

22

Forty-six hours have gone by since the last time they sat in this room. Nancy fiddles with her cell phone to keep busy. Joe sits quietly. And a thousand fearful thoughts battle to suppress the positive ones Jonathan is attempting to generate. Today's the day.

Dr. Mancini walks in and sits behind her desk, looking squarely at Joe. "Good morning, everyone. We have your test results, Joe. I'm sorry to say they confirm the diagnosis of early-onset Alzheimer's." Her words are a poisonous gas hanging in the air, waiting to be inhaled.

Jonathan knows his mother prayed for negative results, but he encouraged her to prepare for this possibility. She won't want to accept it, but he knows she won't stick her head in the sand, either. The slightly rusted folding chair squeaks as Jonathan shifts his weight. He glances at his father, who's slumping and staring at the floor, then onto his mother, who's struggling not to openly weep, eventually landing on Dr. Mancini. Time for the "caregiver" hat.

"What does this mean, exactly, and what are the next steps?"

Dr. Mancini looks at Joe. She never ignores the patient. "Alzheimer's is a degenerative disease, which means it'll continue to get worse over time. Right now, you're in the early stages, Joe. As time progresses, the impact on your day-to-day activities and your memory will increase, eventually inhibiting your ability to complete certain tasks."

Dr. Mancini looks back toward Jonathan. "We'll monitor the progression of the disease, starting with monthly check-ins."

With her focus returning to Joe and Nancy, Dr. Mancini's genuine care for each patient bleeds through the medicine. "You should know everyone's different. No two people have the same journey. It's one of the reasons the medical community's had such difficulty in identifying the cause and, ultimately, a cure."

Nancy's lip starts to quiver.

Jonathan continues with fearful thoughts overwhelming his previous hope. "Is there anything the patient can do to influence the rate of progression?"

Dr. Mancini offers a slight nod. "There are a number of studies that suggest certain changes can favorably impact the pace at which the disease advances. They focus on a healthy lifestyle, including exercise and diet."

"What about treatments?"

"In addition to lifestyle changes, there are treatments that can help manage the disease. Two of the more commonly prescribed medications are Donepezil, commonly known as Aricept, and Memantine, commonly known as Namenda. They each do something a little different, and while they do not impact the progression of the disease, both help with memory and cognition. I recommend we start with Aricept."

Jonathan asks the question that's been on his mind since the moment he read the complaint Joyce Kramer sent him: "What about Antsalemab? I know it was recently approved by the FDA."

"I continue to do my reading on this treatment. As is the case with all medications, Antsalemab has side effects. More studies are currently underway, which will provide additional insight into its long-term efficacy. It's showing promise, and I like what I've read so far."

Taking off her reading glasses and placing them on the desk, Dr. Mancini delivers more difficult news. "But it's cost-prohibitive for most people. It costs $36,000 a year, and unfortunately, Medicare isn't covering it."

Jonathan fixates on one statement: *I like what I've read so far.* He pushes a little further. "What if cost weren't an issue?"

Dr. Mancini is thoughtful before answering. "I might be willing to prescribe it for the right patient, but it has to make sense from a medical perspective first and foremost."

Nancy and Joe look at each other and then at Jonathan. They know what's coming next, and Nancy moves to stop it before it happens. "No, Jonathan. There are other drugs that are covered by insurance."

"Mom, I'm just trying to understand the options. But make no mistake, I'll do whatever's necessary to get Dad the treatment he needs."

Joe pulls his shoulders back and lifts his head as he sits up straight, staring Jonathan in the eye. "I will not take the new drug. End of discussion."

Dr. Mancini interjects before the argument gains steam. "Joe, as I mentioned, I'd recommend we start with Aricept, monitor your bloodwork, and track the impact."

Joe slumps again. "Fine."

Dr. Mancini stands and holds out the packet of information she gives every dementia patient. "Joe, you're not alone.

We'll continue to do everything we can. If at any time you have questions, please don't hesitate to call."

Jonathan considers their "thank you" to Dr. Mancini as they leave. It feels incongruent with the news they just received. As he starts the car, his thoughts shift to solutions and support, knowing this is going to be a difficult road for them to travel.

The real battle begins today, and his resolve won't tolerate anything but success.

23

Joyce sips her morning tea to choke back the disgust of being in a closed room with Vinnie. His presence gives off an "axe murderer" vibe. As he sits, it becomes evident Vinnie's been in the office all night and must have a cheap bottle of whiskey hidden somewhere.

"What'd you find out?"

As Vinnie shuffles in the seat, Joyce notices his body odor as it drifts with his movement, but he forges ahead, seemingly unaware or uncaring of the scent. "My team and I only had a short window but were able to gather quite a bit of information."

Joyce maintains her composure. If he constantly harps on the short timeframe, she'll scream. She knew he'd get help, but to call them a "team" was a stretch. Joyce already wants to throw his ass out. "Tell me what you found."

"First, there's nothin' of interest identified during their time in college or law school. Both got undergraduate degrees in Political Science and then got into Syracuse Law, which is where they met. Solid students, both made Law Review. No criminal records. They were at different firms locally before they went out on their own."

Having done it herself, Joyce appreciates giving up promising careers at larger firms to take a swing at something better. Gutsy move. "What about before college?"

Vinnie looks back at his notes. "They come from different backgrounds. Erickson comes from old money. He attended private schools, eventually becoming high school salutatorian. Silverman comes from a middle-class family. Public school kid who worked at a local grocery store while working to become valedictorian of his graduating class. He was also a solid baseball player. Articles say he could've gone pro. In short, both good little boys."

Joyce nods for him to continue.

"Erickson's some kinda genius. Photographic memory or some shit like that. He's single and likes to travel. He drives a Porsche and has the speeding tickets to prove it. According to my underground network of retired cops turned security guards, he spends a fair amount of time at the swankiest nightclubs around the city." Vinnie looks up for approval.

Joyce's gaze of indifference sends a message. "And Silverman?"

"A literal Eagle Scout. Clean driving record. A woman by the name of Emily Watkins recently changed the address on her driver's license to match his, so I presume she's the girlfriend. Silverman and Erickson purchased the building where they work a couple of years ago. Prior owner carries the mortgage and indicates they're current." Vinnie looks up, knowing Joyce isn't pleased. "Um… Remember, we didn't get a lot of notice."

Joyce struggles to control her rage. "I know that. Now get your ass out of my office and find something. And add that Watkins woman to the list." She refuses to believe there's nothing.

Upon his departure, Joyce pulls a bottle of Febreze from her desk drawer and spritzes the chair and room before returning to her prep for the call with Jonathan. She has no Plan B and has zero interest in hearing Michael scream at her for wasting $25,000 while reminding her that he wanted to interview prospective firms *before* they were retained.

Joyce taps her fingers on her desk as she waits for Jonathan's assistant to transfer her call.

"Hello, Ms. Kramer." She hears the impatience in his voice.

"I know you're busy, Jonathan. May I call you Jonathan?" She figures $25,000 ought to buy her something.

"Yes, that's fine."

Joyce is sitting behind her desk with her shoes off, closing her eyes as she gets down to business. "As I said, I know you're busy. Did you speak with your partner?"

"I did. After considerable thought, we've decided we'll take Propentus on as a client."

Joyce's shoulders finally relax. "That's great to hear, and please call me Joyce."

"Julie will send our retainer letter this afternoon. We expect the $250,000 to be wired before 10 a.m. tomorrow morning. Once we have that, we'll get to work."

"Absolutely. However, there's the matter of the Non-Disclosure Agreement. I'm sorry, but I must insist that anyone who'll be attached to this case execute one. The intellectual property at stake makes this non-negotiable."

"Joyce, there'll be a small number of individuals who'll work on this matter. My partner and I are prepared to sign the NDA as individuals and as the principles of the firm. However, asking every paralegal or legal assistant who may touch the file in some manner is impractical."

Joyce was prepared for pushback. She lets a moment pass for effect. "Fine, I'll modify the NDA and have it couriered over. I'll need wet signatures before the retainer's sent."

"We'll turn the NDA around as quickly as possible. Feel free to return the executed retainer letter in the interim. I look forward to learning more about Propentus."

"Excellent. I look forward to working with you, Jonathan."

The call ends, and Joyce shakes her fist in triumph. She smiles, ecstatic to have landed a firm she can control. Her ability to push them to take the case and sign an arguably unnecessary NDA proves she's got this handled. Fuck Michael!

24

Jimmy paces angrily in his office. Richie just left after delivering unexpected news about the survival of an adversary, leaving him in no mood to be interrupted. Within seconds, there's a knock on the door. "WHAT?"

Vinnie slowly opens the door and nervously hovers in the doorway. "Got a minute, Jimmy?"

The blue snake on Jimmy's neck returns. "What the fuck do you want?" He'll make sure the bartender who let Vinnie through won't make that mistake again.

Vinnie walks in and closes the door. He doesn't sit. You don't sit unless Jimmy offers. The crooked fingers on Vinnie's left hand prove that. "I wanna let you know that Propentus has retained Jonathan Silverman of the law firm of Silverman Erickson to defend them on the lawsuit. I'm doing deep background on the firm, this attorney, his partner, and his girlfriend."

"What'd ya find?"

"Nothin' useful… Not yet, anyway. But I wanted to let you know I'm diggin'."

"You fuckin' kiddin' me? Tellin' me you got nothin', but you're fuckin' lookin'? What the fuck am I supposta do with that? You're wastin' my fuckin' time!"

Vinnie does what he always does, plodding forward blindly. "I guess you could say it that way, Jimmy."

The snake's visibly throbbing. Jimmy wants to separate Vinnie's appendages, slowly and painfully, but he can't. "I *did* say it that way, you fuckin' moron. Now, get the fuck out! Bring me somethin' useful."

Vinnie looks dumbstruck. "Um… okay. Thanks, Jimmy. I'll let you know when I got somethin'." He backs out of the office, slowly pulling the door closed behind him. Everyone knows you never disrespect Jimmy by turning your back to him.

Still pissed off about Richie's bungle, Jimmy slams the top of the desk and contemplates what the moron just told him. He doesn't recognize the name of the firm. Silver and Erick, or something like that?

Jimmy trusts only a handful of people, and Vinnie isn't one of them anymore. He'll ask his guys to bring him information about this attorney. He may need to intervene at some point, and it's always good to be prepared.

25

fter the initial whirlwind started by his father's diagnosis, everything's falling into a new rhythm for Jonathan: home, work, Canton, Newton... Repeat. He's upset with himself for missing dinner the last couple of weeks. It couldn't be helped. He's been slammed at work. But he hasn't missed a doctor's appointment... and today won't be the first.

As he's done before, Jonathan picks up his parents and drives them to Newton. The car ride is quiet except for *Willie's Roadhouse* on Sirius XM. His father loves country music.

They arrive at the office on time but have to wait about ten minutes until they're escorted to an exam room where the nurse records Joe's vital signs. Jonathan looks at his mom who also seems to notice he's lost a few pounds. Other than that, everything is in line.

Dr. Mancini walks in moments later, wearing a reassuring smile. "Good afternoon, Joe. How are you feeling?"

"A little tired, but fine."

She peers over the top of her reading glasses, which are sitting low on her nose. "How are you doing with the Aricept?"

Joe looks embarrassed, but she asked. "It makes me run to the bathroom every five minutes. Everything I eat either runs right through me, turning to liquid and exploding out of me, or it comes right back up." Joe's colorful description makes Nancy look queasy.

"I'm sorry to hear that, Joe. Sounds like a real hassle. Any other side effects? Racing heartbeat? Difficulty breathing? Dizziness? Headache?"

"No."

Dr. Mancini looks at Jonathan to fill in any blanks.

Jonathan gently corrects his father, something he seems to be doing more of these days. "Dad complains of a headache almost daily. Tylenol seems to help, but we're worried he's taking too much."

Dr. Mancini makes note of this. "If he's taking it as directed, he should be fine." She returns her attention to her patient. "Joe, do you know what day of the week it is?"

"It's Wednesday."

From her seated position, Nancy taps Joe gently on the knee. "It's Tuesday, Joe, remember?"

Jonathan cringes. He's read the literature: you should avoid asking someone with dementia if they remember something. Through his research and recent personal experiences, he has learned the patient will say something akin to, "Of course, I remember," to avoid being embarrassed while often becoming frustrated, if not flat-out angry.

Jonathan has spoken to his mother about this at least a dozen times and knows she's trying her best. He places his hand on her shoulder.

Dr. Mancini sits up after leaning over to type in his last answer and looks Joe in the eye. "Do you know who the President of the United States is?"

"Yes, it's Trump," Joe answers confidently. "No, wait, it's the other guy. What's his name?"

He's right, it isn't Trump.

Dr. Mancini moves on, walking Joe through a series of other questions, which he answers somewhat accurately. One of his better days. She then spins the stool to look at Nancy. "Nancy, how are we doing with the lifestyle changes?"

Nancy perks up, and Jonathan knows she is proud of their success on this front. "We're doing well. I've tried to make sure each day looks the same. It's not identical, but it's more consistent."

"That's great, Nancy." Dr. Mancini then returns her attention to her patient. "How do you feel about that, Joe?"

"She gets crazy about us eating at the exact same time every day."

Dr. Mancini smiles gently. "That's okay. It is not about being perfect. Anything else, Nancy?"

"I bought a Mediterranean cookbook and have been trying the recipes. Some we like, some we don't. Although Joe thinks 'Mediterranean' is code for 'Italian' and wants pasta all the time."

Joe looks defiantly at Nancy and then to the doctor. "Italy is in the Mediterranean, isn't it?"

Dr. Mancini joins the laughter in the room. "Yes, it is Joe."

Jonathan enjoys the levity, knowing it's something that will be ruthlessly stolen from them at some point.

"That's great, Nancy. Keep up the good work, and it's okay if there is some variability in the schedule." She looks over her glasses and gives Joe a conspiratorial wink. He winks back in appreciation of the support, then gives his wife an "I told you so" smirk.

Jonathan steers the conversation back to where he wants it to go. "How is your research coming along, Dr. Mancini?"

She looks at Joe again. "As you know, Antsalemab is the newest treatment for dementia. It doesn't cure dementia, but it purports to slow, or even stop, the progression of the disease in cases of early-onset. I've recently prescribed it to two other patients. I'm looking forward to seeing how they do."

"That sounds good, doesn't it, Dad?" After the problems he's having with Aricept, Jonathan wants to get him on board with a new drug.

"Sure." Joe is back to giving short answers; he's done for today.

Jonathan takes a swing. "Dr. Mancini, do you think Dad's a candidate for Antsalemab?" He sees his mother shift to the edge of her chair, anxious yet fearful of the response.

"I've read everything I can find on Antsalemab, and I'm aware of the recently filed lawsuit. I'm a little worried about unknown long-term effects, but I realize patients with dementia are in a different position on that issue. You'll recall I said I'd be willing to prescribe it for the right patients." She hesitates and looks directly at Joe. "I believe you are one of those patients. We could stop the Aricept and move forward with Antsalemab."

Nancy's eyes drop to the floor as the black cape of defeat drapes around her. "Does it still cost as much as you said before?"

Jonathan swallows hard. He can't remember the last time he lied to his parents. It might have been in high school when he swore he wasn't drinking at a post-game party. His hangover the next day almost gave him away, but he knew what he had to do. "I spoke to Medicare. They said they'd cover the prescription."

Nancy's purse falls to the floor as she jumps out of the chair, the cape being stripped away by singing angels. "Really? Oh my god, Joe! This is great news! Dr. Mancini, when can he start taking it?"

Dr. Mancini looks at Joe. He's the patient. "Joe, what do you think about trying this new drug?"

"It's fine, I guess."

Nancy sits back down, gleaming with relief and optimism as her head swivels between Joe, Dr. Mancini, and Jonathan.

Before proceeding, Dr. Mancini looks at Jonathan, who gives her an imperceptible nod. "I'll work out the details with Jonathan."

Jonathan's angst about lying is softened by the elation in his mother's eyes. "Thank you so much, Dr. Mancini."

Dr. Mancini gently returns to the facts. "We'll have to wait and see. There's no guarantee this drug will provide the results we're hoping for. And, given Joe's reaction to Aricept, we'll have to watch this very closely."

As they walk to the car with a new prescription in hand, Jonathan smiles at Nancy, who's bouncing on the balls of her feet like a cat chasing the red dot of a laser pen.

26

With the work she's done the past few weeks, MJ has filled a third of a new external hard drive with information about Michael Riccio, Propentus, and Melissa Cosgrove. As she initiated her Propentus dossier, she focused on how and why Riccio started the company, as well as learning everything she could about Antsalemab.

She's amazed by his ability to raise capital in a short period of time. After hitting big with Genomics, he used his own money as the seed round for his company. A lot of people talk about doing that. Few actually do. That says something.

As the Antsalemab trials progressed, the company continued to raise capital. Michael successfully raised $30 million in the Series A round, a bit higher than you'd expect, particularly given its focus on dementia research, something global pharmaceutical companies have been unsuccessful with for years.

The trend continued in subsequent rounds, with $50 million raised in Series B and another $95 million in Series C.

Once the drug moved into human trials, a Series D round raised an additional $175 million.

MJ can't help but be amazed as she ponders the money question. Antsalemab slows the progression of dementia, possibly stopping it, but it isn't a cure. Dementia diagnoses are growing exponentially every year. Exactly what every investor wants to see: a continually expanding market.

Propentus is a privately owned company, making it impossible for MJ to get her hands on the company's financials. In addition to that frustration, she's finding key investor details difficult to obtain. It's not surprising to see many of the well-known venture capital firms that play in the biotech space involved. However, she's struggling to find detailed information on one of the investment companies from the Series D round. She's dedicated a couple of very late nights with corresponding bottles of Sauvignon Blanc to the endeavor but has come up empty—something she despises. Now, she's forced to do the one thing she hates even more: ask for help.

Knowing most start-ups run at a financial loss, and after doing a little rudimentary math on the top of a pizza box, MJ believes Riccio is leveraged to the hilt. She imagines they all must be eager for the IPO. The projected market cap is mind-boggling.

Melissa Cosgrove is MJ's next research topic. Beyond a GoFundMe page with a small balance, she doesn't have a significant digital footprint. From what MJ's found, Ms. Cosgrove is reportedly a loving parent and grandparent who's been dealt a shitty hand—perhaps shittier than most—but there's absolutely nothing nefarious that MJ's been able to dig up on her or any member of her family. She sounds like the grandmother everyone would wish for.

MJ's never met Michael Riccio, but she gets a weird feeling in the pit of her stomach the more she reads. He grew up a first-generation Italian whose parents gave him everything they had to give. He certainly made the most of his humble beginnings, but if his parents were to read his most recent clippings, she's positive they'd be disappointed in the man he's become.

Prior to his time in Cambridge, Riccio lived a relatively ordinary life as a college and graduate student. Beyond being brilliant, he's willing to work hard to support his endeavors, like holding down multiple jobs throughout graduate school, two traits investors look for before giving someone their money.

She didn't find any record of a love interest, which she found odd given he's on the verge of being worth hundreds of millions of dollars. People should be lining up to be friends or more with Michael Riccio.

MJ views herself a phenomenal investigator, but even she has her limitations. After a few weeks of working on this alone, she reluctantly calls for reinforcements, contacting a team that shares her unwavering commitment to the truth and is willing to use any means necessary to obtain it. An unlikely friendship first brought them together when she was in college.

She reaches out to them infrequently, in large part because she fears the consequences. But most importantly, she can never use the raw data they supply. She must take the information provided and work doggedly to find and confirm it via legal means, something that requires a great deal of time and effort, even when you know for certain it's there.

Instead of giving this team all the details of her research project, MJ kept her request tight this time, solely asking for assistance in researching the investors in Propentus.

27

Jonathan's sitting in his office, doing what he's done for the past week: focusing on the FDA application for Antsalemab. The materials are exhaustive and complex. He's glad he's an attorney and not a scientist. His phone rings with a call from what's become a familiar number.

"Good morning, Joyce. How are you today?"

"I'm well. I was just handed your message from late yesterday afternoon."

"No problem. If it was an emergency, I would've called the cell number you gave me."

"So, you're telling me if I get a call from you after 5 p.m., I should worry?"

Jonathan hears a windy noise through the receiver. "I'm sorry. I missed that, Joyce."

"Sorry. Blowing on my tea. Taylors of Harrogate Earl Grey, if you like teas. Had it my first visit to London and fell in love."

Jonathan's taken aback by the casual banter. "Um, I called because I've been living with the FDA application and approval documentation you forwarded and have some questions."

"What would you like to know?"

"I'm trying to learn as much as I can about the FDA process itself. It's a lot." Jonathan attempts to continue the casualness of their current call, "I thought prepping for the bar was tough." He chuckles.

"Yes. I've tried to forget that period in my life."

Jonathan can't tell if she means prepping for the bar exam or navigating the FDA approval process. He shrugs and keeps going. "I'd like to meet with Dr. Harold Johnson and Dr. Renee Spencer... and you, of course." Excluding her would've created another opportunity for her to remind him who the boss is.

"It might be quicker and easier if you send me your questions. I'll get the two of them to prepare responses. Saves you a trip to the lab and allows them to answer as they have time."

Jonathan slouches back into his leather chair, exasperated. He's accustomed to operating with complete, unfettered access to those he needs to speak with. Time to test the waters. "Joyce, I appreciate that, but I'd like to meet with them face-to-face. If this does get certified, they're going to be key players in the defense. The sooner I start building a relationship with them, not to mention getting a read of them as potential witnesses, the better."

Jonathan's not surprised by the authoritarian tone that follows.

"Good point. Send me the questions in advance so they can prepare. It'll be more efficient for everyone."

"I'll email them to you directly, and you can share them." He hates it but knows he has to throw her a bone. She's going to hear the questions anyway.

"Anything else?" Joyce has completely shifted from casually talking about her favorite tea to pushing for the call to end.

"No, thanks for your time, Joyce." Jonathan ends the call perplexed. His concern with her level of control, something he feared at the outset, goes up a few notches. They're just starting. What will she be like when the case really gets going?

28

The next morning, Jonathan sits at his desk, feeling energized. He slept well, had a terrific work out, and after a long hot shower, he's ready to tackle the day.

Last night's dinner with his parents was the best it's been in weeks and gave Jonathan the very thing he needed: good news. His father was happier and engaged more in the discussions, talking about his favorite topics: the Sox, Patriots, and Bruins.

His mother was as giddy as a schoolgirl with her news. She mentioned Joe working on a crossword, something he used to enjoy but hasn't done in years. He's suggested they take a walk a few times instead of needing to be dragged to the door. While uncertain of the cause, her conclusion is simple: Joe's been more his old self, and he's recalling things more easily. And the best part... there've been no side effects from the Antsalemab.

Jonathan smiles at the memory and sips his coffee, refocusing as he flips page after page of the FDA information Joyce provided with his usual commitment to detail.

With a furrowed brow and mindless gaze across the office, Jonathan searches for clarity and understanding. Every supporting document was signed by either Dr. Harold Johnson or Dr. Renee Spencer. There are thousands of pages. Why just these two? Jonathan also senses something relative to the document chronology, but he can't quite put his finger on what. Did the FDA ask about any of this? If they did, what was Propentus' response? He adds these observations to his continually increasing list of questions as Julie knocks on his door.

"Hey, what's up?"

"I'm sorry, Jonathan, but I'm getting the runaround trying to schedule your Propentus meetings. Hate to ask, but maybe you can call Ms. Kramer?"

He apologizes to Julie; it's not supposed to be this hard.

As Julie walks back to her desk, Jonathan reconsiders his motives for taking the case. He knew from the outset that Joyce Kramer would be an overbearing pain in the ass, and she's lived up to that expectation thus far, so this most recent issue shouldn't be a surprise. Did the dollar signs blur his thinking? Sure, there was interest in the drug that treats a disease he learned is impacting his family's future, but was it more? Perhaps it was the thrill of handling a high-profile case?

As he finishes his second cup of coffee, his phone buzzes. "Ms. Kramer on line one."

He'll never get through everything at this pace. Jonathan rolls his head around his shoulders and shakes his arms out, trying to reduce his irritation for needing to remind his client of their obligations. With a forced smile on his face, he grabs the phone. "Good afternoon, Joyce."

29

Joyce doesn't have time for this bullshit today, nor should she have to placate someone who works for her. It'll be a cold day in hell before she apologizes.

"Fine, Jonathan. I'll ask my team to cooperate in scheduling the meeting with Harold and Renee. Anything else?"

"Thank you, Joyce. I'll ask Julie to finalize the dates immediately."

Joyce's frustration has sharpened her hearing. "Excuse me, Jonathan? Did you say dates? I thought you were looking for one meeting, not multiple meetings?"

Jonathan's aggravation oozes out. "I did. Meeting with Harold and Renee separately will be more effective. You know people are more confident in numbers. I need to see what they're like as individual witnesses. I appreciate multiple meetings make it more time consuming for you, but this is the best approach."

Joyce hates to be patronized and detests that he's right even more. Clenched teeth make it difficult to smile. "Fine. Do you have the questions available, as I requested?"

"Almost. I've created a set for each of them. Some are the same, so I can identify any potential discrepancies we'll have to resolve prior to depositions. After one last review to confirm I haven't missed anything this round, I'll have them to you by end of day tomorrow."

Joyce's worries continue to mount. Maintaining control of Jonathan and the litigation, on top of getting the IPO launched, is testing her limits. "Good." She holds her breath but asks anyway. "Is there anything that's concerning based on your initial review?"

"There are few things I think any idiot, even the 'The King of the Fender Bender,' will notice. We'll have to be prepared with an answer."

She shifts uncomfortably in her chair and grabs a pad of monogrammed paper from the corner of her desk. "What are those?"

"For example, I notice all the documents you've forwarded are signed by Drs. Johnson and Spencer. I find it hard to believe others weren't involved…"

Jonathan is the first to question that. The FDA never said a word. Joyce's regret in her choice of counsel becomes real. He's smart, thorough, and direct. A dangerous combination if left unchecked.

"… And second, it feels like there are gaps in dates. Nothing obvious, but some seem to fall outside the rhythm seen throughout the remainder of the package."

Joyce uses every ounce of energy to avoid screaming. "I'm not sure what you mean, but I'm confident Harold and Renee will be able to speak to that. Anything else?"

Jonathan doesn't hesitate. "Joyce, I believe cases are won and lost on the little things. A simple reference or comment deep in a document can dictate the result, and it's my job to find those before the opposition does."

Finally, something upon which they agree. She's been successful throughout her life by keeping the little things from biting her in the ass. "Agreed. I look forward to receiving the questions."

Joyce ends the call before he can say another word, grappling with the realization that Jonathan Silverman is much more than another little thing.

30

Joyce's sitting with her head tilted back and eyes closed, reflecting on her recent revelation when there's a knock on her open office door.

"Got a minute?" Michael walks in, not waiting for a response.

Joyce sits up. "Absolutely."

Michael doesn't sit. He stands over Joyce's desk as a show of authority. "Where are we with this lawsuit?"

"Interesting you should ask. I just got off the phone with Jonathan." Joyce flinches inwardly but is unsurprised when Michael's face turns red.

Not only did she not speak to him about Jonathan before she hired him, but she also committed the firm to $275,000 without his knowledge.

"Is he earning that huge goddamn retainer *you* gave him?"

Joyce doesn't blink. "He's gotten through a great deal of information and is very, very thorough. He's setting up meetings with Harold and Renee. I'll be at all meetings, of course."

Michael shakes his head. "Not what I'm looking for, and you know it. What's he doing to make this go away? I told you, nothing can derail the IPO."

Joyce stands, her anger bubbling over. "I've spoken to him every single day, Michael. In some cases, multiple times a day. I'm driving him to find the quickest way out, without any type of settlement. And, I'm pushing the IPO forward at the same time."

"Settlement? You've talked settlement?"

Joyce maintains eye contact. "I told him up front there won't be a settlement."

Michael's face twists into exaggerated puzzlement. "I'm not sure that's your decision to make unless the title on your door's changed? If we include an ironclad non-disclosure, how much would it cost?"

"First, entertaining settlement would be disastrous. I'm concerned with the message that'll be sent as we move to launch the IPO. It might inspire others to file suit with the hopes of a quick payout. More suits will kill the IPO." She walks from behind her desk and gets in Michael's face.

"Second, I've given no thought as to value. There's no need unless you're going to consider settling, and we aren't."

Michael muffles his indignation, and inches closer, giving Joyce a sinister stare to remind her of who's in charge.

"Okay, Joyce. Since you chose the attorney without my input, despite my direct request to the contrary, and are the one steering this ship, you'll be the one held accountable if we end up smashing into the rocks."

Joyce swallows hard, his message received loud and clear. "Going forward, I'll give you updates on the status of both the lawsuit and the IPO," she says as her nails nervously scratch her neck.

He steps back and takes a couple of deep breaths. "And I want all options to remain on the table."

"All resolution options will remain on the table."

Michael scoffs and struts toward the door, leaving Joyce to ponder how she's going to keep Michael from making a mess of things.

31

MJ's returning from Snoopy's mid-afternoon visit to the dog park, thinking about what she's uncovered so far when her phone starts vibrating. It's from a restricted number—it's always a restricted number.

"Hey... Whatcha got for me?" MJ isn't much for small talk.

Neither are they. "Not sure, yet."

MJ stops in her tracks, causing Snoopy to be tugged back. "What the hell does that mean?"

He calmly continues. "One of the guys started pulling on a string that's leading to interesting places."

It isn't necessarily a guy. MJ knows "the team" is made up of different genders, races, religious beliefs, sexual orientations, political affiliations, etc. They don't care how you identify. All that's required are superior hacking skills, a lack of concern for the law, and an absolute commitment to secrecy.

"Did you hear me?"

Snoopy is walking in anxious circles around the stationary MJ, entangling her legs with the leash. "Sorry. Didn't want to interrupt again. When do you want to meet?" They'll never give her anything meaningful over the phone.

"Same place. 11 p.m. tonight." The call ends abruptly.

MJ hates the late-night cloak-and-dagger bullshit, but it's one of the quirks she's learned to accept. She's met a few of them during these clandestine meetings. Never the same person twice. They're obsessively careful to conceal their identities.

She tried to track the first person she met using the unique name she was given. How hard could it be? After staring at her laptop for two days, she identified the name as belonging to the daughter of a leader of a small African country who had died from the bubonic plague a hundred years before. Lesson learned. She won't waste her time again.

"Sorry, Snoop, walk's over." Fortunately, Snoopy had already created the little pile of warmth she hates.

As she meanders down the sidewalk toward home, enjoying the sunshine on her face, her thoughts return to the gaps she's been unable to fill. It's unlikely her findings will overlap with what she will hear tonight—they never have before.

That thought causes another sudden stop. Do they watch her? Monitor her searches? She asked them to check her laptop for viruses once. Did they plant one of their own? Not for the first time, she wonders if getting involved with this group is a good thing.

MJ resumes walking and begins mentally reviewing her research on Antsalemab. The initial set of trials seemed to show amazing promise. It wasn't until the human trials that articles started speaking to possible problems. She was surprised to learn that only one in every thousand drugs ever makes it to human trials.

Articles published post-approval highlight the frequency of high blood pressure or kidney stones in trial participants. The onset of these issues occurs within the first three to five months of taking the drug. The addition of high blood pressure medication reportedly resolved that issue, and increased water consumption, a common approach to managing the formation of calcium oxalate kidney stones, significantly reduced those incidents.

One article concluded by stating there are instances where one has to address a medication's side effects in order to continue receiving the benefit of the original medication. MJ knows nothing's ever that simple.

As she walks into her apartment, MJ has a ridiculous thought. She takes the leash off Snoopy, kicks off her Chucks, and makes the call. Saying she's an investigative reporter usually results in nothing more than a dial tone, but she's stunned when she's put through to Joyce Kramer.

She'll employ the "Fernandez method," as she calls it, a tried-and-true strategy. Anyone can hit the fastball, but only the pros can hit the breaking ball.

She sits up, poised over her laptop, ready to throw the first pitch.

32

Joyce despises reporters but decides to take the call as a sign they aren't afraid of the press or the lawsuit. It's also an opportunity to spread positive messaging for the benefit of the flailing IPO.

"Ms. Fernandez, how can I help you today?" If Joyce's eyes roll back any farther, she'll be staring at the back of her skull.

"Ms. Kramer, thank you for taking my call. First, please call me MJ. Second, I know you're busy, so I'll make this quick."

"Thank you, MJ. I appreciate that. I have a meeting in a few minutes. You happened to call at just the right part of my day." Any more sweetness and Joyce will need an insulin shot.

"I'm looking into the class-action lawsuit recently filed against Propentus. I've been reading everything I can find relative to Antsalemab and Melissa Cosgrove."

"Yes, but how may I help you?"

"I'm wondering if you could talk to me a bit about the FDA approval process for the drug. I'm interested in the side effects identified throughout the trials."

Joyce leans back. This isn't hard. "First, I'm unable to speak specifically to the pending litigation. However, the information you seek is readily available. The potential side effects are identified in all of our materials, as required by the FDA."

MJ keeps pushing. "I've read those materials and find no mention of chronic kidney disease as a potential side effect. Why do you think Ms. Cosgrove believes Antsalemab caused her kidney problems?"

Joyce sits back up, paying closer attention. "Again, without specific reference to the pending litigation, you're correct. There's no noted relationship between Antsalemab and chronic kidney disease. That's why we have 100% confidence in our ability to defeat this action."

MJ's relentless. "I did note, however, that kidney stones and high blood pressure, both of which are symptoms of and/or potential causes of chronic kidney disease, are identified side effects. Is there a connection?"

Joyce almost slams the receiver on her desk, regretting taking this call. "Again, without specific reference to the pending litigation, that's correct. Kidney stones and high blood pressure are identified as potential side effects. The incidence rates of those findings are relatively small and easily remedied." Now to end the call without the appearance of avoidance. "I'm sorry, MJ. As I mentioned, I have another meeting. Why don't you speak with my assistant and find some time to continue this discussion?"

"That'd be great. Thanks for your time. I look forward to our next conversation."

"Have a good day, MJ." Joyce ends the call, pissed at herself for being cavalier. It wasn't a complete disaster, but it didn't go as well as it should have. Who the hell's this investigative reporter, and what's she up to?

Joyce gags at the thought but sends a message to her assistant to schedule a meeting with the Head of Security.

33

It's 7:30 p.m. Joyce's been dreading this call, having pushed it off for as long as she dared. She throws the Hermes scarf that matches her outfit perfectly around her neck and heads for her car. She settles into the driver's seat, takes a deep breath, and dials the number that accompanied the one-word note she found this morning. "Today"

It's again answered on the first ring. There's music in the background. For a moment, she wonders if her nerves led to her misdialing the phone.

"You requested a call." A statement, not a question. You never ask a question.

"Where do we stand?"

"I'm working on it."

"Work faster."

"These things take time, but rest assured, I am doing everything possible to resolve the issue."

"You ain't thought of everything. I know three things you ain't considered." His icy monotone rings in her ear.

A cold sweat settles over Joyce's skin, and her body begins to tremble. She's glad she's calling from her car and not her office. She wouldn't want anyone accidentally overhearing the call or, worse, seeing her lose her usual composure. "Every avenue within the legal process is being evaluated and addressed."

"You ain't listenin'."

She knows he isn't talking about the legal process. "Removing obstacles in that manner isn't appropriate at this time." She hopes that signals a full understanding of his comments.

"It's very appropriate if things ain't fuckin' fixed soon."

The call rudely ends. Directive delivered and received.

Joyce turns off the phone and pulls the sim card before getting back out of her car. Looking around, she takes a deep breath to steady herself. She's shivering, although it's seventy-four degrees. After a minute or two, she crouches and tucks the phone beneath the front tire.

Her hands are still shaking as she gets back in and starts the car. Nodding at her objective, she shifts the car into reverse and hears and feels the crunch, with the sound triggering a single thought.

The clock's ticking.

34

Jonathan leans back and sighs. These questions are a good start, with none being overly difficult or tricky. The majority are identical. Those that aren't touch upon Harold and Renee's respective roles and credentials. He pushes send, wondering how much "coaching" the two will receive from their trusted General Counsel. After putting his computer to sleep for the night, he packs his briefcase, excited to get home at a reasonable hour. Tonight's a special night. He finally convinced his parents to go out to dinner.

When Jonathan enters the front door, Emily's already home and enjoying a glass of cabernet cauvignon from a bottle Walt had given them a couple of months prior. She knows nothing about wine but knows this one's expensive.

Jonathan takes a minute to quietly observe Emily, admiring the woman who means so much to him. Despite being alone with country music playing in the background, she's seated on the couch with her bare feet curled beneath her. Presumably to honor Walt's generosity by doing the things he's been teaching them, she swirls the wine in her glass and takes a deep breath through her nose. Finally, she brings the crystal glass to her lips and takes a sip with closed eyes.

As a Keith Urban song starts, Jonathan decides to make his presence known and walks into the room. He bends over, gives her a kiss, and steals a sip of wine. "I am going to take a quick shower and change before we head out." He looks at his watch and then wolfishly back at Emily. "Care to join?"

Emily gives him a provocative smile, tilts her head gently, and responds in a seductive voice. "I would, but I've already done my hair and makeup. But... I might need a shower before I go to bed."

Jonathan winks at Emily and heads toward the bedroom. Emily laughs gently before yelling into the other room, "Would you like a glass of wine? It's one of the nice bottles Walt gave us."

"Nah, I'll wait 'til we get to the restaurant. Hoping to get there earlier enough to grab a drink at the bar before my parents arrive. Just the two of us."

After throwing the keys of his BMW to the valet, Jonathan and Emily walk into the restaurant forty-five minutes before their reservation. While Nancy's always early, there's plenty of time to sneak in a romantic drink at the bar. Emily orders the house cabernet sauvignon, and Jonathan orders a Macallan. They raise and clink their glasses, something they've done since their first date—a simple way to stay connected with one another.

Jonathan closes his eyes and allows the warmth of the scotch to take control for a moment. "Mom says Dad seems to be having more good days than bad. It'll be interesting to see how he is tonight."

"I don't want to be a downer, but you shouldn't get your hopes up."

Jonathan looks at Emily with a tear welling up in his eye. "I won't. I've read the literature from the Alzheimer's

Association. This isn't a disease that gets better. It only gets worse. The only question is the rate of decline, something impossible to predict."

As he wipes away the lone tear, Emily looks like she has something she wants to share with Jonathan, but the shift in her expression indicates she is keeping it to herself for now. Instead, she says, "True, but you're doing everything you possibly can. You're doing what every son should do. I'm proud of you for that."

"Yeah, but you know me. I believe there's always something more that can be done. Always."

They've had this conversation a couple of times. Emily's tried, unsuccessfully, to get Jonathan to realize there's only so much that can be done. He's doing it all. He's a loving son who'll walk through fire for his parents, and they know it.

She reaches over and grabs Jonathan's hand. "You're a terrific son, and you're doing all the right things." She leans in, and they share a tender kiss.

Out of the corner of his eye, Jonathan spies a stranger barreling toward them from the other side of the bar, his face getting redder with each step. "You're Jonathan Silverman, right?"

Jonathan immediately stands. "Can I help you?"

"You're working for that company that gave that woman kidney problems, right?"

Jonathan's protective spirit finds him subconsciously taking a step to one side to put himself completely between the stranger and Emily. "Yes, I represent Propentus."

"My grandmother's takin' that drug. Now she's startin' to have kidney problems. We're callin' that attorney to see if he can help her, too."

"I'm sorry to hear that."

The stranger takes a step closer and lowers his voice to deliver his real message. A small amount of whiskey-infused spittle lands on Jonathan's cheek. "You'll be sorrier if that goddamn drug is makin' things worse for my grandmother." The guy looks at Emily, turns on his heels, and storms away.

Emily watches Jonathan unclench his fists. "You okay?"

Jonathan takes a drink of his scotch. "I'm fine. Are you okay?"

"I'm fine. That was crazy."

Before he can respond, Jonathan sees his parents walking through the door twenty-five minutes early. The guy who was harassing Jonathan bumps into Joe as he exits.

Jonathan gives Emily another kiss and whispers, "So much for a quiet drink alone."

He waves his parents toward the bar. After hugs are exchanged, including one between Emily and Joe that still astonishes Jonathan, given his father's lifelong aversion to hugs, he offers his seat to his mother.

"Would you guys like something to drink before we go to our table?"

Nancy looks at Joe, then proudly proclaims, "No thanks. We've given up drinking alcohol."

Jonathan and Emily look at each other, understanding the message that's just been telegraphed. Before either could say anything else, the hostess came over and told them their table was ready. Jonathan pays the tab before he and Emily abandon their unfinished drinks.

After sitting around the table, the hostess hands everyone a menu and also hands Jonathan the wine list.

Nancy gives him that look all mothers possess. "Thank you, but we won't be needing this."

Jonathan smiles at his mother. Message received and understood.

After hearing the specials, they order, and the usual discussion ensues. Nancy asks about work. Joe complains about the Red Sox... again. As the appetizers are delivered, Jonathan watches Emily chat with his mother. She warned him on the way to the restaurant he needed to be the one who asked about his father. If he didn't, she would.

"Dad, what've you been up to?"

Emily responds to his "I'm trying" shrug with a look of her own. Apparently, you don't need to be a mother to possess that look.

"Not much. Your mother keeps taking me for walks like I'm a dog. Other than that, I'm watchin' the Red Sox sink to the bottom of the AL East. Patriots and Celtics get going soon… Thank God."

Nancy jumps in proudly. "We've been taking daily walks. Your father complains about it, but we're up to a mile and a half each day."

Emily claps gently. "That's awesome! Congratulations. All I do is sit in my office all day. I probably couldn't make a mile without stopping for oxygen and water." That gets a laugh out of the group as Emily looks over, giving Jonathan one last chance to get to the point.

He dives into the deep end. "So, Dad, how's the new drug working out? Any problems?"

After a few seconds of silence, Nancy looks at Joe, who returns the gaze with an eye roll and his standard response. "It's fine."

Jonathan got the answer he expected, but he can tell that his mother isn't satisfied. "Your father's having no side effects. This drug's amazing. It's really helping," she says, beaming.

"That's great to hear." He smiles at Emily.

Emily's glare sends an unmistakable message of disappointment. *Really? That's it?*

Nancy finishes her report. "He's sleeping better and isn't as grumpy as he was before. Our next appointment with Dr. Mancini is next week."

"I'm clearing my schedule so I can drive you there."

Jonathan and Emily both pay close attention throughout the rest of the meal. Joe appears less agitated as he sits there, following the discussion and actually engaging at times, something he has struggled with recently.

As they get dessert and coffee at the end of the meal, everyone's happy. Something they, as a group, haven't felt in quite a while. It's nice.

35

Joyce sits in her office, repulsed by what's about to happen, but this reporter's making her nervous. She knows involving Vinnie in anything's a gamble. He's a weak, pathetic individual who'll sell his soul to the devil if it saves his own ass. She has no choice.

Vinnie stands in the doorway, leaning against the casing with his right arm. His ill-fitting uniform does him no favors. His shirt and pants are wrinkled, but his shoes have a fresh shine. The shit-eating grin on his face is almost too much. "Gooooood morning, Joyce."

"Come in and shut the door," she says pointedly, affirming her control.

Vinnie smirks as he plops into a chair like he owns the place. "What can I do for you?"

The sooner he's out of her office, the better. "Have you learned anything more?"

"Truthfully, those two guys might be the closest things to angels I've ever seen. I've called in reinforcements for a deeper dive, but so far, nothin' interesting."

Joyce isn't entirely surprised. "Okay, keep going with that. I need to add someone to the list."

Vinnie heaves his body forward with eagerness. "Sure. Who?"

She lunges backward in synchrony. "A local investigative reporter named MJ Fernandez. I spoke with her yesterday. She tells me she's looking into the lawsuit and Melissa Cosgrove, and she thinks I'm stupid."

"I'll get right on it. Speakin' of the lawsuit, anything going on there?"

Joyce rolls her eyes. He's so fucking annoying. "Just stay in your goddamn lane, Vinnie… And bring me something useful."

Vinnie relaxes back against the chair and raises his hands in concession. "Okay. Any rush on this new addition?"

"I'd like an update within the next forty-eight hours."

Vinnie stands and fights to button his suit jacket. "Okay, see ya in a couple days." As he reaches the door, he looks back at Joyce with an insincere smile. "Thanks for trusting me with this. I won't let you down."

Joyce stops herself from telling him to fuck off. "Of course. That's why you're the Head of Security." She chokes on the words as they leave her mouth.

Joyce sits back and takes stock of the challenges that lay before her. First, they pushed Antsalemab through the FDA process, positioning them to launch the IPO, when this idiot attorney filed a bullshit class-action, making the investment banks jumpy. Then, she hires an attorney who she thought she could control. Now, she's rethinking that. And she has a CEO, the Head of Research, and the lead researcher who require constant babysitting.

But, most importantly, she has to keep *him* happy. That's priority one.

36

MJ puts on her red Chucks, a lightweight jacket, and grabs an energy drink despite the hour. It's the only black jacket she owns, and for an unknown reason, she feels tonight's secret rendezvous requires such attire.

"Not this time, buddy," she lovingly says to Snoopy as he follows her to the door.

MJ's imagination is running wild as she contemplates the information she's about to receive. Information she's confident is paramount to moving her investigation forward.

She arrives at the designated spot and looks at her phone. It's 10:56 p.m. The light from her screen breaks through the darkness, illuminating her face as she sits quietly. As the clock on the dash flips to 11 p.m., there's a soft knock on the passenger front side window, startling MJ. She unlocks the door and watches a giant squeeze himself into the passenger seat. He has to be at least 6'5". He pushes the seat back as far as it'll go, but his knees still press against the dashboard as he looks over at MJ with a smile.

"I'm Michael."

She has multiple immediate thoughts, none of them positive. *Why do I do this? I'm sitting here with a man I don't know. He's huge. He could kill me and walk away.* She finally says the first thing that pops into her head. "How fuckin' tall are you?"

Michael laughs. "I'm 6 foot 7."

"Shit, had I known, I would've rented something with more legroom." She hopes the small talk will relax her. It doesn't.

"I have an update from 'the team.'"

It's always from "the team." These guys never refer to themselves individually. It's as if they share a brain and a personality. MJ's heart rate continues to race as she grabs the notebook and pen waiting on the dash. Her gut's screaming at her to get this behemoth out of her car, but her desire for the information overwhelms her survival instincts. "Okay."

Michael begins without the benefit of notes. "You asked us to look into Propentus and its investors, including their principles. We have information from their date of birth through today. It's not hard." He says this in a confident, obvious way. "We looked at all of them, but there's one investor that's particularly interesting."

MJ has learned from past experiences with "the team" that she has to let the messenger deliver the information however they want. "Interesting how?"

"It's complicated, and there are a number of intersecting issues."

"Okay." MJ sits, ready to take notes like every teacher's pet she knew in high school.

"One of the investors, Excellence Investments, Inc., has invested in one company and one company only… Propentus. While every new firm starts with its first investment, this company was incorporated in Delaware fifteen years ago. No activity until their investment in Propentus a couple of years ago." Michael slows a bit, allowing MJ to keep pace.

"The CEO and President is AnnMarie Spinelli. The COO is James Spinelli. Robert Picciano, the attorney who assisted with the establishment of the corporation, is Boston-based."

"What do we know about the Spinellis?" MJ had the basics from Dun and Bradstreet, but this is where she ran into challenges. There are hundreds of Spinellis in the United States.

Michael clears his throat. "We have confirmation the Spinellis identified as the executives of this company are residents of an assisted living facility in Florida, despite the PO Box in Boston used in the letters of incorporation. They've been married for fifty-seven years, and a review of their medical records indicates they both suffer from dementia."

MJ's head comes up quickly. "...*review of their medical records indicates...*" Christ, how'd they get those? MJ lets the thought go. "Okay, do they have any children? Who's managing their affairs?"

Michael smiles, a teacher proud of his student's aptitude. "They have one son, Anthony, born in Boston, but he moved to Florida with his parents as a teenager."

MJ writes quickly and flips the page, hungry for more.

"This is where it gets complicated."

"Complicated?"

"Anthony has controlled his parents' finances and healthcare for years. We reviewed the Powers of Attorney and Healthcare Proxies that give Anthony control. They were prepared by the same attorney, Robert Picciano, about twelve years ago."

MJ quickly connects the dots. "So, the Spinellis incorporate in Delaware, with the help of an Attorney in Boston, despite living in Florida. Then, a couple of years later, they use the same attorney to give total control of their lives to their son, Anthony. Have I got that right?" She chastises herself for not looking deeper into the attorney. "What do we know about Anthony and the attorney?"

"Picciano, first. He specializes in corporate law and is listed as the attorney of record in the establishment of a number of corporate entities. His specialization prevents any red flags from being raised. With a cursory review, no one would think anything's amiss. He's licensed in multiple states, although a DUI about fifteen years ago put stress on his licensure."

MJ can't write fast enough.

"Picciano's eventually able to get around the DUI. The evidence got messed up. Happens more than you think. We have information suggesting a woman was in the car with him that night. However, her name was omitted or removed from the arrest report. We're working to secure her identity."

Michael continues to adjust himself in the seat like he can't seem to get comfortable but stays on task. "We tracked Picciano's travel and noted multiple trips back and forth from Florida around the time Excellence Investments was established and incorporated and again when the PoAs and Healthcare Proxies were established."

MJ looks away from her notebook, realizing Michael's eyes are in constant motion, scanning for danger.

"After that, Picciano wanted nothing to do with Florida. He's continued to travel over the years, mostly to the Caribbean, with his favorite stop being the Caymans, but we found no additional travel to Florida or any abutting state." Michael takes another pause. "It's possible he drove into Florida from another state, but his credit card records fail to reflect purchases, like rental cars, gas, or hotels, that would support that theory."

MJ is continually amazed at how routinely they speak of information they secure via illegal methods. It used to concern her, but a best friend from college, Sean Murray, who's an IT genius and the person who introduced her to "the team," has repeatedly reassured her she's safe. She met him when she jumped in and defended him from the jocks in college who were giving him shit. She's always fought for the underdog.

She shakes out her tiring hand and flips the page, knowing she's been scribbling nonstop for an hour, but they're just getting started.

37

Vinnie strolls into The Last Inning, grabs an open bar stool, and orders a double Jack, neat. The loud music overshadows the various sporting events being shown on the large-screen TVs located throughout the bar.

As he sips his drink, he's shocked there's a cornhole tournament on one of the televisions, in addition to the Sox game and a few other MLB games. He scratches his head, asking himself, *When the hell did cornhole, a tailgating game, become tournament and TV worthy?*

Vinnie waves the bartender over, orders another drink, and asks to speak to Jimmy. Out of the corner of his eye, he sees Jimmy talking into another gentleman's ear. Vinnie knows the music is kept loud in an effort to defeat any bugs that might be planted within the bar—the feds are always watching.

Vinnie sees the moment when Jimmy notices him. Jimmy finishes his conversation, gives the guy a hug and a kiss on the cheek, and walks toward his office. He never stops but yells loud enough for anyone within a twenty-five-foot radius to hear him, despite the loud music, "Okay asshole, my office… Now."

The music can still be heard in the office, even with the door closed, but it's much easier to talk with one another. Vinnie knows Jimmy has his office swept for bugs twice a day. The bar's swept regularly, but the office would be the real prize. Anybody can walk into the bar and plant a bug. It's been done before. "Hiya Jimmy, how ya doin'?"

Jimmy leans back in his squeaky chair without inviting Vinnie to sit. "Do you fuckin' have somethin', or are you wastin' my fuckin' time again?"

Vinnie jumps into the deep end. His palms sweating like they always do. "I wanna let you know I've been asked to look into a reporter."

"By who?"

"Apparently, the reporter called the office and spoke to Joyce Kramer, the General Counsel. She asked me to look into her."

"Who's this fuckin' reporter?"

"MJ Fernandez. She's twenty-nine years old. A graduate of the Newhouse School at Syracuse University. She's working at *The Herald*."

"What's she investigatin'?"

"I think she's asking about the lawsuit and the company's new drug."

Jimmy seems to be hearing this for the first time. Vinnie almost smiles, but his level of comfort disappears in an instant. "You 'think'? Why don't you fuckin' know?"

Vinnie's nerves impact his voice. "Joyce didn't say. I was asked to check this reporter out. I started, but I wanted you to know ASAP."

"Me knowin' you're doin' somethin' is useless. You get that, right? I need details." Jimmy leans forward in his chair, no longer holding back. "You're pretty fuckin' useless these days.

I'm beginnin' to wonder why I helped such a fuckin' idiot get the Head of Security job."

Vinnie's now in a full-blown panic. Sweat moving to other places on his body. "Jimmy, you know I'm real appreciative of you helpin' me out. I'm just tryin' to give you up-to-the-minute updates."

Jimmy looks at Vinnie with his dead, black eyes. "You ain't doin' anythin' but tellin' me you're tryin' to do somethin' or startin' to do somethin'. You're fuckin' useless. If you can't bring me information, I'll find someone who can."

Vinnie can be thick most days, but he needs to get out of there, and he knows it. "Okay, sure, Jimmy. I'll bring you somethin'." What else can he say?

Venom and spittle fly across Jimmy's desk. "Goddamn it! Get the fuck outta here. Don't come back unless you got somethin' fuckin' worthwhile."

Vinnie says nothing more as he backs out of the office and all but runs to the front door.

38

"Okay, so what's Mr. and/or Mrs. Spinelli's connection to Michael Riccio?"

"Nothing overt identified, but we're exploring a couple of theories." Michael switches topics. "Ready to hear about Anthony?"

MJ's almost frothing at the mouth. This story's going to be huge; she can feel it. Her eagerness is overly evident. "Yes!"

"Anthony grew up in Florida and graduated from a public high school. No trouble other than a couple of fights as a senior. His grades were mediocre at best. College wasn't pursued. After graduation, he returned to Boston. Postal records show an address in East Boston to start. It's the home of a second cousin. He moved around a bit after that. He got a job as a server at a restaurant in the North End a few days after he landed at Logan."

Michael's fidgeting reminds MJ he's uncomfortable, but he doesn't falter. "We believe Anthony began to reconnect with childhood friends. Some of these friends have significant criminal records. He's listed as a 'known associate' on different reports, but surprisingly, we didn't find any criminal record for Anthony. Nothing in Massachusetts, nor anywhere else."

Michael took a moment and tried, unsuccessfully, to stretch his back. "Anthony eventually moved into the construction industry. He became a member of Local 104, the electrician's union, and worked his way up to become a journeyman. Tax returns reflect he kept the restaurant job until he was making good money as an electrician."

MJ flips over another page. Her arm's killing her.

"There's evidence suggesting Anthony's had a few romantic partners. He's a good-lookin' kid, and he flashes a lot of cash, so his choices are likely plentiful." Michael hesitates before he drops the next data point. "We believe Anthony's gay."

MJ almost drops her pen. She looks quizzically at Michael. "Wait. What? Why do you think that?"

"Anthony's exceptionally careful about this. However, the one place he can't hide from is his doctor. The medical records from his primary care physician reflect frequent AIDS testing. While many people get tested regularly, his pattern of testing suggests recurring checks since his early twenties. He's negative, by the way."

MJ's mortified. This "team" knows no bounds. She thinks about Anthony's departure from Florida. Was he running from his sexual orientation? A few fights in high school? He returns to the city of his birth, joins a union, and starts running with the wrong crowd. Is it all to avoid confronting who he really is?

Sorrow for Anthony overcomes MJ. A friend of hers is gay and shared over martinis and soul-crushing tears her family's decision to shun her when she came out. It was one of the most emotional moments MJ's ever experienced. She makes a mental note to call her friend.

Back to business. "Have you identified any connection between Anthony and Michael Riccio or Propentus? Romantic involvement?"

"We've found nothing that links them directly. Anthony's trail starts to fade a bit once he joins the union. His bank records are limited, which leads us to believe he's a big fan of cash. Of particular note is Anthony's regular trips to Florida for reasons unknown. It's a pattern that's been repeated for years. Perhaps to spend time with his parents, or perhaps go somewhere he believes is far enough away to privately explore the other side of his life. Of note, Spinelli and Picciano were on the same flights to Florida on a number of occasions prior to the establishment of Excellence Investments, Inc. They sat next to each other."

MJ's head is spinning. She's trying to connect everything she's heard with what she's pulled together. There's so much to figure out, but this pushes the rock farther up the hill.

"We'll provide another update very soon."

Without saying another word, Michael opens the car door and unfolds himself. After a few seconds of stretching, he reaches into his pocket and tosses MJ a non-descript thumb drive. "This is everything I just told you. I presume you know how to protect this information?"

MJ's pissed. He could've told her that first and saved her from getting a cramp in her writing hand. "I do. And you could have given me this upfront."

"Yes, but you may not have been as attentive as you needed to be. Besides, you didn't ask." Michael closes the car door and fades into the darkness. She finds it disturbing yet amazing at the same time... How does a 6'7" giant become a ghost, disappearing into the darkness?

39

Jonathan picks up his parents and heads to Dr. Mancini's office. Traffic on 128 is heavier today. With his father's country music playing, Jonathan's mind and attention wander into the realm of the FDA filing. Without warning, the BMW engages its brakes, stopping itself and jarring all three of its occupants. Jonathan looks up, realizing what happened. He paid extra for this option, knowing he frequently gets lost in thought. The front bumper of his old car was proof of that.

Joe's not happy, the anger visible on his face. "Pay attention."

Jonathan reverts back to his sixteen-year-old self, with a shiny new permit in his pocket, taking driving lessons from his father. "Sorry."

Jonathan looks around and notices a gray Honda in the lane next to them. The driver looks familiar, but Jonathan can't place him. As traffic breaks up, their trip continues, with Jonathan now 110% attentive.

They arrive at the office without further incident and walk into Dr. Mancini's waiting room with a lighter step than on prior occasions. To pass the time as they wait to be called back, they chat quietly. The primary topic is what Jonathan and Emily would like for dinner on their next visit.

Finally, after being taken to a room and waiting a little longer for the doctor to arrive, a light rap on the door precedes Dr. Mancini entering. She takes a minute to wash her hands, something Jonathan assumes she does a thousand times a day. "Good morning, everyone."

After some quick pleasantries, Dr. Mancini gets down to business. "How are you feeling today, Joe?"

"Pretty good." A change from his usual response.

"Excellent. Nancy, anything to add?"

Nancy pulls a small notepad from her purse—one that neither Joe nor Jonathan had seen before. She flips a few pages, clears her throat, and proudly delivers her official report. "First, Joe seems to be sleeping better. He still naps off and on during the day, but he's less restless at night." She flips to the next page. "Second, Joe's appetite's good. He still isn't a fan of the Mediterranean diet, particularly the fish, but he cleans his plate most meals." One more page flipped. "Lastly, we've been walking every day and are up to one and a half miles."

Dr. Mancini writes down the information Nancy provides. "That's a thorough update, Nancy. Thank you." With a smile, Dr. Mancini looks up at Jonathan. "Jonathan, anything to add?"

Jonathan's shock over his mother's presentation makes him default to the easy answer. "Nope."

"Okay, great. I noticed today's blood pressure readings are higher than they've been in the past. I'm going to ask the nurse to take them again before you leave. Blood pressure can fluctuate for a variety of reasons, so there is nothing to worry about at this point." Dr. Mancini smiles reassuringly. "Joe, anything else bothering you today? Any new aches or pains?"

"I'm sixty-five. There's always a new pain."

Everyone chuckles.

"True enough. Anything new of particular concern?"

"My feet are bothering me today."

Nancy looks startled by this revelation. She narrows her eyes at her husband and scolds him, "Joe, you haven't said anything to me about that."

Joe looks at Nancy smugly. "You never asked."

Jonathan mentally prepares to put on his "mediator" hat for the ride home.

Dr. Mancini captures this new information. "Okay, we'll watch that. If it becomes a problem, take a couple of Tylenol, but be sure to follow the dosages outlined on the bottle. Anything else?"

"Nope."

Dr. Mancini spends a couple of moments typing into her laptop, a ploy to kill some time before she asks Joe her questions. "Joe, can you tell me which of my offices we're at today?"

Joe stops and thinks hard about the question. "Um... uh... It's the one in..." He finally gives up. "Jonathan drove us today." He looks at Jonathan, pleading for the answer without saying a word.

"Newton, Dad. We're in the Newton office today."

"Ah, that's right."

Dr. Mancini continues. "Joe, are you having pain anywhere today?"

"Nope." Nothing about his feet this time around, surprising Jonathan, given how adamant he was moments ago.

Dr. Mancini asks a few more questions, which Joe answers correctly. Lastly, she asks, "Joe, any problems with the new medication?"

"No."

Dr. Mancini looks at Nancy, who confirms Joe's response. "Nothing so far."

"That's great. Your cognition remains steady, with no adverse reactions. I see no reason to make any changes. We'll continue to monitor, and I'll see you in a month."

Today, the three of them are in unison as they say, "Thank you, Doctor."

The nurse returns and retakes Joe's blood pressure in both arms. While it's lower than when he arrived, it's still higher than it's been trending. She adds the results to Joe's chart.

40

Jonathan arrives at Propentus a few minutes early. He accepts the offer of coffee and is led to a windowless conference room in the center of the building. Harold strolls into the room five minutes late, sighing and shaking his head, apparently annoyed with the need to be here. He's wearing his lab coat, the one that tells everyone his name and that he's a PhD. Joyce quietly enters behind him.

Jonathan stands. "It's a pleasure to meet you, Dr. Johnson."

Harold scoffs as they shake hands. "I don't believe being part of a lawsuit is a pleasure of any sort."

Jonathan smiles. "Certainly not. Part of my job is to make it no fun for the plaintiffs who brought the suit. I need your help to do that."

"Well, *that* I'm happy to help with." Harold sits across from Jonathan, holding his hands on the table with his fingers interlaced.

With three sentences, Jonathan brings Harold's guard down a notch. Jonathan repositions his laptop as Joyce takes a hard copy of the questions from a manila folder.

Jonathan knows flattery often works with pompous people and lays it on a little thick. "Harold... may I call you Harold? Of course, I will always refer to you as Dr. Johnson in front of the plaintiffs and the jury. They need to know you're a well-respected PhD."

Harold's shoulders relax further. "Sure, thank you for asking."

"Certainly. Okay, Harold, we're going to discuss the questions I sent to Joyce. Did you have a chance to review them?"

"Yes. Joyce reviewed them with me."

As expected, Jonathan notes to himself, but he isn't going to poke that bear at the moment. "Great. Why don't we get started?" Jonathan walks Harold through the questions in the exact same order they were prepared, starting with his educational background. The goal is to give Harold a chance to brag with the hope he'll eventually let his guard down fully.

Jonathan is impressed as Harold walks through his credentials and the journey that brought him to Propentus. His CV is impressive, but Jonathan is pleasantly surprised with Harold's ability to present the information in a way that feels professorial. That'll play well to a jury. Maybe he's not the arrogant, *I'm the smartest guy in the room,* researcher Jonathan initially thought.

For the next forty minutes, Harold appears comfortable. Either he's well coached with a lot of rehearsing, or he's a bright researcher, passionate about the process involved in discovering a pioneering treatment. Jonathan periodically writes notes on a legal pad after recording Harold's responses on his laptop.

He notices Joyce watching and presumes she likely knows exactly what he's planning.

"Thank you, Harold. I must say, the way you carried yourself throughout those questions is exactly the way I'd want you to behave any time you're in front of the plaintiffs or the jury. Your answers were easily understood, even for a layman like me. You did a great job not being overly technical."

Harold's grinning from ear to ear. Jonathan guessed correctly on how best to manage him. Time to test Harold's agility and his reaction to pressure. "Harold, you may have noticed me writing things down. I've captured additional questions that are born from the answers you provided. This is common, and rest assured the plaintiffs will be doing the same. We can never fully predict every question that'll be asked."

Jonathan looks at Joyce for confirmation.

"Yes, Harold. You'll recall I mentioned this during your preparation for today's meeting."

"Yes, of course. Ask away."

Jonathan grabs the legal pad, shifts in his seat, and everyone in the room senses the change in his demeanor. In a tone specifically designed to knock the doctor down a peg, Jonathan hits him right between the eyes. Harold never sees it coming.

"Harold, when I asked about Control Group A, you said they were 'selected by you and Dr. Spencer.' However, the paperwork filed with the FDA says the participants in Control Group A were randomly selected from a larger group. Why the discrepancy?"

Harold's mouth drops open. He shifts in his seat, looking to Joyce to throw him a life preserver. She doesn't move. He's on his own, and Jonathan can tell he isn't happy about it. Harold regains his footing, looking at Jonathan with contempt and a smirk. "I'd have to see the document to which you are referring in order to answer that."

Jonathan quietly reaches into his briefcase, pulls out the document, and hands it to Harold. Jonathan catches Joyce's look of disdain. With what, he's not entirely sure, but she knows this is how the game's played.

Joyce appears to be lost in her thoughts when she realizes Harold is speaking to her. "Sorry, what was that, Harold?"

Anger and self-righteous indignation define Harold's new approach. "I asked whether I should answer the question. There's intellectual property involved."

Before she can answer, Jonathan jumps in, returning to the nice guy he was at the beginning. "Harold, as a condition of taking Propentus as a client, Joyce had me and my partner execute an iron-clad non-disclosure agreement, which means you can share anything and everything with me. In fact, Joyce and I expect you to. It's the only way I can effectively do my job in protecting Propentus."

Jonathan watches splotches appear from beneath Joyce's collar as she swallows hard. He's deftly tied her hands.

"Jonathan's 100% correct. He's signed an NDA and, as our attorney, is also bound by attorney-client privilege. Feel free to be completely honest and forthright with him."

Harold seems apprehensive as he looks back at Jonathan. "What was the question again?

Jonathan re-reads the question with the same accusatory tone, then places the document directly in front of Harold.

Harold sits perfectly still, evaluating his options. After taking longer than he should, he decides ignorance is the best approach. "I'm not sure why."

Friendly Jonathan puts his pen down. "Actually, Harold, while I still want to know why, I appreciate your honesty. This is a good teaching moment. If you're asked a question you're not completely sure about, ask for clarification. If it references a document, always ask to see the document before you respond, just as you did. And, simply saying 'I don't recall,' which isn't a great answer, is better than being caught in a lie."

The apparently declining level of trust in Jonathan leads Harold to become aloof as they talk through the remaining follow-up questions. He plays the dunce card a few more times, causing Joyce's neck blotches to spread.

Jonathan's evaluation is straightforward: Harold's a narcissist who views the entire world from an undeserving perch of supremacy. He's not Walt-smart, but he's intelligent. Jonathan finds it implausible that Harold, as the Head of Research, doesn't remember key pieces of information, and those were the simple questions.

Jonathan adds Harold's name to his list of worries about this case.

41

Harold storms out, flying past Renee as she's heading toward the conference room, his lab coat resembling a windblown cape. He spins around. "Don't believe a fucking word the guy says. I can't wait to talk to Joyce. Son of a bitch tried to make me look stupid. He's not on our side."

Harold doesn't wait for a response. He continues stomping toward his office, muttering under his breath. Renee, already nervous, is now petrified. What the hell's she walking into?

As she enters the conference room, Jonathan stands and reaches out to shake her hand. "It's a pleasure to meet you, Dr. Spencer."

"Nice to meet you, Mr. Silverman." Renee sits down across from Jonathan. She fiddles with a button on her lab coat, and her leg begins to bounce before the first question is asked.

"Please call me Jonathan. May I call you Renee?"

"Of course."

"Okay, Renee, I am going to walk through the questions I forwarded to Joyce previously. Have you had a chance to see those questions?"

"Yes, Joyce and I have discussed them a few times."

"Great. I'm going to walk through the questions in the exact order they were provided. If you don't understand something, just ask me for clarification. Okay?"

"Sure." Renee continues playing with the button.

Jonathan seems to cautiously guide Renee through the questions even though she's confident with her qualifications. A PhD in Chemistry from Stanford is only one of the many accomplishments littering her CV.

Jonathan finishes with the prepared questions, writing down notes as Renee patiently waits for the next question. She wonders if Joyce's influence on her responses was obvious. She feels the energy of the mood shift as Jonathan prepares for the next round of questions.

"Renee, you probably noticed I was writing a few things down on my legal pad. They're questions that came to mind as you were walking me through your initial answers."

Renee's head snaps to look at Joyce, who looks as uncomfortable as she feels. "It's pretty similar in science. You test something and get a certain result," Jonathan says, obviously walking her slowly to the real question. "That result prompts you to try something different, right?"

Renee ponders the statement, not having thought about it that way, but realizes the logic holds. She looks at Joyce before saying a word.

Joyce uses a motherly voice, to which Renee responds favorably: "It's true, Renee. This is a normal part of the process."

Renee looks back at Jonathan. "Okay," she says, but she feels like her leg will fall off with all the nervous bouncing she's done.

"I know you and Harold had access to all the data associated with Antsalemab. I also know you both signed almost all of the documents associated with the application to the FDA. What I'm wondering is, who else had access to the data?"

Renee freezes, then gives him the prepared answer in a robotic cadence. "We restricted access to the information to me and Harold. We felt it important to keep it compartmentalized."

Jonathan shifts in his seat and scribbles something else down on his legal pad before he asks his follow-up question. "Okay, is that common?"

Renee again looks at Joyce before reciting her well-practiced line. "We do it that way at times."

"Thanks. I'm still learning the whole process. The data's entered into corporate computers, right?"

Renee's answer flows more easily this time: "Yes, that's the only place we enter it. Propentus takes great pride in protecting its data. We have a top-notch IT team."

"And who's in charge of the IT department?"

Renee again looks to Joyce for help. This time, Joyce speaks up. "Thomas 'Tommy' O'Hara is our VP and CIO."

Jonathan scribbles down that name. "Thanks, Joyce. I'll want to speak with him so I get a complete, step-by-step understanding of how data is collected and stored. The complaint alleges Propentus hid things from the FDA. I need to speak intelligently about how that could never be the case."

Joyce smiles. "Absolutely, I'll have my assistant work with Julie to set something up."

Jonathan turns back to Renee. "I think that's it for today. Do you have any questions for me?"

"Um… How'd I do?"

"You were terrific. We'll spend a lot of time talking to make sure you're fully prepared for any question the other side may throw at you."

Renee notices Joyce flinch at the statement, but that isn't her problem.

They say their goodbyes, and Renee returns to her lab feeling both relieved and worried.

• • •

Jonathan could smell the bullshit coming from across the table at both meetings. But it's his job to get the truth, and of those he has met so far, Renee's naiveté makes her the most likely to go off script and give it to him. Ideas of how to move forward with the case swim through his mind as he is escorted to the exit.

By the time he arrives at his car and throws his laptop bag in the back seat, Jonathan is more convinced than ever there's something being hidden from him. All he has to do is figure out what it is before "The King of the Fender Bender" does.

42

The sound of pitter-patter echoes in MJ's head as she blocks the sunrise from her eyes. Snoopy jumps up on the bed and runs to ring his bell. She's groggy. It's almost noon. She was up late reviewing the material on the thumb drive and creating an expanded list of questions. Questions are good… answers are better.

After Snoopy's third trip between the front door and licking her face, MJ leaps out of bed, throwing on a pair of sweats and a baggy sweatshirt that were lying on the floor. She almost falls over the coffee table as she hops on one foot to put on her Chucks while Snoopy bounces at the front door. He's on a mission.

They barely get outside before he relieves himself at the first available tree. He then pulls her toward the dog park. He has more on his mind. Fortunately, MJ grabbed the pair of sweats she wore last night, the gray ones with pizza sauce on them.

On their return trip, MJ happily discovers the change from last night's pizza shoved into one of the pockets, allowing her to grab a desperately needed cup of coffee. After the first satisfying sip, she and Snoopy fall into their usual pace, and her mind swirls, as it always does. There's so much information to collate and piece together.

She finds herself again facing a complicated issue. How's she going to give her editor information no one should have? She's navigated that in the past, but this time's different. Half of today must be dedicated to connecting the dots for him. The other half would be figuring out how to answer the one question he's likely to ask: "How'd you get your hands on this information?"

Arriving home. MJ heads straight to the Keurig after kicking off her shoes. She pops the blueberry pod into its chamber, puts her mug underneath, and pushes the button that will create the special elixir. A shower will clear her head, and then she'll review everything one more time.

• • •

With wet hair, MJ pulls a t-shirt over her head and retreats to the couch. The first question she keeps returning to is the connection between Anthony Spinelli and Michael Riccio. "The team" promised more, which will include Riccio specifically. Will the connection become obvious once she reviews that material?

MJ tosses that thought aside, deciding to do what she should've done before: learn all she can about Robert Picciano. She reviews every shred of information Michael provided and compares them with her own sparse notes.

Robert Picciano has a limited digital footprint, with only a few articles that mention the local boy who graduated from Boston College and BC Law. He was on Law Review and graduated cum laude. Now, in his late fifties, he seems to have a decent, albeit insignificant, career.

Other than an article in a law journal announcing his ascension to partner at Wallace, Connors, and Ramirez, there are a handful of meaningless articles identifying him as the attorney representing one of the parties involved in a corporate deal.

She finally gets to the good stuff: his DUI. According to the police report, Picciano alleged he was heading home from dinner when he swerved his Audi A6 to miss a pedestrian who stepped off the curb. The maneuver left his vehicle stuck on the curb after striking a street sign and narrowly missing a hydrant. After failed field sobriety tests, he was given a pair of matching silver bracelets and a ride to the station, where blood was drawn and sent out for analysis. He was charged with multiple violations, including felony DUI.

Michael's thumb drive includes photos from a couple of different red-light cameras. Picciano "missed" the light a lot that night. Two building surveillance cameras were his undoing, however. They unquestionably confirmed that no one stepped in front of him.

Just as Michael had said, the DUI charges were dropped without fanfare. Not reduced, dropped. All that's been found is one incidental note at the bottom of a memo: *missing blood*. The non-DUI-related charges followed a common trajectory, including a hefty fine and a few Saturdays in traffic school.

MJ shakes her head, knowing a felony conviction for DUI puts a law license in jeopardy, including possible suspension or revocation. Picciano dodged a bullet.

The RMV record confirms he's kept his nose clean since that night—not even a parking ticket. Picciano never married. Tax returns reflect a couple of women who shared an address with him, but none seemed to make it past one tax season.

Lastly, the report outlined his extensive travel. He definitely enjoys the beach more than the mountains. Other than the trips connected to Anthony Spinelli, "the team" couldn't correlate any traveling companions. They couldn't rule out companions who traveled separately, however. That's impossible to track digitally unless you know who the other person might be.

MJ pulls her feet up and sits on them. Soft jazz plays in the background as Snoopy joins her on the couch. With few answers identified, more questions fill her mind. It's one of those days, but she's undeterred. She always gets there in the end.

43

Jonathan puts the BMW's sport mode to good use as he aggressively weaves through traffic. He hasn't been this pissed in a long time. He's going to call Joyce, but if he does it while he's driving, it'll be ugly. So, he focuses as intently as he can on not causing an accident on the way back to his office.

After parking his car like a stunt driver in a Hollywood film, Jonathan sprints into the building, barely able to contain himself. He flings the office entrance door open, immediately yells for Julie to get Joyce Kramer on the phone, and walks into his office, throwing his jacket and tie over a chair.

"Ms. Kramer on line one."

Jonathan takes a deep breath and snatches the phone from his desk. "What the hell was that, Joyce?" It's the nicest thing he can say. She's a client, after all. An immensely difficult client, but a client nonetheless.

Joyce's tone remains flat. "I understand your frustration, Jonathan. I'd be unhappy if I were you."

"Unhappy doesn't scratch the surface! I can't effectively represent Propentus without access to everything. I know you coached them. Hell, I would've, but either you did a lousy job, or they're idiots. Which is it?" He looks at the note he wrote himself before picking up the phone: *Keep it in check*. So much for that.

Joyce maintains her cool. "Yes, I coached them. They're scientists, Jonathan. This is their first foray into our world. I'd be lost in a lab. We have more work to do than I expected."

His anger erupts like Mount Vesuvius. "Their preparation aside, Joyce, I'm being stonewalled. I don't have, nor have I been told, everything. That ends now. I demand, not request, unfettered access to everything and everyone even remotely associated with Antsalemab. If you're unwilling to provide this, I'm going to reconsider my representation."

"Jonathan, you have access to everything you need. Harold and Renee are skittish. We'll work with them on that."

"'Everything I need'? *I* decide what I need, Joyce. And, skittish? Harold's an arrogant bastard who thinks he's the smartest guy in the room, and Renee's brilliant but a people-pleasing mouse, constantly seeking approval. Both are the kiss of death at trial, and you know it."

Joyce tries deflection. "I shouldn't tell you this, but you'll find out eventually. Harold's going through a nasty divorce. I haven't kept anything from you intentionally, and I can assure you I didn't tell Harold and Renee what to say."

He wonders if she told them what *not* to say. "Joyce, this stops today. I want copies of every single document, whether paper, electronic, or other, within the next twenty-four hours. I also want to meet with the CIO."

Jonathan has pinned Joyce into a corner. If she refuses, she will put his representation at risk. He's aware that this would be the last thing Propentus would want right now: a public onslaught that would follow his voluntary withdrawal.

"Of course. I'll work to get you the materials as quickly as possible. After we hang up, I'll have my assistant call Julie to schedule the meeting with Tommy. Will that work?"

Jonathan looks at the note again. Is she giving him what he wants, or just saying she will? He'll know by end of day tomorrow. "Yes. To be clear, I want the documentation within twenty-four hours, and the meeting with Mr. O'Hara should occur within the next forty-eight hours. There's no wiggle room on this, Joyce."

"Understood. I'll have my assistant call Julie immediately."

"Goodbye, Joyce." He slumps in his chair. No amount of money is worth this.

44

MJ is sitting in Spagnola's office, which reminds her of a fishbowl. She wonders how he'd react if someone stared at him from the outside while tapping on the office's floor-to-ceiling glass.

"What do you have, MJ?"

"First, let me say that while I have a lot of information pulled together, I'm still working to connect the dots."

"Yeah, yeah, I get it. What do you have?"

"Okay. I've learned Riccio led a pretty clean life prior to getting to Cambridge. I have a few calls out, but unless they have some unexpected bombshell, I feel pretty comfortable stating that. His time at Genomics is also relatively benign. I still have a fair amount of work to do from his starting Propentus to the present, but indications are he's become a complete ass."

So far, so good. Now for some of the juicier stuff. "I don't have access to Propentus' financials, but there are plenty of articles that speak to their impressive ability to raise capital. I've been doing deep dives into each of the investors. Most are the usual suspects you'd expect to find playing in this space. Again, I have additional work to do there, but nothing overt is immediately jumping out."

MJ notices his interest lagging. "However, there's one investment firm that's caught my eye. Excellence Investments, Inc. On the surface, they appear to be just like any other investment firm. However, a deeper look reveals a company that's been around less than fifteen years and was incorporated with AnnMarie and James Spinelli being named CEO and COO, respectively."

MJ tries to control her cadence, knowing her pace can get away from her. "It's taken some creative research, but I believe I've found these two individuals. They're husband and wife and are currently residents at an assisted living facility in Florida. I believe both are suffering from dementia. Furthermore, although established years ago, Excellence Investments made no known investments until they invested in Propentus as part of the Series D raise. And nothing since."

Spagnola looks up from his notes, peering over his reading glasses. He's listening again.

"The Spinellis have one son, Anthony, who never went to college and returned to Boston after graduating high school. Anthony has complete control of his parents' life. There are Powers of Attorney and Healthcare Proxies in place for both. Robert Picciano is the attorney the Spinellis used to establish the corporation in Delaware. He's a local kid turned corporate law attorney via BC and BC law. One issue in his past is of particular interest. A DUI which was dropped, presumably because of a chain of custody issue."

She can't mention the woman just yet. She has nothing but "the team's" thoughts on that. "Travel records reflect both he and Anthony traveled to Florida at the same time and often on the same flights around the period when Excellence Investments, Inc. was established."

MJ takes a sip of the energy drink she brought in with her as she decides if Anthony's sexual orientation is irrelevant for the moment. "There's more to do, but police records reflect that while Anthony's been a good boy, his name's listed as a 'known associate' of a number of others who haven't been as well-behaved. In fact, a few of them have taken up residence in Walpole and other facilities throughout the Commonwealth."

She gives him a second to catch up. "Lastly, I spoke to Joyce Kramer, General Counsel for Propentus. I asked her a question about the impact of high blood pressure and kidney stones as potential indicators or causes of chronic kidney disease. She dodged the question by acknowledging the trials showed some incidences of HBP and kidney stones, but those were easily resolved. She's hiding something. I feel it in my bones."

MJ looks up from her notes and waits for Spagnola to say something. He's digesting everything. She knows now's the time to sit and be quiet, something she isn't known for.

After thirty seconds, which feels like six hours, he drapes the two halves of his glasses around his shoulders, playing the role of teacher. "Okay. First, you should've waited on the General Counsel. No need to tip your hand this early in the investigation."

"I know. That was stupid."

"That aside, I agree something doesn't smell right, but it may not be the smoking gun you think. The story may actually be about the FDA's failure to catch any of this in their review. They look at financials as well as the research. Rather than why did..." he flips the page to check his notes, "...Excellence Investments Inc. invest in Propentus as their only investment."

"Agreed. There's a lot here, but there are funny things going on. I've barely scratched the surface on Riccio. That's up next. I need to figure out if and why there's a connection between Michael Riccio and AnnMarie, James, or Anthony Spinelli."

"You bought yourself another two weeks. But I need to see more connected dots."

"Sure."

MJ leaves the news building, relieved he didn't ask what she meant by "creative research." She's standing outside, looking at her phone, when she catches a guy staring at her.

This isn't the first time, and she hopes it isn't the last. But there's a difference. He holds her gaze. Something about his intensity sends a shiver up MJ's spine. After a few seconds, she breaks eye contact, returning to her thoughts of Thai for dinner.

She takes a few steps before looking back over her shoulder. He's gone.

45

Renee sits in her office with her eyes closed, classical music playing softly in the background. It's helped soothe her since she was a baby, and it's working until Vinnie appears.

"Hey, Renee. How ya' doin'?"

Renee sighs heavily and looks up. She's already having a crappy day. She doesn't need him to make it worse. Her response is as snarky as it is uncharacteristic. "Not today, Vinnie."

"Whoa... Just checkin' in on my favorite researcher after her meeting with the attorney."

Renee struggles to center herself as she watches an uninvited Vinnie slither into her office and plop into a chair. Her hatred toward him has been the subject of many counseling sessions.

She musters every remaining ounce of energy. "I've been told by the attorney and Joyce not to talk with anyone." Not entirely true. She was advised not to talk with anyone outside of Propentus. She knows Vinnie's afraid of Joyce. Invoking her name should help.

"True, but I'm the Head of Security. You can tell me any-thing." He smiles, the small gap between his teeth front and center.

"I'm just following orders." Keeping it short usually drives him away.

"Must have been pretty bad if they told you not to say anything, huh?"

Renee takes another deep breath. She'd kill for anyone to stop by her office right now, even her narcissistic boss, Harold. "It wasn't that bad."

Vinnie stares, not blinking. "Not that bad, huh? Means it was a little bad, right? What happened?"

"I told you; I'm not supposed to say anything." Renee's leg starts bouncing, once again confirming that therapy isn't helping her anxiety.

Vinnie changes course without warning. "Attorneys are assholes, even to their own clients."

Renee's head snaps up. How did he know? Was he out-side the conference room? She fights to remain silent as she fiddles with a button on her lab coat.

"You didn't deserve that. They say they're on your side, then attack you when they don't like your answer. I saw that a lot as a cop." Vinnie now sounds like a condescending teen-ager. "I can tell from your body language something happened. Remember, I was trained on that stuff. What happened?"

Renee feels like she's on a deserted island. Harold is a self-centered jerk, and Joyce only cares about the company and controlling every word she says. She has no one, and she can't talk with anyone outside the company. They made that abundantly clear. Vinnie is still a slimy scumbag, but he gets it. With a heaving sigh, she breaks.

Renee starts to cry. "Only because you're in charge of security. Joyce and I practiced the questions we expected him to ask. She told me how to answer them." She wipes her tears and takes a gulp of air as if she were breaching the surface after a deep dive. "But then, he asked different questions. Joyce didn't tell me that would happen. She just sat there. She abandoned me."

The excitement in Vinnie's voice is evident. "What were the questions?"

The words tumble out wildly now. "He asked me why only Harold and I signed the FDA paperwork and who else had access to the data. Those weren't on the original list." She blows her nose louder than someone of her size should be able. "Joyce finally jumped in when he asked who was in charge of IT. Now he wants to talk with Tommy." Renee mumbles, "Joyce should've helped me sooner."

Vinnie stands up and goes around the desk, putting a hand on her shoulder. "Sounds like you did great. And you're right about Joyce; she should have helped. You know, you can always talk to me, right?"

The touch snaps her out of her bewilderment. Renee slaps his hand off her shoulder. "Look… Um… I wasn't supposed to say anything, and I'm sorry I criticized Joyce."

"Relax, I'm on your side. I just wanna help."

Renee regains her composure and her backbone, glaring at Vinnie. "Seriously, forget I said anything."

Vinnie walks toward the door, grinning. "No worries, Renee. Mum's the word."

As he leaves, Renee looks at the reflection on her computer screen. She's ashamed for buckling to his pressure; worse still is the massive wave of nausea caused by his touch. She leaps up and rushes toward the ladies' room, questioning what she's just done.

46

Vinnie shows surprising restraint as he heads to find Harold. If he can get that asshole to break, too, he's hit the jackpot and can again prove his worth to Jimmy.

Harold is covering his cell phone with his hand, whispering, as Vinnie sticks his head into the office. Harold gives Vinnie the finger and turns so he isn't facing the door as his whispers get louder. "You'll get the fucking money."

Vinnie dons a knowing smirk.

Harold hangs up and spins around. "Why are you lurking around listening to other people's calls? Get the fuck out!"

Vinnie heard the word "money," and he could see the fear written all over Harold's face. Time to press. "Fuck you, Harold. I know you met with the attorney. Wanted to see if you're alright." He knows the touchy-feely approach won't work with Harold.

Harold's defiance isn't surprising. "I'm not going to say a word to you about this." Just then, his cell phone rings. It's Renee. A warning call. He ignores it, daggers flying from his eyes. "Nothing, Vinnie. 'Niente' if saying it in Italian will get it through your fucking head."

Vinnie wasn't prepared for Harold to be this irate. "Calm down. I know lawsuits can be fucked up. Renee's shook up, so I'm lookin' in on you, too. That's all." Vinnie's still standing in the doorway, leaning against the doorframe—his favorite pose. He's hoping the pressure of the call will shake something loose.

Harold's steam's fading. "I'm fine. Everything's fine."

Vinnie senses a crack. "I'm the Head of Security, so you know you can always talk to me. Joyce can be a real ball-buster, and I know you can't talk to anyone outside the company." Vinnie crosses his fingers and toes.

Harold redirects the conversation. "Sorry. I have a lot on my mind with the divorce and everything."

Vinnie tries the buddy approach. "Yeah, sorry to hear about that. Shitty situation. Anything I can help with?"

"No. She's dragging me through the muck, is all. I'll figure it out."

Shit! Vinnie thought he'd finally gotten through. "Okay. Hang in there, and remember, don't let the bastards win."

A despicable grin spreads across Vinnie's face as he struts back to the security desk with his newfound knowledge.

47

I t's 6:30 p.m. when Jonathan pulls out of the firm's parking lot after deciding to grab a bottle of wine for a quiet evening at home. He and Emily haven't had one of those in a while. Wanting to hear Emily's voice, he calls her through the car's system. As he waits for the call to connect, he notices a nondescript Toyota Camry pull off the curb behind him.

He quickly forgets the car when Emily answers. "Hey, babe. What's up?"

"I'm just leaving work. Thought I'd stop and grab a bottle of wine for an evening at home. What do you think?"

"Sounds great! Grab whatever. You know me, I have no taste buds… According to Walt."

They both laugh.

"Okay, think about what you want to order in. I'll see you in a bit. Love ya!"

"Love you, too."

Jonathan hangs up and turns on the radio to get some news. He has no idea what's going on in the world. His time has been consumed by his parents, doctors, and the job. The newscaster says something about sabre-rattling by China, threatening Taiwan again, a One China policy, etc. Then, something about North Korea meeting with Russia and what that might mean for the rest of the world.

His mind wanders and lands on his being a lousy boyfriend. Sure, he's taken Emily out a couple of times, but it's always been with his parents. He's been working crazy hours, which she's used to. Or at least that's what she says. And, of course, there's the unexplained nightmare and all that goes with it.

Without warning, he dives headfirst into the Emily rabbit hole.

Jonathan loves her in a way he never expected. His bouts of fear and paranoia are a thing of the past. She accepts all of him: the good, the bad, and the ugly. He realizes he needs to speak with his father about the next step with Emily before he no longer can.

A huge smile and a private laugh follow his decision that there will be a next step. The sense of calm from making a challenging decision releases the tension he's been carrying for far too long. His grip on the steering wheel softens.

He pulls into the liquor store, noticing a gray Toyota pulling in behind him. Was that the same one parked on the street outside his office? Maybe? He's tired. Besides, Toyota is one of the best-selling manufacturers in the U.S. He could throw a rock in any direction and hit five of them. He's almost skipping as he heads for the red wine.

• • •

The next morning, Jonathan gets into the office early. He and Emily enjoyed a wonderful evening with wine, Chinese take-out, and the movie *Casablanca*. His thoughts on the treadmill today focused on making time to visit his father to chat about the future. Just thinking about the word "future" makes him smile.

As he's walking toward his office, Walt hollers from down the hall. "Mornin', Jonny…"

Nothing's going to bother him today. "Morning, Walt. You're in early."

Walt balances an extra-large iced coffee on a file in one hand and holds a half-eaten bagel in the other as he navigates his way down the hallway. "I have an early hearing. You look… how do I describe it… happy? What gives?"

Jonathan can't hide his smile. "I'm always happy. Apparently, the happiness aura is shining a little brighter today."

Walt changes directions, almost dumping his coffee. With a few sidesteps and crazy arm gyrations, he somehow manages to keep it upright. "Bullshit. Now, I have to follow you to your office and find out what the hell's going on."

Jonathan chuckles and leads the way to his office, circling his desk before he sits in his chair.

Walt drops his file on the floor next to the chair opposite Jonathan as he sits.

"Jesus, Walt, you're getting crumbs everywhere. Can you please put something under that sweating coffee so it doesn't drip all over my files?"

Walt devours what's left of the bagel in two huge bites. With the last pieces still in his mouth, he continues. "There. Problem solved. So, what gives?"

Jonathan's smile will not be erased. "Nothing gives. I got a good night's sleep and had a great workout at the gym."

Walt's inner child begins a familiar chant. "Jonny got laid… Jonny got laid!"

Jonathan blushes, giving away the truth. "Christ, Walt, will you ever grow up?"

"Not if I can help it. You don't want me to anyway, and I'd never disappoint you."

Jonathan moves some files around on his desk to avoid encouraging Walt. "Whatever."

"So, what's going on?"

"Waiting to see if I get the materials I requested from Propentus and whether Julie's been able to schedule a meeting with their CIO."

"Not what I was referring to, but okay, that's good." Walt's childish voice returns. "Wanna hear what I did last night?"

Jonathan sighs and starts flipping through some unreturned call slips. "Do I have a choice?"

"Not really. I went to dinner last night and met the most wonderful woman."

Jonathan looks up with a smirk. "Is she a pro?"

"Touché! She's an account executive for a medical supply company or something like that. We had a couple of drinks, and she decided she wanted a nightcap. My place was closer."

"I don't need to hear every little detail." Jonathan has heard so many of these stories over the years he could write the ending himself.

Nothing pushes Walt off-topic. "We get to my place, and I park my car on the street in my usual spot. As I'm opening the door for her, I notice a guy sitting in a Chevy a few cars up. I didn't think anything about it until this morning."

A jolt of adrenaline is released as an image of the Toyota flashes through Jonathan's mind. "Wait… What?" Walt has his full attention now.

"I was too wrapped up in the nightcap at the time, but why would someone be sitting in a car at 1:00 a.m.?"

"Was he there this morning?"

"No. Both he and the car were gone. Maybe I'm paranoid." Walt takes a big slug of coffee as he uses the sleeve of his suit jacket to wipe the water ring from Jonathan's desk.

Jonathan tries to recall every detail of the Toyota. "Maybe, but there was a gray Camry last night I swore I'd seen a couple of times. First at the office, and then it pulled into the liquor store right behind me."

Walt sits up a little straighter. "Okay, you know I'm no fan of coincidences. What the hell's going on?"

"Probably nothing. Let's just be more aware of our surroundings over the next few days, okay? Now I have work to do. Don't you?"

Jonathan's mind is racing to come up with an answer to Walt's question. He doesn't know what to think. The bullshit with this new case, the guy at the bar, the Toyota, and now the guy sitting in front of Walt's place. He pushes the thoughts from his mind. He has a full calendar today.

48

Vinnie is livid. Joyce set the appointment for 8 a.m. sharp for one reason, and one reason only: to bust his balls. He shows up at 8:14 am to make a point, finding her sipping tea from that stupid bone china cup and saucer she reportedly inherited from her grandmother. He strolls into her office with his head held high.

"Good mornin'."

Joyce puts down her tea. "It's not. You're late, and I don't have time for fucking games. You better have something worthwhile this time."

Vinnie opens his little notebook. "Erickson is a single guy who's a creature of habit. Not much of a life outside of work. He spends time going back and forth between the jail, the courthouse, and the office. Then, he eats dinner at one of the same four or five spots. The hostesses and bartenders call him by name." Vinnie flips the page. "He likes expensive meals and wine. No permanent girlfriend. We've seen him bring a couple of different women home. They're not pros. Just someone he picked up in the bar."

Joyce shakes her head, exasperated. "So, we know he eats and fucks. What do you have that's actually useful?"

Vinnie's confidence evaporates as he shares the disastrous news. "Um… you should also know our guy was noticed."

"What the fuck are you talking about? You said these guys were professionals. Ex-military or something."

Vinnie has to redirect her anger. He has enough problems. "The guy waiting outside his house fell asleep. He woke up around 1 a.m. when headlights hit him in the face. He sat there, frozen like the proverbial deer." Vinnie scrambles to continue. "Erickson barely noticed. He was focused on the brunette getting out of the car. He prefers brunettes."

In a quiet, guttural voice, Joyce responds, "Do I look like I give a shit about hair color?" She releases an angry sigh. "And now?"

Vinnie quietly states the obvious. "We back off for a bit."

Joyce takes another sip of tea and closes her eyes. "What about Silverman?"

Vinnie hesitates again. "Not much on him either. He's the definition of a workaholic. He's in the office by 7:30 a.m. every day, some days earlier. He leaves his house, does an hour or so at a local gym—mostly cardio—and then goes to the office. He doesn't usually leave until 7:30-ish." Maybe humor will ease the tension. "Guess you could say he works half-days."

Big mistake.

Joyce yells through clenched teeth. "I don't need fucking jokes. I need information!"

Vinnie is almost as scared of her as he is of Jimmy. "He seems to be spending a lot of time with his parents. He and his girlfriend go to dinner there once a week. We've tailed him and his parents to a doctor's office. We believe one of his parents is seeing a neurologist." He looks at his notes. "A Dr. Mancini."

Joyce is indifferent at this point. "The girlfriend?"

"VP at Santander Bank. She works normal banking hours. She goes to the gym periodically, but not with the same discipline as Silverman. Usually after work. She goes out with girlfriends for drinks maybe once a week. No pattern there, either."

"You're wasting my money! This *team* of yours is useless! Tell me you've had better success digitally."

Vinnie's own stupidity is written all over his face. He was focused on the old-school tactics when he should've hired the hackers he used during his days on the force and still uses to help with a few Jimmy-related requests.

"This team has different strengths."

Joyce throws up her hands, narrowly missing her grandmother's teacup. "All but the fucking guy watching Erickson, right?"

"I'll engage the right people the moment I leave."

"Get the fuck out of my office, and don't come back until you have something useful."

Vinnie slinks away, the familiar words stinging like salt on an open wound. He knows the penalty for letting Jimmy down. He wonders what it'll be if he lets Joyce down.

49

A little more than twenty-three hours have expired when a notification pops up on Jonathan's laptop screen. Joyce has embedded an encrypted message from Tommy O'Hara in the email, including instructions outlining the method to gain direct access to everything Propentus has relative to Antsalemab. He decided last night that even a whiff of continued gamesmanship, and he's going to cut Propentus loose. He has more important things to worry about these days.

After getting an update on his appointment to meet Tommy, Jonathan asks Julie to clear his calendar for the remainder of the day. Jonathan anxiously opens the message with the click of his mouse. It's the moment of truth.

A restrained excitement buzzes around his office. Jonathan has spent the past few weeks searching for one very specific piece of data or information that would cause the defense to collapse, something he's dubbed the "Silverman Linchpin Approach": everything ties to a single point of failure, a strategy he's relied upon in the past. He isn't sure "The King of the Fender Bender" is that smart, but he knows better than to judge a book by its late-night commercials.

After a few failures, Jonathan finally figures out how to enter the portal to Propentus' records. His shoulders relax. This is exactly what he should've had from the outset. Complete access. While the files are in an understandable sequence, their contents are incredibly complex and full of technical jargon.

Jonathan begins by searching for the word "kidney," looking for any material that might be related to the primary injury Ms. Cosgrove and the rest of the class are attributing to Antsalemab. If he can challenge the connection between Antsalemab and kidney disease or create a question relative to typicality, he may be able to defeat the certification. That's where he found success in the *Ackerman* case.

The list that comes up is unbelievable. 286 documents are identified. Most have multiple pages. He starts where he always does… at the beginning.

● ● ●

The next time he looks up, it's 3 p.m. He has already drunk two large coffees and one energy drink, filled twenty pages of a legal pad with notes and questions, and he's only gotten through forty-seven documents. Jonathan stands and stretches. His eyes are strained from reading and deciphering the charts and graphs that are included.

He grabs another energy drink and heads back to his desk when he sees a note's been slipped under his door. His appointment with Tommy O'Hara is in two days. While not their agreement, this gives him time to meet with his own IT team to gain a basic understanding of cyber security and secure a list of questions they deem important.

Jonathan turns on Sirius XM's *The Highway* on the small Bluetooth speaker in the corner of his office, and "Bless the Broken Road" by Rascal Flatts comes on. He picks his head up and thinks about Emily for a moment. The lyrics capture his own journey. He smiles to himself. Could be a nice song to dance to… in the future. Back to work.

A couple of hours later, Jonathan opens the 147th document his search identified. It's a report that indicates five of the twelve initial test subjects developed calcium oxalate stones. The report goes on to outline the efforts taken to address this development. He makes a note to learn more about kidney stones. He rubs his eyes again, grabs a new legal pad, and is opening the next document when Julie buzzes him. "Ms. Kramer on line two."

Jonathan stretches, shakes out his cramped hand, and takes a pull off the energy drink. He puts his feet squarely on the floor and hits the speaker button. "Joyce."

"Hello, Jonathan. I trust you've received the secure link I sent, and by now, know you have an appointment with Tommy O'Hara." She's not glib or snotty.

"I did. Thank you. I've already started to review the documents. You told me there'd be a lot." He takes a quick pause. "Is this the part where you tell me to be careful what I wish for?"

An olive branch extended.

Joyce chuckles. "Not at all. I want you to have confidence that you have access to everything. I thought direct access would be easier than just a huge data dump. It's also safer from a data security perspective."

Olive branch accepted.

"Thank you. I have a legal pad full of questions already. I'd like to have a follow-up meeting with you, Harold, and Renee. I'm sure most of the questions are easily answered."

"Absolutely. I expected you to have questions after your review. There's a lot to understand. Can I ask where you started your review?"

Jonathan finds the question a bit disconcerting but shakes the feeling off quickly. "By searching the word 'kidney,' do you know it's mentioned in 286 documents?"

"I didn't."

"As Ms. Cosgrove's primary medical complaint, I thought it made sense to start there."

"Makes perfect sense. Is there anything else you need?"

"I think I have enough to keep me busy for a while. Thanks again."

"You're welcome. See you in a couple of days." Joyce hangs up.

Jonathan replaces the receiver, rethinking his view of Joyce. He had to play hardball, but she's finally given him everything. Perhaps this is the first step in her becoming the partner he expects all clients to be.

50

Vinnie almost hits three different pedestrians as he weaves his way across the city, racing to The Last Inning. After running his fingers through his hair, he steps out of his car and walks into the bar with his head held high. He nabs a seat at the bar and orders his usual. He doesn't ask to see Jimmy; he demands it. No fuckin' around today. The bartender brings him his drink and tells him to sit tight.

Twenty minutes later, the bartender yells over the music from the other end of the bar to get Vinnie's attention. Vinnie sees him nod toward Jimmy's office. It's showtime. He throws back his drink and drops a $20 bill on the bar before sliding off the barstool, strutting toward the office door, eager to deliver what Jimmy's looking for.

He knocks and waits. He knocks again. Nothing. He knocks a third time. Still nothing. What the fuck? He gets back to the bar and sees the bartender and another guy pointing at him, laughing their asses off.

Vinnie trudges to that end of the bar with a full head of steam. "Very fuckin' funny."

"We thought so." The bartender is enjoying every second of this. "Sit down, numb nuts. Here's one on the house. Jimmy'll be here later."

"Fuck you!" Vinnie snatches the free drink off the bar and heads back to his previous seat.

He orders a third drink and a cheeseburger. As he's wiping ketchup and mayonnaise off his face, he sees the bartender nod toward the front door. It's Jimmy. He decides against throwing back his drink. He needs to be on his game.

The bartender hands Jimmy a soda water with lime as he walks by Vinnie, shaking his head in disbelief. "Okay, asshole."

Vinnie drops his napkin on the bar and follows Jimmy into his office. Tonight, Jimmy points to a chair in front of the desk. This is a positive start. Vinnie sits like a trained dog responding to the command. "Hey, Jimmy. How ya' doin'?"

"I'm busy. Do ya finally have somethin' fuckin' useful?" Jimmy leans back with his fingers laced behind his head. The chair creaks as if it is going to snap and launch Jimmy across the small room.

"I wanna give you an update."

"This ain't a fuckin' board meetin'. Talk!"

"I've been lookin' into a buncha people. Some at the direction of General Counsel and some on my own." Jimmy likes initiative.

"This isn't new information." Jimmy sips his soda water.

"Yea, sure. Anyway, the attorneys first. So far, nothin'. I got someone workin' to hack their phones and laptops. The computer stuff might turn up somethin' we can use."

Vinnie doesn't take a breath. He's building up to the good stuff. Jimmy's going to be so fuckin' happy. "Second, I been pushin' on the Head of Research and lead researcher, and I found out a couple a things."

Vinnie waits for a response. Jimmy's cold, lifeless eyes stare back.

"The lead researcher's a woman. I got her to tell me what she's hearin' about the lawsuit. She stiff-armed me for a while, but I finally broke her, and I convinced her I'm the only one she can talk to."

"And?"

"Oh, yeah. Sorry. She told me the attorney's askin' a lot of questions about the FDA paperwork. He's also askin' questions about the computer system, how they save files and stuff."

"So fuckin' what?"

"It means now I know what the attorney's lookin' at, which is good. I also locked this chick down as a source goin' forward. I'm gonna pump that well for all its worth." An X-rated image floats through Vinnie's mind.

The chair groans in defiance of Jimmy's movements. "You got nothin'. The attorney's askin' questions. That's his fuckin' job! I ain't interested in questions. I'm interested in fuckin' answers."

"You're right, Jimmy. I'm workin' on that." Vinnie feels his excitement slide back toward hopelessness. Before he realizes what he's saying he blurts it out. "And I gotta tell you Jimmy, I ain't so sure the blonde will keep her mouth shut when it matters."

Fuckin' Jack Daniels. He can't screw this up now. "And I think the Head of Research owes people money. I overheard a conversation. I got him on the verge of spillin' it all. One more conversation and he's mine."

Jimmy sits forward. "Finally, somethin' interestin'."

"I've been workin' hard on this for you."

Jimmy lurches forward with the speed of a mongoose, snapping at Vinnie. "You're supposta be fuckin' workin' hard!"

Vinnie's in full-blown recovery mode. His desperation's showing. He doesn't care. He can't. "You want me to check with Richie on the money thing?"

"No. You got anythin' else?"

"Um… No, but I'll keep you posted, Jimmy. Like always."

"Then get the fuck out!"

"Thanks, Jimmy."

Vinnie wipes his hands on his pants as he stands. When he gets back into the bar, there's another guy sitting in his seat, and the burger and drink are gone. The bartender points and laughs at Vinnie for the third time tonight. Vinnie flips him off, which only makes him laugh harder.

All that's left is hammering Harold and Renee to get them to spill everything. Jimmy won't be pissed at him anymore, and then that fuckin' bartender will have to respect him.

51

MJ's sitting at home in her usual spot, doing her usual thing with her usual companion. She's the ultimate creature of habit. She's deep in thought when one of her burner phones rings, raising her hope for more answers. "Hello."

"Hey, MJ, it's Jennifer." Another fake name, but a woman this time.

"Hey, Jennifer, what's up?" She manages to control the excitement in her voice.

"I have something for you. Wondered if you had time tonight to grab it?"

"Sure. I can do that. Usual spot?" MJ crosses her fingers. She hasn't got time to figure out the timing for a new spot.

"Why don't I catch you at the dog park when you take Snoopy for his walk? Snoop's gotta poop, right?"

MJ laughs at the joke. "Perfect."

The line goes dead without an agreed-upon time. Another uneasy feeling blankets MJ as she realizes they know her routine. Maybe it's time to switch it up. Keep them guessing?

MJ sets her phone alarm for 5:30 p.m. She and Snoopy generally take a stroll around that time, so that's when she'll head to the dog park. She's anxious to hear what Jennifer has to add to the puzzle. For now, she continues to read through the articles she's found about Propentus and their IPO. While older articles confirm their intent, she finds only speculation as to timing, with many now referring to the recent class-action as a potentially insurmountable hurdle.

Next, MJ types *IPO launch timing* into her search bar and is surprised to see the various indicators and methods companies use to identify the best launch window. One indicator many use is the Volatility Index, or "the VIX." It's "the fear index," which measures the expectation of volatility within the S&P 500 over a thirty-day period. History reflects the number of IPOs offered when the VIX is higher than 20 is significantly lower. She has no idea how the 20 is actually calculated, nor does she care. A quick check shows the VIX has been fluctuating on either side of that threshold the past few months, leading her to conclude that Propentus was likely ready to go until the lawsuit was filed if they're using this benchmark as a guide.

The more she reads, the more her head hurts. MJ's always viewed attempting to time the market like trying to catch a falling knife. She lets her financial adviser figure that crap out.

After grabbing an energy drink and a couple of aspirin, she tackles the next mind-numbing topic: the FDA approval process. She learns the average timeline is in the neighborhood of three and a half years from application date to full approval. She notes Antsalemab was on the lower side of that timeline, taking about twenty-nine months.

This raised another flag until she discovered that a first-of-its-kind treatment that demonstrates an unmet need for a serious condition can be fast-tracked and designated for "Accelerated Approval." An accelerated approval presumes future trials will result in similar, if not identical, findings. It's enough to bring the new drug to market while trials continue and Propentus seeks full, traditional approval. Antsalemab, as a revolutionary treatment for early-onset dementia, a disease that impacts millions globally, received its approval under this exception.

MJ reaches over and scratches Snoopy behind the ears, contemplating the last few hours of her work. There are hundreds of millions, if not billions, at stake, and her math suggests Propentus desperately needs to refill its coffers.

If the FDA withdraws its accelerated approval or declines to grant full approval for Antsalemab for any reason, Propentus will be just another name that joins hundreds of others on the heap of failed companies. Initial investors, including Riccio, will lose everything. The pressure created by the untimely litigation must be immense.

She's shaken from her thoughts by a beeping alarm. It's time for a walk.

52

Jimmy's sitting in his office with Richie. Their seats struggle under the strain of weight, as both men fight to get comfortable. Jimmy directed Richie to look into Jonathan and Walt. To their surprise, his guys didn't find anything different than Vinnie.

"Jimmy, I'm tellin' ya, these guys got nothin' in their past that we can use to squeeze 'em."

Jimmy can't believe it; everyone has secrets. But he trusts Richie with his life, so he'll trust he's telling the truth on this. "Fine. Keep lookin' in the past, but what about now? What can we fuckin' squeeze 'em with today?"

"Silverman has a girlfriend. Pretty hot. She lives with him, so I am presumin' it's pretty serious. Maybe she's a weak point. The other guy fucks around. Maybe we could get one of the girls to cozy up to him, create some photo opportunities?"

Jimmy sits up. His chair sounds like a barge scraping along a pier. "Finally, someone usin' their fuckin' head. Find out what this girlfriend does. And have one of the girls take a swing at this fuckin' Erickson guy."

"Done."

Jimmy leans forward even farther. "That dickhead Napolitano says the fuckin' Head of Research owes someone. Find out who and how much. Might be worth buyin' that debt if it ain't ours already." The chair protests as Jimmy leans back yet again. "Dickhead also says there's a blonde at the company who might be a problem. Keep an eye on her. He says he's got it covered, but he's fuckin' worthless." Jimmy scratches his head. "Might need to cut our losses there."

Ritchie doesn't blink. "'Might' or 'Need'?"

"Let's keep it at 'might' for now, but my patience is wearin' fuckin' thin. Ain't nothin' gonna get in my way. Capeesh?"

Richie nods and heaves himself out of the chair. He doesn't have to wait for Jimmy to give him permission, nor does he have to say he'll keep him posted—that's a given.

Jimmy pours himself a drink from a bottle he keeps in his desk. It's not supposed to be this fuckin' hard. They said it was as easy as falling off the curb. It's guaranteed. Just a matter of time. He throws back the whiskey as the blue snake on his neck begins to calm.

Jimmy Rizzo gets played by no one. Pieces of those who were stupid enough to try have been found in the Mystic River.

53

MJ arrives at the dog park early. She hopes Snoopy takes extra time tonight to complete his business. At 6 p.m. sharp, a woman approaches MJ. Snoopy barely reacts. He's got other things on his mind.

Jennifer is a tall, bubbly redhead with bright green eyes that are in constant motion, like Michael's. MJ thinks she's in pretty good shape until Jennifer arrives. There's not an ounce of body fat on her lithe, athletic body. As she leans in for a hug, MJ wonders where the hell these people come from.

"Great to see you, MJ!"

MJ returns the hug. "How're things?"

Jennifer bends over and scratches Snoopy between the ears. "Hey Snoop! Busy, like always. You?"

MJ gets the hint. "Busy at the paper. Beyond that, not much."

Jennifer stands back up as her phone rings. She holds up a finger to MJ while she answers the call. The redhead continues to shake her head as the conversation continues. With her phone still to her ear, Jennifer turns back to MJ and mouths, *Gotta run. Sorry.*

MJ goes with it, whispering as if the person on the other end of the phone might hear her, "No problem. See you soon."

Jennifer turns and joins the others, casually walking away from the park and continuing her conversation. MJ isn't surprised that she moves with the same smoothness she saw in Michael. But her thoughts quickly shift from the strangers she's met to her current mindset; she's pissed. She was supposed to get something, but thanks to a goddamn phone call, she stands there empty-handed. If asking for help is what she hates the most, waiting is a close second.

Snoopy begins swinging his head back and forth like he's trying to shake off water. She crouches down to see what's bugging him. She sighs with relief as she removes a thin thumb drive from beneath his collar. "There you go, buddy. Let's finish up and go home."

MJ looks around as she stands back up. Jennifer melded into the surroundings, just like Michael. As if on cue, Snoopy does his business, and after the standard clean-up protocol, they head home.

Back at her apartment, MJ can't get the door opened and closed fast enough and catches Snoopy's leash in the door, leaving him on the outside. After apologizing, she throws her black "spy coat" across the room toward the closet as if it's going to magically open the door and put itself on a hanger. It doesn't, landing in the identical spot from which she retrieved it an hour before.

MJ assumes her customary position on the couch as Snoopy nestles beside her. Jazz on Spotify, a deep breath, and the plugging in of the thumb drive gets things started.

• • •

She stretches her neck, realizing she's been sitting in the exact same position for almost two and a half hours. This report starts with highlights of Michael Riccio's activities, particularly since he arrived in Cambridge.

Once he cashed out at Genomics, he began living like a candidate for *Lifestyles of the Rich and Famous.* He bought himself a convertible Bentley and a huge home, and credit card records show he refreshed his wardrobe with the best in fashion and jewelry.

Her research showed no permanent love interest, but "the team" uncovered a bit more. He enjoys the company of different women: some who caught his eye in the club and a couple with whom he's established regular appointments. The former is of the most interest.

After Michael started Propentus, he began his never-ending battle for capital. He wined and dined investors, regaling them with the amazing work Propentus was doing. Credit card records show him at a different high-end restaurant every night, ordering $500 bottles of wine and eating the finest steak and seafood money could buy—investors are accustomed to enjoying the high life. He'd give them whatever they wanted as long as they gave him their money.

MJ is reviewing a police report when Snoopy hops off the couch to ring the little bell.

"Now? Really?"

She bookmarks the spot and repeats the process she follows multiple times a day. After deciding to grab tacos on the way home, she becomes lost in her thoughts as they trek toward the dog park on autopilot.

When they arrive, Snoopy stops and barks at a man MJ hadn't noticed, snapping her out of her stupor. She looks at the man, who smiles, turns, and walks away. MJ thinks it's a little weird. Snoopy never barks. But, since the guy isn't bothering her, she moves on. She has important information to sort through.

After a quick call, they head to La Vida Loca to find the hostess waiting at the front door. Soft-shelled tacos, a churro, and, of course, a treat for Snoopy.

MJ and Snoopy hurry home, and after inhaling dinner and pouring a glass of wine, she and Snoopy resume their positions. MJ decides to go with Miles Davis' *Bitches Brew* as tonight's background music. It's one of her favorite albums, and not just because she loves the title.

MJ starts again with the police report, which is technically an "incident" report for Michael Riccio and someone named Matthew Smith. "The team" identified Matthew Smith as an investment banker at one of the firms involved in the Series B round. Both men were being obnoxious in a Boston night-club, harassing a couple of women who wanted nothing to do with them. The police were called. They were never charged, but Riccio and Smith were escorted to the door and ordered to never return.

Her heart beats faster as she learns the two women they harassed had records for solicitation and were reportedly connected to a couple of local mob guys. "The team" highlighted a name in the "known associates" section of their records: Anthony Spinelli.

MJ's laptop almost flies across the room as she jumps up.

"Holy shit, Snoop!" She begins walking in circles around the tiny living room as Snoopy refuses to answer her questions. "Did Spinelli know? If so, how'd he find out? Did he do anything about it? If so, what?"

Fifteen minutes later, she blurts out a mantra Snoopy has heard a million times before. "There are no coincidences!" She forces herself to sit back down, reenergized by this new piece of information.

More creative investigative techniques confirm what MJ long suspected: Michael Riccio burns through cash at an unbelievable pace. Had he not sunk every penny he had into Propentus, he would've been broke within twelve to fifteen months of leaving Genomics. He burned through millions living the life most people only dream about. His bank records show a salary draw from Propentus, which barely covers his $18,000 monthly mortgage payment. The investment bank where Matthew Smith works carries the multi-million-dollar mortgage on Riccio's Brookline home.

This information confirms his lavish lifestyle is a front. He charges all expenses, including meals and clothing, on corporate credit cards. The monthly balances are paid by Propentus. In short, Michael Riccio, as an individual, is broke.

Sure, there's a pending lawsuit, but MJ again asks herself why they aren't figuring out a way to launch the IPO. What a nice question to ask if she ever speaks with Michael Riccio. Perhaps it's the next curveball for Joyce Kramer? She shakes the thoughts from her mind, returning to Spinelli and Riccio. Her pacing around the apartment resumes, with a glass of wine in her hand this time. Walking always helps the puzzle pieces tumble.

This situation reminds her of the game, "Six Degrees of Kevin Bacon." Propentus and Excellence Investments. Excellence Investments and Picciano. Picciano and Spinelli and Spinelli's parents. Spinelli to a couple of women, sort of. A couple of women to Riccio, sort of.

She trusts the reporting from "the team" implicitly. If they say the only connection between Riccio and Anthony Spinelli is one that runs through a couple of prostitutes Riccio drunkenly harassed or through Anthony's parents' decision to invest in Propentus, that's all there is.

Could this be the first coincidence she's ever seen?

"The team" speculates on the probability of Spinelli being associated with the mob. The women are, so he may be, too? At least peripherally. Her mind shifts in a different direction. What would the mob do if they found out Spinelli was gay? The thought terrifies her as she again remembers she owes her friend a call.

MJ sits back down, and Snoopy snuggles back in. "Pharaoh's Dance," featuring John McLaughlin, Chick Corea, Wayne Shorter, and Bennie Maupin, starts playing. She leans her head back, closes her eyes, and allows the music to invade her soul. The puzzle pieces continue to bounce, confirming there are still pieces missing.

Suddenly, MJ jumps up—disturbing Snoopy again—and runs to her safe to retrieve a burner phone. Sitting back in front of her laptop, she pulls up a number from the thumb drive Jennifer provided and calls it. The clicks and noises she hears as the call connects make her uncomfortable. It's answered on the first ring, thirty seconds later.

"Yes?" It sounds like a manufactured voice like you get when you talk through one of the toy voice changers kids love to play with.

"I've been reviewing the material. I need the missing pieces."

"Anticipated."

MJ isn't surprised. They share a love for solving puzzles… Finding the unfindable.

"Spinelli, Riccio, Spinelli's parents, Excellence Investments, Picciano, Propentus. Coincidence?"

"There are no coincidences."

"Agreed." Another reason she loves them.

"The situation is being assessed further."

MJ also noted something missing from the thumb drive. "Thank you. The woman?"

"More to follow. There, but not there."

What the hell does that mean? She hates loose ends as much as they do. But before she can follow up, the conversation takes an unexpected turn.

"Beware, others are mining the same data. Safety first."

"Wait, what?"

Silence. MJ stares at the burner. What the hell does that mean? What others? What data? And what's this about safety first? She thinks back to the stranger in the dog park. Is she in danger? They've never left her hanging like that before.

But then again, they've never made a statement like that, either.

54

Jonathan asked Angela, the firm's best paralegal, to sort and prioritize documents, focusing on ties to kidney disease. To better understand what she was reading, Angela spent almost sixty hours researching anything and everything to do with chronic kidney disease. She identified different symptoms, causes, treatments, and contributing factors. After doing nothing but focusing on this for the past week and a half, she jokingly told Jonathan she could pass the nephrology boards.

Jonathan is genuinely impressed with Angela's efforts. He spent hours reviewing the grids and reading the documents Angela identified in this methodical way. Walt's photographic memory would come in handy during times like these.

He begins to see, or thinks he sees, a pattern when it comes to kidney-related complications. Every time a kidney-specific issue was included in a document, it was always followed by a separate document or reference outlining the easy resolution to the issue. Always.

As the attorney charged with defending Propentus and the treatment his father is currently receiving, he takes great solace in his inability to find a smoking gun. If he can't find one, he's convinced "The King of the Fender Bender" won't find one, either.

He asks himself a simple question: Is it possible there weren't any serious issues during the trials? Quite a few trial participants had one or more of the potential symptoms of chronic kidney disease. But there's no specific reference to chronic kidney disease itself. None.

Jonathan knows it's never as simple as it looks. Fatigue, for example, is a symptom of various diseases. Most of the participants reported incidents of fatigue. His father has reported fatigue, and his blood pressure is slightly elevated. Does it mean he has chronic kidney disease?

Jonathan puts those questions aside and stands up from his desk to stretch. He needs to finish preparing for his next interview.

Jonathan's IT team provided him with a series of questions focused on cybersecurity, network security, risk assessment approaches, data breaches, penetration testing protocols, network configuration, data wiping, and a host of other things Jonathan had no idea existed.

• • •

A few hours later, Jonathan arrives at Propentus and pulls into a visitor's parking spot near the front of the building. There are a couple of other cars in visitor slots, including a gray Toyota Camry. Seeing the car triggers the memory of a few nights ago. Again, probably a coincidence, but given Walt's recent experience, he makes a mental note of the car's license plate.

Vinnie is waiting for Jonathan at the security desk. "Nice to see you again, Mr. Silverman. Right this way, please."

Jonathan doesn't remember meeting or seeing this man before but chooses to keep that fact to himself. "Thank you."

Vinnie doesn't let the opportunity pass. "Boy, crazy about this lawsuit, huh? A lot of buzz here in the building, especially when word gets around you're comin' in to talk to someone."

This is a small organization, and this lawsuit is a big deal. Jonathan learned that equity grants were part of every hiring package. As such, everyone has a vested interest in seeing this lawsuit go away. Besides, it doesn't matter how big a company is, word travels. He thinks it was Mark Twain who said, "… *two people can keep a secret if one of them is dead,*" or something like that.

Jonathan smiles at Vinnie and chuckles to ease the tension. "Lawsuits make people nervous. And me, I'm just an attorney, and you know what Shakespeare said about attorneys."

Vinnie likely has no idea what the hell Shakespeare said about attorneys but laughs along with Jonathan just as Joyce comes around the corner, carrying a leather-bound portfolio imprinted with the Louis Vuitton logo.

She smiles and recites the quote. "'The first thing we do, let's kill all the lawyers.'"

"Exactly." Jonathan smiles. "Nice to see you again, Joyce."

With that, Joyce smugly waves Vinnie away. "I'll take it from here. Thank you, Vinnie."

Joyce leads Jonathan to the conference room and takes the same seat as last time. "Tommy should be here in a minute. How's your review coming along?"

Jonathan displays a disingenuous smile while opening his laptop. "Pretty well, actually, but today's questions are going to be centered on document creation, retention, and protection. I've asked my IT team for some questions. I hope to get what I need on this topic in one trip."

Tommy O'Hara walks in. He's a short redhead with a beer belly. His suit jacket is too small and an ugly paisley tie is loose at the collar.

"Good morning, Mr. O'Hara, I'm Jonathan Silverman."

"Good morning. Everyone calls me Tommy." He takes the seat across from Jonathan in what has become "the witness chair."

"Great, Tommy. Please call me Jonathan. I'm sure Joyce has told you that I represent Propentus in this lawsuit. It alleges Propentus purposely hid things from the FDA. I'm looking to understand the process for documents to be created, edited, retained, deleted, and protected. My goal is to paint a very clear and understandable picture for a jury, one that leaves them with a single conclusion: there's no way Propentus could have withheld information."

"Happy to help."

"I have to warn you. I have some questions that my IT team helped me put together. So, the terminology may be correct, but I'll need your help to understand it fully." Jonathan's humility seems to put Tommy at ease.

Tommy pulls at his shirt collar. "Fair enough. I'm sure there's some legal jargon that only you and Joyce know. It's the same thing. Fire away."

Jonathan walks Tommy through his background learning that Thomas 'Tommy' O'Hara graduated from BC High before moving onto Rensselaer Polytechnic Institute where he earned both a bachelor's degree and a master's degree in Information Technology. He's been the Chief Information Officer at Propentus for the past few years, including the years of the FDA submission and approval.

"Okay, now some hard questions. Does Propentus have a CISO and if so, who might that be?"

"We don't technically have a Chief Information Security Officer. We've discussed outsourcing for that role, which smaller companies do. However, we haven't made a final decision. Until then, it falls on my plate."

"Okay, please walk me through Propentus' security assessment approach and current data security protocols."

Tommy spends the next fifteen minutes covering a lot of technical ground. Jonathan scribbles furiously, understanding a tiny subset of what he's hearing.

"Tommy, are there any written manuals, protocols, or other documents that speak to data security in any way?"

Joyce visibly cringes as Tommy answers the question. "Sure. We have some for training purposes. Others we're required to retain and provide to the FDA. There's information that's supplied to the Board, and I know Joyce has incorporated data-related language into the intellectual property section of the non-disclosure agreement."

Joyce answers before Jonathan asks: "Standard boilerplate that every employee and board member has to execute. I'll have Beverly send a copy."

"Thanks. I'd also like copies of the training materials and other documents Tommy referred to."

"Sure thing."

Jonathan notices a hint of distress in Joyce's voice and turns to the next section. "Tommy, please tell me about document and file creation, editing, deleting, and storage protocols."

Tommy launches into another fifteen-minute recitation, giving a comprehensive overview of these areas. Jonathan continues to be impressed with the ease he displays in sharing highly technical information. A bit too much technical jargon, but he's personable and relatable. A jury will love him.

When Tommy stops to take a breath, Jonathan asks, "Please forgive me, but I'm trying to make it simple for myself. Anyone can create a document that becomes part of a research file, correct?"

"Not exactly. Only designated team members have the authority to create documents and folders associated with a specific project. This helps prevent someone from inadvertently dropping a document into the wrong research folder. However, some labs share researchers, meaning some people have authority tied to multiple projects. However, generally, each project team is small, usually no more than five to seven researchers and lab assistants plus the lead researcher."

"Okay, got it. How about editing an existing document? Does the authority work the same way?"

"Basically, but with one major difference. The only people who can edit a document are the original author or someone in their leadership chain," Tommy explains.

"Are the edits tracked?"

"Yes, there's a date and time stamp created when the document's created and every time it's edited. The stamp also identifies who made the change."

"It's based upon user identification and access?"

"Exactly."

Jonathan nods thoughtfully. "Is it possible for me to change the content of a document if I have your user ID and password?"

"Technically, yes. But we take that seriously. We've fired people for sharing credentials. Most employees don't know there's a flag created any time someone enters, changes, or deletes a document from a laptop that isn't assigned to them. So, to avoid the flag, you'd need user ID, password, and access to the person's laptop."

"Okay, so it's difficult but not impossible. How about deleting documents?"

Tommy seems happy to answer Jonathan's questions, a nice change from the last set of interviews. "Authorities are basically the same. However, there's a double-approval requirement to remove documents. This prevents someone who has creation or editing authority from independently removing a document. It could be the original author and their supervisor or any two supervisors in the author's leadership chain. The date, time, and the identity of both approvers are captured."

Jonathan keeps going down the list. "Okay, onto retention."

Tommy recites the expectation from memory. "The FDA requires any research that involves drugs being tested in humans be retained for a period of two years following the date a marketing application for a specific use of the drug's approved. Even if you decide not to file an application or the application is denied, you have to keep all documents for two years after the research is formally discontinued and the FDA is notified. Most companies seek approval from the FDA before they destroy any documentation to be safe. We leverage FDA-approved server farms and redundancies, allowing us to retain documents for decades in order to meet those requirements."

Jonathan tests Tommy's agility. "Is it possible to create a system that can't be hacked?"

"It's impossible to create a 100% foolproof, impenetrable system. If someone wants to get in, with enough time, effort, and skill, it can be done. That said, all of our systems and protocols align with or exceed the FDA's data management requirements."

Jonathan's IT team said the same thing. *Never say never.* "Wow, this sounds pretty thorough."

"Thanks. Data integrity and security are critical, given the intellectual property and patent implications. There's a lot at stake."

Joyce shifts in her seat. "We've been at it for a couple of hours. I could use a break."

Jonathan puts his pen down. "I only have a couple more questions. But I'm happy to take a break."

Before Tommy can answer, Joyce stands up. "Sorry, guys. I'll be back ASAP."

"No problem. I'll use the time to find out if Tommy's a Red Sox fan," Jonathan says with a relaxed smile while flipping to a clean page in his notebook.

As Joyce hustles out of the room, Jonathan notices the angst on her face. He's not sure whether it's driven by her fear of leaving him alone with Tommy or the need to find a restroom.

Tommy laughs, seemingly unaware of the undercurrents in the room. "Yeah, I'm a Sox fan. It's another tough year."

Jonathan puts that aside and refocuses on connecting with Tommy. "My dad's a huge fan. Watches every pitch… Between some brief napping in his recliner."

They both laugh.

Jonathan's not going to waste this rare instance where Joyce isn't around to control things. Hoping she didn't instruct Tommy not to answer anything if she wasn't in the room, he moves quickly. "Tommy, is it possible for two senior people up to Michael Riccio to edit or delete a document without the original author knowing?"

Tommy seems a little taken aback by the sudden shift back to questioning but answers anyway. "Yes, presuming the original author doesn't look at the document again."

"How are the individual human trial results tracked?"

"Very much the same way I described. Those folders have tight access controls."

Jonathan feels the pressure to ask more but suspects Joyce is almost back to the conference room. "But everything's date, time, and individual stamped as well?"

"Yes."

Joyce is winded by the speed of her return. She's smoothing her skirt and sitting back down, working to catch her breath. "So, a Sox fan, Tommy?"

"Since birth. True fans are with a team through thick and thin. I just wish there wasn't so much thin."

"You and everyone else." Joyce looks at Jonathan. "You said you have more questions?"

"I do. Tommy, is there any way to completely purge a document from the system? By completely, I mean, is there a method to remove a document in a way that leaves no digital trail once it's gone?"

"There is, but it is incredibly complex and would require a great deal of skill given the FDA requirements. But theoretically, it can be done."

"Last question." Jonathan suspects this will throw Joyce off-kilter but asks anyway. "Is there a way for you to generate a list of all documents that are removed from a research file and recreate a corresponding copy? I'm presuming it would be a small list, right?"

Joyce almost spits her water across the table. Tommy looks at Joyce, then quickly back toward Jonathan. "Yes, it should be small."

"But you could do it?" Jonathan watches Joyce out of the corner of his eye.

"It would take some time, but yes."

Jonathan got more than he expected. "Great. I think that's all I have for now. Do you have any questions for me, Tommy?"

"No, I'm good." He stands and shakes Jonathan's hand. Jonathan notices that Tommy doesn't look in Joyce's direction before exiting the room.

Jonathan begins packing up. "Thanks for your time today, Joyce."

"I have to run to another appointment. One of the admins will walk you out."

"Thanks again." On cue, Beverly arrives and after Jonathan gathers all of his belongings, walks him down to the security desk where he signs out and returns his temporary badge.

As he gets into his car, Jonathan loosens his tie. For the first time since taking the case, someone was finally open and honest with him. Tommy gave him truthful, understandable answers not filtered or dictated by Joyce.

55

Jimmy looks at the full bar as he walks out of his office. A full bar means a full cash register. A full register makes Jimmy happy. He walks over to Richie, leans over the bar, and quietly says, "Send for the fuckin' idiot."

Richie pulls his cell phone from the back pocket of his jeans and walks toward the kitchen, where it's marginally quieter.

Jimmy grabs a paper and finds an article about the lawsuit against Propentus. More specifically, he's reading the financial section and the article pondering the company's stalled IPO. There's a great deal of speculation around the impact of the lawsuit.

His personal attorney was of little comfort. He walked Jimmy through the legal process, explaining that it was all but impossible to clean up the mess and pave the way for his ascension to the top of the mob history books.

Richie returns and nudges Jimmy's elbow, communicating everything he needs to with his eyes, then backs away, knowing Jimmy hates to wait.

Vinnie made a beeline for the bar, flying through the door exactly twenty-seven minutes after being summoned. Vinnie starts to walk toward Jimmy but stops. He grabs a stool and orders the usual, pulling a $20 bill from his money clip. He sips the drink, nerves rattling his hand.

Jimmy walks toward his office, never saying a word as he passes. Vinnie throws back the rest of the drink and heads to the office with a confidence he doesn't feel. He timidly knocks on the door.

"Come."

Vinnie walks in and stands there—no offer to sit this time. "Hey, Jimmy. Richie said you're lookin' for me."

An unhappy Jimmy leans back in the chair. The creaking's getting worse. "What've you got for me, shithead?"

The shakiness in Vinnie's voice tells Jimmy all he needs to know. "I was gonna press the researcher I told you about, but she called out today. I was headed to her place when I got the call from Richie. I also met the attorney today. When I tried to get something out of him, he clammed up, and before I could push harder, that bitch Kramer showed up."

"So… Nothin'. Is that what you're fuckin' tellin' me?"

The shakiness is followed by the whine of a child. "I know the researcher knows more, Jimmy. I just gotta get her alone. I can get more outta her."

"What about the other guy?"

"I went by his office a bunch of times, but he was always in the lab."

Jimmy's dead eyes never blink. "What I'm hearin' is you only try to get information for me between 9 a.m. and 5 p.m.? No fuckin' OT for you, huh?"

"It ain't like that, Jimmy."

Jimmy loves to make people squirm. "Fuckin' sounds like it. Wish I worked fuckin' banker's hours."

Vinnie's face brightens at the mention of the word 'banker.' "Jimmy... I been makin' progress on the attorney, and his girlfriend. She's a banker. They live together but ain't married or engaged. Maybe we can get to the attorney by gettin' to her?"

Jimmy explodes forward like a bullet from a gun, spittle, and rage flying across the desk. "You think I don't already know that? You're late to the fuckin' party... As usual."

Jimmy watches the realization of what that means plaster itself across Vinnie's face.

Vinnie takes another shot. "Jimmy... The attorney's parents are still alive, too. They live in Canton. More ways to pressure him to get in line."

Jimmy jumps out of his chair with unexpected dexterity for someone of his size. A meaty finger stabs Vinnie in the chest, forcing him to step back in order to avoid falling over. "Again... I already fuckin' know this. What the fuck I need you for?"

Vinnie's back hits the door. There's no escape. The sweat is now bleeding through his security uniform. "Jimmy, I know I can get more from the lady researcher. Like I said, I was headed to her house when I got the call. I'll head over there now."

"This is your last fuckin' chance. Others are gettin' me stuff you should be gettin' me. And they're gettin' it to me quicker. Last fuckin' chance. Capeesh?"

"Capeesh, Jimmy."

Jimmy disrespects Vinnie by turning his back to him. "Get out."

56

onathan smiles as he sees the photo that identifies the caller pop up on his ringing phone. He's more than happy to take a break from reading complex FDA materials.

"Just wanted to say good morning, babe."

"Mornin'. Sorry if I woke you when I left this morning. A lot on my mind with this case."

"You've been working so hard. Maybe you need a vacation?"

"I'd love to take you back to St. Thomas or the Caribbean island of your choice. Hell, I'd take you anywhere. I just can't. This case's taking up every waking second."

"Maybe I can find a way to convince you?"

The seductive tone in her voice triggers a mental image of Emily wearing the lingerie he bought her this past Valentine's Day. Red looks great on her... And even better off. "I'm happy to let you try as many times as you like."

They both laugh.

"Love you. Try to get home at a decent hour tonight, okay?"

He notes the playfulness in her voice. "Love you, too."

Jonathan hangs up and closes his eyes, spending a few more seconds with the image of Emily in the lingerie. He gets up, stretches, grabs a cup of coffee, and picks up where he left off.

Angela's done an amazing job sorting through the materials and cataloging them in a way that makes sense to an attorney. He opens an email from her with the subject line "Peculiar." She relays identifying small gaps in the records. After going through everything, she believes something's missing but doesn't know what. She closes the note by suggesting Jonathan ask Propentus about it.

Jonathan sits back, puts his hands behind his head, and props his feet on his desk. He'd felt there were some gaps in the 250+ "kidney" documents he reviewed but couldn't confirm his feelings. Without mentioning anything to her, Angela also identified something awry in the larger data set.

Tommy O'Hara said he could generate a report that identifies the deleted documents, as well as recreate them. It's time to ask him to do that. Jonathan puts his feet down and heads out the door to find Julie. "Can you please get Joyce Kramer on the phone?"

Julie looks down at Jonathan's shoeless feet and smiles. "Sure, I'll try right now. New dress code?"

"Very funny. Thank you."

Jonathan's grin morphs into a grimace. The question now... How to ask Joyce for this information? He needs to find a reason she can't argue with. He's mulling over various options when his phone buzzes. "Ms. Kramer on line four."

"Hi, Joyce. How are you today?"

"I'm well. What can I do for you, Jonathan?"

"Just a couple of quick things. First, I forgot to mention that Schneider called and poked around the settlement issue. I pushed back, and he played smartass by reminding me of my ethical obligation to speak to my client about these matters before I told him to screw off."

"Asshole."

"Yes, but I was a bigger asshole. I told him no more extensions on discovery. That my client was unwilling to delay this matter further. He didn't like that, made some comment about being a solo and he'd need to secure more resources. Without saying so, he's threatening to turn it over to one of the bigger plaintiff's firms."

"Okay. First, no settlement. Second, what else do we need to defeat the class certification?"

"I have some of Melissa Cosgrove's medical records, but I believe they're incomplete. We're still waiting on interrogatory responses, and I haven't seen the medical records of any of the other plaintiffs. If we're going to challenge typicality, I need those records, too."

"Okay, that's the priority. Press him hard for that information. No more delays. File motions to compel if you have to."

Jonathan's pleased with Joyce's agreement to turn up the heat. He loves applying pressure. Pressure forces errors. "Got it. One more thing." Jonathan closes his eyes and lets it rip. "The records I'm reviewing feel like they're missing something. It's hard to explain, but I think it'd be a good idea to ask Tommy to generate a report that identifies documents that were deleted and recreate them. When we met, he said it'd be some work, but he could do it."

"I don't believe anything's missing, but I'll follow up with Tommy to pull together what we can. Anything else?"

"Still more to get through, but nothing at the moment."

"Great… Let me get with Tommy. Thanks, Jonathan."

"Thanks, Joyce."

Jonathan sits behind the desk, flabbergasted. Joyce doesn't make anything easy. Why no resistance on this?

57

Vinnie flies out of Jimmy's office, knocking into people as he sprints toward the parking lot. He hasn't a second to spare. He's breathing like an asthmatic, fear gripping his lungs like a vice. Starting his car, he wipes the sweat from his face with his sleeve as he begins to contemplate his next steps.

An evening dominated by fear and Jack Daniels finds Vinnie deciding his best approach is to stalk his prey from the building's security desk. With that decision came another—to finish the bottle.

As he does, sadness surfaces with a realization that no one will miss him. Vinnie has no one who'll look for him if he disappears, no one to cry over his casket. His life's purpose is, and has been, all about what he can do for Jimmy and nothing more.

He arrives at his post extra early and determined. They're not getting in or out without passing him today. He's going to corner the two people who can save his life and squeeze every last drop of information from them if it's the last thing he does. And he's convinced himself that if he doesn't, it will be.

Renee's the first to step into his trap. She badges in and walks through the security stanchions.

"Good morning, Renee."

Renee refuses to glance in his direction. "Good morning, Vinnie."

"Got a few minutes?" Vinnie trips over an untied shoelace as he's working his way from behind the desk. If he hadn't caught the side of the desk with his right hand, he'd have ended up sprawled across the freshly shined marble floor.

The unexpected disturbance draws Renee's reflexive look. "Um… Actually, no. I have a department meeting in a few minutes."

"It'll only take a second."

Vinnie hasn't slept or showered, and he knows it shows. As he straightens his wrinkled tie, he glares at Renee, the implication clear.

"Fine, you can have two minutes."

Vinnie struggles to keep up as they finish the trip to Renee's office. She unlocks the door and turns on the light. As they both step across the threshold, Renee immediately puts her laptop in the docking station and sits behind her desk, displaying an attitude of strength Vinnie's never experienced from her. "Your two minutes started thirty seconds ago."

He stands with his hands on the front of her desk, leaning toward her. "I need to talk to you about the lawsuit."

She rolls her chair back the few available inches, using the desk as an unsuccessful barrier between her and the stench of stale sweat and alcohol. "I told you; I can't speak about that."

He's done with pretext. Time isn't his friend. "I need to know what questions the attorney was asking and what your *exact* answers were."

"What do you mean you *need* to know?"

He's a man possessed. His bloodshot eyes unwavering. "Exactly what I said."

Renee holds strong. "I told you. Joyce and the attorney both said not to talk with anyone."

Vinnie snarls through coffee-stained teeth. "I don't fuckin' care. You opened the door, and now I'm walkin' through it."

Vinnie's on the verge of slapping Renee. He doesn't like hitting women, although he's done it a few times in the past... for Jimmy.

Renee sits up straighter. "I shouldn't have spoken with you. I was mad at Joyce. I told you to forget I said anything."

Strike one, Vinnie counts to himself, now understanding what Jimmy feels like when he doesn't have any information. "I don't fuckin' care." A drop of spittle hits the top of Renee's desk.

Her arms start shaking, and both legs begin bouncing uncontrollably. Blotches begin to appear on her neck as tears form in the corners of her eyes. "I have to go to my meeting now." Renee rises, looking like a newborn giraffe trying to stand for the first time.

Vinnie is an angry Rottweiler, ready to tear her apart. He leans farther across her desk. "Sit the fuck down, Renee. We're not done talkin'. Last chance." He has no idea what he'll do if she challenges him.

Renee falls back into her chair, defeated. "Nothing really, I guess. He asked about my education. Then he asked about the research, like who signed the FDA docs, how the data was protected, and who had access to it. Like I told you before."

Not helpful... Strike two. "And?" Vinnie doesn't realize he's clenched his fists.

"I told him access was limited. The system saved everything. Just like I practiced with Joyce. That's it. Oh... And that Tommy's the head of IT."

"That's it?"

Tears are sliding down her cheeks. "Yes."

Vinnie's all but convinced she's about to leap over him to get to the safety of the hallway, but he can't afford to let up. "I don't believe you. There must be somethin' more."

Renee is sobbing at this point. "Really... There's nothing," she sputters between sobs. "He asked where the data was saved and stuff like that. That's it, I swear."

"And what'd you tell him?" Vinnie growls.

"That IT controls it."

Vinnie watches her wipe her runny nose, realizing she knows nothing of value. "You better not be fuckin' lyin'. I'm gonna be checkin'. There'll be fuckin' problems if you lied. And you won't tell anyone about our chats, understood?"

"No... No... Absolutely not. I swear." Renee is still visibly shaking.

Vinnie spins and storms out of her office, angrier than before he arrived. He hears Renee jump from behind her desk and slam and lock the door the moment he clears the casing.

Within seconds of exiting Renee's office, Vinnie's anger transforms into panic. Then, the panic becomes despair. He can't believe his survival rests solely upon the obnoxious asshole in the office next door.

58

arold spins out of the way as a rabid Vinnie flies out of Renee's office. "What the fuck, Vinnie? Watch where you're fuckin' going!"

Vinnie backs Harold toward the wall, getting in his face. "Fuck you, Harold!"

Harold's back hits the wall as he's putting his hands up, palms out, to shield himself. "Take it easy, Vinnie."

Vinnie knows he's spiraling. "We're going to talk."

"I can't. I have a department meeting." Harold moves to his right to try to sidestep Vinnie.

Vinnie quickly steps to his left, blocking Harold, and smirks. "How much you owe?"

Harold's face loses all color as he recoils from Vinnie. His hands start to tremble as he meekly attempts to play it off. "What are you talking about?"

"Your office. NOW."

They walk the twenty feet in silence. Vinnie shoves Harold toward the desk, slams the door shut, and sits down. "Listen, asshole, I don't wanna talk about your debt. But I ain't gonna stay quiet about what I know if you ain't straight with me."

Harold slumps into his chair. His usual bravado is gone. "What do you want?"

A moment of pride hits Vinnie. He's turned Harold into a whimpering kid who's been caught telling a lie. "Tell me everythin' you and the attorney talked about."

Harold is openly surprised by the topic. "He asked about my education. He reviewed the questions he sent to Joyce, and then he asked a couple more he hadn't sent."

Vinnie sneers. Renee didn't mention Joyce having the questions. *Strike fuckin' three, bitch!* "You got a copy of the questions?"

"No, Joyce wouldn't let us have them. She reviewed them with us a bunch of times before the meeting and told us what the answers should be."

A copy of those would be a great gift to Jimmy. "Tell me more about the questions. And your *exact* fuckin' answers, or I might have to let your secret slip."

Harold swallows hard. "He asked me questions about some of the documents. He said there were some inconsistencies and asked me about that."

"You got those documents?"

"No, he put them back in his briefcase."

"You ain't helpin' yourself here, Harold!"

"That's it, I swear."

Vinnie stands up, towering over a seated Harold. "Don't fuck with me, Harold. I ain't in the mood."

Harold repeats himself. "He asked about documents, the differences between their content, and some of my answers. He mentioned something about gaps in dates."

"Gaps? What gaps?" Vinnie keeps jumping around. His lack of sleep is hurting his focus.

"He said it looked like there were some gaps in dates or something."

"What'd you say?"

"I told him that as far as I knew, he had everything."

"And?"

"And nothin'. He wrote down my answers and then asked me a few more questions that weren't previously sent to Joyce."

"Like what?"

"It was stuff I couldn't remember. I told him that. He told me that was a good answer. He told me I did a good job. That's it." Harold is sweating like he's just passed a kidney stone the size of Texas.

Vinnie's pretty sure Harold has been straight with him, but… "Last fuckin' chance, asshole."

"There's nothing. I swear."

Vinnie stands and looks at Harold through bloodshot, desperate eyes. "Listen, you fuckin' pissant, I know exactly what's goin' on. If you ain't told me the truth, or you say anythin' about our little meeting, I'm gonna take a fuckin' wreckin' ball to what's left of your shitty little life."

Vinnie storms out of the office, fear gripping his chest. Now what?

59

Joyce is in her office, frustrated with what she knows needs to happen.

Beverly shared with her that she saw Vinnie hounding Renee this morning, chasing her down the hall, and this wasn't the first time she'd witnessed such behavior. Joyce kicks off her heels and starts pacing, forced to add another ball to those she's already juggling.

Vinnie is employed at Propentus for only one reason: "He" demanded it. Joyce requires Vinnie's services from time to time, and although she despises everything about him, he generally delivers something useful. He has connections locally and a network of retired cops all over the state. She doesn't hate that. What she hates is that Vinnie is her access point into a world that frequently proves beneficial.

Michael's obsession with launching the IPO grows daily, as does "his." She's running out of time to make that a reality.

Renee and Harold are ticking time bombs she's convinced are going to blow at the worst possible moment. She's unsure how to defuse them, and Vinnie's making things more unstable by running around more crazed than normal, harassing the shit out of everyone.

And then there's Silverman... What the hell's she going to do with him? He's smart, relentless, and she must admit... uncontrollable. His questions are too on point for them to be coincidental. If the circumstances were different, she'd love her choice of attorney. But they aren't. He's doing his job with the utmost skill and diligence, but he's becoming suspect, which makes him a problem.

And, while she hasn't heard from her recently, Joyce has some investigative reporter digging into everything.

Joyce closes her eyes in an effort to identify one thing that's gone right since the lawsuit was filed. She can't. She decides to take a walk and get a cup of tea. It'll get her some fresh air and give her the ability to make a call, should she choose to make it.

"I'll be back in thirty minutes. I have my cell," she says to her assistant as she exits her office with her handbag dangling from the crook of her left arm.

Outside, it feels like a different world. The sun feels good. Joyce dons her Prada sunglasses and starts walking toward Starbucks. The warmth of the sun is quickly muted by the problems at hand as she reevaluates the options from every angle. None of them are good, but she must regain control. If she makes the call, what will she say? Will she be blamed, making her a point of vulnerability? She can't have that.

As she walks around the block with her tea, Joyce concludes the best defense is a good offense. She pulls a burner from her handbag and dials the number. As she waits for the call to connect, she clears her throat and takes a sip of tea. She should have gotten lemon. Her voice may need it.

"What."

"We have a security problem." After she says it, she realizes there are multiple possible meanings to that statement. He likes clear and direct.

"Meaning?"

"Our security team's creating problems. Those problems are creating broader security concerns."

"The entire team?"

"Yes."

"It'll be taken care of. Broader concerns?"

She almost choked on her tea. She's never had this type of conversation before. It's petrifying yet exhilarating to wield this much power. "Those should resolve themselves."

"Anything else?"

"No."

Click.

It was that simple. Scary simple. Despite being an English major as an undergrad and three years of law school, she's never realized the power of words until this very moment. She now appreciates the phrase, *less is more.* He said less than fifteen words, yet it's crystal clear what every word meant.

Joyce throws the remainder of her tea into the trash and heads back to the building. She slides her badge across the reader and passes through the stanchions. She smiles at Vinnie, who's sitting behind the security desk, but she doesn't say a word.

As she gets back to her office, she thinks maybe she should have.

60

MJ's mind is filled with questions about Spinelli, Riccio, and the missing woman. What did they mean by *there but not there?* Snoopy stops short, causing MJ to drop her breakfast sandwich as she avoids tripping over him.

"What?"

MJ looks around, watching people walking up and down the street. It's morning, but it isn't the full-fledged hustle and bustle that 8:30 a.m. brings. Nothing stands out, but Snoopy's actions bring the ominous warning from "the team" to the forefront.

Her stomach growls as she bends down and picks up the sandwich, seriously considering the "five-second rule." She's starving this morning, but no. Eating off her floor is one thing; eating off a city street is something else altogether. She drops the sandwich into a trash can, laughing.

MJ doesn't notice the guy walking across the street, half a block behind her, but Snoopy is aware of him. He periodically looks in the stranger's direction, but with foot traffic picking up, his focus quickly returns to the original task—reaching the dog park. Occasionally, MJ tries to follow Snoopy's distracted gaze, but everyone around here looks normal: a commuter with a cup of coffee in one hand, their phone in the other, and earbuds in their ears to avoid random conversations with other strangers.

• • •

Since the majority of her breakfast ended up in the trash, MJ grabs another sandwich on their way home. She gives Snoopy a warning about getting between a hungry woman and her food and holds onto this sandwich a little tighter. After closing the door to her apartment, she engages the four deadbolts. *Safety first.*

As she's taking off her clothes to get into the shower, one of the new burners she pulled from the safe last night starts chirping. She hasn't used this one yet. It must be a wrong number, so she lets it ring. Two seconds after it stops, a different phone in the drawer starts ringing. She throws a towel around her body and heads for the bureau. She answers using her toughest voice. "What?"

"Hi, it's Ralph from the dry cleaners."

Of course, another fake name. Her mind vaguely wonders if they ever change it up and use their real names just because everyone expects the name to be fake. With a shake of her head, MJ snaps back to the current conversation. "Oh, sorry. Hello, Ralph. What's up?"

"Your dry cleaning is ready. We're having trouble getting the red wine out of your blouse, but the rest of the stuff can be picked up today."

"Oh, okay. I'll grab it after work."

"Okay. See you later." Per usual, the call ends abruptly.

Immediately, MJ's thoughts start to swirl. How'd they get the numbers of two newly opened burner phones? She shudders at the possibilities. The thoughts continue as she returns to the bathroom: Which dry cleaner? She uses one near her apartment and another that's close to her office. Since she took the call from home, she'll head there first. She steps into the shower with Snoopy's abnormal behavior triggering "the team's" recent warning, which now dominates her thoughts. Is someone watching her? If so, who? And why? She's nobody.

As she massages the shampoo into her hair, her thoughts shift to "the woman." *There, but not there.* Ralph better have some answers to all these questions.

She steps out of the shower as her excitement becomes torment. It's only 10 a.m.

61

Jonathan is reflecting on Angela's email and his call with Joyce when Walt strolls into his office. "How's our favorite client? Any more cooperative?"

"I'm not sure. They gave me direct access to their research and the FDA application file. Angela has been working day and night, helping me make sense of it all. But she and I both feel like there's still something missing. It's hard to describe. Just a feeling."

Walt plops into the only chair without a file resting on it. "I trust your gut. You should, too. You press the GC?"

"I've poked the bear. Their CIO said he can generate a report that identifies every document deleted from a file by date and by whom. Apparently, there's a two-tier deletion authority process. Seems hard to get around but not impossible. I've asked for that report."

Walt's grin spreads as he leans forward. "Perfect!"

"Yeah, but Joyce agreed to the request without hesitation, which is out of character. She's been fighting me on everything from day one. Why lay down on this? I'm having Julie set up another round of meetings with the Head of Research, the lead researcher, and the CIO. There's something funky going on. I just don't know what it is or what it may mean for the case."

Walt gets up to leave. "Keep at it, Inspector Gadget. And remember, always trust your gut."

Jonathan's phone buzzes. "Ms. Kramer on line two, Jonathan. And she doesn't sound happy."

Walt bolts for the door. "Good luck with that, my friend!"

"Hello, Joyce. What can I do for you?" Jonathan rolls his eyes. He knows what's coming.

Joyce's singularly focused. "For starters, you can do *exactly* as your client directs. All information, coming or going, will come through me. You violated that expectation by asking Julie to set up meetings with Renee, Harold, and Tommy."

Jonathan is sick of the bullshit but needs to keep his emotions in check if he's going to figure out what's going on. "I like efficiency. There's no value in me calling you to request something, just to have you direct me to have Julie call to make the same request. I knew you'd find out, as Beverly works with your calendar to ensure your availability to attend any meeting. Multiple steps are removed from the process, and at least half an hour is eliminated from your bill. A win for everyone."

Joyce isn't giving an inch. "I'm not worried about the god-damn bill! What I care about is the attorney I hired following the rules I've put in place. Yours is not to wonder why."

"Julie was clear you were to be in attendance for all meetings. At no time have I attempted to exclude you." Okay, except for those few questions he asked Tommy while she was indisposed.

Joyce brings the volume down a few decibels. "This will not happen again. Are we clear?"

"Crystal." For the hundredth time since he took this case, he concludes the money isn't worth it. Her need for total control is unmatched, but he'll play her infuriating games. He has to. "I'd like to meet with everyone again as soon as possible."

Joyce's tone is more civilized. "Beverly told me."

Though he knows he should, Jonathan refuses to leave the "I'm an asshole" hat in the closet. "While I have you, has Tommy been able to pull together the deletion report I requested?"

He can hear Joyce clench her teeth. "Not yet. I've asked that he deliver it to me for review prior to it being sent."

Jonathan teases his tweak out further. "Okay. I'd love to have it before the upcoming meetings… If possible."

Joyce seeks a different ending. "Jonathan, make no mistake. I take my responsibilities as General Counsel seriously. I will not let anything or anyone hurt Propentus."

Jonathan bites his tongue and simply responds, "Understood," and ends the call.

Every ounce of his being is screaming to get out. Walt's advice rings in his mind: Trust your gut. Jonathan lets out a long sigh. He has decided he'll tell Joyce to shove the $250K up her ass if she ever speaks to him like that again.

62

MJ arrives at the cleaners at 4:45 p.m. They didn't set a specific time, and she can't wait a second longer. A small bell at the top of the door jingles as she walks in, reminding her of Snoopy. The strong smell of dry-cleaning fluid and starch hangs in the air, and the hissing of the dry-cleaning machines in the rear of the shop is louder than she remembered.

A kid in his late teens, wearing his Celtics cap backward and with full tattoo sleeves on each arm, steps to the register. "Can I help you?"

"Ralph called earlier today and said that most of my dry cleaning's ready."

"Let me check." The kid disappears into the collection of plastic-covered clothing hanging neatly on hooks that correspond with the first initial of the owner's last name.

Another kid, older than the first and also wearing his hat backward, appears. She takes a guess. "Hey, Ralph!"

"Great to see you again, Ms. Fernandez."

"Please, I've told you before, it's MJ." Her acting skills continue to improve.

"Okay. I got your clothes in the back, and I'll show you the blouse."

MJ pushes her lower lip out. "It's one of my favorites."

"I'll be right back." Ralph disappears and promptly reappears with a pair of slacks and another blouse, each individually wrapped in protective plastic. He hangs them up and proceeds to show MJ a blouse with red wine on the front. The owner did a number on it.

"Here you go. By the way, you left some change in the pocket of your slacks. It's in the little envelope stapled to the outside of the plastic." Ralph rings up the order. "That'll be $16.65 with tax."

This is new, but once again, MJ plays along, handing Ralph a $20 bill. He finishes ringing everything in and hands her $3.35 change. "Sorry, we couldn't do anything with the blouse."

"It's okay. I was pretty sure I ruined it. Have a great night, Ralph."

MJ grabs the clothing and heads for the exit. After a few steps down the street, she pulls a small envelope off the receipt and feels a small rectangular object inside. She quickly puts the envelope in her pocket. She also notices the clothing is her size, making her the new owner of a cream-colored silk blouse and black slacks. MJ continues to be amazed at the lengths to which "the team" goes.

Arriving home, she hangs the dry cleaning in the closet and rips open the envelope like a child with a birthday present. It's after 5 p.m., so it's wine, not coffee time. Snoopy walks from his bed half-asleep and jumps into his assigned spot beside her on the couch. MJ starts poring over the contents of the thumb drive. The first section is labeled "Woman." Her pulse quickens.

"The team" got ahold of the evening's bill and payment records, which confirmed it was evenly split between five different people, all men based upon the names. But a closer look at the billing record indicates a sixth person in attendance. There were five appetizers, five entrees, four Manhattans, three Old Fashioneds, two Margaritas, and three very nice bottles of wine. However, there's a notation in the system, a copy of which is included, specifying the need for six wine glasses. It would've been missed by anyone not looking for it.

From there, "the team" scoured nearby security cameras. They pieced together footage that tracked Picciano from his office to the restaurant. As he arrives, he's met by a woman coming from the opposite direction. He holds the door for her as they enter. A few hours later, Picciano and the woman walk out at the same time. One photo confirms she didn't get into his car when the valet brought it around. *There, but not there.*

They tracked her as far as building cameras would allow, eventually losing her. However, they were able to digitally enhance a still photo of the woman taken from a security video. They ran the photo through various databases, including the Massachusetts Registry of Motor Vehicles, coming up with thirty-two possible matches. They worked to narrow the list down, finally concluding the woman at dinner was Joyce Kramer, senior associate at Wallace, Connors, and Ramirez.

MJ springs from the couch, smashing her foot on the glass coffee table and spilling her partial glass of wine. Snoopy ignores her howls as she hops toward the kitchen to get a paper towel. Her mind's churning as her foot throbs, and she cleans up the spill.

MJ is angry with herself. Of course, the unknown woman is Propentus' General Counsel, Joyce Kramer. She recalls reading the various articles involving Picciano, specifically the one announcing his partnership at Wallace, Connors, and

Ramirez. Having done basic research before calling Joyce, she remembers Joyce joined Propentus from the same firm.

As if a bruised foot isn't enough punishment, she slams her hand on the counter, angry with her failure to make the connection. There are no coincidences.

MJ needs to calm down so she can refocus. As she pours a fresh glass of wine, she allows her mind to wander and muses about how the world lived before Spotify. She starts Charlie Mingus's *Changes One* album. Music always helps her focus.

After grabbing Post-Its, push pins, and string, she hobbles toward the empty wall across from the couch. Here, she creates an organizational chart with Propentus at the top. She adds names to separate Post-Its and sticks them to the wall: Riccio, Kramer, Picciano, Anthony Spinelli, Mr. and Mrs. Spinelli, and Excellence Investments, Inc. But she struggles to connect the dots.

Kramer and Riccio are clear. They met at Genomics and currently work together. MJ wraps a string around their corresponding push pins, and for each, it goes directly to Propentus. While Picciano and Kramer were both attorneys at the same firm, they were at very different stages of their careers. Was Picciano her mentor? Were they romantic partners? They get a string.

The lines between the Spinellis and Picciano are also solid. But are any of the Spinellis connected to Kramer beyond the tangential connection to Picciano? No string. What about Anthony Spinelli and Riccio? Riccio harassed a woman who was reportedly connected to Spinelli, and that's the only thing they have, but it's tenuous at best. She places that on hold, too.

She places a piece of string between Excellence Investments and Propentus, but there's nothing connecting AnnMarie and James Spinelli as individuals to Riccio other than their son, which is flimsy. Nothing is added beyond those between parent and child.

Many of the lines connect to Picciano, but MJ can't create a scenario that connects all of them in any meaningful way. There are more question marks than lines. She gulps her wine and returns to the thumb drive.

The second section provides evidence that others are doing similar research. She's confident in "the team's" ability to hide their own digital tracks while following the trail left by others. They're that good and have proven it time and time again.

A police sergeant pulled the Registry and criminal records for Jonathan Silverman and Walter Erickson. The timing is a little odd, having been reviewed after they were hired to represent Propentus. *Wouldn't that need to be done prior?* she wonders.

She physically shivers as if a bucket of ice water was dumped on her head as she reviews the next folder within the section. The same sergeant ran identical searches on her two days after she spoke with Joyce Kramer. There's also a historical view reflecting MJ as the subject of many searches in the past.

While she can understand what she's just read, she can't rationalize what she sees next. The report states that Joe and Nancy Silverman, who were noted to be Jonathan's parents, and someone named Emily Watkins, who was reported to be Jonathan's girlfriend based on her residence, were the subjects of similar searches. There's also a reference to the same effort being undertaken on Melissa Cosgrove and her immediate family days after the lawsuit was filed.

The report confirms comprehensive searches on each, with the work being done from multiple IP addresses, suggesting whoever is behind this is spreading around the work to expedite the effort and possibly avoid detection. "The team's" final analysis concludes these efforts are likely driven by the Head of Security at Propentus, a retired police detective tapping into old relationships to access the information.

MJ is infuriated, then petrified. Her emotions refuse to be contained.

"Joyce Kramer, you fucking bitch!"

She adds the new puzzle pieces to those already tumbling in her head. She understands the two attorneys and herself, but she can find no justification for searches to be conducted on the others.

A knot of fear forms in her stomach as the warning plays on a loop in her head: *safety first.* Something's not right. These people are civilians, so to speak. Why them? Are they in danger? Should she let Silverman know? But how? She can never explain how she came across this information.

The thump of Mingus' bass aligns with her heartbeat as the wine intensifies her exhaustion. She closes her laptop and finishes what's left in the glass, concluding the best course of action tonight is no action.

63

MJ pulls a pillow over her head in an effort to block out the alarm bleating from her phone. She's never been a morning person, and last night's extra glass of wine isn't helping. On top of that, the meaningful sleep MJ was seeking last night never appeared. Puzzle pieces bounced around her head with each toss or turn. No matter where they landed, she couldn't generate a sane explanation for the background work done on the civilians, leaving one conclusion. It was done for unscrupulous reasons. Exactly what those reasons are fall into the TBD category.

As she slides out of bed, Snoopy starts ringing his bell. "Give me a minute, Snoopy."

She brushes her teeth and puts on a pair of leggings and an oversized hoodie before looking in the mirror. It's the best anyone's going to get at the moment. She shrugs and heads to her kitchen to make a coffee before grabbing the leash and the other things she knows she'll need and follows Snoopy to the elevator. She's desperate for the sunshine to help shake the feeling of dread now driving her every thought.

MJ is more vigilant than usual as they travel to and from the dog park. As has been the case recently, Snoopy stops on a dime. Today, she follows his gaze, noticing a man walking on the other side of the street. He's in his thirties, of average height, average build—average in every sense of the word—but he never looks at her. She and Snoopy are both staring at him, yet he keeps looking straight ahead. Most people have a sixth sense when people are staring at them. Eventually, they turn. He doesn't. His inaction scares the hell out of her.

MJ pulls Snoopy along at an abnormally quick pace. Her eyes capture everyone that comes within a block radius. There's danger everywhere and in everyone. She can't get home quickly enough.

As she's about to enter her apartment building, she notices a second individual, also average in every way, standing on the corner. He stares at her... almost through her, refusing to break eye contact.

She races inside to barricade herself behind multiple deadbolts. As the last lock catches, she decides it's time to call Jonathan Silverman.

64

"Jonathan, there's a reporter, an MJ Fernandez, on line three."

"You know I don't take calls from reporters." Nothing good comes from speaking with the press. He learned that the hard way.

"She says it's urgent, and she sounds determined."

Jonathan rolls his eyes and sighs. Why's it always 'urgent' with these people? He doesn't have time for this shit. "Okay, give me a minute."

Jonathan makes MJ wait for a full five minutes. He wants to see just how important this really is. He finally picks up the call. "Jonathan Silverman."

"Good morning, Mr. Silverman. My name's MJ Fernandez. I'm an investigative reporter, and I would like…"

"Ms. Fernandez…"

"Please call me MJ."

He needs to shut this down. "Okay, MJ. I'll keep this short. I have no comment."

"Mr. Silverman, I have information you need. I won't ask a single question. My goal is to give you information I believe to be tied to the Propentus litigation and that directly impacts your family."

Jonathan pauses at the mention of his family but wants this to end. "Thank you. I have all the information I need." As he takes the phone from his ear, he hears her screaming.

"Wait, wait… Mr. Silverman. I have evidence that your parents and girlfriend are the subjects of a covert investigation."

His pause is palpable this time as he revisits the memories of the Toyota and the car outside Walt's home. She has his full attention. "What'd you say?"

MJ takes a breath. "I said your parents and girlfriend are subjects of a covert investigation, as are you and your partner. We need to meet."

Jonathan is torn. He knows reporters will say anything to capture a soundbite that will find its way to the front page, but this seems a bit extreme. "Ms. Fernandez, I don't appreciate your references to my family, and I still have no comment."

"Please call me MJ. I'm a subject of the same investigation, and I believe the investigation is being done by representatives of Propentus. I can meet you anywhere and at any time."

Her plea strikes Jonathan as truthful. There's a deep anxiety in her voice. And she's talking about the four people on the planet who mean the most to him. Either this reporter's figured out how to get to him, or she's telling the truth. He's furious, but he can't ignore this.

"Ms. Fernandez, I don't know what the hell you're up to, but I'll give you ten minutes. I'll have my assistant schedule an appointment for you here in my office for later today."

"It's MJ, Mr. Silverman, and this shouldn't be discussed in your office."

What the fuck? He's incensed at this point. "Okay, MJ. What the hell do *you* suggest?"

"I can be in front of your building in thirty minutes. We can grab a coffee."

"I'll need an hour to finish what I'm working on. I'll meet you then."

"Thank you, Mr. Silverman."

Jonathan rubs his temples as he swivels his chair to face his laptop. He enters MJ's name into the Google search bar. He has fifty-eight minutes before he needs to be downstairs.

65

Vinnie is hiding in his tiny apartment, looking at the notes he's scribbled onto an old pad of paper. He's desperate to find the best way to turn chicken shit into chicken feed. Jimmy put him in his job so he could watch over things, secure up-to-the-minute information, and pass it along. Jimmy no longer believes he's getting what he's paying for. That's never good.

Vinnie wrote down the information he has to offer Jimmy under two headings: "The Bitch" and "The Asshole." Vinnie doesn't have the whole picture but knows enough to ensure "The Asshole" will play ball. Walking in on that phone call was an unexpected gift.

He's already hinted that "The Bitch" has loose lips. He knows another word from him, and she'll suffer the same fate as Luca Brasi. While not a problem for Jimmy, Vinnie fears being the prime suspect if that were to occur. Particularly if she's already gone to HR... again.

With the help of enough whiskey, Vinnie resigns himself to ask the hard question: Does he truly have anything of value for Jimmy? Jimmy knows the attorney is asking questions. They're not important. It's the answers that concern Jimmy, answers that could have devastating consequences.

At one point in the early morning hours, Vinnie's paranoia took control. He questioned whether "The Bitch" and "The Asshole" were honest with him. If they lied, he'd be giving Jimmy bad information, which is exponentially worse than telling him nothing, but at this point, their answers are all he has.

As the sun comes up, Vinnie looks at the sheet of paper and reviews the useless information he's secured and the questions he knows Jimmy will ask. Questions for which he has no answer. *Why didn't you fuckin' know someone's holding a debt over Harold's head? Why can't you control the fuckin' blonde scientist? She's a lab geek. You shoulda gotten it outta her sooner. Why didn't you tell me there are questions about the FDA reports and data?* Vinnie knows he's hinted at this but also knows Jimmy's selective memory will blot that out. *Why didn't you plant a bug in the conference room? Why haven't you done anything with the attorney? Why's the old lady still alive?* He concedes these are valid questions, and while he'd thought about some of these things, he didn't act or talk to Jimmy about them. That's his biggest mistake.

Vinnie takes another long pull from the fifth of Jack Daniels sitting on the coffee table. It was almost full when the evening began twelve hours earlier. After wiping his mouth with his sleeve, he decides it's best to take a shower and get some sleep before he meets with Jimmy.

He stands, crumples the evening's useless scribbles, and tosses them into the trash.

Fuck it. He's pulled off miracles before.

66

Jonathan exits the building fifty-five minutes after his phone call with MJ. As he scans the meager crowd in front of his building, it's obvious who he is meeting with. MJ looks like her online pictures, even though she's wearing sunglasses and a Sox cap is holding back her pink-streaked hair, a detail her photos didn't reveal.

MJ steps forward confidently. "Mr. Silverman, I'm MJ Fernandez. It's a pleasure to meet you." She raises her right arm.

Jonathan stops in front of the reporter, arms crossed across his chest. "I'm not certain I share that sentiment, Ms. Fernandez. Time will tell."

"Please, it's MJ. Do you have a favorite spot for coffee?"

"I'm not picky. Dunks is about a block and a half from here."

"Perfect."

They turn and begin to walk down the street. The sounds of a city street are all that's heard. Two turns and eight minutes of silence later, they finally arrive at their destination.

Jonathan finally says something. "What'll you have, MJ? I'm buying." Despite the anger associated with her references to his family, Jonathan decides to play nice. Nothing good has ever come from pissing off a reporter.

"I'll have a large, hot blueberry, no cream or sugar." She shrugs her shoulders and smiles.

Jonathan looks at her oddly.

MJ starts as soon as Jonathan hands her the sweet-smelling coffee. "Would you like to sit, or would you prefer to go for a walk?"

Jonathan notices MJ's attempt at showing no emotion. Her trembling hand gives away the truth. "Let's take a walk. I missed the gym this morning." A little white lie, but one that seems to make MJ a little more comfortable.

They exit the aroma-filled shop and turn left, taking them farther from Jonathan's office. He gets down to it—he doesn't have time for whatever this is. "So, why am I here, MJ?"

MJ takes a sip from the steaming cup. Jonathan is shocked the heat didn't bother her. Maybe she's tougher than she looks?

"You're here because there are people who've spent a great deal of time investigating you, your parents, Ms. Watkins, and Mr. Erickson. I presume if you had a dog, they'd have investigated them, too."

"And?"

MJ gives it to him right between the eyes. "I'm going to tell you a short story, which is directly tied to your question."

As they casually walk, MJ explains about reading the online article about the class-action lawsuit and how her grandmother's battle with dementia prompted her to investigate. Next, she outlines her research into Michael Riccio and Propentus.

"I believe in following the money, which brought me to Excellence Investments Inc. They were incorporated many years ago, and out of nowhere, they made their first and only investment in Propentus."

She lays out the details surrounding the elder Spinellis and their current health. She notes Anthony Spinelli's frequent trips to Florida and even his sexual orientation. Next, she moves on to Attorney Picciano and how his DUI was dropped due to an evidence problem. "There's a sole note about *missing blood* on the last page of his file."

After talking about the unknown woman, she drops the bombshell. "The woman was a younger Joyce Kramer, who worked at the same firm as Picciano."

Jonathan stops and looks at MJ, saying nothing.

MJ explores her surroundings before proceeding to tell him about Snoopy's new stopping routine and the man on the corner. Lastly, without mentioning her source, MJ outlines what "the team" has found relative to the depth and breadth of investigations being done on his parents and girlfriend. Here, she admits for the first time out loud that she's worried for her safety and for theirs.

It takes her fifteen minutes to walk him through it all. "I don't know how or why just yet, but I'm convinced there's more to the Excellence Investment angle. And that's why you're here."

Jonathan digests and analyzes her statements. His own investigation covered much of what MJ outlined, but the new information she shared is information that could only be obtained via methods he would never explore.. That said, it's very helpful information—or is it? He represents Propentus. He can't talk about the lawsuit or the company.

He chooses his response carefully: "First, I admit to being impressed with your thoroughness and story-telling ability. However, some of the details I believe were obtained—how shall I put this—resourcefully. I don't need or want to talk about your investigative approach."

MJ smiles at the compliment and takes another sip of coffee.

"Second, Propentus is my client, and I cannot—will not—talk to you about them, the lawsuit, or their treatment for dementia. Lastly, thank you for making me aware that you believe there's an investigation happening relative to me, my parents, my girlfriend, and my—"

MJ can't help but interrupt. "Mr. Silverman, I don't *believe* anything. What I've told you are facts I know unequivocally to be true. My team and I are meticulous. We don't say something is fact without absolute certainty."

Jonathan continues to be impressed. She didn't get emotional. She looked him in the eye and made the statements clearly and plainly. He has a million questions but refuses to go down the rabbit hole. "Okay. For the sake of argument, let's accept your statements as true. I ask again: why am I here?"

"First, as a decent human being, I thought I should tell you about the investigation into your parents and girlfriend. I presume you're not surprised that someone is looking into you and your partner. However, the investigation into the others is being done for nefarious reasons. There's no other rationale for that. At least none I could come up with."

Jonathan's starting to like her. She's factual, detailed, and direct. And she's right. He can't think of a logical reason why someone would look into his parents and his girlfriend. "Second?"

"Second, there's something very strange about your case and arguably your client. I know this will sound silly, but I have Post-Its on the wall of my apartment with strings going between them. Each Post-It has a name on it. The string represents an identified connection. Right now, Picciano has the most connection points. I'd be interested in your thoughts if you're willing to share them."

If he didn't like her before, he does now, as a fellow 'Post-It on the wall' thinker. Based on what she's told him, there are a lot of connections to Robert Picciano. But the connections he's most interested in haven't materialized.

"I have an ethical obligation to my client. I will not break this obligation, not just because it would put my law license in jeopardy, but because I, too, believe in doing what's right."

MJ doesn't blink. "I meant thoughts about your family and friends being investigated." She's got him. Jonathan can talk about that without violating his ethics if he chooses.

Jonathan's mind is still trying to absorb everything. Despite the swirl, there's one constant: ensuring the safety of Emily, his parents, and Walt. "My family is, and always will be, the most important thing in my life. I appreciate you making me aware of what you believe is occurring—"

MJ interrupts again, rolling her eyes openly and sighing. "Jonathan, I'm not trying to be difficult, but I told you. This isn't a belief; it's a reality. I only deal with realities. I sort through gigantic piles of shit to get to them at times, but I don't deal in beliefs. Sure, theories, maybe, but those aren't the same as beliefs. Theories either become realities or they're disproven and discarded. Period."

Jonathan looks at his watch. They've been gone for almost an hour. Fortunately, they'd taken a couple of rights along the way, so he wasn't as far from his office as he could have been. "MJ, I have a meeting I need to get back for. This is interesting and… educational, but I'm at a loss as to what you'd like me to do with this." He took the next right and continued walking, albeit at a slightly quicker pace.

MJ reaches into her pocket. "I told you there would be no questions. But I want you to review the contents of this thumb drive. I believe there's serious danger lurking. Why and for whom, I'm uncertain, but I'm committed to finding out. That said, I'm confident your client's involved, and that means danger for anyone digging into their universe."

Jonathan accepts the thumb drive she hands him but doesn't close his fingers around it. Is it wise to accept information that was likely obtained unethically?

"That's it, Jonathan. Just read. My number's included in the documents. I'm here if you'd like to discuss this further. And, not to overstate the obvious, you need to prevent that thumb drive and its contents from being seen by anyone but you. Thanks again for the coffee." With that, MJ turns around and walks away, her pink-streaked ponytail bouncing with each step.

Jonathan's stunned. He's never had a reporter behave like this. They're usually pit bulls, asking question after question. Whether they're searching for answers or trying to trip you up to grab a soundbite, they're relentless. He shakes off the thought, tucks the thumb drive into his blazer pocket, and hustles back to his office. He can't be late for his meeting. He's still trying to wrap his head around the last fifty minutes as he enters the building.

With his mind in a million different places, Jonathan doesn't notice the average-looking man standing across the street, watching him walk into the building—the one with the cell phone in his hand.

67

After grabbing a few hours of fitful sleep, Vinnie showers and throws on a pair of jeans, a t-shirt, his python cowboy boots, and the Sox hat he got at the Home Run Derby in 1999. As he puts it on his balding head, Vinnie remembers the impressive sight of watching those baseballs leave the yard and the electricity in the stadium. It was one of the best nights of his life.

He arrives at The Last Inning full of trepidation. He's convinced Jimmy means it when he says *he's done,* and Vinnie knows what those words mean to Jimmy. He also knows he doesn't have a single piece of information so important that Jimmy will be forever grateful.

But he has a plan.

He grabs his usual seat at the bar and orders a drink. As he sips his double Jack, he reflects on the tough spots he's been in during his life. He's found a way out of every single one. He's spent the past forty-eight hours convincing himself he can pull off another miracle.

Richie is sitting at the other end of the bar, and he smiles at Vinnie. That's a good sign. Richie never smiles.

After twenty minutes, the bartender gives Vinnie the nod. It's now or never. He needs to walk into Jimmy's office confidently and lay out his plan. He'll stretch the truth. Hell, he'll lie if it saves his ass. He's done it before and isn't afraid to do it again. This is a game of chess, not checkers. He takes a deep breath and knocks on the door.

"Yeah?"

Vinnie walks in with a self-assured look on his face. "Hey, Jimmy."

"Why the fuck are you here?" Jimmy doesn't offer him a seat. He's too nervous to sit anyway.

"I got some really good info for you. I was able to corner those two people I told you about, and I did more investigatin'."

"And?"

"First, the two scientists. The blonde told me the attorney is askin' lots of questions about data, how it's created and saved, etc. He's also askin' why most of the FDA documents are signed by her and that idiot, Harold. She says she told him IT does all the data stuff, and the research is compartmentalized. She answered the questions the way Joyce told her to."

Vinnie takes a breath. Jimmy's listening. It's working.

"She says she's sure the attorney believed her. Me, I ain't sure. I'm pretty sure she's fuckin' lyin' to me about some of it. I pressed her really fuckin' hard. She started cryin' and just kept sayin' the same things over and over. And if she caved and talked to me, who else is she talkin' to? She's a risk."

Fuck "The Bitch." She's a sacrificial pawn that's been pushed to the center of the board. Time for the next move.

"I told that asshole Harold I know he owes people, and I was sure his wife would be interested in knowin'. He shit his pants and told me he'd tell me whatever I wanted to know. The guy's got no balls."

Jimmy hasn't interrupted. Vinnie knows that means it's going well.

"He says the attorney found mistakes in the paperwork. He said he couldn't explain why, and the attorney's smart. He could smell the bullshit. The guy's fuckin' scared to death... and should be. I got 'em by the balls. He's goin' through a divorce and has real money problems. I can convince this guy to do anythin' we want to keep me from tellin' his wife."

Another great move made. It's all falling into place. Vinnie's proving he still knows how to squeeze people for information and now has a guy on the inside who's under his complete control. Jimmy's sitting there, occasionally taking a sip of his soda water, listening. Vinnie knows from experience that if he wasn't giving Jimmy exactly what he wanted, he'd throw his ass out of the office.

"I been followin' the lawyer. I had people trackin' him but decided it was better if I did it. This is important shit, and I want it done right for you, Jimmy."

Jimmy nods. It's working. Vinnie's talking faster and faster. "The other day, I saw him talkin' to a reporter who called Joyce Kramer. They grabbed a coffee together. I don't know what they was saying 'cuz I couldn't get close enough, but it can't be a coincidence. I'm stayin' on him personally."

Now for the closing maneuver. Vinnie's positive it'll bring him the miracle he so desperately needs.

"And I figured out the best place to put a bug in the conference room these guys always use. My guy's bringin' me the bug tonight, and I'm gonna install it early tomorrow before anyone gets in."

There it is—all laid out. Jimmy listened and didn't interrupt once. It's all Vinnie can do not to smile. He stands there waiting for Jimmy.

Jimmy gazes at Vinnie and shifts in his seat. It isn't quite a smile, but it isn't the usual sneer, either. "This is good. You say you was gonna place the fuckin' bug tomorrow?"

"Early… Before people arrive."

"Why don't you grab Richie, go pick up the fuckin' bug, and plant it now. Nobody's there, and Richie's good at that shit."

Jimmy's ecstatic! Angels sing! Miracle achieved! Better still, he offered to have Richie help. Vinnie wants to let out a huge sigh of relief, but he can't. He needs to act like this is just another day.

"And this blonde… She knows stuff that can hurt us?"

"She might. She did a couple of things, but nothing major. But she has loose lips."

Jimmy pauses to think it through. "If she spills what she fuckin' knows, that could lead to more questions. Talk to Richie 'bout that, too. He'll figure it out."

"Will do, Jimmy." *Bye-bye, you fuckin' bitch… You shoulda said yes when I asked you out.*

"Okay, now get the fuck out. Richie's at the bar but was plannin' on leavin' to do somethin'. Catch him before he leaves."

"Okay. Sure. Great, Jimmy. Thanks." Vinnie immediately reaches for the door and backs his way out of Jimmy's office, just like he has a million times before.

He won't make it to a million and two.

68

Jonathan brings the thumb drive to his head of IT, where it's plugged into a standalone laptop, not connected to the Wi-Fi in the building or the law firm's network, to check for malware and ransomware. Within minutes, the thumb drive is declared safe, and Jonathan heads to his office. After hanging up his suit coat and grabbing an energy drink, he closes his door and plugs the drive into his laptop.

Jonathan is shocked by the volume of information. He opens a document titled "Summary" that contains links embedded within the text designed to immediately take the reader to the documentation supporting that particular content. The level of organization is impressive. He reads the lengthy summary without the benefit of the embedded links to get a sense of the totality of the story.

During his second pass, he clicks on various links. He finds copies of records and information that could've only been gathered illegally. Jonathan anticipated this based on MJ's verbal summary, but the quantity of such information is unnerving. Having this information in his possession clashes with his personal morals, so he stops reading.

After a few moments of reflective pacing around his office, he decides it's too late and sits down in front of the laptop again. He'll have to figure out what to do with the information later. A bridge he never imagined he'd need to cross.

Everything MJ told him is included, along with its backup. He understands why she pushed back every time he mentioned *believing* something. After completing a comprehensive review he sits back, listening to softly playing country music. As he does so, he remembers he has the Toyota's plate number. Since breaking the law is apparently his new hobby, maybe he should ask Walt to have it checked.

Just then, his laptop dings, notifying him of a new email. He recognizes the Gmail address as one included on the thumb drive. With slightly less appreciation than his hour-ago self would've had, he clicks to open the email. It's a blurry photograph of someone—he can't tell if it's a man or a woman—standing across the street from his office building. The only text is the subject line: "be very careful".

Jonathan yanks his hands away from the keyboard as if the computer had physically shocked him. He stands abruptly and walks away from his laptop as if creating distance between himself and the danger the blurry individual represents. Who's watching him? Are they watching his parents and Emily, too? After a few moments of pacing, he removes the thumb drive, unsure where to store it.

The morning's adventure has cost him more than half a day. He needs to get back to work. Jonathan refocuses and sends Angela a text, asking her to step into his office. They spend the next hour reviewing materials and finalizing responses to discovery demands.

Once again, Schneider has asked for everything under the sun, most of which he isn't entitled to. Jonathan has taken the same approach in the past, knowing *they can't say no if you don't ask.* After reviewing the letter he drafted with Angela, which outlines the reasons why he won't get them, Jonathan asks Angela for her thoughts on the research materials in the portal. Jonathan knows she won't pull any punches.

"Something's wrong. There's a cadence to the dates of materials entered into the files. However, there are instances where the cadence changes. It returns, and then it changes again." Angela spins her laptop so it faces Jonathan and points to two sets of dates on the screen. "I've also noticed that of the documents with edits, a few seem to have far more than others. Harold Johnson and Renee Spencer are the authors of most of those edits. And almost all the heavily edited documents are included in the 286 'kidney' search list. Lastly, of the original twelve participants in the human trials, one individual's file is much thinner than the others. I haven't had a chance to put a lot of time into figuring out what the difference might be."

Jonathan likes Angela. She's bright, thorough, and hard-working. And she gives it to him straight. While she's currently applying to law schools, he'll create a spot for her when the time comes. The firm needs her.

"I hadn't noticed the smaller file. Great catch. I've asked the CIO for a report of all the documents that were edited or deleted. I'm going to see if he can break down the edits in a way that allows us to manipulate the data to look for anomalies. We'll see if Joyce lets that fly." Jonathan shrugs unknowingly.

"I can't explain it," Angela says, her mind obviously still spinning over the details. "There aren't huge, glaring gaps. It is more of a gut feeling than anything."

"Always trust your gut. It's a key tool in an attorney's tool-box, just as it is in life."

Angela stands and stretches. "Will do. See you in the morning."

"Have a good night, and thanks for all your hard work on this."

Jonathan initially thought he was looking for a problem and thus found one. Joyce's steel-fisted control and reluctance to provide information triggered the uncertainty. Harold and Renee's interviews supported his gut feeling. He now has information, albeit illegally obtained, which reinforces his concerns. Angela coming to similar conclusions without prompting confirms that his gut has been right—something is definitely off. But what? His worry for his parents, Emily, and Walt escalates as his concerns about Propentus intensify. Finally, he reluctantly slides the thumb drive into his pants pocket. Where else is he going to hide it?

69

Jonathan peers at the headline as he grabs the morning *Globe*: "Former Boston Police Detective Killed in Carjacking." He slides the newspaper under his arm. As is his habit, he'll read it when he gets to the office.

He's listening to the local news as he drives to the office when he hears: "Former Police Detective Vincent Napolitano was gunned down during an apparent carjacking..." The report goes on to say that Napolitano retired and became the Head of Security at Propentus. Jonathan almost sideswipes the car in the lane next to him. What the hell is going on? Coincidence?

Just then, his cell phone chirps with a text message. He asks Siri to read the message. It's as if the person read his mind: *there r no coincidences.* Is it from MJ? A member of her team? He tries to send back a response, but Siri tells him his message can't be delivered.

Jonathan's head is spinning. He wants to call his parents and Emily to warn them. Should he? What would he say? *A reporter I just met told me you are in danger. The information that led to that conclusion was obtained illegally but can be trusted. And the carjacking death of an ex-police detective is the proof.* It sounds like something out of a Dennis Lehane novel. No one will believe him.

Jonathan gets off the elevator, and before the door to the offices of Silverman Erickson closes, Walt is standing in front of him. "You hear?"

"Yeah, on the way in."

Walt matches Jonathan's pace as they walk toward his office. "I've already made some calls. I'm told they aren't convinced it was a carjacking gone wrong. The detectives are continuing to investigate, but Napolitano has no known family and left the force under a black cloud. He caused a shitload of problems for a lot of people over the years."

Jonathan pauses at the door to his office. "I need to call Joyce. And I need to bring you up to speed on something. I'll come find you after I speak with her." He closes the door, leaving a confused and concerned Walt outside.

Jonathan feels an urgency and tosses his briefcase on the floor beside his credenza. A message from Joyce is in the center of his desk. Maybe he should've called from the car.

"Julie, can you please get Ms. Kramer on the phone?"

Before Jonathan puts down his coffee, Julie announces, "Ms. Kramer on line two."

Jonathan immediately picks up the receiver. "Joyce, I heard on my way into the office. I'm sorry."

"Thanks. Things are chaotic. I have a meeting with HR in a few minutes. We're bringing in grief counselors for the staff. Vinnie wasn't the most beloved guy, but everyone knew him. We're a small company."

Jonathan is taken aback by Joyce's tone. It's more mechanical than emotional. "I'm sure it's a difficult time. I was going to call you this morning because I need a couple of things for the latest round of discovery, but that can wait, given the circumstances. My next call's to Schneider asking for an extension."

"Much appreciated, Jonathan. I gotta run. Call you later."

"Sure, whatever you need. Call my cell if it's after 7 p.m. Good luck."

Jonathan sits down and thinks about everything that's happened in the past forty-eight hours. Before he gets too deep in thought, his cell phone chirps again. *buy u a cup of coffee?*

He is pretty sure he knows who it is, but how the hell did she get his cell number? Anger and paranoia keep his response cryptic. *Sure. Same place? Remind me again, what did you drink?*

hahaha, u know. there in 30.

They dodged the question, but who else would know what he was talking about? He throws his full cup of coffee in the trash and heads out his office door. "Julie, I'm running out for coffee. Would you like anything?" he asks as he passes his assistant's desk.

"No thanks."

Jonathan walks quickly to his new favorite coffee shop and immediately spots MJ sitting at one of the small tables inside. She has her laptop open and appears to be in deep thought when he walks in. He picks up his order and joins her.

MJ peers over her laptop. "Hey, I said I was buying."

"No worries. Besides, I was afraid you'd try to get me to drink some of that blueberry shit you ordered last time."

She barely chuckles. MJ lowers her voice and pulls her hoodie up to hide the distinctive pink streaks in her hair. "Wanna walk?"

Jonathan politely declines. "I'm too tired."

"Fine. We have to remember where we are," she says in almost a whisper.

Jonathan looks around. The distinctive orange décor makes their location unmistakable. He can't forget even if he wanted to. "Yeah, not a problem."

The whispering continues. "This is related." MJ taps the table next to where her phone is previewing an article about the security officer's death.

Jonathan sits back in his chair and takes a sip of his coffee, shaking his head. "We don't know that. My partner is making some calls."

MJ scowls and all but slams her hand on the table. "There are no coincidences. My team's already digging."

Jesus, this woman doesn't mess around. "Okay, so let's say you're right."

"First, I *am* right," she insists, "but I want to know everything I can about this alleged carjacking. Second, this just raised the threat level to DEFCON 2."

"Wait… Is one the worst, or is five the worst? I always forget." Jonathan's attempt to lighten the mood fails.

"Jesus Christ, man. One is the worst. For a smart guy, you don't know shit." MJ shakes her head and looks around. "I didn't move it to DEFCON 1 because neither you nor I have been personally threatened. Or have you?"

The lightness leaves Jonathan's voice. "I have not."

MJ takes another sip, looking around continuously. Her head swivels as the hoodie blocks her peripheral vision. "We need to figure this out quickly. I propose we form an alliance."

Jonathan frowns. "I don't believe that's a good idea." As the silence between the two stretches out, he sighs. "But for the sake of argument, let's say we agree. How would that work exactly?"

"Simple."

Jonathan chuckles darkly. "Nothing's simple. Certainly nothing about this situation."

"No, really. It's simple. We work together and share everything." MJ's eyes scan the room again before she continues. "You have a lot of resources. I have a lot of resources. Combining them doesn't double them; they become exponentially more powerful as long as we avoid overlapping efforts."

"MJ..."

She interrupts him in the loudest hushed tone he has ever heard. "No names!"

Jonathan's eyes roll. "Okay, whatever. Person A, as I've explained, I have obligations that I cannot and will not shirk. What you're proposing is logistically impossible."

"I'll take," MJ looks around casually, her voice barely a whisper, "the lawsuit off the list of topics. We're looking for the same answers. It's foolish to waste time, money, and energy on the same things. An alliance is the obvious solution."

"Again, I'm not sure your proposal is feasible," Jonathan says with furrowed brows, trying to justify her proposal.

"Did you look at what I gave you?"

"Yes." The thumb drive is in his pocket. He almost slept with it under his pillow. But, after this morning's news, he wants to smash it and forget he's ever seen it.

"Then you know I'm not screwin' around. This is serious shit, and we gotta get them before they get us. Or should I say, before we're 'carjacked.'" MJ lowkey makes air quotes, emphasizing more that she believes the death wasn't a random occurrence.

Jonathan is struck by her tenacity, her unemotional, methodical approach to things, and her ability to get shit done. He'll do what he can and must to protect his parents and Emily, but he'll not put his career or the firm at risk. Viewing the thumb drive she gave him was risky enough, but teaming up with a reporter to investigate one of his clients?

That could lose him everything he's ethically worked so hard to achieve.

Jonathan leans forward. "How about this: You email me questions—questions that any detail-oriented investigative reporter would ask. I'll answer those I believe stay within the bounds. The questions you send will tell me what you're working on."

"First, I am not just *any investigative reporter*. Second, other than replying to emails, what will you be doing to contribute to this partnership?"

Jonathan looks around and tries to keep his voice down. "First, it isn't a partnership. Second, I'll be scouring the depths of a complicated FDA filing and the corresponding research to figure out whether my client's playing above board."

MJ is clearly pissed. "So, doing the job you're getting paid to do."

Jonathan shakes his head. What's this woman not getting? He's telling her he'll be digging through all of the records and communications associated with Antsalemab and, most importantly, talking to the key players. "You're missing my point. Yes, I'll be doing my job—a job that neither you nor your 'team' can do."

Jonathan watches it come together for MJ. He can question people she can't, like Joyce Kramer, Harold Johnson, Renee Spencer, and Tommy O'Hara. Her resources do the research behind the scenes, as he operates out in front. And, while he didn't say this, his partner apparently has a pipeline into the police.

"Fine." MJ stands without saying another word. She gently closes her laptop and heads for the door. But after two steps, she returns to the table, grabbing her blueberry coffee. "No need to waste a good coffee."

70

Joyce is in a meeting with Michael and the head of HR when her cell phone buzzes. She casually glances at the number—restricted. "Will you excuse me," she says while declining the call and walks out the door.

She's pissed. These calls aren't supposed to come to her personal cell. That's not the agreement. Joyce practically stomps down to her office, shuts the door, pulls a new burner from her purse, and calls the number that was on the last Post-It note. It's answered on the first ring.

"I call, you answer."

"I was in a meeting," she snaps.

"I don't fuckin' care. Didn't my message make that clear?"

Joyce was expecting this call. He's not screwing around anymore. She feels solely responsible for what happened, and it's made her physically ill. She originally thought having that type of power was thrilling, but now she knows firsthand that reality is anything but. "I have a dinner meeting this evening. It's the only topic on the agenda."

"Where do we stand?"

The question she hates the most. The IPO has stalled because of the lawsuit. A lawsuit takes time. It isn't just going to disappear. "I have another call into our primary contact." It's the only thing she can say.

"And?"

"And… every time I speak with him, he references our current legal troubles."

"Do I gotta fuckin' speak to him?"

Oh shit, she can't let that happen. "I have it handled."

"Your friend kept sayin' the same fuckin' thing. Look how that turned out."

This is bad. The worst Joyce has ever seen it, and she's seen a lot in the past few years. "I'm not him." He always seems to respond well to a little backbone.

"Keep it the fuck up, and you'll be just like him."

No ambiguity there. "Understood."

"I hear the idiot and his fuckin' student are problems."

She knows he's referring to Harold and Renee. Fucking Vinnie. What'd he say? "I told you; they're under control."

"Tick fuckin' tock." Click.

Joyce grabs her trash barrel and vomits for the third time today. She wipes her mouth with a napkin she pulled from a desk drawer and takes a moment to lay her head on her desk. This has gone from bad to worse and has the potential to become the fucking worst if she doesn't figure it out.

Joyce gags as the smell seeps from the trash barrel, but there can't possibly be anything left in her stomach. She smooths her skirt and looks in the mirror on the wall. It's obvious she just puked, but she doesn't have time to fix that. There's too much at stake.

71

Jonathan returns to the office to find Walt patrolling the lobby. "Where've you been?"

"Getting coffee." Jonathan realizes he doesn't have a cup of coffee in his hand. Maybe this spy shit's harder than he thinks.

"Come on."

Jonathan walks toward his office with Walt following so closely behind that Jonathan swears they could be wearing the same shirt. Walt slams the door behind him.

"Walt, what the hell's going on? You're acting crazy, even for you." Jonathan sits at his desk and stares at his partner.

Walt paces the room with his hands jammed deep into his pockets, presumably to keep his arms from flailing around as he speaks. "My sources tell me there are serious doubts the guy from Propentus was killed during a carjacking."

"You told me."

Walt shakes his head. "No, I said it looked like a carjacking, and they might be less diligent since the guy was a piece of shit."

"And?"

"Forensics says the physics are off. They make it highly questionable that he was shot trying to fight someone off. The points of entry suggest an effort to make it look like that. Besides, who'd want to carjack a five-year-old Escalade? And there's chatter this guy's connected."

"It's still a murder, right?"

Walt stands in front of Jonathan's desk. "I didn't say that. Are you fuckin' listening to me? Something's going on. If he's connected, that's a whole new problem. And this is related to a case you're handling."

"Jesus, Walt. Take a breath." After his meeting with MJ and the "extra" things he knows, it surprises even Jonathan that he's the calm one in the room. "First, this guy was the Head of Security. He's not a researcher, nor anyone who has anything to do with the class-action. Second, you said there are questions. You didn't say it wasn't a carjacking. And lastly, no one's said anything about him being tied to the mob."

Walt finally bubbles over and throws his hands up. "I am telling you. This guy's a fucking loser. My guy says he got mothballed early because of excessive force complaints coupled with a bunch of other shady shit. Rumor has it he was Jimmy Rizzo's puppet on the force, probably one of many who fucked around with evidence on mob-related cases, among other things. None of it was ever proven, but you know how these things work. Where there's smoke..."

Jonathan appeals to Walt's logical side. "Okay, okay, got it. But where are they going with this? Let's say it's a mob hit. Will anyone want to draw attention to a guy they should've known was under the mob's thumb? It'd open up Pandora's box."

"I asked the same question. It's been kicked upstairs at Police Headquarters *for further discussion*, which my guy says means they're working on damage control."

Jonathan's original plan was to tell Walt everything. With Walt freaking out, he thinks better of it. Maybe tomorrow. For now, he tries to calm him down. "Okay, until then, let's keep our heads. Besides, there's no tie to Propentus other than his employment. A lot of pieces have to fall into place before any of that becomes a concern. Now, I have to call 'The King of the Fender Bender' to get an extension on some discovery responses. I can't get what I need. Propentus is a mess at the moment for obvious reasons."

Walt frowns but has at least stopped pacing the room like a caged animal. "Thought you said you schooled him when he threatened to farm the case out to a bigger firm?"

"I did. Now, I have to eat crow and ask for something." Jonathan's not looking forward to this call.

Walt takes a deep breath and sits down across from Jonathan. "Well, you know what I say… If you have to eat crow, don't eat it one feather at a time. Take a huge fuckin' mouthful and be done with it."

Jonathan smiled at Walt. "Another 'Waltism.' You should write a book."

"When I retire." Walt stands and nods respectfully at his partner. "Good luck with the call. I'll let you know when I hear something from my guy." He pauses briefly in the doorway on his way out. "Keep your head down. My gut tells me something's going on."

"You too." Jonathan sits back in his chair and closes his eyes for a moment after Walt leaves. Between MJ and Walt, he has a massive headache. He washes down a couple of aspirin with his energy drink before messaging Julie to reach out to Attorney Schneider.

His phone buzzes a couple of minutes later. "Attorney Schneider, how are you this afternoon?"

"Did you finally talk some sense into your client, Mr. Silverman? You calling me with the offer of a lifetime?"

Jonathan rolls his eyes, which doesn't help his headache. He also notices Schneider called him "Mr." when he addressed Schneider as attorney. He doesn't have time for idiotic mind games. Jonathan's crow awaits. "I'm not sure if you heard about a carjacking that took place last night. A retired police detective wound up dead."

"I heard something about that."

"Well, the deceased is—or should I say was—the Head of Security at Propentus. Everyone from the CEO down is shaken. They're a small company. A tight-knit family." The truth's malleable.

Mr. Schneider continues with his disrespectful tone. "And you're looking for an extension on the pending discovery demands?"

"A short one. I spoke with their General Counsel. They're bringing in grief counselors for the next couple of weeks, so anyone who needs it can get support during this difficult time."

"When you were speaking with Ms. Kramer, did you happen to mention our last conversation pursuant to your ethical obligations?"

Jonathan can see his smirk through the phone. He's about to tell Schneider to fuck off when he remembers Walt's wisdom. He takes another huge bite. "I did not. She was running into a meeting with HR to discuss grief support when I called. I offered my condolences and asked her to call me when she had a moment." Partially true.

"Mr. Silverman, my clients are running out of time. They want and deserve justice. The Head of Security has no involvement in this litigation whatsoever, and you know it."

Jonathan is comfortable with silence. It's one of the most powerful tools in the negotiation toolbox. He sits there, chewing on his crow, waiting for whatever comes out of this guy's mouth next.

Once Schneider realizes his ploy didn't work, he jumps back in. "But neither I nor my clients are without compassion. We'll grant an additional seven days for the responses and for you to meet your ethical obligations by speaking to your client about resolving this matter."

"That's appreciated, Mr. Schneider. I'm happy to grant the same extension for the medical records that remain outstanding." Jonathan struggles to keep the sarcasm out of his tone.

"Oh... Um... Right. You'll have them shortly."

Jonathan swears he hears papers shuffling on the other end of the line.

"And, in the spirit of transparency," Mr. Schneider continues, "I'm sending over the next set of interrogatories and discovery demands. I'm looking for every version of any document that's been created, edited, deleted, or stored relating to Antsalemab, including research materials, emails, and text communications between company employees, members of the Board of Directors, investors, and the lead investment bank underwriting their upcoming IPO."

Jonathan's head is throbbing. Before he can tell Schneider to shove his requests up his ass, Schneider takes one last shot.

"I look forward to hearing your client's offer soon, Mr. Silverman."

After being abruptly hung up on, Jonathan begins massaging his temples, wondering if his headache will ever go away.

72

onathan holds the door and watches the stunning woman he's with glide into the restaurant. Tonight, Emily is wearing one of Jonathan's favorites: a black mini with a pair of Jimmy Choo stilettos. He went out of his way to find out who Jimmy Choo was after she moved in.

He quietly enjoys watching the heads turn as they enter. Men and women gawk at her as she follows the maître d' to their table. She's with him, and he's decided he'll do whatever it takes to keep it that way, reminding him, yet again, that he needs to speak with his father.

Jonathan was planning to tell Emily everything over dinner, but on the drive to the restaurant, he decided not to rob her of the wonderful evening she deserved. It could wait until tomorrow.

The hostess ushers the couple to their table, and Jonathan orders a bottle of Hourglass Cabernet Sauvignon. He remembers Walt talking about it, but beyond that, he's clueless. The waiter smiles and leaves to retrieve their selection.

Emily didn't bother him about it at home, but it seemed like dinner was the appropriate time to bring up the news she—and everyone else in the city—heard. "Wow... crazy thing that happened to that guy from Propentus, huh?"

Jonathan told Emily he had taken on the Propentus case, so of course, she would bring this news up with him. "Yeah. I spoke with Joyce Kramer, their General Counsel. I met him once and candidly got a weird vibe."

The waiter returns with the wine, showing Jonathan the bottle to confirm their choice. He hands the removed cork to Jonathan and pours a small amount into his glass. Jonathan won't smell the cork—that part of the process is stupid. He swirls the wine in the glass consistent with Walt's training, then takes a sip. After nodding his approval, the waiter decants the bottle at the table. Walt would be proud.

Emily leans forward and quietly asks, "What does this mean for the lawsuit?"

Jonathan lowers his voice as well. "Technically, the Head of Security has nothing to do with the lawsuit. He was in charge of physical security, not data security and isn't part of the research team, so he has no connection to the suit." Guilt burns deep within his chest for not being completely honest.

"That's good, I guess."

They both spend a few moments reviewing the menu, settling quickly into their established routine of negotiating the appetizer and entrée choices. The waiter returns, pouring them each a glass of wine after getting their orders. They clink their wine glasses and take a sip as Emily moves the conversation to a more positive topic.

"Your dad seems to be doing well. Looks like the new drug's working."

Jonathan has been struggling to maintain positivity toward Propentus given the past forty-eight hours. "Maybe. Dad's memory is better, according to Mom, but we all know it's technically not better. At best, it's not getting worse. I think any noted positive change is tied to the strict routine she has him on versus the drug. But, whatever the reason, Dad's stable, and Mom's happy."

Emily looks left and then right before asking the next question. "Have you told the people at the company your dad's taking Antsalemab?"

"No, I'm keeping everything separate. Neither Walt nor I see it as a conflict, so no need to disclose it."

Jonathan returns to the menu, his mind slipping into the murky waters of his dad's situation. He hasn't shared the depth of his despair with anyone, not even Emily. He must continually remind himself that the treatment is not a cure. His father's abilities will deteriorate over time. Jonathan often thinks about the difficult journey that lies ahead, and it terrifies him. Some call it "the long goodbye."

As he's lost in his thoughts, a buzzing sound emanates from Jonathan's sports coat. He glances at the number and quickly stands. "I'm sorry, it's Joyce. I should take this."

"I'll be fine, sitting here and enjoying this *exceptional* wine." This is their long-standing private joke, the one that drives Walt mad.

Jonathan smirks at Emily before heading toward the door and hitting "accept" on his phone. "Hello, Joyce. How are you doing?" Jonathan is genuinely concerned. Joyce is a total pain in the ass, but this is a daunting situation and an unrelated issue. Or is it? Either way, now's not the time.

"It's been a helluva a day. After working to take care of the staff, I spent most of the afternoon with homicide detectives. They wanted to know everything I knew about Vinnie, what he did at work, and what I knew about his life outside of work, etc."

"I'm sure that was difficult. Did you know him well? On a personal level, I mean?" Without realizing it, Jonathan switched from an empathetic supporter to an anxious individual, looking for information MJ or Walt could run with.

"I didn't spend time with Vinnie outside of work. He tried to establish a relationship years ago, but I shut that down. HR's come to me more than once to discuss his attempts to build what he called 'friendships' with a number of women within the company." A faint chuckle escapes Joyce, but Jonathan doubts she finds anything humorous about the situation.

"Oh... sorry. Didn't mean to pry." That's a lie.

"This falls within attorney-client privilege, right?"

"Absolutely."

Jonathan senses her relief as Joyce prepares to unburden herself. "The guy was a pig. He spent most of his time wandering the halls, chatting with every pretty woman in the place. I guess, in a twisted way, I should feel special. He chased me, too." Another forced chuckle escapes.

Jonathan's taken aback by the honesty. "Yeah, I got a weird vibe when I met him. I thought it was because he was a retired cop. Those guys always have a vibe."

"True. But that's not why I called. I'm on my way to have dinner with Michael to talk about Vinnie, and I'm sure he'll be looking for the most recent status of the lawsuit. I want to make sure I have up-to-the-moment information to share."

"I'd put it this way: discovery's progressing, and Schneider's playing games. He agreed to a seven-day extension for the pending discovery responses but keeps pressing the topic of settlement. He's mentioned more than once to remember my obligation to ask my client."

Jonathan is standing on the sidewalk outside the restaurant. He catches himself looking around to see if anyone's watching him or, worse, trying to eavesdrop on his conversation. "I've been spending a lot of time tearing through the records. I have questions about some of the documents, which I hope will be answered when I get Tommy's report. And I have a bunch of new questions for Drs. Spencer and Johnson. But you already know that."

"Okay. First, I'll mention the settlement to Michael tonight at dinner so that you can tell Schneider to shove his obligations up his ass. Second, I think the meetings have been set, although they may need to be pushed, given today's developments."

Jonathan wants the meetings to occur as soon as possible. "Understood, although I …" Suddenly, Jonathan notices a guy standing at the end of the block who's waiting to cross the street. The traffic is light—he could've gone any number of times. Jonathan is working to absorb every detail he can when the stranger catches Jonathan watching him. The stranger looks both ways and jogs across the street without hesitation, never once looking back.

"Jonathan? Hello, Jonathan? Did I lose you?"

"Sorry. Someone was walking by, and I didn't want them to overhear our conversation." The hair on the back of Jonathan's neck is standing up. Did he follow him and Emily? Are there others watching them? Are there people in the restaurant assigned to surveil him? MJ's information has his paranoia skyrocketing. He regains his composure to answer Joyce. "As I was saying, I expected that. No problem." The stranger's presence makes him desperate to get back to Emily.

"Okay. Thanks for the update. I'm pulling up to the restaurant. I'll let you know if anything comes up during dinner. Enjoy the rest of your evening, Jonathan."

"Thanks. You, too."

Jonathan scans the street, not seeing anyone else who looks suspicious but notices a security camera on one of the buildings on the corner where the stranger crossed.

Jonathan walks with purpose as he re-enters the restaurant. The knot in his stomach tells him there's more to this, and his gut is rarely wrong. He hates to admit it, but he needs to come clean with Emily. And although Walt is a nervous wreck, he needs to know everything, too.

Jonathan takes a deep breath and returns to the table, sits down, and immediately drinks the entirety of his wine as he tries to tamp down his fear. As he reaches for the decanter, he notices a plate of fried calamari that's almost empty.

"Sorry, I didn't wait. I'm starving." Emily smiles, reading the concern on Jonathan's face.

"That's fine. Thanks for saving some." He returns the smile, hating himself for what he's about to do... What he needs to do.

73

J oyce valets her Mercedes and saunters into the restaurant, fatigue growing with every step. Michael arrived before her and secured a booth in a dark corner, one that allows him to keep his back to the wall.

"Michael." Joyce slides around the half-moon-shaped booth so she's facing Michael. She notices the empty tumbler in front of him just as a waiter in a starched white tuxedo shirt with a perfectly-tied bow tie approaches.

"Good evening, ma'am. May I get you something to drink?"

Joyce enjoys a nice glass of wine but rarely drinks hard liquor. Tonight's different, though. It's been a horrendous day and has the makings of being an even worse evening. "A Woodford Old Fashioned, please."

"Yes, ma'am. Another sir?"

"Double, Johnnie Blue... Neat," Michael casually instructs before waving the waiter away. He throws back what's left of his drink and gives Joyce an odd look. "Gonna be one of those nights, huh?"

Even a casual observer can tell Michael has enjoyed more than one beverage, putting Joyce on high alert. "It's been an impossible day. You have car service, right?"

"Yup, I left the Bentley at home."

"Good."

The waiter places a small drink napkin in front of Joyce and sets down her drink. He then replaces Michael's empty glass with a fresh scotch. "Do you have any questions about the menu?"

Frustration bleeds through the exhaustion as Joyce refuses to let an intoxicated Michael control the evening. "We're going to enjoy our drinks right now. I'll flag you down when we're ready to order," she snaps.

"Yes, ma'am." The waiter fades into the background without a sound.

Joyce takes a sip of the Old Fashioned. The sweetness of the bourbon tastes amazing. She's already contemplating a second. "We need to talk."

Michael toasts her with his scotch. "Yeah, yeah, yeah…"

"Shut the fuck up and listen." Joyce looks around to see if anyone overheard her.

"Unless you're here to tell me the lawsuit's quashed and the IPO will be launched tomorrow, there's nothing left to discuss."

"How about Vinnie, you cold-hearted prick?"

Michael's dismissive tone proves her description is correct. "Not a big deal. We need a new Head of Security. HR will take care of that."

Joyce has had enough, and the bourbon's taking hold. "You're a heartless bastard. This is fucking serious!" She ignores the surroundings this time, staring straight at Michael. "His death is a message."

"A message? I don't need a goddamn message. I know what needs to be done, and you're the one that's supposed to do it. I've been telling you that for weeks." Michael inhales half of the liquid in his glass.

Joyce is livid, her neck ablaze with anger. Everything to do with both the IPO and the litigation sits in her lap—as does Vinnie's death. Although Michael doesn't know that piece. The last thing she needs is this stupid son-of-a-bitch reminding her of the monumental task she's facing.

As her dark side rears its ugly head, Joyce looks around and lowers her voice. "Need I fucking remind you that I'm not the one who was given 20 million dollars? It was you—not me—who is expected to pay it back. With interest." They've talked about this too many times, and she's done with his bullshit antics.

Michael doesn't even try to keep his voice down. "If you do your job, I'll do just that."

Joyce realizes the scotch now controls the conversation. She's upset with herself for not having anticipated this and gotten to the restaurant sooner. "Listen and listen closely. Billington keeps pushing back. This lawsuit is the stumbling block."

"Then get rid of the lawsuit, or get rid of Billington."

Joyce scratches the blotches on her neck. "How many fucking times must I tell you? It isn't that easy."

"Settle the case, launch the IPO, everyone's fuckin' happy. Sounds easy to me." Michael finishes his drink and waves the waiter down while holding up his empty glass, the universal sign to request another.

She's infuriated by Michael's apparent ignorance as to how the world works. "I'm going to say this for the last fucking time. We can't settle this case. Not only will it bring more lawsuits, the insurance companies aren't willing to pay what it'll take even if we throw our million-dollar self-insured retention on the table." Joyce takes another drink. "And before you ask, settling without the insurance companies creates other problems. To do so may result in a complete loss of insurance coverage, and that would be disastrous. Again, this situation isn't easily resolved."

The waiter delivers Michael his next drink. "Would you like another, ma'am?"

"I won't be here much longer."

"You were hired—for a hefty fuckin' price, I might add—to get Propentus through an IPO," Michael says, slurring some of his words. "Now, you're controlling the lawsuit that stands in the way, using the attorney you, and you alone, selected. And you can't get Billington to do his goddamn job. I'm happy to share these facts with anyone who fucking asks."

Joyce sits back. Is that a threat? Does he really not know who has the power in this relationship?

"You *really* don't want to go there, Michael. Trust me," Joyce says as she grabs her handbag from the booth seat and slides out. Although she walks out calmly, she hopes that Michael is paying attention. She's far angrier with him than she ever was with Vinnie.

74

The waiter delivers their entrées and refills Emily's wine glass. After offering fresh ground pepper, he fades into the background.

With a mouthful of ribeye, Jonathan looks up and asks, "How is it?"

Emily smiles back. Shrimp scampi is one of her favorites. "It's delicious. However, I can't remember. Does red wine go with scampi?"

They both smile.

After his experience outside, Jonathan can't wait another moment. He takes a deep breath, and with a look so caring he feels it run through every fiber of his being, he puts his fork down. "There's something I need to tell you. I know you'll have questions, but if you let me finish, some may be answered."

Emily looks up, confused and concerned. "Is everything alright?"

Jonathan looks around as his paranoia provides another adrenaline spike. Maybe they should be at DEFCON 1? "For the moment."

Jonathan takes a sip of courage from his wine glass and scours the restaurant for danger before telling Emily everything. He relays his concerns about Propentus and, to a lesser extent, Joyce, careful not to violate attorney-client privilege. He eventually tells Emily about his various Toyota sightings, the guy outside Walt's house, and the guy on the street moments ago.

Jonathan glances around the restaurant again and continues. "I'm not extremely worried, but Walt's connections tell him that Vinnie Napolitano's death may not be the result of a carjacking. Napolitano had a terrible reputation. He's reportedly connected to a certain group of people and did corrupt things while he was on the force."

Emily leans forward. "Can I ask questions now?"

"Of course." Jonathan didn't mention MJ and doesn't know why.

"Are you safe? Are we safe?"

The panic in Emily's voice cripples Jonathan. He can't bear to hurt her, yet here he is. And he hasn't shared the big stuff yet.

"Truthfully… I'm not sure." Not entirely true. "Walt has his guys keeping an eye on everything. He and I have become more attentive to our surroundings. That's why I noticed the guy on the corner when I was talking with Joyce. He's probably no one."

"But he may be someone?" Jonathan notices the tremble in the wine as Emily lifts the glass to her lips.

"Yes, I suppose so." He hates to admit it, but she's right. Jonathan answers a few more questions, mostly about Propentus, Joyce, Vinnie, and the lawsuit, knowing that Emily senses there's more. She's always been able to read him.

Emily reaches across the table and takes his hand. "Look, I'm in this with you no matter what. I can tell you're trying to protect me. Please don't hold anything back. I'm a big girl. I can handle it."

Jonathan's heart is exploding. If he mentions MJ, he worries that it will intensify Emily's level of alarm or, worse, put her in greater danger. But MJ's the one who told him what's going on. She's one of the good guys.

Jonathan goes for broke. "Okay, there's one more thing. I fear telling you will make things worse, and I refuse to put you, Walt, or my parents, in danger. If that's really what we're dealing with."

Emily looks at him with strength and compassion. "Please tell me. You need to talk with someone. I want to be that someone."

Jonathan opens his mouth to continue but doesn't. "Let's get out of here. We'll have a drink at home, and I promise I'll tell you everything."

• • •

After a tense end of their meal and a quiet ride home, they both change into something comfortable. Emily pours Jonathan a scotch. A double. She pours herself a glass of red wine and sits on the couch with her legs tucked beneath her… Waiting.

Jonathan sits next to her. Tonight's clinking of their glasses has never been more meaningful. He takes a healthy gulp of his drink before beginning. "An investigative reporter named MJ Fernandez contacted me about the case. She's told me we're all being investigated and likely watched. She works with a team of people who provided much of what she's shared."

Another sip of scotch. "She gave me a thumb drive full of information, a large percentage of which could've only been obtained illegally. That said, the information fans the flames of my own trepidations with Propentus, the case, and if I'm honest, the drug Dad's taking."

No holding back now. His pace quickens. "And MJ believes the death of Vinnie Napolitano is somehow connected."

Emily moves closer and gives Jonathan a hug and a kiss on the cheek. "Okay, now I'm scared."

"I'm so sorry. I don't mean to scare you. I've been wrestling with this. But it's important we're all attentive. Walt knows a little but doesn't know everything I just told you."

Emily stiffens. "You've gotta tell him."

"I know. He's already freaking out. I don't want to make it worse."

Emily leaves him no choice. "You *will* tell him. Now, what about your parents?"

"I promise I'll bring Walt up to speed. As for my parents, I'm not going to say a word. It's the last thing they need to be worried about. My priority is keeping everyone safe, but I have to get to the bottom of this. There's something there. I feel it in my gut. MJ has the same feeling, and the two of us are starting to work together to solve the puzzle."

Jonathan notices a tremor in his own hand as he takes another sip before continuing. He's sure Emily sees it, too. "We have the security system here. You have your pepper spray. If you're attentive as you come and go, I think that's all we need."

Emily smiles at Jonathan, finally winning a long-standing debate. "I told you I needed pepper spray."

Jonathan smiles back and raises his scotch. "Yes, you did." He finishes his drink.

The moonlight coming through the window is ominous, bathing them in uncertainty as they sit quietly in each other's arms. Jonathan rests his chin atop Emily's head, silently vowing to get to the truth.

75

Jonathan has won a number of cases here, but this courtroom has never been his favorite. It's poorly lit, small, and located in the bowels of the 200-year-old courthouse. His steady hands smooth the front of his Hugo Boss three-piece suit, the one he saves for closing arguments, as he scans the gathering. Jonathan's eyes stop briefly on his parents and Emily, who are eagerly anticipating the tale he will expertly weave.

After taking a deep breath, Jonathan strides confidently across the courtroom to stand in front of the captive audience in the jury box. "Ladies and gentlemen, the right decision in this case, exonerating my client, leaves the plaintiffs without further recourse. That may seem harsh, but it's the right decision. The only decision."

As he continues reviewing the facts of the case with the seven women and five men, he keeps their thoughts on the importance of always doing the right thing, even when doing so might feel wrong. To emphasize his point, he randomly gestures toward the image of the blindfolded woman holding the scales of justice carved into the wall behind the judge.

Suddenly, the judge stands and stares with annoyance at Jonathan. "Decide," she demands.

The courtroom seems unfazed by the interruption. The court reporter continues to capture every word while the jury watches him, awaiting his next point.

Jonathan is fazed, though. He shifts his weight between his feet and looks to the judge, working to mask the confusion caused by the unexpected demand. The frustration of losing the momentum of his closing arguments comes through in his response. "What decision are you looking for me to make, Your Honor?" he asks through gritted teeth. Being an experienced attorney, the agitation quickly diminishes, and he forces a smile, swallowing his pride.

"How dare you!" the judge snaps. "You know what it is, Mr. Silverman. Do not disgrace yourself before this court by pleading ignorance." She opens her robe to remove a handgun. Spectators begin gasping and ducking in desperation to hide themselves from the bewildering danger.

For a moment, Jonathan wonders how she got the gun past the metal detectors, but then his eyes flash toward his family, who are sitting in the corner with their hands folded in their laps, pleading with their eyes for him to do whatever the judge demands.

Jonathan opens his mouth, but nothing comes out. The eloquence he exhibited in his statements to the jury disappears the second he grasps the gravity of his situation. Fear clouds his mind.

The judge smirks in disgust, then points the gun at his family and pulls the trigger. The thunder of the shot ricochets around the courtroom.

Jonathan awakens with a singular thought: *Why the hell is Vinnie Napolitano now part of the dream?*

76

MJ is finally sitting at her desk for the first time in a while. She's continuing her background work on the Spinelli family as her phone rings. Without looking, she answers the call.

"Hey, MJ, it's 'Andy.'"

Another member of "the team." "Hey, Andy, great to hear from you. It's been a while."

"It has. Would love to catch up if you have time."

"That'd be great! I can break away for lunch if that works."

"Yeah, I think I can make that work. The usual place?"

MJ doesn't know where the usual place is but doesn't want to give that away. "Sure. Say 12:30 p.m.?"

"See you there."

MJ tosses the phone on her desk and sighs. She now has sixty-four minutes to figure out where "the usual place" is and get there. She starts going through the various places she's met members of "the team" before. Did they leave her a new location somewhere? After frantically searching her mind, she's stymied. She can't miss this meeting.

For the next few minutes, MJ drives herself crazy until a thought cuffs her in the back of the head for not realizing it sooner. She enters "the usual place" in her browser's search bar. To her surprise, there are no less than fifty locations identified as "the usual place," mostly bars and restaurants around the country. After scrolling a bit, she finds what she's looking for. Without another pause, she grabs her laptop and phone and sets out on this adventure.

Her hustle gives her the time to circle the block once, searching for anything or anyone that looks out of place before entering The Usual Place, a new bar that recently opened a few blocks from her office. Nothing obvious catches MJ's eye as she completes her reconnaissance.

Less than a minute after MJ walks in, a man walks in wearing an old army jacket, jeans, and spit-shined army boots. She looks his way, and he smiles at her. "Hey, Andy. So glad we could connect on such short notice."

"Me too." Andy is all business.

MJ asks for a booth for two, preferably in the back. They get one in the middle of the dining area. Andy sits with his back facing the wall, giving him a full 180-degree view. MJ watches in awe as he evaluates patrons and counts exits without the slightest turn of his head. His demeanor convinces MJ he can handle whatever arises.

There's small talk until their draft beers arrive and the server leaves. Andy starts the conversation in a low voice. He continues scanning the room in a way that only another pro would identify. "You're in danger."

MJ chokes on her beer but plays it off. "I'm always in danger."

Andy's steely eyes deliver the most intense look she's ever encountered. "Genuine danger. That's why I'm here."

Holy shit! She knows things are getting a little hairy, but this is the first time they've sent someone to personally relay a warning. It must be bad. She's aware that "the team" always knows things she doesn't. She looks at Andy, whose army jacket hangs loosely. He must be carrying, right? She smiles back with uncertainty. "That's troubling." She's trying to keep the conversation short, although the five key questions that begin with "w" flood her mind.

"You've kicked over a hornet's nest. The swarm's angry."

"Options?"

"A few. Outlined within." He nods toward her beer.

MJ never saw him do it, but somehow, he slipped a thumb drive beneath her cocktail napkin. "What now?" She hopes the answer is he'll come home with her and be her bodyguard forever.

"Steps are being taken that will either further anger the swarm or see them migrate to a new location. Either way, they'll show themselves fully."

She knows she can't show it, but MJ is freaking out. What the hell's Andy talking about? What does the phrase *anger the swarm further* mean? "I choose what's behind door number two."

Andy speaks loudly, startling MJ. "Great catching up. I gotta run, but I'm going to be in town for a few days. Let's grab another beer before I leave."

"Sounds great!"

MJ hopes that's code, meaning he's watching her back as this sorts itself out—a thought that sends her anxiety to new heights. As MJ remains seated and sips on her beer, Andy slides out of the booth and immediately on the balls of his feet, ready for anything. He scans the entirety of the room in less than a second and calmly strolls toward the door.

After about ten minutes, MJ catches the eye of their waiter across the room and mimes writing in the air. He nods and returns with the bill. She pays and then snatches the thumb drive. As she gets up to leave, she almost flips over her empty pint glass. MJ looks around, puts her hands in her pockets, and leaves.

She gets outside and ratchets the threat level to the most serious level. She's scared to death, but all of this must mean she's close. But to what exactly?

77

onathan and Walt head to The Jury Room for a quick lunch. After ordering their wings and beers, Jonathan scans his surroundings before beginning. "Walt, I need to bring you up to speed on the Propentus case."

"What's up?"

Jonathan walks Walt through the new information in detail. In addition to reviewing the problems he's personally faced with Propentus and his own suspicions, he tells Walt about MJ and the conclusions she and her team have drawn as a result of their "creative" investigative techniques. Walt is so captivated by the tale Jonathan is weaving that he finishes his beer without realizing it. "You want another beer before I continue?"

Walt gazes at his glass. "Looks like I need one. You want?"

Jonathan shakes his head and takes his first sip. "This one's plenty for now."

Walt returns from the bar with the larger 22 oz. beer this time. "Okay, let's see if I have this straight. Propentus discovered this groundbreaking drug, which is fast-tracked through the FDA. It's poised to launch an IPO and, arguably, make hundreds of millions, if not billions, of dollars. Then, a class-action lawsuit is filed by an ambulance chaser, all but killing the IPO talk. The suit alleges the drug causes chronic kidney disease, a fact that was hidden during the application process."

Walt wipes the foam from his upper lip before he continues. "We're hired to defend them. They're less than cooperative and aren't forthcoming. You and Angela believe there's something funky with the paperwork but haven't been able to put your finger on anything solid."

Walt downs a third of the beer. "One of their investors is a company established about fifteen years ago. The principals of that investment company are a married couple who are battling dementia in an assisted living community in Florida. The attorney who helped them set up the corporation subsequently set up powers of attorney, healthcare proxies, etc., giving their son complete control. A few years after he's given control, the firm makes its first and only investment in a biotech start-up: Propentus."

Jonathan continues nodding as Walt recites exactly what he just told him, knowing his friend needs to speak it aloud to process it. He is, however, darting his eyes around the room to see if anyone is listening to them.

Walt chugs another third. "The son has suspected ties to organized crime but has kept himself out of trouble. He might be gay, which may be the reason he's keeping his head down. The attorney had his own problems. He gets popped for a DUI, which somehow gets dropped. The GC worked with said attorney at the same firm before she moved onto Propentus."

Walt pauses again to take a breath and finish his second beer. "And the Head of Security, who's a piece of shit ex-cop known for screwing around with evidence and other shenanigans, gets killed during a botched carjacking. To top it off, you've gotten much of this information from an investigative reporter nobody knows. That about cover it?"

Jonathan isn't surprised at how succinctly Walt pulls it together. "More or less."

Walt scoffs and shakes his head. "This is unfucking believable. It sounds like a damn movie script. Can Matthew McConaughey play me in the movie?"

Leave it to Walt to bring lightheartedness to the situation. Jonathan shakes his head and closes his eyes. Walt's right. This is too crazy to believe, and they aren't remotely close to figuring anything out yet.

As the wings are delivered, Walt orders another round of beers. "You tell Emily?"

Jonathan has no interest in the wings today. "She knows everything."

"Your parents?"

"They don't need to know right now. Antsalemab seems to be helping Dad, and Mom is happy. She thinks Propentus is the greatest company out there."

Walt aggressively taps his empty glass, his anger roiling. "Now what?"

Jonathan has thought about this a lot. "You follow up with your contacts—discreetly—and see if you can get us a little protection. I'll connect with MJ. I want her to know I've spoken with both of you. I'm gonna ask if her team can use their creativity to identify the guy I saw the other night. There's a camera on one of the buildings."

Walt has a full head of steam now. "Good. This is no time to be a fucking Boy Scout. You know that, right? They've threatened the family. Time to drop the fuckin' gloves."

Walt's right. Someone's changed the rules. But Jonathan has to protect everyone he loves, take care of his client, and keep his own ass safe. All while figuring out who the hell that someone is.

78

It's a beautiful day, and normally she'd walk. Not today. MJ's never this unsettled. She takes a cab home and locks the multiple deadbolts as soon as she crosses the threshold. Her landlord wasn't happy when she demanded it but agreed since she was willing to pay for it. Today, she is glad she was so insistent.

She starts *Miles Davis' Greatest Hits* playlist on Spotify while grabbing a glass of water. After retrieving the external hard drive from the safe, she settles in with Snoopy. His presence brings extra comfort today. She pops the thumb drive into her laptop, having no idea what she's about to see.

As the first page displays on her screen, MJ commits to memory the phone number atop it before reading the contents. This report starts with a list of steps recommended for her safety, many of which she already follows. There are new suggestions, including securing a handgun. Her heart skips a beat at the prospect. For the first time in her life, she's at DEFCON 1, but she wants nothing to do with a gun.

After recovering from a near panic attack caused by reading the warning, MJ continues scanning the document. Anthony Spinelli has done a nice job staying off the radar, which is difficult in today's digital world. But "the team" has tracked his movements for the past few years. They have addresses, credit card statements, tax returns, and travel manifests. He owns a very nice four-bedroom, five-bathroom brownstone in the Back Bay, mortgage-free. He continues to travel to Florida frequently, usually flying first class and staying at the Ritz Carlton near his parents' assisted living facility. His spending habits create questions for anyone who's paying attention, but no one appears to be.

After reviewing the information, Anthony Spinelli remains an anomaly. Where does he get his money? His travel suggests he cares for his parents, but is he stealing from them to support his lifestyle? Where do they get their money? From the investment company? Is there more to the "known associates" issue? MJ puts all other questions aside and recommits to her proven method: following the money.

Next is Joyce Kramer's folder. They've provided everything from her birth certificate to her last gynecological visit. Joyce grew up locally, following the same path many have: high school, college, law school, law firm, and finally, corporate General Counsel. There's nothing in her professional journey that would generate a raised eyebrow. Her spending habits demonstrate a love for luxury. Her clothing expenses alone are more than MJ has made in the past three years combined.

She enjoys diving and has traveled to some of the best dive locations on the planet. She's also spent a fair amount of time in Florida, but there's only been one instance where her time and Anthony's time overlap. He was in Key West, and she was attending a conference at the Ritz on Amelia Island, hundreds of miles apart.

Vinnie Napolitano is the subject of the next folder. It includes the entirety of his police department personnel file and investigative reports associated with his death. Following Vinnie's money is simple: he didn't have any. MJ is astonished at the level of debt he leaves behind. She'd be puking blood if she had that much red on her financial ledger.

She spends time with his personnel file, looking for something... anything. She notes his first three years out of the academy were spent walking the beat in an area that includes The Last Inning. For her, this highlights the question about Napolitano's rumored connection to organized crime. His career path is littered with fits and starts. She questions how he ever made detective. Next in the file are copies of multiple reprimands. Atop this list is one associated with Robert Picciano's DUI case.

Vinnie was one of the officers who responded to the accident. The reprimand, although extremely vague, suggests he caused a break in the chain of evidence for Picciano's blood sample. That break led to the dropping of that charge. Why would he mess with that particular case? Her adrenaline surges as she adds a new string to the wall between Napolitano and Picciano.

After securing the string, MJ pauses to examine the mess on the wall, asking herself the big question: *What's missing?* How does a scientist CEO, his General Counsel, her former law partner, an infirm couple, and their son all come together with a corrupt former police detective? Picciano's Post-It looks like it has spaghetti hanging from it. For a moment, she wonders if he should be at the top instead of Propentus.

The questions swirling in MJ's head come to a sudden halt when Snoopy rings his bell. Her thoughts shift, causing terror to overcome her. She doesn't want to leave the security of her apartment. MJ gives herself a pep talk as she adds pepper spray to the items she grabs for this trip. She'll keep one hand on that while keeping the leash in the other. She hides her freshly dyed hair beneath her hoodie and heads out the door.

MJ keeps her eyes moving as they travel their usual route. Everyone she sees is a threat. Snoopy finds one of his favorite spots and does his thing, and MJ suddenly realizes she needs to let go of the pepper spray to clean up after him. She bitches at people who don't. She won't be one of those people. As she bends over to pick up what Snoopy left behind, a man with no dog approaches. MJ pops back up, drops the poop bag, and points the pepper spray at the would-be attacker, ready to give the bastard a face full.

The man stops short and says, "Andy sent me," and then disappears as quickly as he had appeared. MJ hurriedly tosses the bag into the trash and races home. Snoopy's legs have never moved so fast.

Once safely behind her deadbolts, she leans against the back of the door, sliding down until her ass hits the floor. Tears flow freely as the stress of DEFCON 1 is released.

79

Jonathan is convinced that Tommy O'Hara holds the key. He and Angela agree it's not about the thousands of pages they've reviewed—it's about what's been deleted. While running on the treadmill this morning, he concocts a strategy designed to push Joyce into a corner, giving her no choice but to allow another meeting. He puts his plan into action as soon as he gets to the office.

"Good morning, Joyce."

"Good morning, Jonathan. How can I help you?"

"I'd like to speak with Tommy O'Hara later today. We're under the gun with Schneider; he's filed additional discovery demands. I need to know what I'm dealing with to prepare responses effectively."

Joyce's displeasure with the request is evident in her tone. "I don't believe today's possible."

Jonathan and Walt agreed that if she refuses access to Tommy, Silverman Erickson's out, and Propentus can find new counsel. "I'll send you the questions as soon as we hang up. In addition, I'd like Tommy to walk me through the reports I've requested. I'm sorry, but it has to be today. Schneider's refusing another extension."

Joyce says nothing. Jonathan knows she's mentally weighing her options. Eventually, she comes to the only viable conclusion: "How's three o'clock?"

"See you then. The questions are on their way. Thanks, Joyce." Jonathan pushes send on the email containing his questions, knowing that Joyce will want as much time as possible to prepare Tommy, but it doesn't matter. Today's focus is the edit/delete report. Immediately after sending the email, he sends a message asking Angela to come to his office.

Angela knocks gently on the open door. Jonathan waves her in. "I'm meeting with Tommy O'Hara at 3 p.m. This might be our only shot. What are the most significant questions, in your opinion?"

Angela steps into Jonathan's office and shuts the door before sitting across from him. "First, I'd like to know what they're hiding." They both smile, knowing that's the key question and wishing they could be that direct.

"Very funny. Seriously, how do we get there?"

"I'd start with having him walk through the 'create,' 'edit,' 'delete,' and 'save' process again," Angela says. "Let's see if he's consistent. It'll also put him at ease because it's his area of expertise. He can pontificate all he wants. Next, I'd ask if he generated the edit/delete report you requested. You have to get that report. How we validate its content is a different challenge, but we can worry about that once we see what they give us."

"Agreed," Jonathan says as he nods at Angela. "It could be horseshit, and we won't know. What else?"

"Tommy will be helpful with the process. You'll have to go back to Johnson and Spencer or others to validate what he gives you. What is it you're always saying?" Angela smirks, obviously teasing him. "Oh yeah: *don't get out over your skis.*"

Jonathan smiles at his protégé.

They spend another hour strategizing. Finally, Jonathan stands and stretches. "The meeting isn't until three. If you think of something before then, let me know. By 5 p.m., we should have more information and hopefully more answers. Thanks again for your hard work on this, Angela. I mean it. Couldn't do any of it without you."

Angela smiles proudly and stands too. They both know today's the day.

80

onathan arrives to a somber environment. The eeriness of death surrounding him as he signs in at the main security desk is disconcerting. His level of sympathy for a man he didn't know, particularly given the developments of the past couple of days, is surprising. He blocks those thoughts as he's led to the conference room where Tommy and Joyce are waiting.

"Tommy. Joyce. I'm sorry for your recent loss. Terrible situation," Jonathan says sincerely as he walks toward his usual seat.

Joyce stands and reaches out to give him a handshake. She's emotionally drained, and cracks in her façade are showing themselves. "Thank you. Needless loss of life. With time, we'll bounce back."

Tommy follows Joyce's lead. "Thanks. Joyce said you wanted to see me again?"

Jonathan shifts gears and initiates the plan. "Did you get a chance to look over the questions? I know this is last minute, but we have some deadlines."

"Yes, Joyce and I reviewed them. I think I am ready to go."

Jonathan wonders about that choice of wording. He *thinks* he's ready to go? Jonathan expected the same confident guy he met previously. Maybe he's reading too much into it? "Great. I'd like to start by having you walk me through the 'create,' 'edit,' 'delete,' 'save,' and storage process again."

"Sure." Tommy clears his throat and goes through the entire process again. Step by step. He talks about the limited access, the even more controlled ability to edit, and the double-approval deletion policy.

Jonathan stops him as he begins to talk about data storage. "Sorry to interrupt, Tommy, but I want to commend you. Everything lines up with my notes from our prior meeting. Consistency is important when it comes to depositions and live testimony. Well done."

A huge smile spreads across Tommy's face. Angela pegged it. The way to Tommy's heart is appreciating his expertise.

"Before you jump into the storage piece, I'm hoping you brought along the reports I asked Joyce for." This is it.

"Yes." Tommy reaches into the folder he brought with him, and before Joyce can stop him, he slides it across the table to Jonathan.

"Excellent." He takes a quick peek and looks at Joyce. "Can we take fifteen minutes so I can review these? There may be some immediate questions that jump out. I don't want to waste your time by scheduling another meeting if we can avoid it."

Jonathan knows it's impossible for Joyce to say no. "Absolutely. However, we'll need those back before you leave. I'll have them added to the portal."

During his meeting with Angela, they role-played various versions of this discussion. He hopes the plan they came up with works. "I understand. Please give me ten or fifteen minutes with these, and I'll make sure you get them back before I leave."

Just then, Beverly knocks on the conference room door and sticks her head into the room. "Excuse me, Joyce. I hate to interrupt, but there's an urgent call for you."

Joyce stands. "Thanks, Beverly. Jonathan, I need to ask you for your phone. I can't have you taking pictures of the documents. I'm a stickler for this type of stuff."

This is playing out as he and Angela rehearsed. The hard part of the plan is getting Tommy out of the room. Time to see if their preparation pays off.

"I have to tell you… I'm offended by the implication. If you can't trust me as your attorney, we have a bigger issue that needs to be discussed." They practiced his resentment, too.

"It's not that I don't trust you. From day one, I've been cautious, some say obsessive, in protecting the company's intellectual property. Isn't that right, Tommy?"

A genuine look of camaraderie appears on his face. "Yeah, she's tough on that with everyone. It's not you."

Jonathan reluctantly gives Joyce the phone he placed on the table when he arrived. "It isn't a problem, anyway. My phone died on the way over. Lousy battery life. I was going to ask Tommy if he had a charger that might work."

Tommy jumps up, eager to please. "Sure, I have a charger for almost every phone. Let me see which one you have, and I'll grab one from my office."

Jonathan fights the urge to smile. This is falling into place better than he could've hoped. "That'd be great. It's an iPhone 12. I can charge it when Joyce returns."

Joyce grabs Jonathan's phone as Tommy heads toward his office to get a charger. "Beverly, would you mind sitting here with Mr. Silverman while we're gone?" She looks back at Jonathan. "Company policy dictates all visitors be accompanied by an employee at all times."

"Sure, I can do that. The call's on your direct line." Beverly sits down.

"Great. Thanks."

Jonathan begins reviewing the reports in silence. As he and Angela suspected, there are records that have been deleted that'll seemingly fill in some of the date anomalies they noticed. What he really needs is the actual content of the documents to determine their significance, if any. The list is much longer than he expected, further feeding his suspicions. He thought it'd be relatively small, with Propentus giving the FDA everything and letting them sort it out.

Jonathan has another phone with which he intended to take photos. With Beverly babysitting him, that won't be possible. Joyce's craftier than he expected. Where's Walt and his photographic memory when you need him?

Jonathan begins to write down dates, authors, editors, and deletion approvers for each of the documents. Harold Johnson initiated many deletions, with Joyce Kramer identified as the second-level approver. He flags those in his notes. Deep into the report, Jonathan notices an entire folder has been deleted. He tries to determine what it might be by piecing together what's in front of him. He can't.

Jonathan has no way of knowing if this report is accurate or complete. He has no idea what he'll get via the portal, so he decides to capture as much as he can. He hasn't written this much, this quickly, since the bar exam. Tommy comes bounding back into the room. Beverly gets up and leaves, her babysitting job complete.

"Tommy, you said you could recreate the actual documents that've been edited or deleted, right?" Jonathan asks as he continues to scribble notes.

"Yes, we're required to keep everything pursuant to the FDA guidelines I previously shared."

Jonathan decides to go for broke. "Can you please recreate every document on this report?"

"Sure, and I'll make sure you have every version, not just the final, so you can see the specific edits, too." Tommy makes himself a note.

Joyce comes back into the room, visibly upset.

Jonathan plays dumb. "Everything okay?"

"I'm not sure. The police want to speak with me again about Vinnie Napolitano. They're headed this way."

Jonathan asked Walt to pull a few strings. It didn't play out perfectly, but it did give Jonathan a couple of additional minutes alone with Tommy. Now, he'll see if he can cash in on those. "Can either of you tell me why an entire file would be deleted? Not just individual documents?"

Joyce almost jumps out of her seat to speak before Tommy opens his mouth. "Yes. Sometimes, a document or folder is created, and its contents become more appropriately housed in a different file. The materials are moved, and the original folder's deleted."

Damn it. Neither Jonathan nor Angela contemplated the possibility of documents being shuffled like three-card Monte.

Tommy provides confirmation. "Joyce's right. It can happen that way. I have no idea how often it happens, but theoretically, the process remains the same as long as the person moving the documents has the right access."

Jonathan makes a note and looks back up. "Tommy, I'd like you to recreate all of the documents, files, and folders that have been edited or deleted."

"Sure, I'll add those to the portal, like we discussed."

Bingo! Jonathan locked it down before Joyce could say anything. He's laying it on thick, but he needs Tommy to remain cooperative. "That'd be great. I really appreciate it, Tommy. This IT stuff makes my head hurt. Glad you're on the team."

Jonathan has gotten all he can and isn't surprised by Joyce's reaction to the last two minutes. "Jonathan, I hate to do this, but the police are on their way, and I've no idea how long they'll be here or what they want, for that matter. May we reschedule?"

Forgetting about the ruse of pressure from Schneider, Jonathan cooperates. "Sure. It works better that way. I'm sure I'll have additional questions after my review of the recreated documents. Tommy, thanks again for pulling that together."

"No problem," Tommy says with a smile as he stands.

Joyce slides Jonathan his phone across the table and lets him know she's in charge… again. "Jonathan, I'd be remiss if I didn't remind you that the information to which you've been given access is proprietary. And you and your firm are operating under an NDA over and above your attorney-client privilege obligations."

Jonathan knows she used the word "obligations" to tweak him, but the shot glances off him. He swallows his belligerence this time. "Yes, Joyce. I recall executing the NDA, and of course, I'll maintain my obligations relative to attorney-client privilege. I take that very seriously." They shake hands, and Joyce escorts Jonathan to the exit without exchanging another word.

As Jonathan settles into the car for his drive back to the office, one thing is apparent: he needs the details. Will Joyce let Tommy provide it? Regardless, Joyce's reminder sealed it. There's no other reason to make that statement but as a threat. Jonathan's a lot of things, but stupid isn't one of them.

In truth, he isn't overly concerned. He knows there are exceptions to the attorney-client privilege rule, including the "Crime or Fraud Exception." He's confident defrauding the FDA, either by editing, deleting, or purposefully omitting information, qualifies as a crime. But he needs the proof for what he intuitively knows to be true.

81

onathan is racing back to his office when a call from an unknown number interrupts his thoughts. He contemplates letting it go to voicemail but answers it anyway. "Jonathan Silverman."

"We need to talk."

The heavy breathing is unmistakable. "You okay?"

"Yes."

"When?"

"ASAP."

Jonathan has no idea what's going on, but there's something very different in MJ's voice. He could swear it's fear, but she strikes him as a woman who'd have no issue slugging it out with a Navy SEAL to get to the truth… And his money would be on her.

Another call comes in.

"Hey, my mother's calling, which's never good. Can I call you back?" Jonathan asks.

"No, this number will no longer be active once I hang up."

"Um… Okay… Pick a spot, text me an address, and I'll see you there at 6 p.m." Jonathan clicks over to his mother. "Hi, Mom. What's up? Everything okay?"

"Jonathan. I've told you time and again, I don't just call when something bad happens." Jonathan would challenge that argument, but there's no point. Maybe today will be the first? "I'm just checking on you and Emily. We haven't seen you two for dinner in a while. Your father and I miss that."

"How's Dad doing?"

The lilt in her voice tells him all he needs to know. "He's doing great! This new drug is a godsend. He's happier and isn't forgetting as much. It's amazing!"

Jonathan knows she's stretching the truth but can't determine how far. "How about you?"

"I'm fine. Are you guys free this week? Your father's been begging me to make lasagna."

Jonathan could hear the pleading in her voice. His mother was technically correct; she didn't call for something "bad," but she did want something. Well, there's nothing bad, as far as he knows. The last time she called, offering lasagna was not a positive experience.

"I think so. I'll check with Emily tonight. It'll have to be toward the end of the week."

"That'd be great!" The smile on her face infects her voice.

"Okay, Mom. I gotta run. Call you later. Love you."

"Love you, too."

Jonathan disconnects the call, his thoughts returning to his disturbing conversation with MJ. She sounded anxious. His cell phone chirps again. He glances to see a text from another unknown number—nothing but an address.

● ● ●

After completing her newly needed reconnaissance efforts, MJ sees Jonathan walking toward her from where she saw him park a block away. She waits impatiently outside the restaurant's entrance. When he walks up, they say nothing, but Jonathan smiles and opens the door for her. Against their request and preference, they're led to a booth near the front windows.

After a quick order, Jonathan smiles. "Not sure I like the hair. Pink suits you. What's so urgent?"

MJ delivers the bad news as calmly as her nerves allow: "I circled the block three times before you arrived. Thought I saw something on the second pass, but it was gone on the third. We're at DEFCON 1, and I have a guardian angel. At least for a little while."

Jonathan's mouth drops open with shock. "What the hell are you talking about?"

"My team's pulled some things together. In short, this all revolves around Riccio, Kramer, all three Spinellis, Picciano, and Napolitano. It seems this group's attempting to pull off something big, and it has to do with Propentus."

"That doesn't sound very much like new information," Jonathan says with trepidation.

MJ looks around and then lowers her voice. "How's this for new information? Napolitano used to walk the beat near The Last Inning bar, which is owned by Jimmy Rizzo. Everyone within a twelve-block radius of that place is connected or wants to be. Second, it looks like Napolitano's the one who fucked up Picciano's evidence, forcing the DA to drop the DUI charge. Shortly thereafter, Picciano worked with the Spinellis to set up Excellence Investment, Inc., which years later invested in Propentus, their sole investment."

MJ quickly glances around, then takes a sip of her beer. She hates beer. "And Kramer's squeaky clean. Not even a speeding ticket. They found nothing in her background, and these guys find everything. No one's that perfect. Anthony Spinelli is living far beyond his reported income. Appears to have paid cash for a $2,000,000+ brownstone. Where's he getting his money? Lots of questions, and he's been very quiet beyond continued travel to Florida, presumably to see his parents, given the location of the hotel where he stays."

MJ chokes back another sip, continuing in a clipped fashion. "My new friend, Andy, gave me a dire warning. I'm convinced Andy is ex-Special Forces. Average build, nondescript in every way. There's an electricity in the air that surrounds him. His foreboding eyes are dark and never stop moving. I'm convinced he's a very dangerous man. And he said he was sent *because* of what they're finding. Thus, the elevation to DEFCON 1."

Jonathan sits back and remains quiet. It's obvious he is evaluating the information MJ just shared. Without Jonathan adding anything to this one-sided conversation, MJ continues. "My team's not fucking around anymore. They're tearing through every document, and I mean all of them, associated with the drug: initial research, every trial, FDA application, FDA investigative notes, approval, and post-approval research. It's their intent to compare everything the FDA has to what Propentus has in their system and to what you've been given."

MJ looks around the room and stares out the window as she delivers the last piece of news: "I took my dog to the dog park and met a new friend, someone who looks exactly like my other new friend. All he said was, 'Andy sent me,' and then vanished into thin air." MJ's hands are shaking like she's terrified—and she is.

Jonathan obviously sees her distress. "Okay. First, I want something a little stronger to drink. Actually, it's a need, not a want. You?"

"Nope. I have to stay sharp. Andy made that clear. That and I should consider getting a gun."

• • •

Jonathan's mind reels with all that MJ's shared. It doesn't surprise him when he sees a tear slide gently from the corner of MJ's eye, but the sight still knocks the air from Jonathan's lungs. He's had crazy clients who made all sorts of threats, but this is next-level shit. He thinks of Emily and the imperative of protecting her. Jonathan waves the server over and orders a Macallan.

They sit in silence until the scotch arrives, although MJ's eyes continuously scan the room.

Jonathan takes a long drink of his scotch and gives the brown liquid a moment to work. "Okay, that's better." He takes a breath before he delivers his information to MJ. "My partner has contacts within the police department. They think it was staged to look like a carjacking. I've been pushing my client for documents, specifically documents that were edited and/or deleted. My paralegal and I both believe there's something amiss, and we hope the recreated documents will shed some light."

Jonathan finishes the scotch and continues tap dancing along the edges of his attorney-client privilege obligations. "The CIO can and has created a report that contains what's purported to be a complete list of everything that falls into those two categories. He also agreed to recreate the actual deleted documents as well as the missing folder's information. And…" He joins the surveillance sweep. "... Kramer threatened me before I left, which tells me I've hit a nerve."

Jonathan's stunned by his openness with a reporter. He's in uncharted waters and knows there's no going back. With the scotch's help, he decides to follow Walt's advice. He doesn't drop the gloves; he throws them violently onto the ice. Just like eating crow, he's all in.

"Listen, can your… team… check on something? I think I was tailed the other night. The guy walked off, but there's a camera on one of the buildings." Jonathan writes the address on a napkin. He slides it across to MJ, who just stares at it. "Maybe they can ID this guy and tie him to someone else. We need to figure out who's behind this."

MJ gradually moves the napkin toward the edge of the table.

Jonathan wants another drink, but Andy's warning is echoing in his head. "Have you told anyone?"

MJ places the napkin in her pocket without looking. "There's no one else for me to tell. I can't go to my editor yet. He'll call the cops and the paper's internal security team. No one needs that." The fatigue in her drained tone belies her attempt to change topics. "Okay. This file that was deleted. What do you think's in it?"

"No idea. Hoping to know by tomorrow, but given Joyce's threat, I don't hold out much hope."

Jonathan watches in awe as he sees the terror and exhaustion in MJ's eyes morph into confidence and anger, the fuel that now feeds her drive to find the truth. "I'll make sure we do."

Jonathan noticed her use of the term "we" in that statement. "MJ, I think you need to get clear of this…" Before he can continue, she throws up a hand and interrupts. He unwittingly awakened the Kraken.

"No fucking way. This is the story of a lifetime. Pulitzer kinda shit. Besides, I'm the conduit between you and my team. You can't do this without me."

She's right. Most of what they have is because of her and the creative effort of her team. Sure, he's working on everything, but it seems like she has a hundred people who know no boundaries, sitting at computers around the world with nothing but time on their hands. "I really think…"

MJ's determination is back with a vengeance. "Stop fuckin' thinking. The topic's closed. End of discussion."

Jonathan's father's face flashes before his eyes as the call with his mother's replayed. *This new drug is a godsend.* He shakes his head, trying to clear cobwebs. "Okay. One step at a time. Let's get the deleted stuff first."

MJ stands to leave. "Thanks for the beer, counselor. And by the way, fuck you. My hair looks great." She puts her hand on her pepper spray and walks out the door with an energy that frightens Jonathan.

He drops a 50-dollar bill on the table and heads toward his car, finding himself adding MJ to the list of people he needs to protect.

82

J oyce locks the doors, checks every window, and turns on the
security system. While this is her normal routine, tonight
it brings no comfort. The pressure is overwhelming. She
hopes a shower will wash away her problems and her sins.
She pours a glass of wine and heads to the bathroom.

After standing in the shower until the hot water runs out,
Joyce puts on a pair of leggings and a comfortable, oversized
sweatshirt. She heads to the kitchen, grabs the bottle of wine,
and eventually collapses on the couch, relaxation finally fighting its way to the surface.

She's enjoying the peace and quiet when her doorbell
rings. She's not expecting anyone, so she ignores it. It rings
again, and this time it's accompanied by a heavy knock.
Someone is eager to get her attention.

Joyce tip-toes to the door and peers through the peephole. Fear grips her chest as she almost drops her wine glass.

"Open the fuckin' door. I saw the light comin' through the
peephole change when you looked out. I fuckin' know you're
in there."

Joyce stands frozen, her mind swirling with dread.

"You gonna open the fuckin' door, or do I need to open it for you?" The voice is louder and angrier this time. The last thing she needs is for him to be angry or for her neighbors to see him.

Joyce is about to open it when she remembers she'd set the alarm. All hell would've broken loose, and he'd be beyond pissed. She turns off the alarm, takes a deep breath, and opens the door.

His smile reminds her of Jack Nicholson looking through the bathroom door in *The Shining*. "Ain't you gonna invite me in?"

She needs to keep this short. "Come in."

He walks in and looks around. He's been here before, but it was a long time ago. "Love whatcha done with the place."

A disingenuous smile appears on her face. "Thanks. Drink?"

"Bourbon."

"Sure…" She should've remembered. It's been years since they've been in the same room. The last time didn't end well—okay, it could have ended worse—she's still alive. Joyce goes to the kitchen and pours Basil Hayden into a rocks glass. For a moment, she considers ditching the wine and pouring herself one but decides against it.

She hands him the glass and watches as he takes a large sip. "Ahhhh… Fuckin' love bourbon. Don't usually drink on a weeknight, but seein' tonight's a special occasion and all," he says as he walks over to one of the couches, sits down, and puts his feet on her handmade, live-edge coffee table. "This is fuckin' nice. You done good for yourself, counselor."

She needs to get him out of her home. "What can I do for you?"

He's a rattlesnake ready to strike. "You fuckin' know what!"

Oops… Wrong question. "Yes, I suppose I do."

"And?"

She repeats herself… Again. Her annoyance is evident. "As I've explained, the pending litigation is creating concerns. They talk about market volatility, but right now, it's this lawsuit that's scaring investors. No one wants to invest in a company that's facing that type of liability. Launching an IPO under these circumstances is a fatal mistake."

"Can you think of another fatal mistake?"

Joyce shudders at the memory from all those years ago. "I'm working with the investment bankers."

Without warning, he throws the expensive tumbler against the wall. The crash is deafening. Bourbon-coated shards of glass twinkle as they skitter along the tile floor. "Not fuckin' fast enough."

Joyce flinches, having experienced his rage before. Rather than using what courage she has left to ask him why he's sitting in her living room instead of Michael's, she makes a feeble attempt to drag Michael back into the boat. "We understand."

"You got thirty fuckin' days. Not thirty days and one minute. No more discussions. Capeesh?"

"Yes."

He gets up with the demeanor of a dear friend and heads to the door. "Great to see ya again, Kramer. Thanks for the drink."

She closes the door behind him, saying nothing. It's better than screaming the truth… *It's never been great seeing you!* She's shaking so badly that wine spills from her glass. It gets worse as she realizes that the thirty-day clock started the moment she shut the door.

83

S noopy barks wildly at the unexpected knock on the door. MJ grabs the Louisville Slugger signed by "Big Papi" that leans against the wall for occasions like these. She peers through the peephole.

Seeing Andy standing there causes her to physically leap backward, almost stepping on Snoopy. No one from "the team" has ever come to her home. While she isn't surprised that they know where she lives, the fact that he's standing there is terrifying and would move her to a DEFCON 0 if it existed.

MJ leans the bat against the wall and takes a few seconds to unlock the deadbolts. As she opens the door, Andy looks back toward the elevator and walks into her apartment without waiting for an invite. He glares at Snoopy, who immediately turns tail and heads to another room, whimpering.

MJ closes the door, finding herself whispering, "What the fuck are you doing here?

"The nest you kicked over is much larger than initially thought, and the swarm's getting angrier by the minute."

She's too tired for games. And the whispering's over. "Enough with the fucking code, already!"

Without saying a word, Andy takes a small device from one of the many pockets in his ancient army jacket and strolls through her apartment. After walking through the two bedrooms and the bathroom, he continues his recon in the kitchen and around the perimeter of the living room. "Appears to be clean."

MJ realizes he and his little toy are searching for listening devices. "Again, what the fuck's going on?"

"You've stumbled upon something extremely dangerous. Document comparison ends with problematic findings."

She gives up on fighting the code. "Dangerous? Problematic? How? To whom?"

"To everyone taking the drug, to you, and anyone who's associated with the lawsuit and likely their friends and family."

It may be the confidence bolstered by the personal ninja standing next to her, but MJ's panic flips to excitement. She knew there was a story here. She could feel it in her bones. Her heart races. "Okay, so give me what you know."

"Not here."

"You just walked through my entire fucking apartment without permission, I might add. Your toy didn't beep once, so why not here?"

"Open spaces are less problematic. We need to be outside. Somewhere you don't usually go."

MJ's spinning out of control. The questions are bombarding every neuron. She needs answers and will do whatever she must to get them. "Fine. Come on, Snoopy. Let's go for a walk."

Snoopy peeks out from the bedroom where he's been hiding since Andy walked in. MJ puts the leash on him, grabs a couple of poop bags, and throws on her spy jacket, which feels more appropriate than ever right now. Lastly, she makes sure she has her pepper spray.

"I suggest you grab your AirPods, too."

MJ rolls her eyes, retrieves her AirPods from her night-stand, and returns to find the front door open and Andy already walking toward the elevator.

After speed-walking to catch up, they stroll to the eleva-tor with only Snoopy's leash clanking on his collar, filling the silence. Andy is on high alert. MJ notices he's barely making contact with the floor as he walks. Definitely Special Forces.

Outside, Snoopy tries to make the traditional left turn. Not today. MJ tugs on the leash and starts in a different direction. After a couple of blocks, she can't take the silence anymore. "First, do you have a thumb drive for me?"

"Keep facing forward. Put your AirPods in," Andy commands.

While she's doing that, her cell phone rings.

"Listen to me closely. I'm right behind you. Keep walking and talking, just like you would with any other person. Don't look back. I'll be there; you don't have to worry about that."

"Whatever. Do you have what I asked for?" MJ's distaste for this cloak-and-dagger bullshit grows with each step.

"Before it's delivered, there are a few things you need to know."

"Okay." MJ's shaking as the adrenaline's surging.

"This thing's huge and involves people who play by their own set of rules. Rules brought to the U.S. by Italian immi-grants years ago."

MJ almost stops and turns around. "Holy shit… The mob? Are you fucking kidding me?" She thinks about the references to Anthony Spinelli, Jimmy Rizzo, and Vinnie Napolitano in prior reports. Questionable connections have just become pieces of string to be added when she gets back to her apartment.

"Keep walking and looking forward. These people have already eliminated one threat. We have no doubt they'll continue down that path if forced."

MJ desperately wants to turn around and ask questions. She's struggling with this communication style. "And?"

"What you'll see is inconsistencies in the documentation."

"What kind of inconsistencies?"

"The kind that would've likely led to a different decision."

MJ can't help herself. She stops and turns around. Andy is a full block behind her. She would've sworn he was two steps behind.

"I thought you said you had my back?"

"I can run the length of a city block in less than ten seconds. I have your back." He sounds annoyed.

"No more bullshit. I'm sick of walking. I want answers." MJ stands her ground, staring at him.

"That's not how this works. Particularly if you want what I have in my pocket."

Shit! "Okay, okay, I'm going." She turns around and starts walking again.

"These are serious people. There's significant money involved, and they'll do anything to keep a lid on this, as proven by the recent carjacking that's made the headlines."

MJ knows the answers to the questions bouncing around in her head are probably on the thumb drive. Her mind shifts toward something much more personal. "How long will you be my bodyguard?"

"My friends and I have been around for a couple of days and plan to stay around for a few more."

"Will I know when you decide to leave?"

"Yes."

"Thank you." This makes MJ feel a little better, but she thinks of something else. "Are any of your friends working with the attorney?"

Andy sidesteps the question. "He must never know about us. Never. To do so creates significant danger and will jeopardize any future working relationship you may seek."

MJ has already taken a step she's never taken before in telling Jonathan her team has been the source of some of the information. And he was quick to realize they're ready, willing, and able to cross any line to follow where the data leads. She knows it's a risk trusting Jonathan, but he's taken a huge risk by trusting her. He's put his career at stake by possessing the information she's shared. As long as the mutual trust remains, she's confident she hasn't put any stress on her long-term relationship with "the team." "How do I legally confirm what you've provided?"

"Not our problem," Andy replies flatly. "Our arrangement has been clear from day one. You've navigated the issue before. We trust you'll do it again."

"Understood. Can I get my present now?" MJ was anxious to retreat to the safety of her apartment. Even Snoopy seemed anxious to get home. A creature of habit, for sure.

"One more thing. Whatever you're going to do with this information, it needs to be done quickly. Their patience has worn thin."

"Got it. The present?" MJ asks again.

"It's sitting on your coffee table." The call ends.

MJ spins around, finding Andy gone. She's energized yet petrified. This emotional rollercoaster is unlike anything she's ever experienced, and she's convinced it's just getting started.

As they head toward her apartment, Snoopy lets MJ know he has some business of his own to attend to. She tightens her grip on the pepper spray as they walk past her building. Her eyes in constant motion, methodically scanning for "hornets."

84

Jonathan throws on a pair of khakis and his favorite Peter Millar polo. He sits on the small bench near the front door to put on his loafers. "You ready?"

"Yeah. How'd your mom sound?" Emily asks. Jonathan finds it endearing how much she cares, another reason for the conversation he plans to have with his dad.

"Great, actually. I don't think there's anything waiting for us tonight besides lasagna. That reminds me, no wine until we get home. Mom's holding strong for Dad."

Emily gives Jonathan a kiss and a wink. "Wine when we get home, then."

"I want to stop for flowers, though. Like a strong hand-shake, bringing your host a gift is a moral imperative," Jonathan says with a grin. "Add being a gentleman to that, and you have 50 percent of the conversations I had with my dad as a kid."

Emily laughs at the visual.

Despite the stop, they meet another necessity: arriving on time. Jonathan knocks on the door, and they walk in. The scent of sauce and garlic creates a warm embrace, welcoming them into a loving and compassionate home.

"These flowers are beautiful," Nancy says as Jonathan enters the kitchen and hands her the bouquet. "We'll put them in water and display them on the table. How are you, Emily?"

"I'm good. You seem to be in a terrific mood." Emily embraces Nancy.

"I am. Life's good," Nancy says as she releases from the hug. "Joe's doing great, and I have my son and his beautiful girlfriend here for dinner. It doesn't get any better than this."

Jonathan turns his smile into a pout. "What, no hello for me?"

Nancy smirks and then winks at Emily. "Oh, hello, Jonathan. You have a lot to be happy about, too."

Jonathan holds his ground. "Yes, but not as much as Emily."

Nancy doesn't miss a beat as she takes a playful swipe at Jonathan. "You're the lucky one if you ask me. She's out of your league."

Jonathan smiles but doesn't disagree—internally. "I'm not going to stand here and take this abuse." There's laughter in a kitchen that was somber just a few months ago. He heads to the living room, still laughing.

"Hey, Dad."

"Oh, hey there. How ya doin'?"

"The real question is, 'How are *you* doing?'" Jonathan says, taking a seat on the couch facing his father, who sits comfortably in his recliner.

"I'm pretty good."

"That's great to hear."

Just then, Nancy hollers from the kitchen, "Come and get it!"

Throughout dinner, Jonathan watches his parents. The smile on his mother's face has never been brighter. His father smiled a few times, too. Despite this, he can't help but fall into the hole of despair, knowing these days will become fewer and farther between as time does what it does. His father's struggles will grow, eventually stripping the smile from his mother's face. He buries the thought and strains to embrace the joy and happiness of the evening.

After an amazing dinner, Jonathan and Emily clear the table. As Nancy checks to see who might want coffee, she notices Joe heading to his recliner. She leans in and, in her best conspiratorial voice, whispers, "Don't tell your father, but I switched the coffee to decaf months ago. He still thinks he's getting the real thing." Nancy winks at them.

Emily winks back and whispers, "Your secret's safe with us."

Jonathan loves to see his mother like this, but woeful thoughts crawl back to the surface. His mother is strong, but he worries about the toll this is taking on her as a primary caregiver. When Dr. Mancini said those fateful words, her world shifted on its axis. She was lower than he'd ever seen but has rebounded, happily focused on taking care of the love of her life. He dreads the next plummet, which they all know hovers on the horizon.

He has read articles about the stress on caregivers and the importance of taking care of them, as well. He often wonders how his mother deals with the fear and uncertainty when she's alone. Jonathan hasn't shared his fears with anyone; he can't. The isolation he feels fuels his daily struggles with the thought of losing his father.

Taking the case and defending the drug that he's seen positively impact his father's life was supposed to be another way to help. But the information MJ has provided, coupled with his own observations, makes him question everything.

Nancy pours the coffee. "I didn't want to say anything in front of your father because it upsets him when we talk about it, but he's doing great. We go for our walks. He doesn't argue with me when I give him egg whites, fish, or anything else that's good for him. Well, not as much anyway."

"That's great to hear, Mom. And you seem to be doing better." Again, Jonathan drew on techniques he'd learned from the materials he'd read.

"Yes, as I told you on the phone. This new drug is a god-send. And it's all because of you. If you didn't fight with Medicare to get it covered, we'd be in a very different place."

Guilt's pressure on Jonathan's chest makes him wonder if he's having a heart attack. For a split second, he thinks about coming clean. He glances at Emily, whose look suggests she knows what he's thinking. The imperceptible shake of her head sends a clear message.

He nods in acknowledgment as his gaze returns to his mother. "A lot of the credit goes to you. You're driving the lifestyle changes which have a favorable impact on the disease's progression. He wouldn't be doing any of those things if it weren't for you."

"I can only do so much," she concedes. "It's the drug. I know I've said it a thousand times and will say it a thousand more, but thank you for fighting for your dad. You've made the difference. I love you." Nancy gives Jonathan a hug as a tear rolls down her cheek.

Jonathan looks over and sees Emily watching them with love, pride, and admiration as he's pulling back from the hug. "I'll do whatever it takes for both of you. That's my job. Now, enough of the mushy stuff… What's for dessert?"

As Jonathan and Emily head home to enjoy a glass of wine, Jonathan's thoughts drift to the mission he and MJ have undertaken. There's something going on with his client that's put everyone he loves in danger. He has to figure out what's going on, who's behind it, and how to resolve it. And time isn't his friend.

He's pulled from his thoughts as Emily reaches over and grabs his hand. "You're a terrific son. You know that, right?"

"I'm just doing what any son would do." Jonathan is glad Emily can't see him blushing in the darkness.

"You never questioned funding this drug for your father. That's no small thing. Yes, you have the means, but not everyone would be willing to do what you're doing. I love you for that!"

"I love you, too." Jonathan's attention returns to the road as he realizes he missed a chance to speak with his father about the future.

85

MJ unhooks Snoopy from the leash, bolts the door, launches her spy jacket toward its usual spot on the floor, and rushes to the coffee table. Andy's ability to leave the drives without her noticing is amazing. The guy's a magician and a ghost. MJ wriggles out of her bra without taking off her shirt—a woman needs to be comfortable.

She shifts to get comfy, grabs her laptop, and settles in on the couch for a long night. There are thousands of documents on the drive. The first section she's led to compares the actual FDA file with what Jonathan's been given access to: they're identical. The FDA file includes the documents that Jonathan requested from Tommy. The FDA must've asked for them, too. Jonathan will come to the same conclusion the FDA did: There's nothing of significant concern. MJ checks this twice. There must be a mistake.

After spending a considerable amount of time on the first file, MJ stretches and grabs some caffeine before moving on to the next folder, which focuses on the human trials. It, too, has thousands of pages, including the medical records of each trial participant. Again, the FDA file and Jonathan's file match exactly. MJ's beyond confused at this point but trudges forward, trusting clarity will emerge from the darkness.

Over the next few hours, she learns about each participant. The level of detail is unnerving. She's vicariously witnessing how dementia ravages an individual and their family. Each fear, frustration, and moment of anger is captured in the records, as is the power of love.

MJ knew it was a horrific disease before she started investigating this story, but after reading document after document, every step of the tragic journey is revealed in great detail. It's obvious no two are the same. The records reflect a positive impact on those who took Antsalemab versus those who didn't, but the depth of the impact varies greatly. Some saw no further deterioration, while others continued to deteriorate but at a slower rate.

MJ doesn't notice her shirt's wet. Her eyes have been leaking as she wades through each personal tragedy. She eventually realizes the documents don't support what she and Andy discussed.

"And what you will see upon your review is inconsistencies in the documentation."

"What kind of inconsistencies?"

"The kind that would've led to a different decision."

MJ steps away from her laptop for a minute, chooses a random jazz channel on Spotify, grabs a cold slice of two-day-old pepperoni pizza, and returns to the couch to redouble her efforts. The next folder holds the consolidated information relative to trial participants with kidney-related side effects. She's surprised to see every participant taking the drug saw an increase in blood pressure. Each received a blood pressure medication, which helped, but pressures never returned to pre-trial levels. The majority of those on the placebo experienced no blood pressure increase. A small number of participants in both the test group and the control group developed kidney stones.

The ambiguity is clarified, finally, in the last section. It wasn't what was given to the FDA or what was given to Jonathan that mattered. It's about the research, documents, and communications Propentus tried to erase. "The team" discovered failed attempts to permanently delete records. The removal attempts were exceptional but not quite good enough.

MJ has never been prouder of the work she's doing, as her entire mindset shifts. It's not about awards or a front-page byline. This is about righting a horrific wrong—a wrong driven by a few money-hungry motherfuckers she's going to make pay. If she can move fast enough... and stay alive.

86

"We didn't agree to this communication approach."

"What, no 'hello?' Fine. I'll make it quick. Coffee in twenty." The line goes dead.

Jonathan stares at his phone in disbelief. Does she expect him to drop everything whenever she demands? Not going to happen, and he vows to make that clear as he's racing to the coffee shop around the corner. He arrives, but she's nowhere to be seen. Now, he's pissed. He walks back outside.

MJ rounds the corner and makes eye contact with Jonathan a couple of minutes later. Her hoodie is up, and she walks past him without saying a word. He follows, his anger building. He doesn't have time for this spy bullshit, which is the second thing he'll tell her when they get to wherever they're going. Two turns and ten minutes later, they end up in a sandwich shop.

They're both in line when MJ drops something on the floor. Jonathan instinctively moves to pick it up.

"Hey there. You're kinda cute," MJ says in a flirty tone. "I don't see no wedding ring. How 'bout I give you my number?

Give me your phone." MJ cocks her hip and holds her hand out for his phone.

Jonathan catches on fast. Without hesitation, he smiles and hands her his phone. A few others in line witness the exchange, but it's too commonplace these days to register with anyone. She enters a phone number, then opens a box for a new text message and types something but does not push send. There's no record if it's never sent.

"Hope you call soon. Bye!" With a longing look, MJ leaves Jonathan standing there with his phone in his hand, blushing with embarrassment. He looks down at the text screen. He deletes what's been typed but follows the instructions to the letter.

Jonathan casually walks to the rendezvous spot, trying not to draw unwanted attention to himself. When he arrives, he sees MJ coming from around the corner, probably completing a security sweep.

She looks down at the bag he's carrying and holds her hand out. "Thanks for lunch. A girl's gotta eat."

Jonathan compliantly hands her the bag, completely forgetting the vow he made as he left his office. "Are you going to tell me what the hell's going on? And you're welcome."

"I am, and you're not going to be happy. Call the number I gave you and start walking. I'll be following."

Jonathan begins walking, blindly following her every direction. He's never done this with any other person in his life. What is it with this woman?

MJ answers on the first ring. "Keep walking, and don't turn around. We'll talk to each other like the thousands of others who do it on these streets every day."

Jonathan holds the phone to his ear, modulating his tone and volume. "Listen, I'm not at your beck and call. I have things to do."

"You sure do. Your client's not a great corporate citizen, and I have the proof."

Jonathan stops but doesn't turn around. "What are you telling me?"

"Do. Not. Stop," she says forcefully. "Keep walking, and pay attention to your surroundings. I'm telling you what you suspect occurred definitely occurred. My team has delivered the smoking gun."

"Is it really that bad, or has this spy shit gotten to you?"

"First, fuck you. I'm trying to help you. Second, it's that bad. In fact, it's worse."

Jonathan's mind jumps from thought to thought. He should've never taken the case, nor had his father start the drug. It takes a millisecond for him to leap to the danger his actions have created for everyone he loves. He slows his pace. "I need to see the proof."

"That would put you in jeopardy both personally and professionally."

He's already thrown the gloves onto the ice. There's no going back. "I need to see it."

"Meet me at Fenway. The Sox are playing tonight."

Jonathan mentally reviews his plans for the evening. He's grateful that Emily knows everything going on. He would hate to add the stress of lying to her about where he was going to his long list of stresses. "Okay, where?"

"Our usual place. And thanks again for lunch." MJ disconnects the call, turning the corner before Jonathan spins, finding her long gone. How the hell is he going to find one woman out of 37,400 people?

87

Jonathan deciphers the clue and buys a ticket to the Sox game through Ace Ticket. His seat is in the bleachers, right below the Dunkin Donuts sign. He may have a general idea where she'll be, but finding a woman in a crowd this large will be difficult, particularly since she took the pink streaks out of her hair.

Jonathan arrives early and heads to the Red Sox Team Store, where he springs for a hat and a jersey. He completes the disguise by grabbing a beer. He needs to be hard to spot, too.

As Jonathan strolls through the area beneath the park, a petite woman dressed like every other fan walking the opposite way bumps his shoulder, jostling his beer. He can't tell if it's MJ but decides to follow her. His sunglasses hide his nervousness and the constant scanning of his eyes. As he catches up to the woman, who has better luck navigating the crowd than he does, he realizes it's not MJ.

As if she sees him through eyes in the back of her head, she stops and spins around. She looks at her phone, then back at him. Jonathan's angst spikes as she steps within a foot of him. "Excuse me. I'm sorry, I spilled your beer when I bumped into you. I'm happy to buy you another."

Every spy novel he's ever read comes to mind, and alarm bells are ringing in his head. "It happens." He moves to get away from this stranger, but she's persistent.

"Let me buy you a Sam Adams. I think the stand's down this way." She heads off in search of a beer vendor when Jonathan yells over the crowd, "I'm meeting someone. Thanks anyway."

She returns, and as Jonathan's about to do the thing he's never done in his life—shove a woman—she reaches into her pocket, pulling out a folded $20 bill. "Okay, but please take this, then." She pushes the bill into his hands and melds into the crowd.

Jonathan unfolds the bill, which holds the key to locating MJ.

The game is getting ready to begin, so the direction he needs to go is against the tide of people. The crowd isn't happy as he pushes through, but he doesn't care.

By the time Jonathan arrives at the location, there's little beer left in his cup. At least twenty-five people, besides himself, have some of it on their clothing. He sees MJ standing in a concession line, looking like all of the others eagerly waiting for a sausage or a Fenway Frank. He hates hotdogs but admits they always taste better at the ballpark.

Jonathan walks up and puts his arm around her waist, eliciting grumbles from those waiting in line behind her. "Hey, wasn't sure which stand to meet you at."

Once they get to the front of the line, MJ orders a sausage with extra peppers and onions and a bottle of water. Jonathan orders another beer. Forty bucks later, they're walking toward the bleachers.

MJ doesn't drop a single onion as she walks through the crowd, eating the sandwich. She looks around and then at Jonathan with a mouthful of sausage. The crowd noise provides cover. "It's fucking bad. There's no other way to say it."

"I need to see it," Jonathan says, trying to act casually, and takes a sip of his beer.

"You will. But you need to prepare yourself. We have to agree on the next steps. We can't go our separate ways on this."

"Why not? It's safer."

"We'll both end up dead." MJ makes that statement without emotion. It's a fact. She takes another bite and keeps walking.

Jonathan's spent enough time with MJ to know she's careful with words. He knows she believes it to her core, but he still needs to see it himself. The stakes are too high. "I need to draw my own conclusions."

MJ stops on a dime, angering the people behind them. Without another word, she spins and walks in the opposite direction. Jonathan finally catches up.

She's visibly seething. "You're pissing me off. I've been straight with you from the jump. Your 'holier than thou' routine's going to get me, you, and everyone you love killed. You need to accept the facts and stop fucking around."

MJ finishes her sandwich, takes a couple of napkins out of her pocket, and wipes her mouth. She hands the napkins to Jonathan and stomps away. He's disgusted until he feels something wrapped in the napkins.

A group of twenty-somethings laugh at him as he slowly puts the napkins in his pocket and makes his way to the exit. He needs to get to his laptop.

88

"Good morning, Michael. How are you feeling today?" Michael looks up with bloodshot eyes and places his pen on the desk. "I'll feel better if you're here to tell me the IPO's launched. Better still, if you also tell me that the lawsuit's been quashed."

Joyce sits in one of the chairs in front of his desk. "I called Billington and told him the IPO will be launched within thirty days. Period."

"And?"

"I hit him where it hurts—the wallet. I told him we'd take our business elsewhere if he can't make it happen."

"Excellent. The greedy prick stands to lose big money should that happen. Do you think he can do it?"

"What I do know, based upon a conversation with a visitor to my home—to my fucking home, Michael—is that this has to happen."

"Better you than me." Michael chuckles. He obviously finds himself hilarious.

Joyce does not. "Not fucking funny. He can't risk being seen anywhere near you, and you fucking know it."

"True. So, he put you on a thirty-day clock?"

"He put *us* on the clock, which started ticking the moment he left my house. He showed up after you and Johnnie Blue prevented us from chatting."

Michael puts his feet up on the desk. "Relax, Joyce. Think it through. There's nothing they can do to us."

Michael's dismissive tone causes Joyce to lose control. "You smug fucking idiot. How the hell did you get this far in life? Maybe, and that's a huge maybe, we're okay until the IPO is launched. Have you thought about what happens once the debt's paid?" Joyce spells it out clearly for him. "There's no longer a need to keep a pain in the ass CEO and his hot-shot General Counsel around."

Michael seems like he's had enough of her shouting for one day. He stands, allowing him to peer down on her. "Calm the fuck down. Nothing's going to happen. Debts are paid, and everyone walks away happy and filthy fucking rich. Including you."

Joyce can feel the telltale blotches taking over her entire neck and face. "I'm fucking done. You're not only an idiot, you're naïve. You're going to get us all killed."

She storms out of his office. Michael's smugness made his true feelings transparent. He didn't care if he was an idiot as long as he was an extremely wealthy idiot. Joyce understood that a billion dollars can make a lot of problems go away, but she didn't share Michael's confidence about their futures.

89

Jonathan marches straight to Walt's office. He doesn't want to drag him deeper, but he needs someone other than MJ to help him think through this. "Walt. I need to speak with you about something." He's never given Walt a more serious look in his life.

"Sure. Now?" Walt looked like he was in the middle of prepping for a trial. Case files littered his desk, not that it was normally neat and tidy.

"Yes, but not here," Jonathan says cryptically.

"What gives?"

"Do you remember where I took Emily on our first official date? Don't say it out loud."

Walt leaps up, tipping his desk chair over. "What the fuck's going on, Jonathan? You're never this serious. And yes, I remember. I remember everything, right?"

In his singular focus, Jonathan forgot. "Oh, yeah. Anyway, meet me there in an hour. Don't be late. And Walt, I mean it. No fucking around." Jonathan returns to his office and grabs his laptop; the thumb drives are in his pocket. He walks out without a word to anyone.

They arrived at TD Bank Garden five minutes apart. Jonathan took Emily to a concert for their first date. She said she liked music, so a concert it was.

"Let's walk." Jonathan's head swivels slowly from side to side as he strides off.

Walt doesn't do cardio every morning and struggles to keep up. "Slow the fuck down!"

Jonathan keeps up the blistering pace, forcing Walt to do the same. "I'm going to tell you the specifics at the highest possible level. After that, you can ask questions."

Walt nods while trying to catch his breath. Jonathan looks around one more time and spits out a summary of everything he read the evening before. "Propentus hid information from the FDA. Information that confirms that Antsalemab has a high frequency of serious kidney-related issues. In short, it's very likely the drug gave Ms. Cosgrove and the others chronic kidney disease. Also, one of Propentus' key investors, to the tune of approximately $20 million, is tied to organized crime."

Walt gives himself whiplash as his head snaps to the side to look at Jonathan.

Jonathan continues as if he's talking himself through it out loud. "My guess is everyone's banking on the IPO, which stalled because of the lawsuit. Once launched, the O.C. connection will probably cash out and move on. Their payday will be huge if previous estimates are close. I believe Propentus and or the mob are following us and the investigative reporter I told you about. Questions?"

Walt returns to staring straight ahead. Jonathan watches him, trying to wrap his head around this.

Finally, Walt looks back at Jonathan. "I could almost see something being withheld from the FDA, but organized crime being so brazen as to secretly invest in the company before the drug is approved suggests a legendary level of conspiracy and balls." Walt's worry is evident. "How many people know about this?"

Jonathan finally slows down. "There are a number of people who know, but I believe the question you're asking is how many people outside the criminals know about this. To my knowledge, the answer's three plus MJ's team."

"Jesus. You, me, and a reporter?"

Jonathan couldn't tell if Walt was astonished, angry, or worried. "Yes," he replies simply.

"What happens now? What about the lawsuit? What about Propentus? Do you know who at Propentus is a part of this? This would require a few players—the right players."

"The 'what happens now' discussion is why we're here. I agree, but it would be as few as possible. My guess is the CEO, that bitch Joyce Kramer, and apparently Vinnie Napolitano are involved. After that, I'm not sure."

Walt's definitely shaken. "I need a drink."

It takes a minute, but they find what they're looking for: an out-of-the-way dive bar, complete with a sticky floor and a trough in the men's room. Hiding in a booth in the back, they order a drink. Bottled beer is the safest option.

Jonathan lowers his voice. "I need help thinking through this. I wanted it to be someone I trust implicitly and who's the smartest person I know. They aren't available, so I'm picking you."

Walt groans at Jonathan's weak attempt to lighten the mood. "Yeah, yeah. So, back to the question. What now?"

"My first thought's to just blow this whole fucking thing wide open. Let the reporter get a Pulitzer and then deal with the litigation fallout after. But that doesn't work for a couple of reasons. First, the moment that occurs, the company is done. No IPO, no more drug, no more anything. Second, the employees of Propentus who are involved with this will likely suffer some tragic event, like a carjacking. Once that's done, the person who reports the scenario will be next on their list."

They've barely touched their beers. "In addition to defending Propentus, I've been seen with said reporter, which means I'm probably on that same list. They'll presume I know everything and that I would've confided in my law partner. Lastly, they'll take vengeance on everyone I love." Jonathan gulps at the thought. "It's what they do, right?" He was hoping for a confident "No" from Walt.

"I'd like to say you've watched *The Departed* one too many times, but there are millions, maybe billions, at stake." Walt shakes his head in disbelief. "These guys will whack their brother over a $1,000 debt."

Jonathan erases the vision of Martin Sheen falling from the top of a building in that movie. "Okay, so we agree this is really fucking bad. The question is, how do we get out from under this?"

"Well, you could keep your mouth shut, pretend you know nothing, and bill the shit out of the client," Walt suggests. "But you'd also have to convince the reporter to kill the story."

Jonathan cocks his head and looks at Walt.

"Yeah. I know. The 'Dudley Do-Right' part of you will never do any of that."

Jonathan looks down. "I can't let others get hurt by this drug. I know some are being helped by the drug. They'll suffer, too. But for the opposite reason."

Walt can obviously read the look in Jonathan's eyes and connects the dots. "I'm sorry, Jonathan."

"There's so much at stake. So many lives in jeopardy on all sides." Jonathan rubs his temples to relieve some of the stress he feels.

Walt watches the weight of the world crashing down on Jonathan. "Look. There has to be a solution. We're gonna sit here until they make us leave. We'll figure this out."

Jonathan takes a sip of his warm Sam Adams. "We have to." His mind has been running through scenario after scenario… He can't see it.

90

There they sit, with ties loosened, sleeves rolled up, and empty beer bottles and coffee cups in front of them. As always seems to be the case, Walt has somehow spilled coffee on his tie. After five hours of talking, thinking, evaluating, and even scheming, they've hit a brick wall.

Jonathan refuses to give up. "Okay. Let's go through the options one more time."

Walt's frustration erupts: "Enough. We've looked at this from every possible angle. They all lead to two choices: blow it up or don't. Both have devastating results for someone, and both leave our loved ones in jeopardy."

Jonathan decides to look at it through the one lens he's never used: selfishness. "Maybe we're looking at this the wrong way. Maybe there's only one question we need to answer: What's the best way to protect my family and friends?"

Walt returns to where they started. "The best way? Do absolutely nothing. Completely ignore what you've been given, and let the shit flow down the path it's on," he says matter-of-factly. "Let the company figure out how to launch the IPO, and who knows, maybe the ongoing trials will achieve the right result. Everyone wins."

"No, they don't. And my family and friends will always be in danger." Jonathan is tired and frustrated that the conclusion always returns to this. "What's to say our Italian friends won't decide to clean house, including our house, after MJ runs her story?" Jonathan cringes and mumbles the thought that's plagued him since learning the truth. "I was wrong to take this fucking case, and I never should've pushed to put my father on this fucking drug."

Walt looks directly at Jonathan. "Whoa... Hold up. Don't do that. You've done everything a good son, no, a great son, would do. There was an opportunity to secure a treatment, and you took it. You can't blame yourself for that."

The stubbornness the Silverman men are known for comes out. "I can, and I will. Now, I have to figure out how to fix this and protect everyone in the process."

Walt sighs, having seen his best friend display this ugly trait many times before. "Fine. I have an idea. We aren't going to solve this tonight, no matter how hard we try. We've been here for a few hours, and I'm starving. Let's find a nice steak and a great bottle of wine."

The depth of Jonathan's despair is profound. Worse still, Walt's right. "I'm not saying you're right. I'm saying I'm hungry. If you need something that extravagant, you're buying."

Walt cracks a smirk. "Whatever, as long as we get a decent meal. Come on, let's get the fuck outta here."

As they move to leave, Jonathan stops just outside the door. He scans the street, looking for anything out of place. Once satisfied they're safe, he walks silently next to Walt, dwelling on the monumental decision in front of him—a decision no one should have to make.

91

I t's a glorious day! Joyce is smiling as the hot water and steam envelop her body. She can't wait to get into the office. After a couple of glasses of wine last evening, the answer came to her as if by divine intervention. She's been focusing on the wrong thing. Everyone knows *perception is reality*. Her focus needs to be on influencing perception, which is a hell of a lot easier than changing reality. It's about spin, and she can do spin. If Silverman does what she instructs, she'll have this spinning like a tornado in Kansas in no time. She can't believe she didn't think of it before.

"Ms. Kramer on line one."

"Hello, Joyce," Jonathan says.

"Jonathan, I've been thinking about the lawsuit, and I wanted to get your thoughts on two things." She decides to play nice in the sandbox and keep the client card in her back pocket.

Jonathan's voice cracks a little. "Sure. What is it?"

Joyce is excited to share her brilliance. "I'd like you to file a motion to dismiss the case. We'll time the filing to allow you to hold a press conference with me by your side immediately thereafter. We'll tell the world why the case has no merit and that you've filed the motion accordingly."

"What are you talking about? We haven't come close to completing enough discovery to succeed with such a motion." The unwillingness in his voice is clear.

"Jonathan, this is a strategy, one that serves multiple important purposes. Before I go further, I must remind you of your attorney-client obligations as well as the terms of your NDA."

Jonathan explodes. "Joyce, I've acknowledged my responsibilities multiple times. If you don't trust me, we should part ways. It's that simple. If you do, I don't want to receive another reminder. Are we clear?"

Joyce wasn't expecting the rebuke. There's only one person who gets away with speaking to her like that, and Jonathan isn't him. But she needs Jonathan if she has any chance of meeting the deadline imposed. "Understood. What I'm about to share with you is tangentially connected to the litigation. Propentus is on shaky financial ground and needs this IPO to move forward now. The motion's a strategy to create space for that to occur."

"This is not a good idea, Joyce. We don't have enough to create a remotely viable basis for such a motion. Second, now's not the time to get in front of a camera. There are too many variables we can't control."

"I fully expect the motion to fail. But it must be filed for the greater good. There's no ethical concern here. If ever questioned, you can argue the filing was designed to force that idiot Schneider to outline his case to the court. And let's be honest, he doesn't strike me as someone skilled at crafting a cohesive argument, verbally or in writing."

"Joyce, this is premature. You know that. Hell, a first-year knows that. 'The King of the Fender Bender' doesn't have to be a literary giant. All he needs to do is provide a list of the discovery that hasn't been completed. He doesn't need to show his hand, or at least not much of it. Motion denied."

No more playing nice. The clock's ticking. "Jonathan, as your client, I am instructing you to file the motion within the next forty-eight hours."

Jonathan swallows hard. "Joyce, I want written confirmation noting my disagreement with this step and your direction to do so. That's non-negotiable."

"Fine. I'll have the letter messengered over within the hour. Anything else?"

"Forty-eight hours isn't a lot of time. I can assure you the motion will be well written, but from a support perspective, it's going to be exceedingly weak. If you're looking to create some breathing room for the IPO, it has to have teeth, wouldn't you agree?"

Joyce does agree and has come to the discussion prepared. "I have executed affidavits from Harold, Renee, and Tommy. The content of those will be the basis for the motion."

Jonathan can't keep the amazement from his voice. "Joyce, I want to review their content before I agree to file the motion. I will not knowingly file a motion based upon inaccurate or false information."

"I wouldn't ask you to do that. You'll see the content is in line with the conversations you've had with them." Okay, there may be a few "inaccuracies," but Joyce knows he isn't able to identify them.

"Send everything over within the hour, Joyce. I'll review it and let you know."

"Jonathan, this motion must be filed within forty-eight hours. I'll get back to you with the details for the press conference."

Her next call will be to Andrew. It's all coming together.

92

onathan's in a stupor as he walks from behind his desk. In the moments since hanging up, his emotions are all over the board. From disappointment in himself for getting involved to abject fear for the safety of those he loves to outrage for what Propentus and their mob friends are trying to get away with. He's baffled by his conversation with Joyce. She can't possibly be serious, can she?

He and Walt discussed how he'd approach all future interactions with Joyce to ensure he didn't tip his hand. He was going to kill her with kindness, following her lead no matter where it went, but neither of them contemplated this possibility. While the motion isn't against the rules, knowingly filing a motion based upon patently false affidavits is.

Joyce tested Jonathan's resolve, reminding him of his obligations… again. He was close to throwing the phone—and anything else within arm's reach—across his office. Under more traditional circumstances, this would've been a watershed moment. If he was going to step away, this

conversation would've been the trigger. But these aren't traditional circumstances.

Jonathan finds Walt in his office. He doesn't ease into
anything. "Joyce has demanded I file a motion to dismiss
within the next forty-eight hours, using affidavits from the
CIO, Head of Research, and lead researcher. I pushed back,
and after I basically said they were fraudulent, she played the
client card."

"Holy shit!" Walt drops his pen on his desk and gives
Jonathan his undivided attention.

"Then she wants the two of us to hold a press conference
about it to put investor concerns at ease."

"The IPO must be right around the corner."

"That's my thought." Jonathan still didn't have a good
feeling about this and was hoping Walt would have words of
wisdom to offer. When nothing else came, he said, "I gotta
run to give Angela a head's up, but I wanted to let you know
the clock's ticking." Without another word, Jonathan turns to
head to Angela's office.

The pressure of not knowing what the hell to do with the
information they now possess is bad enough, but this change
in plans has Jonathan feeling like a piece of coal that needs to
become a diamond within forty-eight hours.

93

Joyce moves the next piece on the chessboard. "What've you come up with, Andrew?"

"Joyce, I told you there's not much that can be done until the litigation's resolved," Andrew explains. "The underwriting banks remain concerned. Some have threatened to pull out of the deal."

Michael strolls into her office. Who told him she would be on the phone with Andrew? She refocuses on the task at hand. "Christ. If I waited for you, Andrew, we'd all be in trouble. I can't give you specifics, but I am working on that with our attorney. The next step in the litigation will be made public in the next forty-eight hours. You'll be ready to launch the IPO immediately thereafter. That's a statement, Andrew, not a question."

"Joyce, it can't occur that quickly."

"Bullshit, Andrew. That's not an answer." Joyce pinches the bridge of her nose and steadies her voice. "You do your part, and let me worry about the rest." She slams the phone's handset onto the receiver.

Michael's face reveals his pleasure with the overarching conversation, but he obviously wants details. "You didn't tell me you had a resolution plan?"

Joyce is sick of placating this idiot and blurts out the first thing that comes to mind. "First, who the hell let you into my office while I'm on a call? And second, I told you I was taking care of everything. That's all you need to know."

Michael's jaw drops at her insubordination. "Excuse me? What'd you say? This is my goddamn company, and you work for me. Don't ever fucking forget that."

She's had enough macho bullshit. The clock's ticking. If she can't pull this off, it's over in the most final way possible. "Michael, I don't have time to play fucking patty cake with you. You want—. Strike that. You *need* this to happen. I'm making it happen. A simple 'thank you' will be sufficient."

Michael's not happy, but she can see he knows she's right; it has to happen. "Cut the shit, Joyce. I want to know exactly how you're going to make this happen."

"You'll want plausible deniability if it comes to that, so specifics aren't important. Within the next forty-eight hours, Silverman is going to file a motion to dismiss. That'll be followed by a press conference outside the courthouse. This should calm investor concerns. I'll force Andrew to launch the IPO. Everybody wins."

Michael looks at her incredulously. "Do you really think it'll work?"

Joyce thinks of Vinnie and about making another call. "Get the fuck out of my office, Michael."

94

Jonathan's mind refused to stop spinning long enough for him to sleep. He gave up and headed to the gym early. The euphoria he gets from running always brings clarity, and he's pleased today's no different. His hour on the treadmill was spent wrestling to identify the next best step. While he had reluctantly agreed to remain in lockstep with MJ, the role of decision-maker was never agreed upon. It's time for him to tell her what that next step's going to be.

After calling three different numbers, he finally finds her. "Good morning."

"Good morning," MJ answers quizzically.

"Lunch. Noon. Your favorite sandwich shop." Jonathan hangs up, not wanting to give her an opportunity to ask questions or, worse, disagree. He returns his focus to drafting the ridiculous motion his client demanded.

A few hours later, Jonathan heads to the rendezvous spot to meet MJ. Not long after arriving, she shows up with her dog in tow. He wasn't expecting to meet someone with a dog and almost missed her. He spots her standing with her back pressed against the building's wall, with her hoodie obscuring others' view of her but giving her a 180-degree line of sight. She's near one of the large windows, which allows those outside to observe the sandwich-making occurring inside.

MJ's getting better at looking around without it being noticeable. "Snoopy needs to walk."

"Fine, but no phone bullshit."

Jonathan bends down and scratches Snoopy behind the ears before they start walking down the street. After a block, he speaks softly but firmly. "I have a plan, and you're not going to like it."

MJ's head turns more quickly than she likely intends it to. "Oh?"

"I'm going to speak with my father today. Not my mother, just my father. I've always relied on him to give it to me straight. He always has, although many times I didn't like the way it felt."

MJ looks at him, puzzled. "I thought you wanted to keep them clear of this."

"Adding him at this stage is non-negotiable. I have two paths in mind. The path I follow will be driven by what he says," Jonathan states.

"Says to what?"

"That's between me and him."

Jonathon can tell she realizes there's no use arguing.

MJ walks, looking straight ahead. "I'll say it again: this shit's real, and this type of bullshit will get us killed. When are you seeing him?"

"I'm headed to their house as soon as I am done here. What's your plan?"

"Guess it doesn't matter until 'daddy' tells you which righteous path to walk."

Jonathan can see she's as on edge as he is. "Cut the shit. This is serious for all of us. There's no time for pettiness. You're the one who said we need to be in lockstep. We can be once I have this conversation."

"Whatever. Here's a new number." MJ turns and storms away without another word. Jonathan reads her body language clearly.

None of them has come up with a solution that checks all the boxes. He hopes his father's guidance will bring them one step closer.

95

Jonathan pulls into his parents' driveway. He's played this conversation over and over in his head; it's now or never. "Knock, knock. Anyone home?"

"Hi, honey. I wasn't expecting you. Can I pull something together for a late lunch?" Nancy wipes her hands on her apron.

He gives his mother a quick hug before she turns and opens the refrigerator. "I appreciate that, Mom, but no need. I had a big lunch before I came over. I was hoping to chat with Dad for a few minutes."

Nancy's voice is muffled as she's rummaging through the refrigerator. "Are you sure? It's no trouble."

"Yes. I'm sure. Dad?"

"He's in the living room." Jonathan hears the disappointment in her voice. Maybe he should've let her make him a sandwich.

"How's he doing today?" Jonathan knows his mother's been overly positive each time they've met with Dr. Mancini. He needs honesty today.

"He's good. We took our walk, and he hardly complained. He ate his lunch without a problem, and now he's watching an old John Wayne movie."

Same old optimism. He'll soon find out for himself. He smiles and heads toward the living room. "Hey, Dad…"

Joe looks up, startled, rubbing the sleepiness from his eyes. "Oh, hey there. What are you doing here? Everything okay?"

Jonathan looks behind him to make sure his mother didn't follow. "Yeah, everything's fine. I need to talk to you about something. Something you can't share with Mom or anyone. Can you promise me that?"

Joe pulls the recliner's handle and puts his feet firmly on the floor. He sits upright, and his eyes don't leave Jonathan's as Jonathan settles on the end of the couch nearest Joe's chair. "Of course. What's going on?"

Jonathan leans over, his forearms on his thighs. He takes a deep breath, and the words begin to flow. He tells his father about the lawsuit and the hidden documents but leaves out how he came by those documents. He shares his trepidations about the investors but leaves out the organized crime connection. He also omits his concerns about their safety. He concludes by saying he has to make a decision. "So, I'm here to get advice. I'm not sure what to do."

Joe takes a deep breath. He's listened intently for the past fifteen minutes and didn't interrupt to ask a single question. As he exhales, he turns his head toward the kitchen, presumably to make sure Nancy isn't nearby, listening in. In the fatherly voice Jonathan remembers from his childhood, he says, "Let's start where we always start. What's the right thing to do?"

Jonathan expected this. It's been like this his entire life. It's ingrained in everything Jonathan does and will do. And this is the reason Walt refers to him as "Dudley-Do-Right."

The words gush forth. There's no holding back now. "The right thing for whom? What's right for one person may be wrong for another."

Jonathan can feel his father rummaging for the right question, like looking for a light switch in a dark closet. "Okay, let's try it this way. What option causes the most damage?"

Jonathan's exasperation bursts forth. "Again, the most damage to whom? There are people who are being hurt by the drug, and there are people who are being helped. Someone gets hurt either way."

Joe's calmness is palpable. "From the day you were born, your mother and I have preached doing the right thing above all else. And remember what we've always told you. The right thing isn't always the easiest or the most popular. But it isn't about easy or popular. It's about what's right."

Jonathan glances at his feet. This is the moment of truth. He has to say the words. There must be absolute clarity relative to what's at stake. He wipes away another tear with the back of his hand and looks his father in the eye, with hopelessness in his own. "Dad, I only have one shot to get this right. If I expose this company's failure to provide all the information to the FDA, it will ruin the company and, in all likelihood, bankrupt it. Even if it doesn't, the FDA will immediately withdraw its approval, and the drug will be recalled and stop being produced. It'll be gone. Forever."

Jonathan sees the look of realization appear on Joe's face, yet his father's conviction to do what's right never wavers. Not for a second. "Is exposing the company the right thing to do?"

"In the eyes of those it's hurting or will hurt, yes, it's absolutely the right thing to do. In the eyes of those the drug is helping or will help, it probably isn't the right thing to do."

"I know you're worried about me. But take me out of the equation. Does that change your analysis?"

There it is—the immovable obstacle Jonathan's been unable to get over, around, or through—his father's dementia and the benefit this revolutionary drug seems to be providing. Jonathan's discussed all his other concerns openly, but the benefit to his father has always been lurking at the forefront of his mind, yet remained unspoken. His father's words squeeze every ounce of love from Jonathan's heart.

"I can't. You're my father. The man who raised me to be the person I am today. We've all noticed this drug's amazing impact on your life. Even you would have to acknowledge that. Taking you, and Mom for that matter, out of the equation is impossible."

"Jonathan, there are meaningful moments in a man's life when he faces hard decisions. Decisions that not only require but demand sacrifice. And yes, it's true that some sacrifices are greater than others. I've had those moments in life, and this is one of those moments for you, and for that, I'm truly sorry. The only advice I will offer is to do what you believe is right."

Jonathan looks again to make sure his mother isn't nearby as he wipes away another rogue tear. "I've made difficult decisions before, Dad. You know that. But this one's different, and you know that, too."

Joe reaches over and gently places his hand on Jonathan's knee. "Have you considered this? If those documents had come to light initially, which was the right thing to have occurred, the FDA wouldn't have approved the drug. No drug. No one hurt, nor anyone benefiting."

Jonathan is now second-guessing himself. His father is right: this is his decision to make, and his alone. It wasn't fair or right to involve him. "Dad, I'm sorry…"

"Jonathan, I love you, and I believe in you. You'll make the right decision. Of that, I'm certain. You always have, and this time will be no different." Joe pats his son's knee and smiles reassuringly.

Jonathan looks at the amazing, selfless man he's lucky enough to call his father. They both know exactly what Joe's saying. Jonathan's unable to keep the monumental grief he feels from showing on his face.

Joe stands and leans down to give Jonathan a warm embrace. Jonathan feels the security he felt as a child and never wants this moment to end.

Jonathan knows what must be done and what ramifications will be born from this decision.

He leans back from the embrace, taking one last look toward the kitchen. With a glint in his eye, he whispers to his father, "I'm going to ask Emily to marry me."

Joe's mood shifts instantly into inquisition mode. "She's a wonderful girl. What makes you so sure she's the one?"

"Dad, she's become everything to me. She accepts me for who I am, warts and all, and I accept her. I've never felt like this before, and truthfully, I never thought I would. If this is what love feels like, I never want to spend a day without her."

Joe's wrinkled brow morphs into a wide smile of understanding and affection. "Although it took me a lot longer to get there, that's how I felt about your mother and still feel today. So, if that's truly how you feel, *do not* let her get away. I'm thrilled for you!"

Jonathan stands. They share another hug, and Jonathan sees, for only the second time in his life, a tear slide down his father's cheek. With a look that encompasses the enormity of their conversation, Jonathan winks. "And remember, you promised not to tell Mom about *anything* we just discussed."

Jonathan says his goodbyes as his mother makes him promise to bring Emily over for dinner the following week. He collapses into the driver's seat as his emotions erupt. He spends fifteen minutes sobbing like he hasn't in years, praying his mother doesn't look out the window.

The discussion sears into Jonathan's soul as the full weight of his father's words is felt. He's caught off-guard as the overwhelming sorrow quickly transitions into immense pride. His father knows the decision Jonathan has to make will return him to the horrifying path in front of him. Worse still, it will steal the renewed smile from the woman who's been his everything for over forty years... Yet, he never wavered. Not once.

Jonathan wipes his face with his shirt sleeve and starts the car. He has a lot to do and less than forty-eight hours to do it. He makes a mental checklist as he drives back toward the office, forgetting to be vigilant of his surroundings.

Despite the gut-wrenching, emotional conversation with his father, Jonathan's leaving his childhood home energized. He's decided. All that's left is the how and the execution while keeping everyone safe.

It's time for MJ and Walt to meet. He's sick of being a go-between. MJ isn't going to like it, but the James Bond bullshit consumes time they no longer have.

● ● ●

Because of his lack of awareness leaving his parents' house, Jonathan didn't notice the Ford Explorer parked down the street. It followed him as he left and remained a quarter of a mile behind him.

96

"Yes?"

"He's met with the reporter again."

"And?"

"They're acting nervous. I think they know they're being followed."

"And?"

"And this can be concluded as a package if that's the desire."

"I'm told the attorney's playing ball."

"'Bout fuckin' time, right?"

"Anything else?"

"The reporter?"

"Everything's on hold at the moment. But remain ready."

"Understood."

Anthony Spinelli disconnects the call. He's in Florida visiting his parents. The sim card and the burner both skip and bounce along the shoulder of I-95 about twenty miles apart. He knocks over his bottle of water and almost finds himself in the ditch while trying to retrieve another phone from his

359

glove compartment. He dials a newly memorized number. It's picked up after the fourth ring.

In a hushed tone, he hears, "What?"

The screaming begins. "You answer on the first fuckin' ring."

Joyce is still whispering. "What do you want?"

"Answers."

"Already provided."

"Not the most important one. When?"

"Press conference, day after tomorrow."

Anthony jerks the Cadillac across two lanes of traffic while somehow demonstrating the ability to flip off those who challenged his maneuver. "What the fuck? Press conference? This is supposed to be a quiet operation. Are you fuckin' kiddin' me? No fuckin' media!"

"It'll get you what you and your boss want."

Unknowingly, his foot's pressing the accelerator closer to the floorboard, commensurate with his building anger. "I shoulda knocked some goddamn sense into ya the other night. Nobody needs a fuckin' spotlight."

"The spotlight's the diversion, which will give what you want."

"Tick fuckin' tock…" He launches the phone out the window without disconnecting the call. It hits the pavement at 90 MPH, shattering into a thousand pieces.

97

Joyce is in the ladies' room, more scared than she's ever been. She peeked under the door of each stall while she was whispering with Anthony. She's alone, but she doesn't know for how long. This has to happen so that all of the craziness stops. They promised she would never hear from them again once she delivered.

She turns the phone off and then looks at herself in the mirror. She hates what she's become. She gently wipes her face and neck with a damp, cold paper towel before returning to her office.

Beverly looks up from her desk. "Are you okay, Joyce? You look a little flushed?"

"Yeah... Um... I'm fine. Just a lot going on." Joyce smoothed her blouse in an attempt to compose herself more. "Can you please bring me a cup of tea?"

"Sure. Messages are on your desk."

Joyce walks straight to her desk and looks through them. She is surprised to see one from Andrew. Immediately, she picked up her desk phone and dialed his number.

Joe Salerno

"Thanks for returning my call, Joyce."

"Got good news for me, Andrew?"

"Sort of. I've been able to keep all the players at the table. I had to give a quarter point to each of them to ensure they stop asking questions and remain on board."

Joyce is surprised by his ingenuity. Finally, this guy's thinking bigger than just his fee, which, by all accounts, will still be huge. If it was her, she would've squeezed him for more than a measly quarter point. "And the launch date?"

"About that... I'm not sure I can get it done within the requested period of time," Andrew reluctantly admits. "I need to update some information and revise the prospectus. Particularly as it relates to the litigation. I'm hoping you can provide additional insight to make things run a bit smoother and, most importantly, quicker."

"Non-negotiable, Andrew. I told you that." Joyce all but slams her fist down on her desk.

Andrew's nervousness is coming through loud and clear. "Um... What can you tell me about how you're going to take care of this?"

"There will be a motion filed, followed by a press conference from the courthouse. I've invited the media. Should make the evening news," Joyce proudly reports.

"What kind of motion?"

She's incensed. This fucking guy won't quit. Joyce appreciated that attitude when he was pushing the IPO process along, but she hates it when she's on the other end of the shoving. "The kind that'll ease concerns and create a window to launch the IPO. I'll be commenting on the IPO at the press conference." She smiles to herself. That should light a fire under his ass.

"Wait. What?" Andrew's nervous tone becomes full-blown panic. "You can't do that."

362

"I can, and I am," Joyce says with finality. "So, you need to come through on your end, or I'll blame you and your firm for everything that goes wrong."

"Joyce, let's be reasonable."

She cuts him off mid-sentence. "I'm done being reasonable. I told you; this gets done. I'm opening the door with this motion, and you need to drive this fucking IPO straight through it. Is that clear enough for you?"

The simpering fool responds. "You won't see the level of return you'll see once the motion's successful."

It won't be. But Joyce can't admit this out loud. "There's plenty of wiggle room if you do your job. Your fee may suffer, but how does the saying go? Oh yeah… *The client's always right*."

"Got it, but I need a copy of the motion before it's filed. Or, at the very least, between the filing and the press conference? It'll help me generate enthusiasm ahead of the launch."

He's finally getting the hint. "Fine. And you know what? You should be giving me a quarter point since I'm doing your goddamn job for you."

She disconnected the call before he said another word. By sending it to him, he would be able to say he was aware of it before it was filed. It's intended to reduce fears and regain the fervor that surrounded the IPO announcement, and if this lets him save face with the other underwriters, all the better.

Joyce tips her head back and closes her eyes. She's the conductor of an amazing symphony, directing the timing of each instrument, the tempo, and the sequence. As long as everyone hits their notes at the right time, this just might work.

98

As he merges onto 128, Jonathan asks Siri to place the call. He doesn't let the recipient speak. "Where are you?"

"At the office. What's up?"

Jonathan can tell by Walt's tone that his face is scrunched. "Stay there. I'm on my way. Details to follow."

Jonathan disconnected the call and dialed another new number. MJ picks up before the first ring ends. "Did you have your conversation?"

"Yes."

"And?"

Jonathan knew she wanted more than a one-word answer. "And you need to be at my office in thirty minutes. I'll bring the blueberry coffee. It's going to be a late night."

MJ's pause indicates she appreciates Jonathan's attempt at an apology for their last conversation. But she comes back with a firm: "No office."

"This isn't a negotiation, nor is it an option. See you in thirty." Jonathan turns the phone off.

• • •

MJ sits on her couch, staring at the phone. She's spooked. What if his office is bugged? An office is a confined space with no place to run if the mob shows up. Maybe she should've gotten a gun.

She doesn't have much time to contemplate these questions and heads to the bedroom to change. She has to take a few risks right now. They're part of the job, although the downside this time is literally life-altering. Woodward and Bernstein took risks, right? She stares at herself in the mirror, burying the fear. *They'll have to settle for a hoodie, jeans, and Chucks*, she decides as she grabs her keys and pepper spray and departs.

As MJ arrives at the offices of Silverman Erickson, she notices an average-looking man standing in the same spot where she had noticed someone before. She watches him climb into the Ford Explorer that just pulled over to the curb. Hopefully, it's a friend of Andy's and not someone else.

The assistant at the desk gives MJ a temporary badge and provides directions to Jonathan's office. Another woman is waiting for her at the elevator and ushers her directly into the conference room before either can say a word. The smell of the blueberry coffee fills the space.

Jonathan and another man, who she presumes is his partner, are already there. They're quietly talking, but it looks intense. Hand gestures and body language suggest a heavy debate, but MJ can feel the trust they have for each other. For a second, she wonders if she can ever be that trusting. "Alright, I'm here. Where's my coffee?"

"MJ, this is my partner, Walt. Walt, this is MJ Fernandez." They exchange quick hellos, and she refocuses the discussion.

"My coffee? You know how I get." An attempt at humor. Something to break the ice.

"On the credenza," Jonathan says as he motions with his hand. "I actually got you two."

MJ walks over and grabs the coffee. She inhales the aroma and takes a sip. It's crazy hot—just the way she likes it. Playtime's over. "Thank you. So, everything worked out with your father?"

Walt looks at her and then to Jonathan. He appears to approve of MJ or maybe her direct, no-bullshit approach. Or maybe… No. This wasn't the time to have straying thoughts.

"Yes. I was filling Walt in on the latest happenings. Why don't we sit down and discuss everything?"

MJ walks to the end of the conference table where the two of them are standing and takes the seat at the end of the table where the person who's leading the meeting usually sits. MJ takes another sip of coffee. "Okay. Talk."

Jonathan walks them through his conversation with Joyce. They agree on one point: She's hell-bent on getting the IPO launched as quickly as possible, and that creates a serious problem for their timeline.

Jonathan waves a few documents around. "As expected, the affidavits from Renee Spencer and Harold Johnson are patently false. Perjury at its finest. Tommy O'Hara's affidavit is technical and procedural but still smells like bullshit. Joyce is smart. They'll take the heat for perjury, as she claims ignorance. She hung them out to dry."

Walt states the obvious. "She must have something major on these guys."

Jonathan scowls while shaking his head. "Maybe it's nothing more than the huge sum of money they all stand to make with the launch."

MJ takes another sip of coffee. "We know Johnson's in the midst of a divorce. My sources tell me he owes the wrong people a lot of money. If it's Kramer's other friends, that's enough to get him on board."

Jonathan jumps in. "Spencer's a different story. For someone that intelligent, she's incredibly naïve. She might be just following orders. O'Hara's the wildcard."

Walt shakes his head. "Maybe. But the motion's a moot point. They signed, and Kramer expects you to file the motion using them as the basis. The reasons they signed are immaterial at the moment. What are we going to do about Propentus and Excellence Investment, Inc.? That's what's relevant. That's the question that needs to be answered."

Jonathan looks at both of them and, without a moment's hesitation, declares, "We're going to do what's right."

99

As Emily heads home, she passes a man sitting in a gray Toyota at the end of their street. Her heart races as she recalls Jonathan mentioning a gray car. She takes a deep breath before exiting her car.

Unsteady hands drop the keys as she unlocks the front door. She uses their retrieval as an opportunity to take a casual look up and down the street. She swallows her fear and enters the house without a care in the world. Her entire body quivers as she locks the deadbolt and calls Jonathan.

Emily whispers as if the person down the street might hear her. "There's someone sitting outside in a gray car." Her voice is shaking as much as her hands.

"Okay, try to stay calm."

She appreciates the comfort just hearing Jonathan's voice provides, but Emily still feels herself shaking. "I'm scared. Should I hide somewhere? Should I leave?" She peeks out the window. The car's still there.

"Sit tight. I'm at the office with Walt. He'll make a call and get a cruiser to swing down the street."

Emily hears Walt say something in the background before Jonathan replies to her, "It's okay. Walt just made the call. They're on their way."

"Jonathan, please don't hang up." Emily reaches into her handbag, hoping her pepper spray will bring her comfort.

"I won't. Are you downstairs?"

Emily suddenly questions her hiding choice. "Yes."

"Okay, go upstairs and carefully peek out the window in our bedroom," Jonathan explains. "That'll give you a better vantage point."

Emily crouch-walks up the stairs and trips over the last step. Her phone flies out of her hand, skittering across the floor and slamming into the wall.

She can hear Jonathan yelling from the floor ahead of her. "Emily! Emily! Are you okay? Oh my God! Emily!"

Emily gathers herself and grabs her phone. "Yes… Sorry. I tripped and dropped my phone. Sorry," she says, gasping for air.

"Are you okay?" Emily hears the panic rising in Jonathan's voice but appreciates his attempts to remain calm and keep her calm.

"Yeah, other than a banged-up shin." Emily crawls on her hands and knees into the other room. "Okay, I'm at the window. Still no cops. What's taking them so long?"

"They should be there any minute."

It's been three minutes, but it feels like thirty. Emily ignores her throbbing shin and crouches near the window in the dark room. She's holding her phone in one hand and pepper spray in the other. Finally, she sees a police cruiser turn onto their street. The cruiser's moving slowly, patrolling the neighborhood.

The Toyota turns on its lights and leaves before the cruiser reaches it.

Emily finally feels like she can breathe again. "He's gone. He just left." She holds back the tears, knowing the impact they will have on Jonathan.

"Okay. Good. Walt says they'll continue to sweep the neighborhood. I'll be home as soon as I can. Are you going to be okay?"

"Yes. The doors are locked, and the alarm's on. I should be fine. A huge glass of wine will help," she says it but isn't convinced.

"Okay. Call for any reason... I love you!"

"Love you, too."

• • •

Jonathan rubs his hand over his face as he hangs up. "Okay, guys. We need to get this done."

A chill fills the room as the atmosphere flips like a switch. They're no longer in a conference room... they're in a war room.

MJ looks at both men and quietly says one thing: "DEFCON 1."

100

While she doesn't know Jonathan's girlfriend, she's read enough about her in the files and feels genuine empathy for him as he paces around the room in an effort to burn off the stress created by the phone call.

As the energy in the room settles, they get back to work—urgency drives their every movement. Initially, the three of them focus on a high-level summary.

First, a new biotech firm develops a revolutionary treatment for early onset dementia, which is fast-tracked by the FDA. The firm was sued prior to the launching of its IPO, with the plaintiffs claiming the company withheld information from the FDA and their new drug is causing chronic kidney disease, among other things.

Next, thanks to the people in the room's combined efforts, they have concluded the allegations in the complaint are true. While they cannot disclose their sources, they have enough to support a belief the FDA wouldn't have approved the drug had all of the information been provided.

Then, a couple of years ago, the mob made a play by investing in the fledgling pharmaceutical company and is the force behind the current drive to get the IPO launched. Jimmy Rizzo, the known head of the local mob, is presumably done waiting for his money and has killed people to make his point.

Finally, they conclude that "The King of the Fender Bender" stumbled blindly into the case. There's no evidence linking him, nor any of the plaintiffs, in a way that suggests they have inside information. None of the three believe in coincidence, but they're hard-pressed to reach a different conclusion on this point. What started out as just another class-action lawsuit has unraveled into an unbelievable story of lies and deceit driven by the oldest motive of all: greed.

"I've been working on my article for a few weeks. With another three to four hours' worth of focused effort, I'll have a front-page story that'll bring these assholes to their knees."

Jonathan looks at her with an intensity she hasn't seen before. "That's good, MJ. You should spend time tightening up the story. But you *cannot* run with it until we all agree. Understood?"

MJ hesitates but knows he's right. This is the story of a lifetime. One that could get her a Pulitzer, the one thing all investigative reporters covet. But none of that's important now. This is about innocent people who've been lied to and hurt as they search for a miracle in their battle against a devastating disease. It's about righting a terrible wrong.

She told Jonathan from the beginning they must be in lockstep. "Agreed. But I refuse to get scooped. I need your commitment to that in return."

There's no hesitation in Jonathan's response. "Agreed. Now, we need to come up with the end of your story."

Walt's sitting quietly when a smirk comes across his face. "I have a crazy idea. Actually, it's a fucking stupid idea."

Jonathan shakes his head and smiles. It was obvious to MJ, even without having read their files, that the two have a history outside of their business partnership. Seeing that kind of comradery is different than reading about it. "Of course you do. Do you have any other kind?"

"Seriously. It's off the wall," Walt says, probably a reflex of being an attorney for so many years—counteracting plausible deniability. "Let me put it all out there. Then you can shoot it down. Okay?"

MJ gets up and grabs her second coffee. She looks at Jonathan, shrugs, and then looks back at Walt. "Okay, whatcha got?"

Walt stands and clears his throat. It's his turn to pace. "Okay, we know the mob's pulling the strings here. They've threatened to eliminate anyone who gets in their way. In fact, they've already killed to prove their point. This is about money. They don't give a shit about any of us as long as they get their money. And, from what MJ's friends tell us, it's a lot of money." Walt starts his second lap around the table when he suddenly stops and blurts it out. "What if we help them get their money?"

Jonathan's head snaps up, looking at MJ and then toward Walt. "What the…?"

Walt looks at his best friend and then at MJ, pausing his gaze on her for slightly longer. "Seriously, what if we just let this move forward, at least for the moment, so they get their money?"

Jonathan is about to respond when MJ jumps in. "Seriously? It's that simple?" She frowns darkly, not sure if she's impressed or horrified by the suggestion.

Walt holds up his hand, asking them to stop. "I'm not suggesting it's simple. What if we get the word to the right people, and in exchange for all of us remaining safe, we agree to let this play out?"

Jonathan and MJ exchange disbelieving glances.

Walt continues before they can object further. "They're instructed to cash out on day one. They confirm they've gotten their money, and then we tear the whole fucking thing down."

A deep silence follows. Thoughts are tumbling like puzzle pieces when the picture starts coming together for MJ. She'd need the help of "the team," but she sees what Walt's suggesting.

Jonathan is shaking his head from side to side. "You're out of your fucking mind, Walt," he says, but MJ notes respect in his tone. "I've said that for years, but you've just proven it once and for all. Are you actually suggesting we collude with the mob? What happens once they get their money? They're very good at making people be quiet—and stay quiet."

Walt shrugs. "I didn't say it's without risk, nor that it's easy. I'm trying to think outside the box."

"Outside the box? This blows the box to smithereens!" Jonathan's agitation is growing.

But MJ sees the value in Walt's plan. She stands, almost dumping her coffee all over the conference room table. "Why's it too far outside? We could all get what we want. First and foremost, personal safety. The company's malfeasance comes to light, the FDA pulls their approval, the drug stops being made, and in all likelihood, the company goes belly up."

Jonathan continues to challenge the hypothesis. "I see nothing but danger. First of all, who are the 'right people', and who the hell's going to meet with them? Second, how do we stay safe forever? Lastly, if the 'right people' can cash out, what prevents the people at Propentus from doing the same thing?"

From the countless hours MJ has spent investigating this from every angle, she knows exactly how to respond. A small smile pulls at the corners of her mouth. "First, the right person is Anthony Spinelli, or if we really want to go to the top, Jimmy Rizzo," she says. "Second, we hold disclosure of their involvement over their heads. They don't want the feds poking around." Now, MJ fully smiles and glances at Walt. "Lastly, the others aren't going to cash out. Their wealth is tied to the stock. They may want to get out, but they won't do it immediately. In fact, they may not be able to, depending on how the grants were issued."

Walt catches MJ's glance and holds her gaze. "Okay. How do we make contact with Spinelli or Rizzo? Call The Last Inning and ask for an appointment?" Walt stands there with his arms crossed, waiting for her response.

MJ doesn't blink. "I'll take care of the contact."

Walt's arms relax to his sides, and he smiles appreciatively at MJ.

"Okay… Hold on," Jonathan interjects. "Let's pump the brakes here. We haven't agreed to this strategy. There are other considerations. What happens to Ms. Cosgrove and the other plaintiffs when this gets blown up? What happens to those who are taking the drug currently and are seeing benefits? It isn't just about the assholes. It's about all the good people this company's fucked with, too."

The excitement that's building in the room nose-dives into the depths of reality. They've been focused on their own safety and the company itself. What about the innocent people this company has hurt?

Walt looks at Jonathan with the eyes of a loving brother and tells him the cold, hard truth. "You're right. But those who have been hurt are already hurt. I know it sounds harsh, but we can't change that. We can, however, stop others from suffering the same fate. It's a little harder for those that are seeing benefits from the drug."

Jonathan pleads his case further. "Yes, we can prevent further damage. But those who have been hurt, arguably intentionally, by the company will lose on all fronts. They have dementia and the problems Antsalemab has created. Every insurance company will disclaim coverage based on fraud, leaving those people without the ability to recover financially. We can't help them."

MJ re-enters the fray. "True, but we can't change the past, only the future. The more difficult question is about those Antsalemab is helping."

The three have a lot more to discuss before they can agree and move a plan—any plan—forward.

101

It's approaching midnight when fear grips Jonathan's heart like a vise. He places the call he meant to make much earlier. "I'm so sorry. Did I wake you?"

"No, I'm lying on the couch with an empty wine glass and my pepper spray, watching a documentary about a serial killer on Netflix."

Jonathan is relieved to hear Emily's voice, but he's stunned by her viewing choice, given their current situation. "Interesting selection... I'm really sorry I didn't call sooner."

"I'm okay. I've seen a police cruiser pass by every thirty minutes or so, and no unusual cars at all. Go take care of business. I love you."

"I love you, too. I'll be home as soon as I can."

As Jonathan ends his brief call, MJ and Walt walk back into the conference room with coffee and an armful of stale snacks from the vending machine in the lunchroom.

MJ drops her cache on the table and looks over the selection. With a shake of her head, she says, "I'm starving. Can we order a pizza?"

Jonathan stands, helping them move their supplies to the credenza, eyeing the choices. "I'm hoping we won't be here that long. We're all tired, and I need to get home to Emily. Let's keep walking through this crazy idea of Walt's." Despite the hours of looking for other options, Walt's proposal was still their most viable option. "Going step by step helps me identify holes in the strategy. Um… I'll be right back."

As Jonathan hurries out of the room, he overhears MJ, saying, "I need to get home to Snoopy. He's probably left me a present or two to show me how much he misses me."

Jonathan wasn't intentionally eavesdropping, but it was a quiet office, and voices travel. "You're pretty badass. Smart, good-looking, and tough as nails. You're not going to take any shit from anyone. Strong attributes."

Jonathan chuckles to himself. Walt's being Walt. He is equally unsurprised when MJ holds her ground.

"Easy, big guy. Not gonna happen," MJ says, although he can't help but notice something in her tone that suggests she might be interested. He hopes that both Walt and MJ appreciate that this isn't the time for that.

Before Walt can say another word, Jonathan clears his throat and walks back in, his hands filled with packages of Post-Its and pens. "Okay, let's go through it. I'll write the steps down and put them on the wall. We will use a green Post-It for the step and the red to identify potential dangers associated with the step."

MJ bursts out laughing. "I thought I was the only person who put shit on their walls."

Walt looks down and shakes his head in disbelief. Jonathan looks at him, smiles, and looks back at MJ. "Nope, every smart person in this room who doesn't have a photographic memory does it this way."

They share a momentary, much-needed laugh and begin to map out the strategy.

The steps are relatively clear. However, the timing of each is critical, but they believe that can be controlled. The real danger is getting Anthony Spinelli and Jimmy Rizzo to accept their offer and, most importantly, trusting them to live up to their end of the bargain long-term.

MJ eagerly embraces the daunting task of making contact and explaining why this is in their best interest. "I'll reach out to my team. Finding them won't be hard. We know Spinelli's in Florida at the moment, and Rizzo is always hanging around his bar. Getting them to talk will be the challenge."

Walt's face scrunches with concern. "MJ, you aren't going to be the one who talks with them, right?"

MJ tilts her head, using a fake, high-pitched voice as if she has a schoolgirl crush. "Oh, Walt… You care." She flutters her eyelashes at him.

Walt apparently didn't pick up on the sarcasm and blushes before composing himself. "No, um… Not what I meant. If you're going to write the article, it can't be you who makes the direct contact."

"The journalist in me wants to be the one," MJ states simply, all teasing removed from her tone. "There's no confusion that way. But I'm going to leave the mob connection out of my article as much as it kills me. It's the only way this works. So, no need for me to be there."

"You trust your team with this?" Walt asks, using his down-to-business voice again.

"Yes. I've worked with them before. Although, not in this way nor on anything this complicated or risky. I'm pretty sure they'll be on board." MJ nods to reassure them, but Jonathan is sure she's trying to convince herself, too.

Walt's demeanor changes. "Wait, only 'pretty sure?' I thought you said you had it handled?"

MJ looks confidently at Walt. "I do. All I'm saying is this is new territory for me with them. I am 99.9% certain this won't even make them blink. I get the sense their worldwide activities have taken them into much darker places."

Jonathan is anxious to keep this moving forward. "When will you speak with them?"

"I'll make contact tonight. They dictate location and time after that."

"You'll need to stress the urgency," Jonathan emphasizes. "I need to have the motion drafted and in Joyce's hands by the end of the day tomorrow, and I have no idea what she's going to say at the press conference."

Walt looks like the last kid picked for dodgeball. "What do I do while you two are busy saving the world?"

Jonathan adds a couple of additional Post-Its to the wall. "Walt, your job's protection. You need to leverage every contact you have to ensure we're safe. That includes the three of us, Emily, and my parents. Can you do that?"

"That I can do. Not for too long, but I can make it happen."

The electricity of nervous energy sparks throughout the room as Jonathan says, "Last chance. We're doing this, right?"

They look at each other with unwavering commitment, all shaking their heads in the affirmative.

"Okay. Let's all go home and get some rest."

They stand up and take the Post-Its off the wall. Before exiting the room, MJ produces two burner phones and hands one to Jonathan and Walt.

Jonathan takes the gathered notes and shreds them before he leaves. As he gets in his car, Jonathan hopes his father will be proud and that his mother never finds out.

102

"Good afternoon, Joyce."

"Is the motion prepared, Jonathan?"

Right to the point. Why am I not surprised? "I'm putting the finishing touches on it. Although it may be a little after normal business hours, you'll have it before I leave today."

"I trust you found the affidavits helpful?"

Jonathan desperately wants to tell Joyce he's going to burn the place to the ground. However, he and Emily thought a different approach might be more effective at keeping Joyce calm. "Yes. Thank you. By the way, did I tell you my father's taking Antsalemab? He's been on it for a few months, and it seems to be helping."

Emily was right. Jonathan catches Joyce's slight stumble of surprise. "No, you didn't mention it. I'm glad it's helping. Now you know what we're fighting for."

"Yes. He started taking it after I took the case. I get it and am personally invested in seeing this come to the right conclusion." He fails to mention what he believes the right conclusion to be.

"Excellent. I'll be watching for the motion to land in my inbox." She ends the call.

Any shred of doubt that remained is gone; Jonathan's convinced he's doing the right thing. Joyce's sense of relief, or maybe it was success, solidified it for him. Before he can give Joyce another thought, the burner phone MJ gave him last night rings. "Yes?"

"The initial discussion is taking place tonight. As agreed, I'll stress urgency and send them to make contact unless I hear differently before 10 p.m. tonight." The call ends.

And with that one statement, Walt's ludicrous plan is in motion. The reality of what they're attempting lands on Jonathan like a collapsing building. He heads to Walt's office, walks in, and closes the door. He flops into one of the chairs as serious doubts flood his mind. "We're a go. We have until 10 p.m. to change our minds. You still think this is the right approach?"

"This is a fucking ballsy move. No doubt about it, but I don't see another way that keeps us safe and prevents thousands, maybe millions, of people from being harmed by these greedy bastards. All we have to do is trust the bad guys." Walt chuckles.

Jonathan knows Walt's right. Everything hinges on criminals who don't hesitate to kill. Even the external hard drives full of information MJ's putting together for each of them to maintain the leverage needed for their individual safety won't protect them if this doesn't go perfectly. He begins to think about his dad.

Walt tilts his head, eyeing Jonathan's face. "Your father will be, and should be, proud of you."

Jonathan looks at Walt with profound sadness. "I spent my entire life hearing him talk about doing what's right.

That's all well and good until doing what's right is so wrong for the people you love." Jonathan pauses and sighs. "Why does it have to be this way? Why does he have to be getting benefit from this drug? What's my mother going to think?"

"Your mom will never know," Walt says reassuringly. "And, even if she finds out someday, when she understands all of it, she'll be just as proud. She and your father are the type of parents every kid should want."

"I've sworn to do whatever I can to help my dad. This doesn't feel like I'm living up to that commitment."

"You're protecting him long term." Walt walks over to Jonathan and places a reassuring hand on his shoulder. "You don't know if his taking this drug will lead to a more serious side effect, one that shortens his life even further. What you do know is right from wrong, and this is the right thing to do."

"It still feels wrong," Jonathan admits. "I'm not sure how I'm going to come to grips with this as I watch dementia steal my father from my mother and me."

Walt squeezes Jonathan's shoulder and then leans back against the desk. "You'll take solace in the fact that you had the chance to talk to your dad about it. You'll remember he's an honorable man, one who understood the decision you were forced to make and that he's proud of you for the way you've handled it."

"Thank you. I appreciate the pep talk. I really do." Jonathan stands to leave. "I have to send Joyce the draft motion. Remember, we have until 10 p.m. to change our minds. So, if you are having second thoughts, let me know ASAP."

103

The short email is all Anthony can think about. Only four men in the world know this email address exists. He can't ignore the subject line… *we know.* He has no choice.

Anthony's crew quickly confirms that the building at the address he was given is being renovated and provides the privacy that a meeting like this requires. Fearing the topic to be discussed, Anthony wants to go alone, but after a lengthy argument about safety, he agrees to allow Bruno to join him. He'll figure out what to do with Bruno after the meeting… if it goes as he fears.

After walking the perimeter twice, Anthony follows Bruno into the building, using him as a shield. In the center of the cavernous space, they find a giant standing quietly with his arms at his side and his hands empty.

Bruno steps forward to set the tone for the meeting. "Who the fuck…?"

In a split second, Bruno lands face down on the concrete floor. Michael is poised to shatter his elbow. One ounce of additional pressure, and Bruno won't be able to use his arm for anything more than a limp filler for his sleeve. Michael looks at Anthony and speaks in a calm voice. "I've been asked to communicate a proposal and bring back your answer."

Anthony's never seen Bruno get beat, even when it's four-on-one. He rightfully concludes the giant is no one to be trifled with. For a moment, he wonders if the stranger in the army jacket is willing to solve his Bruno problem when they're finished. "Let Bruno the fuck up and speak."

Bruno moves to stand next to his boss, his face red with embarrassment, anger, and pain. He's holding his arm, wiggling his fingers, evaluating the damage to his arm and shoulder.

Michael continues, addressing only Anthony. "I represent a group of individuals who seek an agreement that benefits both parties, but not all parties who have an interest in the issue."

"Stop talkin' in fuckin' riddles. Get to the fuckin' point."

In a matter-of-fact tone, Michael lays out the details, confirming for Anthony their full knowledge of the Propentus-Spinelli-Excellence Investment-Rizzo relationship. He goes on to include the location and medical status of his parents, citing the dates that Anthony has flown to Florida.

"My clients propose an arrangement, one that preserves their safety while concurrently protecting your significant financial interest."

The messenger's level of detail is exactly what Anthony feared when he read the email. They must know. "Supposin' what you said's accurate. Whatta they want?"

"As I said, they're looking for assurances relative to their long-term safety. In exchange, they'll ensure you and your business associates recover the monies they've invested."

Anthony grinds his teeth. "We're expectin' a lot more than just our original fuckin' investment."

"Understood. The IPO will move forward. You'll be given enough notice so you'll be able to recoup your equity and make a significant profit. But you'll have one business day to fully extricate yourself from the relationship, pocket what you can, and walk away."

"Then what?"

"Propentus will be destroyed. The company will be worthless within forty-eight hours of the IPO launch."

"What keeps me from cleaning this mess up entirely?"

"What you decide to do on that front is entirely within your discretion. However, should certain individuals find themselves being harmed in any way, from a carjacking gone wrong, for example, a comprehensive dossier will find its way into the hands of federal, state, and local law enforcement."

Anthony throws up his hands. "Jesus Christ... Don't tell me that fuckin' bitch Kramer put you up to this?"

Michael's tone never changes. "She's not my client. Nor is anyone else employed by Propentus."

Anthony runs through the options. If not the bitch or her boss, this highly skilled gargantuan must be here on behalf of the reporter or the attorney—or both. He's impressed not only with their ability to get to the truth but also their audacity in making this play.

"What if I decide to send you back to your clients in fuckin' pieces?"

No emotion. Just facts. "If Bruno's the best you have, I'm not concerned."

Anthony laughs. "Yeah, yeah. So, me and my associates leave a few fuckin' people alone, and we get the fuckin' money we've been waitin' for? Or we don't leave people alone and lose our fuckin' money?"

"Not the way I'd put it. My clients are poised to communicate with federal, state, and local authorities. However, they're more than happy to give you the ability to recover your funds without fear of a badge knocking on your door in exchange for their ability to lead an undisturbed life."

Anthony sees no way out, particularly if he wants to keep his secret buried. "Fuck it. What do we care about a handful of nobodies as long as we get our fuckin' money? This is business."

"You'll have access to your money within the next few days. The IPO launch date will be identified in a press release. Remember, you'll need to act the day of the launch. After that, there are no guarantees as to your funds." Michael looks Anthony in the eye. "What's guaranteed is my clients have taken the steps necessary to ensure everything they know is shared, should even a whisper of potential harm come their way."

Anthony recalls his discussion with Joyce about the press conference. "Fine."

Michael looks at Bruno and then back to Anthony. "One more thing. This arrangement cannot be communicated to anyone other than your boss." Michael turns to leave without looking back. He's obviously confident that Bruno isn't *that* stupid.

104

During an early-morning breakfast meeting, Jonathan and Walt discuss how the firm could become a pariah for defending an unethical company. On top of that, their law licenses would be at risk for possessing the information MJ's team provided. After healthy servings of bacon and eggs and a couple of Bloody Marys, they agree on a solution designed to provide a layer of protection to each of them and the firm.

While Jonathan is handling his assignments, Walt takes responsibility to consult with a friend from law school whose specialty involves corporate malfeasance. After that initial meeting, he and Jonathan executed retainer letters as individuals and on behalf of the firm. Walt hand delivers the signed retainers and one of the external drives MJ created to their new attorney.

Jonathan's next task is waiting for Emily to come home from work. She and Jonathan agreed she'd leave town before the press conference and take a couple of weeks off to visit some out-of-town friends—they'll re-evaluate her return after the exposé comes out. She told co-workers she was heading to California to spend time with friends from college. Not entirely true, but it'll send anyone looking for her in the wrong direction, at least initially.

Emily's hands tremble as she reaches to straighten Jonathan's tie. "Please be careful today."

Jonathan tries to reassure her through dry humor. "It's a press conference. The worst thing that'll happen is I trip over a microphone cord."

It worked. Emily smiled. "Well, we both know what a klutz you are."

"True enough." Jonathan takes her in his arms and gives her a long, passionate kiss, one he hopes conveys how much he loves her. Now, down to business. "You have the phones I bought you?"

"Yes," Emily responds with a playful groan. "The sunglasses, wigs, and the Groucho Marx nose with glasses, too."

Jonathan is sharper with her than he intended. "This isn't funny. Everything has to fall exactly into place. Any deviation will be disastrous." Jonathan again questions his decision to make a deal with the devil.

It's like Emily knows what he's thinking. "This is the right thing," she says as she squeezes Jonathan.

"I know, but…"

Emily interrupts and smiles. "No buts. I love you. End of discussion."

Jonathan holds her tightly. She's right. Besides, they've already rolled the snowball off the peak of the mountain. "I love you, too. And thanks for the pep talk."

They're interrupted by a chirping cell phone. It's the driver letting Emily know he's arrived. Jonathan carries her bag to the car, and they kiss one more time before Emily climbs into the back. Jonathan's palms begin to sweat as the car pulls away.

It's showtime.

105

Joyce's excitement is off the charts. "That went really well, don't you think? You did a terrific job. Clearly, it's not your first time in front of a camera."

Jonathan smiles at the compliment, wondering if she's sincere. "The reporters seemed focused on the IPO launch more than the litigation or the motion."

"That was the hope. With what we presented today, the investment banks should regain the confidence needed to move forward with the IPO. And, between us," Joyce leans a little closer, lowers her voice to a whisper, and says, "It has to move forward."

Jonathan's brow shoots up. "Why?"

Joyce's volume returns to normal. "The investors are extremely restless. The company's a couple of months away from going bankrupt. The IPO was supposed to be launched long before that became a concern. The timing of the lawsuit couldn't have been worse. It fucked everything up."

Jonathan's shocked by her sudden openness. "I know you mentioned financial trouble, but I didn't realize it was that bad. What happens now?"

"You deal with Schneider and whatever bullshit he throws. He's a TV whore. That's where he's at his best, so don't underestimate him." It looks like even the mention of the plaintiff's attorney causes bile to rise in Joyce's throat. "Me, I'm focused on the IPO and only the IPO. In ninety-six hours, Propentus will be one of the most valuable biotechs on the planet."

Jonathan remains in character. "Okay. I'll let you know if I hear something. I wouldn't be surprised if he takes another run at settlement."

"He won't. He'll smell the money associated with the IPO and emphasize that Ms. Cosgrove and the others are 'David' and Propentus is an even bigger 'Goliath.' He and his slingshot can both fuck off."

In that moment Jonathan wonders what went wrong for Joyce. She's a smart, talented attorney. She was on the partner track following the Genomics IPO, but somehow, Michael Riccio convinced her to leave that all behind. How?

"You're probably right. I'll see you later, Joyce." Jonathan can't help but snicker to himself as he walks away. He knows the real story with the "investors." The next essential piece of the puzzle is the actual launch.

At the press conference, Jonathan paid close attention to what Joyce said. She told reporters what she'd hinted at through a few well-placed leaks: The IPO will occur next Tuesday, four days from now. He knows the key is investment bank confidence. They've done all they can on that front. It has to be enough.

Jonathan starts the countdown clock in his head. Ninety-six hours from now, the first day of trading for

Propentus stock will be over, and the release of MJ's article confirming the allegations within the complaint will be in the public realm. The stock will begin to tank in after-hours trading, and the company will implode.

The snowball is about to become an avalanche.

106

After living on cold coffee and days-old pizza for the past forty-eight hours, the time's come for MJ to bring her full story out of the shadows. After going to painstaking lengths to carve out any possible reference or innuendo that might suggest the involvement of organized crime, her eighth and most challenging draft is saved to a new thumb drive. On top of that, she had to knit together the limited data points she'd been able to independently confirm. It wasn't the easiest thing to do this time around, but she's pleased with the final product.

MJ has been sitting in her editor's office in silence for more than an hour. He is reviewing her story and hasn't looked up once. While he's seen pieces of the story along the way, clearly, MJ wasn't able to share everything in those early drafts.

"MJ, this is a helluva story. There's a lot here that I haven't seen before. I have to re-read it for final edits, but I want to run it within the next twenty-four hours, if possible. The IPO announcement at the press conference puts this on a different clock."

"Agreed," MJ says, feeling excitement and nervousness battle for dominance in her stomach. "I'm pulling the motion from the public record to see if there's anything that I should address in the article. And I have calls pending to Attorney Silverman and the company's General Counsel. I'm hoping to get a couple of quotes. I'm not optimistic, but it needs to be done." She knew he'd want to push this quickly, but she needed to keep the timing on track with the larger plan. It'll be close, but she's confident she can do it.

"Agreed. Okay. Follow up with the motion and the calls. Then, take a stab at breaking this into a three-part series. Once the first piece is published, the wheels are going to come off, and every other media outlet on the planet is going to start chasing this. Lastly, you know I need to get legal involved. The feds will be busting down our door."

MJ also expected this. Legal will want to slow this down, which will help manage the timing to a point. She has a little more than thirty-nine hours.

Spagnola is smiling and winks at her as he picks up the phone to call upstairs.

MJ excuses herself and heads to her desk with a determined look on her face. So far, so good. It was time for her to execute the next part of the plan. With a voice loud enough for everyone within a ten-foot radius to hear her clearly, she begins. "Attorney Silverman, please. MJ Fernandez calling."

The line clicks over, and Jonathan says, "Ms. Fernandez. I've told you before: 'No comment.'" MJ knew he'd nail his lines, too.

"Yes, I know," MJ says in her most investigative reporting voice. "I'm looking for additional insight on the motion you just filed."

"We feel very confident with the filing. This case should be dismissed with prejudice. As Ms. Kramer said during the press announcement, this is an FDA-approved drug, which is the first of its kind in providing unprecedented relief to those who suffer from a disease that plagues society." Jonathan quoted Joyce verbatim—just as he and MJ had agreed.

Their carefully scripted dance continues. "I understand. But isn't this filing premature?" MJ begins to draw some attention as a few nearby heads turn in her direction, even though they're only hearing one side of the conversation.

"It's not premature," Jonathan says flatly.

"Don't you expect the plaintiffs to make that argument?"

"Yes. That's an obvious response. Not an accurate response, but it's an obvious one we believe has no merit. I'm sorry, Ms. Fernandez, but I have no further comment." Jonathan hangs up abruptly, giving her no opportunity to respond but also giving her plenty of cover with those who may be listening.

MJ shakes her head in disgust and hangs up the phone. She dials another number and is shocked when Joyce takes her call.

"Ms. Kramer, MJ Fernandez. We spoke previously about the class-action litigation."

"Yes, I remember. What can I do for you, Ms. Fernandez?" Joyce has obviously planned for calls from reporters.

"I'm following up regarding the recently filed motion to dismiss, as well as your announcement regarding the IPO." More interested cycs—and ears—are focused on MJ.

"We are extremely confident this filing will be successful. So much so, we've decided to move forward with the long-overdue initial public offering."

While she rehearsed these questions with Jonathan, Joyce is a loose cannon. MJ keeps her cool and presses forward.

"Why don't you believe this filing's premature? There haven't been any depositions or other forms of discovery you would traditionally see before such a filing."

Joyce responds immediately. "There's been a great deal of paper discovery that's been exchanged, and it's more than sufficient to grant the motion."

MJ smoothly switches topics. "What can you tell me about the IPO timing?"

"As you know, we were very close to launching the IPO before this suit was filed. We believe now is the right time. Investors have access to the public records associated with the litigation, and after reviewing our motion, we're confident they'll agree there's no merit to the case."

"Ms. Kramer, I'll ask again about high blood pressure and kidney stones and their direct link to the disease Ms. Cosgrove's suffering from."

MJ can practically hear Joyce trying to rein in control of the conversation. "As I said and our literature reflects, there are limited incidences of those side effects, and they're easily addressed."

MJ's smirk and rolling eyes are seen by those sitting near her. "So, you're saying if people choose to take Antsalemab, they'll be forced to take a second medication as a normal course?"

Joyce won't be deterred. "Ms. Fernandez, that's not what I'm saying, and you know it."

One last shot. "Ms. Kramer, what do you know about Ms. Cosgrove's current condition or the condition of the other plaintiffs?"

"As I have said previously, Propentus has empathy for what Ms. Cosgrove and the others may be going through. However, there's no evidence that our FDA-approved treatment has played any role whatsoever in their current situations. Now, Ms. Fernandez, I'm sorry, but I have to run. Thank you for your call."

MJ watches the countdown on her phone progress. Justice will arrive soon.

107

I t's Tuesday morning. MJ hasn't spoken with Jonathan and Walt since the plan was set in motion, but she assumes they are in the conference room watching Michael Riccio stand alongside Joyce Kramer as they ring the opening bell for the stock market. Propentus stock surges to 165 percent of the initial offering price within minutes.

Meanwhile, MJ is sitting in her editor's office. They're ready to run with the first part of the three-part series. They've spent the last twenty-four hours fighting with legal about the release of this information without first giving the FDA a heads up. Ultimately, legal decides they'll prepare for the onslaught of calls from the FDA, the FBI, and the SEC but will not notify them in advance. It's going to be crazy, but they're prepared for the forthcoming chaos.

"Congratulations, MJ! This is an amazing story! Great job! Final formatting is taking place right now. Any further updates?"

"My calls with both Silverman and Kramer regarding the motion were uneventful. Nothing new. They repeated information essentially verbatim." MJ pauses briefly. "Plaintiffs' response to the motion isn't due yet. That may shed more light, but for now, we have what we're going to get."

"Okay. Have you seen the stock price? Everyone seems to be buying this stock. It's going through the roof. Apparently, people aren't afraid of the lawsuit."

"They don't want to miss out on the biggest medical discovery in decades. They're willing to risk the lawsuit to get in early." MJ decides to drop questions that she already knows the answer to. "What will be interesting is what the end of the day looks like. Will people buy in early and harvest their profit today? Or will they hold onto the stock?"

Spagnola chuckles. "If they're smart, they'll harvest their profits today. It'll drop through the floor once your article hits the wire."

"Probably." MJ maintains her composure like a pro. "I'm ready to call Kramer for comment once you tell me the formatting team's set to go."

"They're telling me they should be set within the next hour. You should try to call her now. Do you have her cell number? She isn't in her office. Obviously."

"I don't, but I am certain once I tell her staff who I am and what I want to speak with her about, my phone will be ringing immediately thereafter."

"True. Exciting day for you, MJ." Spagnola beams with pride.

"Thanks for believing in me," MJ says sincerely. "I know I can be a pain in the ass sometimes."

"Sometimes?"

They both laugh.

"Okay, okay, I get it. I'm going to my desk to make the call. Wish me luck," MJ says as she prepares to leave his office.

"Not sure you need it, but good luck."

MJ is grinning from ear to ear as she heads to her desk. This is the best story she's ever written. She knows Joyce won't say anything once she's confronted with the truth. She can't. There are eighty-two minutes left on her countdown clock as the one remaining hurdle approaches: Filing the story at exactly the right time.

She can't give anyone a reason to believe they haven't lived up to their end of the bargain.

108

Joyce and Michael leave the trading floor and head to the conference room they've reserved. There, they meet with Andrew and other commercial investors. The celebration's in full force, as the sound of popping corks can attest. The Dom Perignon and Cristal are flowing, with handshakes and clinking champagne flutes all around.

"Congratulations, Michael. And to you too, Joyce."

Joyce didn't appreciate the true level of stress she was under until it was gone. She's done it. She'll sleep like a baby tonight. "Thank you."

Michael's grin couldn't be any wider. He raises his glass. "Thanks, Andrew. Couldn't have done it without your support."

Joyce's phone rings in her hand. Seeing that it's the office calling, she pushes the call to voicemail and drops her freshly silenced phone deep into her handbag. She'll call later. Nothing's going to ruin today.

After the national media outlets Joyce selected had set up their cameras and microphones in different spots around the room, they began interviewing Michael. The sound bites being captured will be on every major network in the country within the hour. The European and Asian wire services have already picked up the story, and Joyce presumes calls are flooding the switchboard at Propentus.

The most frequent question Michael faces isn't about the efficacy of the drug but the cost. The press release he and Joyce prepared speaks to the issue. He parrots the content to ensure consistency. There are a few questions relative to Nobel Prize consideration, but Michael handles them with a surprising level of humility. Joyce can't help but wonder what others would think if they knew what she knew: he's a fucking narcissist who hasn't a humble bone in his body.

With the first round of interviews complete, Joyce grabs her handbag and looks at her phone. There are eighteen missed calls and one voicemail from the office. There are also eleven text messages, all of which begin with 911. Joyce walks out of the room to where it's quieter and calls the office. "What's so goddamn urgent?"

"Sorry, Joyce, but that reporter, MJ Fernandez, says she's going to run an article saying the allegations in the lawsuit have been confirmed. She's looking for your comment and says you have until the end of the day to speak with her. Otherwise, she's going to publish without comment."

Concern barely registers as Joyce looks at her watch. The market's going to close in the next thirty minutes. More importantly, there's no way this fucking reporter has anything they'd need to worry about. She's bluffing to get a soundbite.

"First, not a word from anyone. Any person who says anything to anyone is ruined. Not just fired but *ruined*. Got that?" Joyce waits for a confirmation of what she just said. "Good. Make sure everyone knows it. Second, give me her fucking number. I'll put this to rest."

Joyce begins pacing as she looks around, hoping no one has overheard her—especially a reporter. She knows she has to call Ms. Fernandez, but what can she say that'll prevent the article from running? Probably nothing, but to ignore this now would be even more disastrous.

Fear overtakes joy as Joyce heads to the restroom to splash cold water on her face. She takes comfort in knowing there's no possible way this reporter has anything. It's all been permanently erased. But as she gently dabs the water from her face, she reflects on her own effort to manipulate perception, knowing it can be duplicated by others. Any article that even hints at the truth would crush the value of the stock.

After several minutes of staring at herself in the mirror, Joyce gathers herself and exits the restroom, heading to a quiet corner. She takes a deep breath and makes the worst call of her life. It's the first of two horrible calls, but this one must be first if she wants to stay alive.

"What?"

"There's a problem."

"Problem?"

"A reporter says she's going to release an article that will be devastating." Joyce cringes as the words leave her mouth.

"And?"

"There's only a little time left, but you should sell everything now. It'll be worthless this time tomorrow."

"I know."

"What?"

The phone call ends. Joyce's knees buckle as terror grips her soul, and the blood drains from her face. How's this possible? How could he know about all of this?

Michael is walking toward her, clearly having had his share of the champagne. "What's going on? Why aren't you in the room?"

Intellectually, Joyce knows it's useless, but she needs to create as much distance as possible for herself. "I have to leave. Something's come up at the office, and I have to take care of it ASAP."

"Get your ass back in here. You aren't going anywhere," Michael brazenly demands. "The market closes in less than twenty minutes, and every reporter on the planet's watching." Michael holds up his half-full champagne glass. "Besides, you're a multi-millionaire. I'm sure you can afford to pay whatever it'll take to fix the problem."

"Shut the fuck up, you idiot. I'm sick of your ignorant bullshit. I quit."

Michael tilts his head; the words Joyce said take a while for him to comprehend. When it does, his face reddens as his jaw drops. "What the fuck are you talking about?"

Joyce's entire body slumps. She's physically and mentally exhausted. "I'm going to make one more call. After that call, there's nothing any of us can do. It's fucking over."

"Fuck you, Joyce. Nothing you say or do is going to ruin this. If you wanna quit, fucking quit." The country's newest billionaire whips around, empties his champagne flute, and struts back toward the conference room with the confidence money buys.

Joyce looks around, her heels clicking on the tile floor as she sprints toward the nearest exit. She has to get the hell out of the building and think. The first thing she needs to do is call the goddamn reporter, or does she? It's going to run anyway. She goes back and forth in her own head, eventually deciding that if there is any possible way out of this, she must continue to play the part. She'll leave Michael and the others holding the bag. She's positioned things in the event of a cat-astrophic event, and what's more devastating than this? This is about her now.

Every possibility races through her mind as she steadies herself and punches in the numbers. The call is picked up before the first ring ends. "Ms. Fernandez. I heard you're looking for me?" Joyce's carefree tone is strained.

"I'll be brief, Ms. Kramer. We're running a story that details how Propentus hid important data and information from the FDA. A story that confirms the allegations made by Ms. Cosgrove and others is accurate. I want to give you a chance to comment before we go to print."

Joyce takes a deep breath. She'll plead ignorance to the very end. There's absolutely nothing that connects her to this. Vinnie's gone. Michael, Harold, Renee, and even Tommy are done, and she can't think of a single thing that connects her to all of this. She's worked very hard from day one to insulate herself.

Joyce decides to do what all lawyers do. "Ms. Fernandez. There's nothing to comment on. Your sources are wrong, and once we identify them—and we will—we'll be filing suit for defamation, libel, and slander against them, you, and your employer."

"Joyce. This is your last chance. I know about your connection with certain investors. I have confirmation you attempted to erase and intentionally omit research results that document the harm this drug inflicts. You've defrauded investors, the FDA, and patients. This drug causes irreparable damage, and you know it. Propentus is done as soon as this hits the wire."

The words rip the air from Joyce's lungs, but she holds steadfast. "Ms. Fernandez, I have nothing to say."

• • •

A smile comes across MJ's face. "Good luck, Joyce. You're going to need it." MJ hangs up and looks at the clock. It's 3:58 p.m. She punches in her editor's extension and says two words. "Run it."

109

Jonathan has one last difficult discussion for today. He knocks and walks in. "Mom? Dad? Anyone home?"

Nancy is almost running as she meets him at the door. "Oh, Jonathan, I was just going to call. Did you see the news? The company that makes your father's new drug lied to the FDA. Did you see it?"

"I heard it on the news," Jonathan says. It wasn't a total lie. "That's why I'm here."

Jonathan is shattered by the look of fear on his mom's face. He knew it would be bad, but this is much worse. What has he done?

She fires more questions at him as they head back to the living room. "What are we going to do? What does this mean? Will your dad be able to keep getting the drug?"

Jonathan quietly follows his mother, agonizing over his decision. Joe sits up in his chair, his feet firmly on the ground. Fox News has switched from their normal broadcasting to tackle the *Fox News Alert*. The reporter is talking about the IPO and notes the stock has plummeted in after-hours trading. So much so that all trading of Propentus stock has been halted. "Let's sit, Mom. Hey, Dad. How are you doing?"

"I'm fine."

"That's good. First, I don't know all of the details yet, but my guess is the FDA will issue a statement in the coming hour, withdrawing their approval while they sort this out. That'll be followed by a recall of the drug," Jonathan explains as he splits his attention evenly between his parents.

Nancy is transfixed on the television with tears running down her cheeks, searing a path through Jonathan's soul. He knows she understands what this means.

Jonathan continues the only way he knows how—the only way he can. "I'll call Dr. Mancini first thing in the morning. My guess is she'll advise to immediately discontinue taking the drug. But let's take it one step at a time, okay?"

Nancy stands and walks over to Joe. She leans over and gives him a hug and a kiss, refusing to let go. "I love you. We'll figure this out. I promise."

Joe looks over her shoulder, directly at Jonathan. He smiles proudly and nods. He says it all without saying a word. "I love you too, Nance. Don't worry about me. I'm good."

Jonathan's cell phone rings. He looks at his parents as he stands and says, "I need to take this." After receiving an understanding nod from his parents, he walks toward the kitchen and answers the call. "Hey."

"How are your folks?"

Emily's voice is a comfort he needs right then. Jonathan releases his breath and says, "I'm here now."

Jonathan glances to make sure his parents remain in the living room, assuring that he can speak openly. "I wish you were here. I'm struggling right now. Mom's a mess. Dad's as stoic as ever. This is going to be fucking hard."

"What about everything else?"

"Our attorney has already communicated with the FBI and FDA. Walt and I are meeting with them at nine tomorrow morning. We're as good as we can be on that front." Jonathan closes his eyes, trying to imagine himself and Emily relaxing on their couch, sharing a glass of wine, speaking about anything but this.

"And the other front?"

"Only time will tell."

"Please be safe. Call me later. I'm proud of you, Jonathan, and I love you more than you know."

"I love you, too." Jonathan pauses for a moment after he hangs up before returning to the living room.

Joe and Nancy's eyes are glued to the live reports from Propentus that are on the TV when Jonathan returns. He sits on the couch to watch as the FBI is locking down the building. As the employees are led from the building, Jonathan notices Harold and Renee walking out, wearing only their white lab coats and knowing grimaces.

There's a split screen showing Michael Riccio's home. Michael fights his way past reporters to get into his driveway, just to be stopped by the FBI, who's blocking the entrance to his home. While there's no audio, the video's clear. Michael holds the crumpled search warrant in his hand and is wrestling with agents in a futile effort to find refuge in his home.

Jonathan looks at his father, who's trying to keep his mother calm. Everything in their world is crashing down around them because of the decision he's made. It's worse than he ever imagined.

Apparently, this is what doing the right thing looks like.

110

Joyce shifts quickly into survival mode. She knows if she can speak with him, it'll be bad, but she'll survive, just like she did years ago. It rings and rings. No one picks up. That's not a good sign. She screams and slams her fists against the steering wheel over and over. The fucking reporter knows everything. How? As she hits redial for the twentieth time, she reflects on the decisions she's made in her life.

• • •

It started with her ambition to make partner. Joyce spent as much time as she could with a man who took her under his wing. Robert Picciano was a few years her senior, but he brought her in on a number of the deals he was working on and even invited her to dinner with other partners from time to time. She had even tried sleeping with him, believing that was what it took to advance. He was too much of a gentleman for that.

The first deal he let her take the lead on was the establishment of Excellence Investment, Inc. As the senior partner, he'd review and sign off on everything. He'd be the attorney of record, but she got the experience that comes from doing the actual work. A few years later, the Spinellis' son contacted Robert asking for a favor. His parents were diagnosed with dementia, and he needed Powers of Attorney and Healthcare Proxies drafted before the disease progressed too far. As a pro bono favor, Robert asked Joyce to take the lead in their preparation. This was when she met Anthony Spinelli for the first time.

After the Genomics deal went through, Joyce was recruited to Propentus by a charming Michael Riccio. While she's attending a conference, her office passes on a phone message from Anthony, who she hadn't spoken with in years. She returns the call that has led to this moment.

Anthony asked to meet with her to discuss Propentus' work on dementia. He explained he was in Florida visiting his parents. Witnessing firsthand the impact of the disease is devastating, and he decided to find a way to help. He advised that he controlled his parents' investment firm and was very interested in making a sizeable investment in the company, given their promising trial results.

Joyce immediately called Michael, who emphasized the company's significant financial woes and demanded that she immediately step away from the conference to meet with him. Human trials had begun, and Michael was lining up as much money as possible.

Since she was in Florida, albeit hundreds of miles away, Michael ordered her to do whatever it took to meet with Anthony and lock down the funding. Bright and early the next day, she rented a car and drove hours to meet with Anthony. They had dinner, and after a couple of bottles of wine, she got Anthony to commit Excellence Investments, Inc. to a $20 million investment.

Paperwork was finalized, and they wired money to Propentus, all within forty-eight hours. Michael was ecstatic. They weren't able to celebrate their newfound partnership until weeks later when Anthony returned to Boston. At that dinner, Anthony revealed his true colors and intent. He explained that while his personal commitment to fighting dementia is real, the money Propentus had accepted into their coffers came from a lifelong friend of his, Jimmy Rizzo. Joyce was mortified, but Michael couldn't care less. He needed the money to keep his dream alive.

Months later, Anthony showed up unexpectedly at Joyce's home. She reluctantly let him in. Over a bourbon, he laid out the facts: her life depended upon Propentus getting their dementia drug to market and their IPO launched. While shaking uncontrollably, she told him the trial results were trending unfavorably. He stood and smiled; that wasn't his problem. They needed to figure it out, or she would die. It was that simple.

The next two years were a blur. Each decision saw her ethics and integrity erode to the point of non-existence. Over time, Joyce realized that the devil owned her soul, and there was only one way out: through.

Using photos Anthony provided, she forced Tommy to delete certain records and create a completely separate set of documents for the FDA application. It was easy once Tommy saw the naked pictures of himself kissing another man's wife.

Harold was eager to jump on board in exchange for keeping the photos of him gambling at a mob-controlled poker game from his wife. Renee's insecurity was all she and Harold needed to rope her into the scheme. Page by page, the serious kidney issues that were being identified were erased. The necessary edits were completed by this small band of miscreants. No one the wiser.

The FDA was very thorough, and while they were close to catching on a couple of times, Joyce was impressed by her ability to get around their concerns, eventually pushing them to provide the accelerated approval. The next step was the IPO, which was flying down the track until…

• • •

Suddenly, someone taps on the passenger side window, startling Joyce. She recognizes the face. Blotches and a cold sweat follow. He was with Anthony the first time he came to her home. After a few more seconds, she takes a deep breath; her trembling hand pushes the button to unlock the door.

He gets into the passenger seat. Without emotion, he states the obvious: "This has come to an end."

Joyce makes a feeble attempt at salvation. "I delivered what was asked."

"Others delivered. Start the car."

"Where are we going?"

"Just drive. I'll tell you where to turn as we go." He reaches under his jacket. The message is easily understood.

Joyce accepts the inevitable. A tear trickles softly down her cheek as she starts the car for what she knows will be the last time.

111

MJ is sitting on her couch, re-reading the third segment of her story. She hasn't slept and knows a shower and a clean pair of sweats is more than just a good idea, but she refuses to take the time needed to make either happen. The entire series has gone viral, and she's getting calls and job offers from around the country. Everyone wants to work with the woman who uncovered the conspiracy that has shaken the biotech industry to its core. Every biotech stock has tumbled on fears that if one company can do it, others may have, too.

In the forty-eight hours since her story broke, the FBI and the FDA have done some of their finest work. She's shocked to learn Jimmy Rizzo's conspiracy contaminated the FDA as well. "The team" never mentioned that. Did they know? The committee member who pushed for the accelerated approval disappeared immediately following the initial article's release. Her car and a note were found near Lake Winnipesaukee. Divers continue searching the lake.

MJ's personal cell phone rings. It is a restricted number. "Yes?"

"Your request has been received and approved."

"Thank you."

"There's a massive clean-up effort underway."

MJ knows Joyce Kramer's body was found in her car the day after the IPO launch with what's been reported as a self-inflicted gunshot wound. MJ knows and fears the truth. Will all parties live up to their end of the bargain? "I noticed."

"We look forward to our next collaboration."

"It'll be a while."

"Until then…"

112

As today's dialysis takes place, Melissa Cosgrove watches the news, smiling with supreme satisfaction. The company that caused her and others so much pain has been beaten. She'll have to live with the consequences and all that entails, but she's pleased her personal actions have saved so many others from the same fate.

Attorney Schneider has told her that a recovery from Propentus, or rather their insurance company, is impossible at this point. Their fraudulent behavior takes that prospect off the table. Now, he's talking about a big payday from suing the FDA for negligently doing their job. He made promises before, and she begrudgingly admits her daughter Alexa was right. They'll have to figure out what to do next, but "The King of the Fender Bender" will not be part of it.

Melissa's cell phone rings. It's her daughter, Alexa. "Hey, honey."

"Mom. Oh my God. Mom! You're never going to believe it! You're rich!"

Melissa is confused. "Slow down. What are you talking about?"

Alexa starts crying. "I just got an alert. Someone donated to your GoFundMe account. When I went in to look, I found a $5 million donation from 'Anonymous.'"

"That can't possibly be correct."

"I called GoFundMe, and they confirmed it's legit. Mom, you're rich! You'll never have to worry about money again!"

Over the course of the coming days, Melissa learns the handful of plaintiffs initially represented by Attorney Schneider in their suit against Propentus each received the same compensation. For those who didn't have a GoFundMe account, one was established by an unknown person. They then received an untraceable email notifying them of their new account, its password, and its balance.

113

onathan and Emily arrive at his parents' home. They're excited to see Joe and Nancy and sprint to the front door. It's his favorite for dinner, and he probably shouldn't have, but Jonathan has his mother's favorite Chianti in his hand.

They knock and walk in like they have every time before, but this visit is different. Both Joe and Nancy meet them at the door—smiles and hugs all around. Before a single word can be spoken, Emily lifts her left hand and shows them the ring. A breathtaking 2.5-carat solitaire set in platinum.

Tonight's an event. The conversation never stops. Most of it revolves around the upcoming wedding. The level of happiness in this home has never been higher. As Emily and Nancy clear the table and put coffee on, Joe and Jonathan head for the living room.

"How you doing, Dad?"

"I'm good. I'm glad you finally came to your senses. You should've put a ring on her finger long ago," he teases.

Laughter fills the room.

Jonathan shifts the conversation to a more serious topic. "Really, Dad, how are you? Any problem with the new meds?" Despite efforts to conceal it, Jonathan knows his father can see the guilt on his face.

"Nothing serious. I told you I'm good." As he settles into his chair, Joe looks back toward the kitchen to confirm they're alone.

"Jonathan, I couldn't be prouder of you. You've become the man I always knew you would be. It was the right decision. You've saved a lot of people."

Jonathan looks at the floor. "Dad, I'm sorry. I…"

"Stop. You did the right thing. I love you. End of discussion."

Emily and Nancy return with coffee and dessert, and the wedding conversation picks up where it left off. Talk of churches and honeymoon locations dominate the discussion.

Jonathan takes a moment to reflect and embrace what's happening. His mother's overjoyed. Joe and he exchange smiles and winks. With his beautiful fiancée by his side, Jonathan's happier than he's ever been. He'll treasure this evening forever.

114

onathan has won a number of cases here, but this courtroom has never been his favorite. It's poorly lit, small, and located in the bowels of the 200-year-old courthouse. His steady hands smooth the front of his Hugo Boss three-piece suit, the one he saves for closing arguments, as he scans the gathering. Jonathan's eyes stop briefly on his parents and Emily, who are eagerly anticipating the tale he will expertly weave.

After taking a deep breath, Jonathan strides confidently across the courtroom to stand in front of the captive audience in the jury box. "Ladies and gentlemen, the right decision in this case, exonerating my client, leaves the plaintiffs without further recourse. That may seem harsh, but it's the right decision. The only decision."

As he continues reviewing the facts of the case with the seven women and five men, he keeps their thoughts on the importance of always doing the right thing, even when doing so might feel wrong. To emphasize his point, he randomly gestures toward the image of the blindfolded woman holding the scales of justice carved into the wall behind the judge.

Suddenly, the judge stands and stares with annoyance at Jonathan. "Decide," she demands.

The courtroom seems unfazed by the interruption. The court reporter continues to capture every word while the jury watches him, awaiting his next point.

Jonathan is fazed, though. He shifts his weight between his feet and looks to the judge, working to mask the confusion caused by the unexpected demand. The frustration of losing the momentum of his closing arguments comes through in his response. "What decision are you looking for me to make, Your Honor?" he asks through gritted teeth. Being an experienced attorney, the agitation quickly diminishes, and he forces a smile, swallowing his pride.

"How dare you!" the judge snaps. "You know what it is, Mr. Silverman. Do not disgrace yourself before this court by pleading ignorance." She opens her robe to remove a handgun. Spectators begin gasping and ducking in desperation to hide themselves from the bewildering danger.

For a moment, Jonathan wonders how she got the gun past the metal detectors, but then his eyes flash toward his family, who are sitting in the corner with their hands folded in their laps, pleading with their eyes for him to do whatever the judge demands.

Jonathan opens his mouth, but nothing comes out. The eloquence he exhibited in his statements to the jury disappears the second he grasps the gravity of his situation. Fear clouds his mind.

The judge smirks in disgust, then points the gun at his family and pulls the trigger. The thunder of the shot ricochets around the courtroom as Vinnie Napolitano steps in front of the bullet.

Jonathan sits up in bed. The dream that's haunted him is now clear. The monumental decision the judge demands is about justice. His parents and Emily all pleaded with their eyes to do what was right, even in the face of danger. He followed his heart and did the right thing. And he found a way to protect the ones he loves, even if it meant partnering with the most unlikely of people.

He smiles, convinced he no longer has to worry about Jimmy Rizzo holding up his end of the bargain. Jonathan lays back down, curls up with Emily, and sleeps like he hasn't in months.

115

Jonathan carries a hot coffee to MJ, who's waiting at a table in the coffee shop that served as their command center.

It seems appropriate for this conversation to take place here. MJ opens her laptop, poised for the interview. She smiles. "Aww. You remembered."

"Hard to forget," Jonathan says with a chuckle and sets down the steaming cup. "I think you are the only person on the planet who drinks blueberry-flavored coffee."

They laugh, something that was missing from their prior meetings here.

"I'm pretty sure that's not the case, but point taken." MJ bows her head respectfully and takes a sip of the hot beverage.

Jonathan sits down across from MJ, sensing her reclaimed confidence. He notices the pink has returned. "By the way. Love the hair."

"Fuck you... I can't make you happy, can I?"

More laughter.

MJ looks around and lowers her voice a bit. "Off the record... have you been contacted?"

Jonathan's turn to look around. It's been a couple of weeks. "No. You?"

"I got one call from 'the team.' Other than that, nothing. Although it still feels like I am being watched." To emphasize the point, MJ's eyes make a quick scan of the room.

"I get it. I feel that way, too."

"They're cleaning things up quickly."

"Seems so. First, Joyce. Then Michael being attacked by a supposed investor who lost their life savings buying into the IPO. According to what I've read, it's unlikely he'll come out of the coma. And the woman from the FDA still hasn't been found."

Jonathan looks around the small shop. He knows his attention to his surroundings will never return to prior levels. He can't believe he was ever so cavalier with that part of his life.

MJ enjoys the coffee and continues. "With Riccio, Kramer, and Napolitano gone, it leaves Johnson, Spencer, and O'Hara to fend for themselves. I hear the Feds have them buried in a dark hole somewhere."

Jonathan takes a sip of his coffee. "So, are we back to DEFCON 3?"

MJ shakes her head, smiling. "I'll never be better than that, but yes, we're back to DEFCON 3."

Lightening up their conversation, Jonathan says, "I heard you've been submitted for a Pulitzer? Congratulations."

"Yeah, my editor did that. He can be a real pain in the ass, but I have to give him props for standing behind me on this one."

"You should be proud. It was great work, MJ. You're a shoo-in."

"Stop. Now, what's this I hear about an engagement? Who's silly enough to agree to spend the rest of their life with you?"

"You just erased your name from the invitation list." Jonathan smiles.

"Fine by me. I don't have a pair of wedding sweats anyway." MJ clears her throat and prepares to take notes. "You ready to start?"

"I'm limited in what I can say because of the pending 'whistleblower' matter, but happy to answer what I can."

Through their attorney, Jonathan and Walt provided complete copies of everything, excluding any mention of the mob, to the FBI, the FDA, and the SEC. Now, they're aiding in the investigation into Propentus.

MJ sits poised over the keyboard. "Mr. Silverman, please walk me through the emotional rollercoaster you rode while deciding what to do once you confirmed Propentus lied to the FDA?"

Jonathan sits back in the seat. "Jesus, I thought you said you were going to go easy on me?"

MJ laughs. "Have you met me? This *is* easy."

Epilogue

While *The Decision* is a work of fiction, many of the statistics and information cited within are not. Currently, more than six million Americans are living with Alzheimer's disease, and eleven million more provide unpaid support and care.

With one in eight Americans over sixty-five living with Alzheimer's, it's likely you already know someone impacted by the disease. Should you or someone you care about find themselves facing the daunting battle that is dementia, please know you are not alone.

The Alzheimer's Association is the leading voluntary health organization in Alzheimer's and dementia care, support, and research. Please see alz.org for more information. There is a **Helpline – (800)272-3900** available 24/7/365. The Helpline is manned by highly-trained counselors who stand ready to listen with a compassionate and supportive ear.

They'll provide answers to the questions that arise as loved ones navigate this challenging journey.

Treatments and therapies are being identified and evaluated across the globe on a daily basis. We will not rest until we achieve the Association's vision... *a world without Alzheimer's and all forms of dementia.*

A portion of the proceeds from this book will be donated to the Alzheimer's Association.

About the Author

Joe is a retired insurance executive who lives in Rhode Island with his wife of over thirty-four years. They have two talented daughters and relish any opportunity to spoil their two amazing grandsons.

When not behind the keyboard working to bring stories and characters to life, Joe can be found at any number of golf courses searching the woods for an errant shot, sitting at the bridge table sharpening his burgeoning skills, or at an airport waiting to board a flight to whatever locale his wife has identified as their next destination.

Having witnessed the staggering impact of dementia firsthand, Joe has become a passionate and engaged advocate of the innovative work done every day by the Alzheimer's Association. He's an active Board member of the MA/NH chapter and firmly believes the first survivor of Alzheimer's is out there.

Connect with Joe at JSalerno.com

Made in the USA
Columbia, SC
20 November 2024

47000842R00257